Praise for Barbara Cleverly's Joe Sandilands series

'Spectacular and dashing. Spellbinding.' *New York Times*

'Smashing . . . marvellously evoked.' *Chicago Tribune*

'A great blood and guts blockbuster.' *Guardian*

'Stellar – as always.'

'British author Cleverly out-Christies Agatha Christie . . .'
Publishers Weekly (starred reviews)

'A historical mystery that has just about everything: a fresh, beautifully realized exotic setting; a strong, confident protagonist; a poignant love story; and an exquisitely complex plot.'
Denver Post

'Evocative narrative, sensitive characterizations, artful dialogue and masterly plotting.' *Library Journal*

And for *The Tomb of Zeus*

'Award-winning author Cleverly debuts a captivating new series. In the tradition of Agatha Christie, the characters are complex and varied. Amid the picturesque history of the island (of Crete), mystery and murder abound in this riveting novel.'
Romantic Times

'For readers who love Elizabeth Peters and Jacqueline Winspear, Cleverly demonstrates a knack for creating full-blown historical puzzlers with complicated plots and engaging characters in unusual settings.' *Library Journal* (starred review)

'Tucked into the wealth of archaeological and historical detail is a full-blown English houseparty murder . . . with a spirited, intelligent heroine, a glorious exotic setting, a clever plot and a touch of romance . . .'
Denver Post

Also by Barbara Cleverly

The Last Kashmiri Rose
Ragtime in Simla
The Damascened Blade
The Palace Tiger
The Bee's Kiss
Tug of War
Folly du Jour
The Tomb of Zeus

Bright Hair

about the Bone

Barbara Cleverly

ıdon

Constable & Robinson Ltd
3 The Lanchesters
162 Fulham Palace Road
London W6 9ER
www.constablerobinson.com

First published in the USA 2008 by Bantam Dell
A Division of Random House, Inc
New York

This edition published by Constable,
an imprint of Constable & Robinson Ltd 2009

A copy of the British Library Cataloguing in Publication
Data is available from the British Library

ISBN: 978-1-84529-917-0

Printed and bound in the EU

1 3 5 7 9 10 8 6 4 2

PEFC
PEFC/16-33-111
CATG-PEFC-052
www.pefc.org

This is for my son, Jesse, who found the name of a lost soldier in a Cambridge graveyard.

Prologue

The priest smoothed down his white robe and prepared to make his entrance into the village hall. Fastidiously, he twitched into place his carefully chosen girdle – a narrow length of cloth sewn for him by the ladies of this village. They would recognize it and welcome the discreet compliment to them. The door swung open and he caught the buzz of many voices, a whiff of wood smoke, and the scent of home cooking. Bracing himself for the heat and hysteria generated by an overcrowded room full of emotional people, he turned, a few steps short of the door, and looked back over the countryside.

He'd known better days for a funeral.

The summer day was still flooding this side of the valley with mellow light, quite out of keeping with the solemn occasion that demanded his presence inside that dark bee-hive behind him. He stole a few moments, opening his senses to Nature, saying his own silent farewell to the lady he had loved, admired, and – on occasion – feared. It was unfitting that such a woman should be consigned to her grave, mourned by humankind, on a day when all of Nature was smiling and fertile.

The priest was a country boy by birth; though schooling and theological college had taken him away from these hills for many years, he had never ceased to read the land with an experienced eye. And the scene he was now contemplating enchanted him. Had he ever seen orchards so

1

heavy with fruit, meadows and pens so full of healthy young animals? The late afternoon sun was slanting over the cornfields, gilding them with an illusion of ripeness. He examined the stalk of wheat he'd plucked absentmindedly on his way through the village and was surprised to find he was still holding. Green and hard. Another week or so, he calculated, before they would hear the cry of 'Harvest home!' along the valley.

And yet, he would expect this farming community to be growing daily more active, more involved with the preparations for the heavy work and its reward – the week of feasting and celebrations, the highlight of the year. This ill-timed death must surely have broken the rhythm. The funeral and the following wake would take up three days, and then everyone would be back at work in the fields according to schedule, though no doubt with headaches all round if he correctly remembered the strength of the local beer. But once the carousing was over, it was the loss of confidence that this lady's passing would impose on the local people that concerned him. Simple, superstitious, and trusting, they found themselves without warning prematurely bereft and he feared for them.

'Oh, My Lady,' he muttered, 'how long did I know you? Twenty years? And how often have I known you to mistime a single word or action? Never. How am I to make sense of this death – early and unseasonal?' He smiled sadly. How much more appropriate if she had died in November, at the beginning of their year. *Earth to earth . . . From decay comes renewal . . . The seed is Goodness . . . the conception: Silence . . .* In winter, the sermon would have come readily to his lips and the congregation would have understood and been reassured. The rhythm of the seasons would have been unbroken.

But here he stood, as unready as the wheat in his hand, casting about for a message. He was certain that there would be purpose even in her dying, and if he could open his mind he would see it.

And then he smiled. This forthcoming abundance was her gift and would be her memorial. Yes, that's how he would present it in his oration . . . something on the lines of how *fitting* it was that her mortal remains should return to the womb of earth at the very moment when that which she had cared for was full of the promise of fecundity. And then he would send up a silent prayer that summer storms should not come along and ruin the harvest . . . making him look a fool.

No one can be saved until she is born again . . . Yes, it would be wise to finish on a triumphant note: *She is not dead but lives* . . . But in whom? It would be up to him to discover. He would be watchful. Pose a few well-aimed questions. It was likely that she had handed down her gifts already.

He turned and approached the door of the hall, where a gaggle of children had been set to watch for his arrival. Ducking his head under the lintel, he entered and pulled himself back up to his impressive six feet four inches, standing, ceremonial staff in hand, scanning the crowded room with a searching eye. He noted, without surprise or offence, the subtle movement of the now silent crowd away from him. Who, of these countrymen and -women, would be comfortable to be caught standing close to a priest of his rank? The ones prepared to meet his gaze held it for a proud moment before looking deferentially away. A good sign. If all was to go well they would have to talk to him. He needed their information. Most of them, men and women, were clutching tankards of ale; a few more hours of steady drinking would loosen tongues.

But his immediate need was to break through the barrier created by his awe-inspiring presence. He looked around for a child and chose, from among the reception committee by the door, the smallest one, inquisitive enough to be caught staring. He beckoned him forward. Bravely but slowly the child approached. 'Take my staff, would you, young man?' the priest asked pleasantly. The child took it as though it might turn into a snake between his hands. He held its length awkwardly and failed to make an allowance

3

for the weight of the carved head, overbalancing and scurrying to gain control. For a few agonized seconds he struggled with the implement, dragging it along the floor like a hobbyhorse, and, finally, was helped by an older girl who descended on him with all the clucking concern of a brown hen, to prop it up against the wall.

The priest's shout of indulgent laughter at the performance had its calculated effect: it was echoed instantly by the crowd. 'You have learned a valuable lesson in life, young man,' said the priest to his red-faced helper. 'In a tight spot, always enlist the aid of a big, capable girl.'

The ice broken, a woman of the village approached, bringing him a drink. Not the mug of ale he yearned for, but a silver goblet filled with red wine. He thanked her warmly and, as she stood awaiting his response, he swirled the wine gently, admiring its rich colour and bouquet before tasting it. He sipped again, drawing out the moment, then sighed. 'I believe this may be the best wine I have ever drunk! Italian? I would guess from Etruria, perhaps?'

She giggled with pleasure, nodded, and hurried away.

The Mayor moved forward to greet him. 'My Lord Aeduan, may I say how honoured we are that ... er ... your lordship should ...'

The priest turned toward him benignly and cut through his hesitations. 'She was an incomparable lady and if I may mark her passing by my presence, then the honour is mine. I see you've got all the bigwigs of the diocese under your roof, and I passed hundreds of folk gathering in the square. The arrangements are all made, I trust?'

'Certainly. The bier is prepared and will start on a signal. As you requested, our own village priest is here, ready to assist with the practicalities and accompany you on the journey to the grave. Bran!' The Mayor beckoned to a slender young man in linen robes, whose belt was heavily hung with ceremonial gear.

Aeduan tried not to stare at his assistant, though the bleached hair, fashionably spiked upwards over his head,

4

was clearly intended to mark him out for attention. He had all the charm of an albino hedgehog, Aeduan decided, amused, but he looked clever.

'The equipment you called for is to hand, my lord,' Bran murmured in a quietly efficient tone. 'Though there'll be little enough for me to do, you'll find, sir. She requested no animals at the burial. The last convention she'll overturn? Of course . . . if you should wish to counter that order, sir . . .? I'm sure we could provide even at this late stage . . . No? Ah, well . . . the hearse will be drawn by six lads of the village . . . Oh, there is an exception . . . She asked particularly that her dog be allowed to accompany her. He's over there.' He pointed towards a group of three young girls sitting together by the hearth. The two older ones, arms locked together for comfort, were whispering to each other, subdued; though heavy-eyed with grief, their blonde beauty drew everyone's gaze. The youngest girl, barely ten, was small and dark and absorbed by her own thoughts. As he watched, she put out a hand to stroke the grey-coated hound lying across her feet. A handsome dog. What else? Aurinia had known her horses and her dogs. This one, alert and fierce-looking, was of a breed he'd admired across the sea in Britain. They could run down a deer and snap a bone with ease in their grinning jaws or, as now, play guardian to a child.

'These are her daughters?'

'As you say. The two fair girls, Beth and Saillie, are twins.'

Silver Birch and White Willow. The names echoed their fair colouring and the slender grace of their limbs. Aeduan smiled his approval.

'Orphans now, of course,' Bran confided. 'Their father died in battle. That little spat with the Germans twelve years ago.'

'I remember him. He was one of the bravest and best. But the third child? I have no recollection of her.'

The assistant priest smiled dismissively. 'The Lady's sole mistake. After the death of her husband she took up

5

with . . . showed favour to . . . a stranger, a foreigner. Charming fellow. He would turn up here every couple of years, selling things. Luxury end of the market.' He pointed to the wine cup Aeduan still held. 'That was one of his. The red silk dress she's chosen to be buried in . . . the amber necklace gracing the bosom of the Mayor's wife . . . my own belt . . . he left many markers of his passage through the village!'

'Including the third daughter?'

'Yes, sir. I'm not surprised you were unaware of her. She was not much paraded.'

'What is her name?'

'Sirona, sir.'

'Sirona? The Star? How exotic! And what happened to the father to whom I take it she owes her intriguing dark looks?'

'He was a traveller.' Bran shrugged a shoulder. 'He travelled. He didn't speak much of himself but we all guessed that he was from the south, beyond Marseille. Africa? Egypt, most likely, but we can only speculate.'

'I should like to express my condolences to the girls.'

'Of course, sir. If you'll follow me?'

Aeduan spoke soft, sad words to the fair daughters, causing a further flow of tears, and touched each one comfortingly on her bowed head. It didn't escape his sharp eye that both girls cast swift glances under damp lashes at the gathering, seeking assurance that no one had failed to witness the honour being done them by the priest. At close quarters the pair were even more lovely than he had guessed. They had chosen to wear short dancing skirts and heavy belts from which dangled a single silver disc. Aeduan was impressed and reassured. With their looks, their parentage, and what he guessed to be their wealth, they would have no difficulty in marrying well. They must be very near the age of choosing and there were many young men present from all corners of the province, he noted, young men whose heads turned all too readily, drawn to the swing of a silver disc.

As he approached the youngest, the dog at her feet growled a warning, abruptly cut off at a sharp command from the child. To all appearances unaware of the priest's presence, this daughter remained, head bowed, staring into the hearth. The shapeless grey dress that reached down to her ankles was clearly chosen to deflect attention. Her sole ornament was a sprig of yew fastened to her shoulder with a simple pin. Yew. The tree that grew at the gateway to death. The symbol of rebirth and immortality. Now, who was this?

'Sirona!'

At the sound of her name, she looked up at him, unafraid, preoccupied. Through his surprise at what he saw when she did so, Aeduan struggled to maintain his expression of kindly concern. Under the thicket of springing black hair he had expected to find matching black eyes with perhaps an eastern cast, but these eyes were light grey: her mother's eyes. The child even had the same disconcerting trick of regarding him in a slightly unfocused way, as though she were looking not at or past, but in some strange way, *into* him.

With a certainty he could only wonder at, he reached on impulse for the wheat stalk he'd stuck in his belt and held it out to the child. She struggled to her feet and he saw with a pang of tenderness that she was indeed quite small. She could with ease have ridden on the tall shoulders of the hound which had risen with her and now stood flexed and ready for attack, held back only by the power of a slender right hand on the upstanding scruff of his neck. Aeduan thought the time had come to establish precedence: he murmured to the dog until it sank back with a muffled whimper on to its haunches.

But the girl's whole attention was on the stalk of wheat. She looked from it back to the priest, then put out a hand and took it from him, her face suddenly alight with a smile that he would have sworn was complimenting him on his perception.

* * *

7

The service, held out-of-doors in the village square, was a triumph. How could it fail to overwhelm the congregation? The Lady had earned their deep love; the priest himself was visibly moved, his oratory unsurpassed. At the close, a cortège formed up, ready to make its way up the hill towards the burial place. Aeduan's rich baritone voice rang out over the valley, echoed by the mourners' traditional responses, lusty and tuneful. The six young men chosen to pull along the bier with its gold-inlaid wheels and lavish decorations took up the strain and heaved. On it had been placed a couch spread with rich fabrics and on this lay, open to view, the body of the Lady. Her feet in gold-embroidered slippers were just visible under the drape of her red silk gown. Her arms were heavy with gold bracelets and around her neck she wore a ceremonial gold necklace. They had placed a pillow under her head so that the sight of her pale beauty could bless them for the last time.

Many people lined the way to the burial place, calling out farewells and throwing flowers on to the bier. Aeduan, acknowledging their sorrow with graceful flourishes, reckoned that many in the crowd had travelled a considerable distance to say their farewell. The Lady's influence had spread far wider than this valley. Well, he would ensure that the pilgrims had tales to tell when they returned to their own hearths. A bit of theatre was always welcome on these occasions; the antics of the threshing-floor were always remembered and reported. As they passed the last cornfield he held up his hand and murmured a command over his shoulder to his assistant.

Puzzled – for this was not part of the ritual – Bran obeyed at once, and, selecting a knife from his belt, the young man grasped a handful of wheat by the stalks and sawed at them until the bunch came away in his hand. If he'd had warning of this he could have brought a sickle along, he thought resentfully. The priest took it from him and, with a conjurer's gestures, slipped the girdle from around his waist and wound it tightly around the stalks.

The assistant was uneasy. What on earth was going on? Had old Aeduan been seduced by some esoteric eastern cult? Been spending too much time in Greece?

He watched, entranced like everyone else, as the priest addressed the crowd.

'You see me gather from the field, not the customary *last* bundle of wheat but the *first*.' He brandished it over his head for all to see. 'It is unripe. The ears are slender and there is no sustenance in them. But, my friends, they are well formed and they are whole. With the waxing of the moon they will be ready. They will feed you and your children for the coming year. This is the parting gift of Our Lady.'

In the holy grove, Aeduan filled a beaker with water from the spring that jetted from the red rock-face and they started on the steep final ascent. He timed the last notes of his hymn exactly to the arrival at the cave in the hillside. The village women had done well. The entrance had been decorated with branches of greenery and white flowers to brighten the darkness. Above the mound a wraithlike crescent of a moon was starting its climb into the still-bright sky. Aeduan noted its position and the absence of clouds, with satisfaction.

The shadows had already gathered at the burial place and he was relieved to see that the Mayor had arranged for a chain of lads to hold up flares deep inside the cavern. The entrance faced the east. She would be laid to rest facing the rising sun.

With rehearsed ease, the hauling team took the couch reverently on their shoulders and carried it into the cave's wood-lined interior. In moments, the wheeled bier was dismantled and all its parts carried into the chamber. There it joined the arrangement of rich gifts already in place. Aeduan, his assistant, the twin daughters, Sirona leading the dog, along with representatives of the village, entered to perform or witness the last rites. While Aeduan sprinkled the corpse with water from the holy spring and sang a final hymn before the silver-gleaming image of the Goddess,

Bran moved objects about here and there, finally nodding that he was satisfied.

Aeduan lingered, kneeling by the body for a few last moments. He contemplated the strong features, framed and softened by the cascade of pale hair and now, in the light of the last flare, gleaming with an illusion of youth restored. He mastered his startled reaction when, with a clink of gold bangles, her right hand fell from her bosom and swung limply in front of his face. No one heard his murmur. 'Aurinia, Lady, forgive me my slow wits! One last time you show me the way.'

A further sign. His certainty was growing.

He tugged a bloodstone ring from her finger and returned the hand to its place across her breast.

Bran approached clutching a deep silver bowl. 'Excuse me, sir . . . one more thing before we close down . . . The hound, sir. Shall I?'

'Ah, yes. Carry on, would you?'

At a nod, Sirona led the hound forward and commanded it to lie down at the feet of its dead mistress. Swiftly the assistant priest placed the bowl on the ground in front of it. Assuming that it was being offered water, the animal stretched its neck forward. Then, from behind, the young priest seized the dog's muzzle tightly in one hand, jerking it upwards. With the blade in his other hand, he cut the throat in one practised stroke. The blood spouted cleanly into the bowl.

Duty done, the party moved back on to the hillside path and the priest cast a measuring glance at the heavens, checking the height of the moon, now an emphatic horned presence poised over the mound. All was perfectly positioned.

In the view of the crowd below, Aeduan caught the small girl by the sleeve. She was already moving towards him and made no demur as he drew her forward a few paces, along the path to the summit. He knew that at the moment he offered her to her people she was colluding with him in the presentation and perfectly aware that those below were seeing her silhouetted against the darkening sky and crowned with a silver crescent. With slow ceremony, he took her hand and slipped the bloodstone ring on to her finger, then, bowing, held out the bunch of unripe wheat. She took it from him, steady and gracious, and held it before her with the pride and solemnity of a girl taking possession of her bridal flowers.

Chapter One

Fontigny, Burgundy, 1926

The Englishman groped his way along the dark hallway and hesitated by the front door, listening to the nighttime sounds of the house. Nothing to be heard but the creaking of ancient timbers in the autumn wind gusting against the structure. Hand halfway to the key in its place in the massive lock, he stopped to check once again the contents of his pockets. All present and correct. The all-important postcard was readily to hand in the right pocket of his tweed overcoat. The letter in the left he took out and considered for a moment before stowing it away again.

'Can't imagine what you'll make of this, Johnny, old man,' he said to himself. 'If it reaches you – well and good. Let's hope I'll have a chance to explain one day. Face-to-face. We'll sip a brandy in one of those sleep-inducing armchairs in your club and you can make fun of me. I'll be only too delighted! And if it doesn't get through . . .' He suppressed a bark of laughter. '. . . at least I'll have scared them shitless!'

He tugged a black felt fedora down snugly over his brow, concealing fair hair heavily streaked with silver. Amongst the dark denizens of Burgundy he'd stand out like a harbour-light if the full moon out there penetrated the rain clouds. He listened again to the heartbeat of the house: sleeping . . . sleeping . . . sleeping. Then he froze. His straining ears picked up a slight sound from above. The same sound, repeated, identified itself as no more than the familiar overture to the nightly basso profundo performance from old Capitaine Huleux on the floor above. Could the man's wife possibly sleep through that? Had any of the other sleepers in the house been disturbed? He waited. When he was confident that he was unobserved, he turned the key twice in the lock, glad that he'd taken the precaution of oiling it the previous day, and slipped out into a chilly Burgundy night.

An hour to go before dawn and the sky was still black. But at least the rain had stopped. He glanced to right and left down the deserted street, unable for a moment to move on.

'Brace up! You don't want me to call you a Cowardy Custard, do you?' His nanny's voice sounded in his head, still sharp over the distance of half a century. Funny how the old girl still rallied round when he was in a tight spot.

He made his customary silent reply. 'Bugger off, Nanny!'

'Don't be a crybaby . . . Once begun is half done . . .'

He stepped into the street, cutting off the comforting clichés, and set off towards the centre of town, hugging the deeper shadows along his way. Every inch was familiar to him, every street gutter to be jumped, every jutting window box full of rusting geraniums to be eased around, every stretch of cobblestones slippery underfoot. As he approached the central square, he thought he could well have done without the vivid moonlight that lit up the scene in a glassy theatrical glow.

Agitated though he was, the artist in him lured him into pausing to admire the gleaming façades of the medieval houses lining the square, standing pale against a sky swept clear of the last remnants of tattered clouds fleeing the Mistral towards the south. Was this the last time he would hold his breath in wonder at the loveliness of this corner of France? Could be. Pity, that. He'd grown fond of it. In spite of the unpleasantness. His lips twisted in a humourless smile. He was being absurd. He was still alive in spite of everything, wasn't he? They'd let him go. For the moment.

His fault, of course. He'd been dealt a poor hand but he could have played it more carefully. His wretched temper had got the better of him again, and he'd been rash. Thrown down gauntlets, issued ultimatums. If he'd had his sabre on his hip, he'd have rattled it. He'd made it impossible for them to let him get away back to England with the knowledge he had. A man of his standing with friends in the government and the military would be listened to – in spite of the enormity of his discoveries. There'd be shocked disbelief, followed by concern for his sanity and perhaps even gentle ridicule, but he knew how to weather that. In the end, they'd hear what he had to say. Alarms would be sounded. The French ambassador would be called in to give an explanation. He smiled with grim satisfaction at the thought of the mayhem he would cause. But, just in case he didn't make it, he would ensure, at least, that England was alerted.

But was this still possible? A rush of doubt shook him. One by one his options had been closed down; there remained just this one last despairing throw of the dice. He ought not to involve her in this disgusting, dangerous business but, in the end, it had all come down to a few dreary words on an innocent-looking postcard. It would make its way, unsuspected, just one of the many cards put into the box by tourists near the abbey at weekends. He'd been careful enough to choose a photograph of the abbey ruins, and to send it to her at a Cambridge address unknown to them, he did believe. It ought to evade even their vigilance.

From the shelter of the doorway of the *boulangerie*, he located the Café de la Paix on the opposite side. Wrought-iron tables and chairs were still laid out on the pavement, pathetically promoting the illusion that summer was not over. The postbox stood next to the café, jauntily lit, eerily blue.

Resigned and steadier now that he was so near his goal, he felt in his pocket and grasped the postcard, concealing it in the palm of his hand.

'Quick's the word and Sharpe's the toffee!' exhorted Nanny.

His mood changed to one of impatience. The English-man was unused to creeping around the periphery of any scene or any battlefield; the frontal attack was his usual style. He squared his shoulders, stepped into the moon-light, and walked purposefully across the wet cobbles. A few feet from the letter box, however, he paused.

A sharp cry had rung out behind him. He gasped in dismay. The cry was taken up by others and echoed with harsh derision around the square above his head. Wretched jackdaws! He'd forgotten about *them.* For a moment, heads emerged aggressively from nesting holes in the decaying stonework. Wings flapped. Complaints were made at full raucous pitch and he stood exposed, hating his inconveni-ent hecklers.

They fell silent as abruptly as they had awakened and he dared to move forward.

And then he heard it: a shuffling sound from the alley beside the café, the dull clang of a foot hitting iron and a swallowed curse. His blood churned in his veins, trigger-ing his body into familiar battle-ready reactions.

Overture and beginners.

He went smoothly into his rehearsed movements. Swiftly he covered the distance to the box and, breathing heavily, made play of leaning on it for support. Screening the narrow slot with his body, he slipped the postcard inside. His girl would understand. She'd understand and sound the charge.

Pantomime time. Turning and looking furtively about him, he took the letter from his left-hand pocket with a wide gesture, but, in doing so, dropped it clumsily to the ground, swearing loudly – but not too loudly – as he bent to retrieve it. The oblong of white paper reflected showily in the moonlight, scuttering along the pavement, carried by a complicitous gust of wind. It came to rest by a café table.

Confident English handwriting flowed in black ink across the envelope: *Brigadier-General John McAndrew,*

15

Directorate of Military Operations and Intelligence, The War Office, Whitehall, Londres, Angleterre.

The address was clearly visible a second before a black boot stamped down on it.

Running, crouched, towards it, he was still two or three yards distant when he was jerked upwards from behind by a silent presence. A sinewy hand stinking of horses and leather closed over his mouth. He fought back with an outburst of energy, welcoming the declaration of hostilities. Hand-to-hand combat. So that's how it would end! Well – he could oblige one more time! He kicked out violently at the shins of the man restraining him and relished the stable-yard oath he provoked. It took a second attacker, darting out from the shadows and dragging his feet from under him, to subdue the Englishman. Fingers yanked back his head exposing his throat. In the moment the point of a cold steel blade trailed over the skin seeking its target, his upturned eyes focused on the slender spire of the abbey outlined against the dark blue of the sky and he grimaced with satisfaction to see the precision with which the full moon dotted its *i.*

'I told you this would end in tears!' His nanny's voice was reproving. Regretful. Very close now.

His stretched senses became aware of the clatter of hooves and the jingle of harness in the distance and, as the stiletto slid into his jugular, his last thought was *'Got you, you bastard!'*

Chapter Two

Cambridge, 1927

'A Miss Talbot, you say? *Laetitia* Talbot? Certainly not! I won't see her! What possessed you, Claydon, to let her get as far as my door?'

The college servant, an under-porter, looked anxiously behind him and made to reply, but was cut off with what he considered unwarranted brusqueness. 'Tell her to remove herself from the premises at once. Escort her from the college by the least public route. You understand me? The River Stairs, perhaps?'

'"And, while you're at it, Mr Claydon, why don't you just dunk the minx in the Cam?"' came the amused suggestion from the doorway. '"If she floats, she's clearly the witch we always suspected she was." Dr Dalton! So good to see you again! A year? Can it *really* have been a year?'

The young woman advanced into the room, peeling off her gloves, sending the unmistakable signal that she was not to be persuaded to leave. She turned graciously to her uniformed escort who stood looking uncertainly from the don – now rising with automatic good manners – to the elegantly clad lady, who seemed to be treating the situation with a casualness amounting to levity. Behind his mask of disapproval, Claydon's shrewd eye was assessing the situation and calculating the relative strength of these two antagonists. The under-porter was skilled at this. His job depended on it. And the pecking order here was becoming

17

clearer by the second. He noticed that young Dr Dalton was lurking behind the protection of his desk, a formidable redoubt of polished mahogany piled high with books and papers.

With lazy assurance the intruder extended her rolled umbrella like a billiard cue, playfully, and swept a stack of books on to the floor. 'That's better! Now I can see what you're doing with your hands, Felix.'

The don cringed. Claydon looked thoughtfully at the ceiling.

Miss Talbot settled into a chair. With a wave of her hand she invited Dalton to resume his seat. 'Do sit down. This may take some time.'

She turned to Claydon with a dismissive smile. 'Thank you. You may go.'

Claydon made his judgement. 'Certainly, Miss. Thank you, Miss.' And, in a belated attempt to atone for his lapse in allegiance: 'Shall I whistle up some tea, sir?'

'Thank you, no. This is not a social occasion. That will be all.'

Felix Dalton glowered at the girl smiling across the desk at him. Why the devil had she come? After all these months? Had she found out? Did the young madam still bear a grudge? He sighed. The ball was in her court and he would just have to hear her out. And now, of course, she had nothing to lose. Impossible to threaten her – they'd surrendered their trump card last year. Against all his advice. He decided to go on the offensive.

'You look well and happy, Miss Talbot. The disgrace of being sent down from the University does not appear to have dimmed your spirits.'

'No indeed.' The topic seemed not to disconcert her.

At such a calculated piece of rudeness any other girl would have fled the field in tears. Not this one. She even peered at him flirtatiously from under the dipping brim of her green hat. 'As you observe – ejected from the gloomy

18

groves of Academe with its lurking serpents, I've been enjoying sunshine, open spaces, wide vistas . . .'

Was there a literal meaning to be inferred here? She certainly did look . . . well, *browner* than he remembered.

'Away from the confines of the corridors of learning, I thrive. I find that, after all, the uncorseted life is the one that suits me.' An unladylike wiggle of the shoulders accompanied the remark.

Dalton cleared his throat and fought down an urge to loosen his collar. Stung by her comment, he wondered whether he was blushing. Just as she had intended, the memory of Laetitia Talbot in decidedly uncorseted state returned to torment him. A vision of alabaster and gold had been his first impression as she rose, steaming gently, from her bath before the fire; his second that he was witnessing a very Edwardian scene. Both impressions had been abruptly dispersed when, becoming aware of his presence, she'd hurled a wet sponge at him and pushed him bodily from her room whooping like a bloody banshee. Dalton shuddered at the memory. He'd never be able to look a Botticelli maiden in the eye again.

Now he eyed warily the supple figure opposite. Her short linen walking dress was, as far as he could judge, in the height of fashion and revealing an extent of silk-clad leg as disturbing as ever. He'd been a damn fool . . . misinterpreted the signals . . . if there had been signals. He was no longer sure. And he rather thought he'd been badly informed at the time. That bloody know-it-all Wetherby! And he hadn't been the only gossipmonger to offer comment and advice: 'So you're invited to Melchester for the weekend? A Talbot house party? Oh, my! The literati are to meet the celebrati, then? Guest of Sir Richard?' Asked with a slightly raised eyebrow. 'Or his daughter? Miss Talbot *is* in your supervision group, I understand?'

And: 'The lovely Laetitia! You want to watch out for that one! She'll have you on a cocktail stick, old boy! But surely you've heard? You cannot be unaware . . .? Artistic family . . . Bohemian, you might say. Town house in Fitzroy

Square. Handy for the British Museum. As well as other conveniences less appetizing. Rumour has it that little Miss Talbot . . . much indulged by her papa . . . was allowed liberties no proper young girl of eighteen should ever have been allowed. Mother long dead – no restraining influence – and a constant parade of the loucher low-life of London trailing through the house. She was getting close to some of those appalling scarecrows at . . . what's that school of art? The Slade. That's it. Word is she was sent up to Cambridge – strings pulled of course! – more as a place of safety than of learning, but not before . . .' Wetherby had finished his tale sotto voce although they were alone together in the combination room, his voice getting lower as his excitement rose, his face gleaming in the candlelight, '. . . not before she had arranged to lose her virginity. In an upstairs room at the Café Royal. With a *Satanist*!'

Felix thought he'd replied casually enough. 'Heard that somewhere before, I think. Old story. And you've got the wrong girl.'

But below the astonishment and disapproval a trickle of excitement had begun to flow.

And one thing had led to another. He'd gone happily to the family home on the river Granta, south of Cambridge, impressed by the rambling and ancient manor house almost hidden from sight in a froth of apple blossom. Disconcerted at first to find he was not the only academic of the party – the Dean of his college was also present, all acerbic wit and fluent conversation – he'd settled quickly into the role which appeared to have been assigned to him: up-and-coming young poet. His appearance helped. Whilst not quite in the Rupert Brooke class, it was inevitable that comparisons would be made. He rather affected the floppy blond hair, the misty blue-eyed gaze vaguely wandering the horizon; he'd treacherously implied that his own verse could perhaps be considered – by those with an ear – more vigorously masculine, less obviously the tinkling tunes of a music box. People who'd never read a line of Dalton's verse hastened to agree. They were especially appreciative

20

when the verses were being spoken by the handsome young poet himself as he punted them along the river with seemingly effortless ease. Would he ever forget the audible catch in the breath of one of his passengers – the wife of the Lord Lieutenant – when, without a pause in his recital, he'd ducked sinuously under the overhanging branches of a may tree? With a careless gesture, he'd shaken the almond-scented blossoms from his golden hair, enchanted with the happy timing of his next line: *And the young god, starlight-crowned, outshining Baldur* . . .

A precious moment, quite spoiled by Laetitia who, with breathtaking insensitivity, had chosen that moment to throw an apple core at a passing squadron of ducks. The ensuing racket had drowned out his next stanza.

He'd been flattered that he'd been chosen to take the daughter of the house in to dinner. 'Felix, you'll take in Laetitia?' (All Christian names here for the duration of the party.) Surely there'd been meaning in this? And he'd been flattered, too, by the attentions of the other weekend guests, all distinguished figures. He'd affected not to hear when he'd caught the edge of murmurings behind raised hands: 'Neo-pagan is what they're saying, my dear!' And he'd fostered the glamorous image, salting his talk with the odd guttural phrase of Anglo-Saxon, his speciality. His Viking warrior looks impressed the ladies; he set out to impress the gentlemen with his deep-drinking. In that unbuttoned hour after dinner when the port circulated and the conversation picked up a masculine pace, he'd showed off. He'd been unwise.

Emboldened by four glasses of port and two of brandy, he'd retired upstairs, slipped into his silk dressing gown, and watched from his doorway as her maid said good night. Then he'd crept along the corridor and entered her room.

He flushed with anger and shame at the memory of the scene that followed. He'd never even heard before some of the curses she'd directed at him along with the sponge. Of course there'd been a rumpus. Guests had inconveniently popped out of their rooms in various stages of *déshabille* prepared to repel burglars or preserve a girl's honour; the Lord Lieutenant had brandished a revolver. But, amongst the retired military, politicians, and lions of London literary society, he'd been aware of one face only: the darkening features of the Dean of his college.

The chill command had rapped out with all the authority of a school housemaster: 'Dalton! See me in my room! *At once!*'

You can hear the closing of ranks as far off as Fen Ditton when the University decides to protect one of its own. The outcome was never in doubt. The honour of the college is paramount. There was no question that the matter would be swept under the carpet and one of the two parties removed. On the trumped-up accusation of a manufactured offence against the college – *'Just leave this in our hands, Dr Dalton'* – Miss Talbot was required to leave a week or two before she was due to take her final examinations. He savoured some of the phrases: *'... conduct bringing the name of her college into disrepute ... behaviour likely to redound to the dishonour of her sex ... setback to the integration of females into the University ...'*

Sir Richard had stormed and threatened but had accepted the inevitable. A product of the University himself, he understood the rules.

Ah, well ... in all conscience, the girl would have achieved nothing more than title to a degree at pass level, Dalton judged. Quite rightly, Cambridge had held out against the women walking away with a full degree on equal terms with the men. In any event, this woman was never about to scale any academic heights. And perhaps in the end she had been conscious of that? She had certainly accepted the decision of the authorities and departed with surprisingly little fuss, he remembered. *Suspiciously* little fuss? He tried to read the bland, friendly face across his desk. Comeuppance time? He didn't doubt it.

'I hear that congratulations are due, Felix? In my absence, I understand, you have succeeded in securing the affections of a certain Miss Esmé Leatherhead? The publishing family Leatherhead? Peregrine is her father? What a fortuitous connection for an up-and-coming young poet! You *are* still up and you are still coming, Felix? I wonder if you are aware that Esmé and I are old chums? No? She and I were at school together. A dear girl, though something of an idealist, I always thought . . . fastidious . . . exacting . . . she carries the burden of a Quaker upbringing, poor child! Have you not found so? I really must make a point of looking up my old friend – so much gossip to catch up on . . . And so far it seems you are managing to retain her affections?' There was no mistaking the menace in her sweet voice as it trailed away leaving thoughts unspoken.

'You unprincipled hussy! You wouldn't!'

'I most certainly would.'

He assessed his options. 'What do you want of me?'

'A very undemanding little favour. Something you do every day as a matter of course, I expect. I want you to write a letter of recommendation on college writing paper . . . I'm sure you have a supply buried somewhere in a lower stratum of this rubbish heap?'

Well, the girl had always been direct.

'I'm afraid I could not recommend you to any man or to any organization, Miss Talbot,' he answered frostily, 'whatever you threaten. I am amazed that you have the temerity to ask.'

She dismissed his bluster with an understanding smile. 'Just as well, then, that that is not what I am seeking. You jump the gun, Felix. It seems to be a trait of yours. I am just recently back from Egypt. Indeed, I spent the autumn and winter there. I had gone to lick my wounds, bury my anger in the sands, and see if some hard physical work would take away the sting of injustice. I've been digging. Under the direction of a friend of my father – Andrew Merriman, the archaeologist. Perhaps you've heard of him?'

23

Dalton nodded. 'So – you've been doing a little tomb-robbing?' The sneer was barely concealed behind the polite smile.

'If you've been doing a little versifying.' She sighed. 'It would take up too much of our time to attempt to convince someone who makes a parade of his scorn for the sciences of the value of the new discipline. The Romance of the Past has ensnared me, and I'm not talking about your deeply unattractive Anglo-Saxon warriors. I've learned all Andrew could teach me about the techniques of archaeology and I've read a good deal of ancient history. I can even decipher a line or two of hieroglyphs . . . I see I'm boring you?'

'No, no. My expression is one of incredulous fascination. I quiver with curiosity to know where you are leading me with all this.' He took from a drawer a sheet of college writing paper, unscrewed the cap of his fountain pen with a provoking flourish, and sat, head tilted, all compliant cooperation. Anything to get rid of the girl.

'Good. We're ready then. My intention is to foster the career of a friend and colleague, a Miss St Clair . . . Stella St Clair.'

'Sinclair?'

'No. Not quite.' Laetitia spelled out the surname. 'Miss St Clair is a talented, though at present unqualified, archaeologist, and she is seeking to fill a position which has recently come vacant on a dig in France. This is where I hope to enlist your help. I won't presume to dictate – I'll leave the wording to you. Choose whatever formulae come most readily to mind, but the substance of your letter should be this: You are recommending to the attention of the recipient – more of him later – the bearer, a Miss Stella St Clair, graduate – yes, I said *graduate* – of this University. Having covered herself with glory during her time here . . . no . . . better, I think, say that she achieved title to an honours degree of the second class . . . Miss St Clair has subsequently spent a year in Egypt working with the celebrated archaeologist Professor Sir Andrew Merriman (who will

24

also bear testimony to the good character and capacity of the said lady) and is certainly well fitted for a position with a foundation of the highest order and international reputation. Now – you are writing specifically to an American academic. Here are his details.'

She handed a note over the desk and he read, intrigued despite himself, *Charles Paradee, Directeur, Fondation Archéologique Américaine.* The address was in Fontigny, Burgundy, France.

She paused for a moment, then added, 'And you'd better assure Mr Paradee that your protégée speaks perfect French.'

'French?'

'I understand it to be the lingua franca of Burgundy,' she replied annoyingly. 'And that is one point at least on which you need have no bad conscience. Miss St Clair's mother was French. Felix, stop puffing and blustering and what-iffing and get on with it! No one will ever find out. And if they do, you may say I held a gun to your head. I'll confess to it.'

Ten minutes later, a final draft was approved, folded, and tucked away in her bag, which she closed with a triumphant click.

'And what guarantee do I have that this little show of pettiness is to be the end of your attempts at coercion and not merely the first of a succession of demands?' Dalton wanted to know.

'Guarantee? None at all. I am no gentleman, Felix. If there's anything more I should need, I shall be back for it. And . . . would you really call it coercion? I'd call it black-mail. You should pray that the pursuit of my career takes me away from this snug academic world of yours and distracts my attention from your affairs.'

'Look here! I would like your Miss St Clair, whoever and wherever she may be, and any other performers in this Grand Guignol you are staging, to understand,' he said carefully, 'that should there be repercussions, I shall take steps to protect my reputation.' Then, catching a cynical grey eye, he shrugged and adjusted his tone. 'I wish her every success and you also, Miss Talbot. I shall watch your future career with some interest. I hope your success will lead you on to further – and farther – triumphs in lands distant from Cambridge. I believe wonders are to be unearthed in Italy ... or Crete ... or Ur of the Chaldees! The scorching sands of the Mesopotamian desert conceal many things an enterprising girl might lay hands on – golden crowns, precious jewels ... *scorpions*!'

Abruptly the sleek professional mask slipped and Laetitia caught a glimpse of the spiteful schoolboy he must once have been.

She replied coolly, 'I find the creatures in the most surprising places. Just as well I have become immune to their sting.'

He rose to his feet but did not offer to shake her hand or see her out.

Laetitia Talbot paused, her hand on the doorknob, and turned with a charming smile to the pale and deflated don. He readied himself for her Parthian shot, always, he remembered, her speciality.

'By the way, Felix ... the story that has circulated amongst you ...'

Dalton looked puzzled.

'The alleged loss of my most precious possession ...'

'Ah! That? Great Heavens! You were aware ...?'

'Naturally, since it was *I* who initiated the story. It has always annoyed me that such a sprightly tale could have become so garbled in the retelling. I'm afraid it will shock you even further, Felix, when I tell you that the gentleman in question was not a Satanist – he was a *scientist*.'

Chapter Three

She closed the door gently, adjusted her hat to a less rak-
ish angle, then stood for a moment or two struggling to
achieve a level of control. Disgust both for her own subterfuge and for Dalton's treachery expressed itself in an
inconvenient inability to pull gloves on to shaking hands
and a sudden loss of impetus.

She had conducted her business with such ruthless haste
she found herself with an hour to spare before her next
appointment. A walk by the river would calm her. And she
could say good bye to this most lovely, most gracious spot
in the world. She made her way along to Garret Hostel
Lane, tormenting herself with the memory of her eight-
year-old self careering uncertainly down the path on
her first new bicycle. An impetuous purchase by her godfather, Daniel, who'd taken her into the bike repair shop
in Laundress Lane a week before her birthday. They'd
gone in to pick up a new brake cable for him and had come
out with a gleaming, two-wheeled, dark green wonder for
her. Daniel had run behind anxiously shouting advice.
'Don't look back! Keep pedalling, Letty!' He'd caught up
with her on the sharp upward slope of the bridge at
the end of the lane where, finally, she'd run out of courage
and puff and they'd hung laughing and gasping over the
parapet.

Now, she paused in the same place. Turning the knife in
the wound. There was no one else around to enjoy the
fresh spring day. With examinations looming, undergraduates were all closeted away with their books, desperately

filling in gaps and plastering over the rough surfaces of three years' study. She was glad to have the river to herself for a bit. She watched as a black swan, all too conscious of his exotic good looks, was joined in a pas de deux by a white swan. She almost applauded as they dipped and bowed and exited left, behind a curtain of yellow willow boughs.

A punt approached going at quite a clip. Four young men in blazers were singing a boating song and drinking champagne. Their companion working on the pole joined in the chorus, apparently unaware that he was moving off course and about to collide with the arch of the bridge. Laetitia knew this stretch well. With the authority of one who'd taken part in the Saturday morning seven o'clock punting classes for women and had the valued certificate of competence under her belt, she called out a warning: 'Oy! Watch out! Pull to starboard!'

The punter took time to doff his boater gallantly to the pretty girl on the bridge before correcting his course with a flourish, sending the boat skimming with a swift fish-tail through the arch. Laetitia crossed to the other side and waved a friendly acknowledgement of his skill, then wandered on over the bridge and along the riverbank. Why was she doing this? Tormenting herself with the sight of all that she'd lost? This was a world that had rejected her without compunction largely because she was female, and because she had challenged authority's model of female behaviour. To survive in this hostile environment it was wise to pin back your hair, wear spectacles and clumpy shoes. It was prudent to acquire a taste for lisle stockings, weak tea, and earnest conversation, and never to hanker after silk, champagne cocktails, or racy talk. And it was no disadvantage to gain higher marks than the men. She had found she could do none of those things.

She followed the winding western bank of the Cam through the beech trees until she came upon the sight of King's College across the river. The light was so intense she had to squint up into the gem-hard blue of the sky to

28

admire the slender thrust of the pinnacles of the Chapel. For an unsettling moment a pillared temple at Karnak standing out against an equally brilliant sky superposed itself. But the sun-scorched vision was dispelled by the movement of a herd of black and white cows, up to their udders in buttercups, lazily munching their way across the lush meadow grass in front of the college.

She knew why she loved this place. The monuments, the pillars, the carved temples of Egypt were not on a human scale. They towered; they threatened. You lowered your eyes before the stones of Egypt. But the golden architecture she now looked at raised the eyes as it lifted the spirit. Every line of the Chapel pointed heavenwards; every pinnacle exhorted the onlooker to praise God. But it was the secular buildings clustering about – Clare, classical and handsome with its pilastered front smiling genially on to the river; the graceful Wren Library; the balanced and elegant Senate House – which gave out the confident statement: 'If praise is due – praise Man.' Not one single potentate, no Ramses, no Thutmosis, demanded the onlooker's abasement; the name of no single vaunting personality came to Laetitia's mind as she stood, smiling and admiring. A few English kings and queens had attempted to secure immortality here by their benevolence perhaps, but she could never remember their names. And none of the architecture rang a martial note; no brazen trumpets sounded – just the deep and jovial swell of the chapel organ. This was a place that celebrated learning, progress, and creativity. It celebrated Humanity.

Distantly, a cracked bell dinged the three-quarter hour and Laetitia walked on along the path skirting the lawn towards the gate leading into King's Parade. The scene of her crime. She'd foolishly accepted a challenge from a group of male undergraduates, some of whom she had counted her friends. Of course she was bold enough to light a cigarette and walk across the middle of the lawn! The Proctor and his two Bulldogs must have been lurking close by. Her companions had mysteriously melted away:

29

she'd been left alone to face the wrath of the college hierarchy.

She paused, tempted for a moment to repeat her crime. No. Time to grow up. The cigarettes stayed in her bag and her feet on the path.

This was not and never would be her place. She heard again in memory her godfather's voice: *'Don't look back, Letty!'* and she kept her face determinedly set towards Trumpington Street and her second meeting of the morning.

Fitzbillies tea shop was strangely empty when she arrived, and she hardly needed to hear the welcoming voice calling, 'Over here, Letty!' to locate her friend. Laetitia hurried over, weaving between the tables towards the small brown-haired, brown-eyed girl jumping to her feet in excitement. They clasped hands and kissed each other warmly before settling down on either side of the starched cloth.

'Train on time? I hope you've not been waiting long?'

'No, no, Letty! I took a taxi from the station and I've only just got here. Tell me at once! Were you successful! Did you get it?'

Laetitia looked with amused affection at the anxious face and decided it would be cruel to spin out the tension. 'Yes! It worked like a charm!' she replied. 'Oh, we'll have a pot of tea for two, Miss, and two of your Chelsea buns, please.'

When the waitress had gone off with their order, Laetitia took the letter from her bag. She passed it to her friend, watching her reaction as she opened and read it.

'Perfect! This is perfect! I couldn't have written a better recommendation myself. Well done! Gosh, it took some courage to face him down like that. I say, Letty, did he fall easy victim to the blackmail?'

'He did! I laid it on a bit thick – I mean, I made out that I understood him to be your fiancé ... Hope you don't mind? Esmé, I have to warn you that he made no attempt to deny the relationship. In fact he looked rather smug, I thought, when I brought it up. Anything you feel you ought to confide?' She looked anxiously at Esmé Leather-head. 'You will be careful, won't you? Dalton's a vindictive little twerp. I hope you've not got into an entanglement for my sake?'

'Don't worry!' Esmé hurried to reassure her. 'He's never actually proposed to me, so that's all right. The minute he does, I shall turn him down. But he's much more con-cerned to spend his time sweet-talking my father. And you know my father! He's getting pretty fed up with the over-tures, I can tell you! Felix and his verses are hanging by a thread and he's tolerated only because I've been kind to him. One more ambling alexandrine, one more halting hexameter, and Father will set the dogs on him! I think I'll wait until you're safely in France and then complain that he's becoming a pest.'

She took up the letter again and her smile faded. 'I won't ask you if you're sure you know what you're doing, Letty – I expect you've got it all worked out to the last move – but *I* shall ask for some reassurance! And what's all this nonsense about the name?'

'You know perfectly well that my mother's name was St Clair before she married my father. And the French half of my family have always called me by my second name – Stella. You should hear them trying to pronounce "Laetitia"!'

'Aren't you being just a little . . . um . . . over-careful?'

'You're trying not to say "hysterical"?'

Esmé grinned and nodded.

For a moment, Laetitia looked uncomfortable. 'Believe me – I have good reasons for the deceit. And, anyway – the identity does belong to me. It's going to be my professional name. I can do this, Esmé! Whatever they ask of me. Andrew Merriman is a pretty harsh taskmaster, you know; he would have put me on the next boat home if I'd not been pulling my weight. I can do it! I've learned tech-niques and methods. But I'm adaptable – if anonymity is what seems to be required, I can always fade into the background.'

31

Esmé, plumply pretty, looked in disbelief at her statuesque friend, wondering what could possibly be the background into which Laetitia Talbot could fade. 'It's not that that concerns me, Letty. I'm sure you'll integrate like anything. It's the danger. Dead man's shoes, that's what you're proposing to fill. A *murdered* dead man's shoes! And not just any man. *Daniel* ...' She leaned across the table and squeezed Letty's hand. 'I know you were very fond of him.'

'Fond? Oh, more than fond. I loved him,' said Letty. 'He was my father's best friend and *my* best friend. My father was off soldiering for most of childhood. It was Daniel who was always there when I was growing up ... teaching, explaining, joking, getting me into hot water. And – do you know? – I suspect the old thing's still doing that!'

'From beyond the grave?'

'Just that!'

She rummaged in her bag and took out a dog-eared postcard. 'Have a look and tell me what I'm to make of this! Much delayed in the French postal system apparently, it was delivered while I was away in Egypt. Judging by the date, Esmé, this looks like my godfather's very last message to me. Or to anyone. It appears to have been stamped the day after he was murdered. And that's odd enough, but it's by a long way not the oddest thing.'

Chapter Four

Esmé looked carefully at the photograph on the front and made no comment. She turned it over and studied the postmarks and then finally read the written message. Still silent, she looked doubtfully up at her friend.

'Tell me what you're thinking,' Letty urged.

'Well, Fontigny looks very pretty. Jolly good abbey, I'd say . . . The sender has dated it the second of October and the first of the postmarks bears the date of the day following. As you said. So far nothing remarkable.' She was keeping her voice deliberately neutral. 'Um . . . just a couple of things . . . For a start, this card wasn't sent to you and it wasn't Daniel who sent it. I see it's addressed to a Miss Tabitha T. c/o Mrs M. Cartwright, thirty-five Albert Place, Cambridge. Don't you think you should hand it back to one or other of these ladies?'

'Of course it's for me! Maggie Cartwright is my old governess. She lived with us at Melchester and taught me until I went to school and she retired. She used to call me Tabitha after the nursery rhyme . . . you know . . .

> 'Tabitha Twitchit is grown so fine
> She lies in bed until half past nine . . .

'On account of a period of slothful late-rising I experienced in my youth.'

Esmé nodded, comprehending instantly. She glanced back down at the card. 'Now I begin to understand the game. So – thanks to the insight and kind offices of your governess, this made its way on to Miss Twitchit.' Her mouth tightened with the effort to suppress laughter. 'Using my deductive powers and my sketchy knowledge of the works of Beatrix Potter, I will guess that the signature at the end: – *your loving Jeremy F. –*'

'Fisher,' muttered Letty, ill at ease. 'He was fond of fishing in the meadow by the river. Maggie Cartwright invented that one, too.' She glowered. 'Well – what do you expect, Esmé? If someone's checking his mail, he's hardly likely to sign it *Lt.-Col. Daniel Thorndon, D.S.O.*, is he? Clearly, Daniel was trying to avoid interception by someone who was aware of *my* name and address – and *his.'*

Esmé stared in disbelief for a moment, then continued her commentary in a deliberately bracing tone: 'Well . . . No bloodstains on the postcard, I see. So you couldn't say it had been snatched from his lifeless hand and put in the box by a tidy-minded killer? No . . . but I suppose you could say it looks rather battered?'

'It was retained by the police for a while. Daniel's body was found near a postbox in the middle of the night. No reason for him to be walking the streets of Fontigny at that hour . . . the assumption was that he'd not been able to sleep and had spent a wakeful night writing up notes and had dashed off this postcard, which he popped into the post during his walk. They sealed the box and checked the contents. This must have been retained as evidence, inspected, and then sent on with all the rest of the mail the box contained some weeks later.'

'So it was waiting for you when you got back from Egypt?'

Letty nodded. 'That terrible time last year. I'd been sent down from the University. My father and I were exhausted from fighting a force much stronger than we were, and then the bombshell of Daniel's death exploded over us. His body was sent back for burial and after that we geared ourselves up for another impossible struggle – with the French authorities this time. Daddy went out and made a fuss but

34

had to come back with the official judgement intact – Daniel had been tragically stabbed to death by a street-robber.'

'Now that is odd. A robber out and about at five in the morning? Whom would he be expecting to rob? Perhaps it's different abroad, but surely any successful thief would choose more fruitful hunting grounds – crowds on city streets in broad daylight? Markets? Tourist spots?'

'Exactly! My father's nothing if not thorough. He made the local police reveal their crime records. No street robberies since the war, and not many during and before either. The usual *crimes passionnels* – a lot of those in the aftermath of the war . . . husbands returning unexpectedly – and that's it. It's a quiet cathedral town, not a place where a stiletto-wielding assassin lurks round every corner in wait for unwary somnambulists! Though some of his possessions had been taken.'

'Ah!' said Esmé knowingly. 'That's very probably a distraction.' The House of Leatherhead made a great deal of money from one of its less celebrated branches – crime novels – and Esmé cheerfully admitted to reading each title as it rolled off the press. She knew what to ask next. 'Who found the body? Do you know?'

'Oh, that at least is well documented. He was discovered by a contingent of cavalry! Daniel would have approved. He was in the Royal Horse Guards during the war.'

'Cavalry? At dawn? Good Lord! A scene of quite surprising activity, the square of Fontigny, it seems. It only lacks an operatic bass-baritone strolling on, belting out a lament, and you could stage it at Covent Garden.' She broke off in embarrassment. 'Oh! Sorry, Letty! I wasn't thinking . . .'

Letty laughed. 'No – you're right. It certainly must have looked very dramatic. The cavalry who came galloping up on this occasion arrived just a few minutes too late, according to the pathologist. They were actually twelve young soldiers out exercising the horses of the local Haras.'

'Haras?'

'It's the state stables. A sort of central stud-farm serving the whole of France. The cream of the country's horseflesh spends half the year there. These young lads were riding them through the square on their way out to the hills when the lead horse sidestepped to avoid something on the ground. The rider dismounted to investigate. The lads did everything you could have hoped for – they summoned the police and the local doctor, they even split up into teams and searched the alleyways running from the square. They put in a full report, which impressed my father. And really, I have to say it: we couldn't find fault with the French authorities. Though the name of Talbot is not exactly unfamiliar in law-and-order circles in Fontigny.' She shuddered.

'I see,' said Esmé. Her grin was amused and appreciative. 'I know your father! He'd roust them out. Stand no nonsense. They've probably got a thick file with TALBOT spelled out on the spine. They may even have added TAKE COVER! Yes, I can understand why you had to choose a different name! But, I have to say, if Sir Richard, redoubtable old thing that he is, couldn't make any progress, I don't reckon *your* chances can be very high.'

'I intend to go about it differently. Father goes in full tilt, bellowing a challenge. I shall employ tactics of a different nature.'

'Sneaky, you mean.'

'Say, rather – subtle.'

Esmé sighed. 'Have you thought about a motive, Letty? Any ideas? Your godparent was an inoffensive old bean, wasn't he? No one had reason to want him dead, surely? Could he have been mistaken for someone else?'

'It was a bright moonlit night. And you have to be pretty close to your target to put a knife into his throat. You'd know if you had the right man.'

'He didn't have any dangerous habits?' Esmé persisted. 'Habits which could have brought down such a vicious attack? Lost a fortune gambling and couldn't pay up? Seduced the mayor's wife? He hadn't suggested Napoleon

36

had feet of clay at the end of his short legs? That would get you killed in France!'

'You know he was a blameless teddy bear. A charmer, yes. And I understand quite a ladies' man in his earlier days, but discreet. No one ever ambushed him to deliver a horsewhipping on the steps of his club!'

'Then it must have something to do with his work. Doesn't he mention his work in the card? Let's read it again.' Esmé shook her head, puzzled. 'This is becoming a two-pot problem, I think,' she said, beckoning the waitress. 'Miss! Would you please bring us another of whatever that was? Darjeeling? Thank you. Oh, and two slices of marmalade cake . . . Thinking always makes me hungry.

'Now.' Esmé began to read aloud the message, written in tiny letters to squeeze it into the available space:

> *'Fontigny-Sainte-Reine.*
> *'Dearest Tabitha, Beautiful abbey isn't it, even in ruins? Not too late to wish you success in your new venture, I hope? Look forward to comparing notes when next we meet! All going splendidly here in Burgundy..*
> *'Met your old friend Lady Uffington here the other day. She sends her regards and insists you look her up when you visit. Incredibly ancient these days (aren't we all!) but the old girl can still show you young 'uns a thing or two! If you do come out – bring good company. Suggest Judy and her friend. Plenty for them to do in this town! Your loving Jeremy F..*

'What do I make of this? Well, honestly, Letty, not much. Can this *really* be from Daniel? It seems a perfectly ordinary message. Rather dull, in fact, when one remembers what an entertaining man he was.' For a moment Esmé's face dimmed into sadness. 'Do you remember when he tried to teach us to smoke? Oh, sorry, Letty . . . not the time or place . . . Now I'll concentrate. First: it's not his style. Second: it isn't exactly a last desperate call for help, is it? I

37

mean, it's hardly a case of words hastily written on the last page torn from the family Bible . . . in blood . . . in ancient Greek . . . got out of the country carried in a cleft stick by a trusty native bearer?'

'Are you just going to mock? Or are you prepared to look at this seriously?' Letty asked stiffly.

'Yes, of course. Let me see . . . Sudden death is clearly not on his mind, is it? He's looking to the future. He wishes you luck; he's happy with his work in Burgundy; he's even setting up a sort of awful English society get-together with mutual friends.'

Letty leaned closer over the table and whispered, 'What would you say, Esmé, if I told you that what *I* see there is indeed a cry of distress?'

'I'd say you were nuts. Too many hours under a tropical sun without a topee.' She poured out more tea from the fresh pot. 'Very well. Tell me what I've missed. What have you seen in this very ordinary communication?'

'Look at the fourth sentence. *All going splendidly* . . . That one.'

'Rather gives one to suppose that he was happy in his work. No murderous clouds on the horizon?'

'No. The reverse! What do you see at the end of the sentence?'

'A full stop, of course!' Esmé looked again. 'Well, actually, *two* full stops. Getting old? Spluttering pen-nib?'

'No. Fully intentional, I believe. It's a code. I didn't know you before we were eleven, but when you were about eight, Esmé, I wonder if, like me, you went through that phase of yearning for secret societies, passwords, codes?'

'Good Lord, yes! With three older brothers, my sister and I depended on that sort of thing to survive. We even invented our own language.'

'When I was about that age – just when the war broke out – my godfather used to write me notes and postcards to cheer me up. My older brother had answered the call to war and my mother had died and I was a lonely little girl. Daniel helped to fill a gap . . . before he went off, too . . .

38

Anyway, one day he left a note on the hall table. It was the butler's day off or the disaster would not have occurred! It said: *Dear L., Watch out! Your least favourite great-aunt has just telephoned. Lillian finds she is able to come down to spend the weekend and will be here in time for tea. Alert your Pa and Mrs Hascombe to this terrible news. I'm heading for the hills. Love, Daniel.*

'Unfortunately, Great-Aunt Lillian arrived before I returned from my music lesson and found the house empty. But she did find the note.' Letty shuddered. 'I decided that leaving notes about the place was a dangerous business and I devised a simple way of communicating with my godfather. The trick was this: a double stop at the end of a sentence negates it.'

Esmé looked puzzled.

'Imagine this,' Letty explained, *'Dear L., I know you'll be delighted to hear your favourite aunt can come for the weekend..* (Dot, dot!) *She'll be here in time for tea.* You see, the double fullstop after "weekend" indicated he knows I'll be anything *but* delighted?'

'And presumably you are the only person in the world who would be aware that the presence of an insignificant little dot turns this third sentence into: *Everything is going disastrously* wrong *in Burgundy?'*

'I'm sure that's what he meant. And why bother with a childish code anyway? For the first time in fifteen years? Why not whiz off a series of letters or phone calls to someone in authority? Daniel had lots of friends in high places in London. He could have written a message in Phoenician or ancient Assyrian to one of his cronies at the Museum if that was his fancy, and they would have understood. Someone was watching him. Intercepting his communications. I had thought that his letters to us were growing increasingly distant . . . impersonal. Daddy even said one day, "Good Lord! Daniel appears only able to talk about the weather and the cooking these days! What's got into him?" And one letter, I do believe, had been tampered with, resealed, then sent on.'

'Heavens! This is disturbing. It speaks of someone with a good deal of influence in the community. Someone with authority. Local power? In France that would be the mayor? The police? And what about this site director he worked with?'

'Daniel admired Charles Paradee. He was always very complimentary about him.'

'Paradee? Odd name?'

'Charles Paradee is American. Ambitious, able, lots of dollars behind him and his project. It's the rest of the message I can't make head or tail of.'

'Can't you contact this Lady Uffington he mentions? Ask her if she can shed any light?'

'Well, that is the strangest thing: the lady doesn't exist. Esmé, I've never heard of her.'

'One of Daniel's old flames, I should think. It may not have occurred to him that you'd never met her. You know what they're like, that generation – they think everyone knows everyone else. I bet she's in Debrett.'

'I've checked. I've even looked in *Who's Who*. I rang the editor of *The Times*. There's no such person.'

'She seems real to Daniel. She sends you her regards and asks you to look her up when you go to Burgundy. How did he know you were going there?'

'He didn't. I think that's a suggestion. No, marching orders. He's telling me to go.'

Esmé lost interest in her marmalade cake. 'Dangerous stuff! If the French police with all the resources at their disposal can't bring it to an acceptable conclusion, why on earth do you suppose a lone English girl could succeed? No!' She shook her head vehemently. 'You meant the world to Daniel. He would never expose you to the dangers of a situation like this. Show me where it says so.'

'Right here,' said Letty, pointing. '*If you do come out – bring good company. Suggest Judy and her friend. Plenty for them to do in this town.* I warned you this was very nursery-oriented! Daniel knew I would not only understand but would be alarmed by the references to the past. *Judy and*

40

her friend. I was given a Punch and Judy set of wooden puppets one Christmas. I absolutely hated Mr Punch and threw him away, but I kept Judy and her friend. Now do you see?'

'Sorry. You'll have to tell me.'

'Judy's friend and protector was a *policeman*. This is Daniel's way of telling me I shouldn't go out there by myself and that I should take the precaution of somehow setting up police involvement ... That there was something criminal going on there.'

Esmé handed back the postcard. 'So what have we got? Daniel's in trouble. Hating something about Burgundy – a well-founded sentiment in the light of what was to happen – and suspecting that something was about to go badly wrong, he encourages – no, *requires* – you to inveigle a Scotland Yard Inspector into accompanying you to this benighted spot. Once there you are to locate this Uffington woman – a phantom – who will obligingly lead you further down into the awful maze. Am I getting this right? Well, it's quite clear then, Letty. I see no problem. There's only one action you can, in all conscience, perform, isn't there? More tea? You pour.'

'Oh, right. And what action do you have in mind?'

Letty, with cup in one hand and teapot in the other, could do nothing to prevent her friend from making a sudden lunge across the table to snatch her letter of recommendation to Charles Paradee.

'You tear *this* to shreds! I'll do it for you. And you go nowhere near this wretched Fontigny. You write a polite note to this Paradee person telling him that, after all, you find you will not be available to come and dig with him. I don't want to hear a second body's been found oozing its lifeblood away into a medieval gutter!'

41

Chapter Five

Sir Richard Talbot lounged in his favourite armchair, the remains of a glass of Talisker at his elbow, the latest Buchan novel on his knee. After a good day's hunting and a congenial dinner, he should have been at ease. Fretfully, he poured himself a second whisky and calmed himself with the familiar gesture of holding up the cut-glass tumbler to the glow of the fire, the better to admire the amber liquid. His agitation persisted and he glowered across the hearth rug at the cause of his state of unease. Four narrowed eyes returned his glower.

'You can't hide behind that glass for much longer, Daddy,' said Letty. 'You're going to have to give us your answer. Just say yes and we'll leave you in peace to go back to your shocker.'

'Pay no attention to her, Sir Richard! You know what she's like! Say no, or there'll be another coffin coming back from France,' insisted Esmé boldly.

Sir Richard looked at the two earnest faces on the sofa opposite and sighed. Why these two had remained such firm friends over the years was a mystery to him. They never agreed about anything. He'd not bothered to count the occasions on which he'd been called on as final authority to decide which one of them was right, only, having announced his decision, to be set upon by both of them. Laetitia, tall and fair-haired, had all the stalking elegance of an egret when seen next to her small friend, who was as bright-eyed and neat as a robin. He decided to bluster a little more. Sometimes they got bored and left him alone if he went on for long enough.

'One more word and I'll ship the pair of you off to darkest Burgundy and have you chained up like Andromeda – to a postbox! You deserve it! I can hardly begin to believe what you've done today. If that young thug Dalton takes it into his head to open his mouth – and we all know how discreet *he* can be – bang go *my* dining rights in several colleges. You ought never to have made contact with this American and offered your services, which I'll bet is what happened. I don't believe a word of all that nonsense about a post being advertised, my girl. My suspicion is that *you* approached this Paradee and said you'd go and work for no recompense and he replied saying thank you very much and requesting testimonials. Am I right?'

Laetitia's cross face told him all he needed to know. 'I curse Daniel for putting such ideas into your head, Letty, and I'm not at all convinced that you're reading him aright anyway. It all sounds a bit thin. Two full stops indeed! Where'd you get hold of all this *School for Spies* stuff? What rubbish! And what about poor Andrew Merriman, who was gracious enough to nurse you through a year's apprenticeship in Egypt? You're getting *him* to vouch for you too? How did you manage that?' Catching a deepening of Letty's colour, he groaned. 'Oh no! More blackmail! Well . . . it can't have been difficult, I suppose. Andrew would always be a very easy target for blackmail. Dash it! More fences to mend!'

'But, Daddy! We owe it to Daniel to do as he asked us with his last words, don't we?' She thrust the postcard at him. 'Won't you listen to him? One last time? We'll never hear his voice again! Are you silencing him forever?' After an hour of explaining, cajoling, and reassuring, it had come down to this. She had no more tricks left. But her father had always listened to Daniel.

He took the card and silently read the words again. Finally he looked up. When he spoke, his voice was husky with emotion. 'Soppy old thing! Very well . . . I concede.

We'll hearken to what the old reprobate has to say. But, my girl, we'll stick to the letter of what he says or we'll take no action at all. Is that agreed?'

Letty nodded solemnly, disguising her satisfaction at hearing a sally port creak open.

'Then it all comes down to Mr Plod, the Policeman. The character stipulated by your godfather. I would never allow you to go abroad, not even as far as Deauville . . .' He considered for a moment. '. . . and perhaps rather particularly *not* Deauville, without a reliable escort. You find yourself a suitable companion – and I'm not offering any assistance here, you're on your own! – and you can go. There will, of course, be certain requirements . . .'

'Requirements? What sort of requirements?' Letty asked with misgiving.

'The lucky candidate for this journey to Hades and back must be elderly – a retired officer of experience and heavy with years, sufficient years to put him beyond the range of your allurements and blandishments, my girl! He should be the male equivalent of the college bedders – what is the phrase? *De aspecto horribile.* That's it.' He laughed, beginning to enjoy himself. 'Ugly as sin! And he must have an unblemished record, be in full possession of all his faculties, able to speak French, and willing to take on the guise of chauffeur and general factotum for a spoilt young English miss. I'm prepared to offer a remuneration of five pounds per week plus living expenses. Over-generous perhaps, but the sum reflects the particular demands of the position. There you have it. Daniel's own words, clarified and expanded a little by me. I'm sure my friend would have wanted nothing less than this,' he added piously.

Esmé chortled. 'In other words – no, you won't go, Letty! A victory for common sense. Well done, Sir Richard!'

When the two young women arrived next morning in front of the colonnaded façade of the Fitzwilliam Museum and tethered their bicycles to nearby iron railings, Esmé turned towards the steps and the entrance.

'No. This way,' said Letty, pointing towards Downing Street. 'Something to do before we go in, if you wouldn't mind.'

'Now, I ask myself: how disappointed am I to postpone the pleasure of gazing at ancient potsherds, rusty arrowheads . . . loom weights?' said Esmé with heavy sarcasm. All Letty's attempts to make her friend see the fascination of ancient articles dug from the earth had so far been unsuccessful, but she never stopped trying. 'So – where are you taking me?'

'To the police station.'

'Letty! Why?'

'Because that's where we'll find policemen,' replied Letty patiently. 'And if we ask the right question of the right officer, that's how we'll find a *retired* policeman.'

Esmé scampered angrily after her friend as she crossed the road into Downing Street, heading for St Andrew's Street. 'If you think you can track down ex-Sergeant Ebenezer Gotobed to his retreat in Garlic Row and talk him into going to France with you, you're barmy, Letty! He'll be far too busy with his pigeons and his leeks. And I very much doubt that Mrs Gotobed would be able to spare him. I'm sorry I spoke slightingly of the loom weights! I adore loom weights! Can we go back and admire them now?'

She was still complaining when they arrived in front of the imposing and uncompromisingly austere police headquarters.

'I'm not going in there,' declared Esmé firmly, looking up at the heraldic carving over the mighty front doors. 'I've heard about this place! Don't they have something in there called the Spinning House? When the Proctors arrest unaccompanied young ladies of the town, they lock them up in it without telling their families. And make them do hard labour!'

'I think it's closed down. And anyway – we don't look like tarts of the town exactly, Esmé. I rather think it was the

45

fact of being *accompanied* by male members of the University that got the Proctors excited and the young ladies into trouble. But, just in case . . .' Letty patted her bag, 'I've got my cards with me.'

But Esmé noticed that she straightened her hat and tucked away a stray lock of hair.

As they hesitated outside, peering through the open double doors into the oak-lined, marble-tiled interior, a group approached from the direction of the city centre. Two burly policemen were dragging along between them a third man. Esmé's attention moved at once from the smart getup of the constables to the abject appearance of the down-and-out they were hauling along with such little ceremony. He was frail, grey-bearded, and unkempt. His clothes were second- or even third-hand and seemed to consist mainly of an overlarge greatcoat and shabby boots. Tramps and beggars were a common enough sight on the streets even now, eight years after the war, and Esmé was always being reminded to pay no attention to them.

'Letty! Look! You must speak to them!'

Letty's eye swept over the group. 'They're just constables, Esmé. And they're busy. They won't do. We're going to have to go inside to get our information.'

'No! Look properly! They're being beastly to that poor old man. Can't you see? His nose! It's bleeding! They've been hitting him.'

'I do believe you're right. Well, why don't you go and remonstrate with them?'

'You know very well they'll take no notice of *me*! Oh, he's limping! They've been kicking him!' Esmé's pity was turning to anger. She pointed an accusing finger in their direction. 'Go for them, Letty!'

'Really, Esmé! Where is this going to end? You had me rescue a three-legged tortoise from the market, the runt of a litter from the puppy van, and the knife-grinder's asthmatic donkey, and now you're trading up to human flotsam and jetsam.' She sighed. But Esmé noticed that while she was speaking, Letty's back had straightened, her

46

chin had come up, and she was watching the three men coming towards them with a searching eye.

The two girls positioned themselves side by side, blocking the pavement in front of the constables and their prisoner.

'May I help you, ladies?' one asked as they halted in surprise.

'You most certainly may, Officer. Release that gentleman! We, as members of the public whom you serve, take exception to the manner in which you are handling him. Observe, Miss Leatherhead, would you, the nosebleed, the limp in the left leg, the bruise appearing on the left cheekbone.'

Esmé moved closer to the prisoner, dutifully observing the alleged wounds as they were itemized, and tut-tutting primly.

'May I suggest, ladies,' said the constable, exquisitely polite, 'that if you are easily affronted by scenes of this nature, you do not loiter in the doorway of the local nick? A pleasant walk in the Botanic Garden may well be more in tune with your sensibilities. They do say as how the peonies are a sight to behold at the moment.'

'Oh, I dare say, Officer,' agreed Letty. 'Unfortunately, we have business with the Chief Inspector. I have been charged by my father – Sir Richard Talbot, Justice of the Peace . . . you are aware of Sir Richard? – with the delivery of a most urgent message. Here's my card.'

One officer wiped his hand on his trousers and took the proffered card, glancing at it briefly. He nodded lugubriously at his companion.

'And now, perhaps you would care to enlarge on the problem you are having with this man?'

'He's a down-and-out, ma'am. No visible means of support. Picked him up in the graveyard behind St Mary the Less. Just routine. We'll take him in to the desk, book him, and he'll be sent up Castle Hill to spend a week in the House of Correction.' He gave a conspiratorial grin. 'That

47

should convince him it's time to move on away from Cambridge.'

'If 'e can still move, after a week in the Correction!' chortled the second constable.

Letty flinched but retained her polite smile. She shook her head. 'Something tells me you may have misconstrued this matter, gentlemen. Can you be quite certain that he is penniless? Or have you merely assumed as much from the state of his, er, toilette?' She reached a gloved hand into the pocket of the man's filthy greatcoat. When she pulled it out again, a silver half-crown piece glittered between her thumb and forefinger. 'There! Visible means of support! The price of five days' accommodation at sixpence a day. You ought to have declared it,' she reprimanded the tramp. 'They'll add wasting police time to your charges if you're not more careful.' She dropped the coin back into the man's pocket.

The policemen looked at each other glumly over the prisoner's head. Then, without a word exchanged, they released him. 'Very well, ma'am,' said the spokesman. 'Have it your way. I hope as how he's properly grateful for your intervention. Cell'll keep for another day or two. Now, we'll go and inform the Governor that you are expecting to see him. Perhaps you could wait in the lobby?'

'Inform the Guv?' muttered the second in a voice he intended to be overheard. 'Sound the alarm you mean! Poor old sod! Wonder if he has *any* idea what he's in for?'

The girls were left on the pavement looking uncomfortably at the newly freed man. The tramp didn't jump for joy at the unexpected release or amble away but stood quietly staring back at them. Finally, he fished around in his pocket and held out the half-crown. 'I couldn't be quite certain that I would find the coin in there,' he remarked. 'It seems to come and go at will. And may I say that I am, indeed, properly grateful?' His voice was low and without accent. A surprisingly pleasant voice, Letty thought. She shook her head and gestured that he was to keep the coin.

Esmé rummaged in her bag and produced a clean handkerchief. He did not refuse or make a fuss but took it gracefully. 'Ah, yes. It seems I resisted arrest! Unconsciously – literally – for I was sleeping when they came upon me in the Saxon graveyard. Oh, no need for concern, Miss – I managed to roll with the punch. The nose was broken many years ago.'

'What on earth were you doing in a graveyard?' Letty asked.

'Lying in the sun on an ancient tombstone, amid the wild grasses, sheltered by the old walls of Peterhouse. It brings peace to my bones and is much to be preferred to a hammock in the Mill Road shelter. But I must not detain you from your meeting with the Inspector.'

'Oh, I think I can say we've decided to put that off for the moment,' said Esmé with some confidence, sensing her friend had been distracted from her purpose. 'Miss Talbot and I are actually just off to the Fitzwilliam to look at loom weights, aren't we, Letty? We'll walk back with you to St Mary the Less – it's on our way. If we run into any more predatory policemen, I'll unleash Letty again.'

He gave her a smile which managed at once to convey sadness and a sense of humour. 'Then I will be proud to accept. But may I propose the slightest detour? If you will follow me – I suggest a good few paces behind ... being downwind of me is, I admit, most challenging – we will walk through Petty Cury and I will find the means of repaying your contribution to my welfare.'

As they walked along behind him, Letty remarked to Esmé, 'Old soldier, wouldn't you say? The minute he started to walk in front of us his back straightened, did you notice? What on earth do you suppose he's planning to get up to in Petty Cury? Rob a bank?'

He stopped and waited for them to draw level with him outside the bookseller Heffer's shop. Then he pointed to a box containing a job lot of mixed secondhand books on display on a trestle table by the door. 'Have you got a shilling in your purse, Miss?' He spoke to Esmé.

'Yes, I have,' she said, producing one.

'Then pick up that leather-bound book – yes, that one – and check that the price pencilled on the front page is indeed one shilling.'

'Yes, it is.' Esmé inspected the dull brown book with its spare gold lettering with misgiving. 'Walden? Thoreau? Which is the author and which the title? It says *1854* on the spine . . . can this be of any interest?'

Catching the concentrated look of longing on the tramp's face and a quickly controlled twitch of his dirty fingers towards the book, Letty decided to compensate for her friend's ignorance. 'Certainly, Esmé. Henry David Thoreau – the truest American who ever existed, according to Emerson, and I suppose he would know. The author spent some time living a rough life and a solitary one in the woods by a lake at a place called Walden . . . somewhere in the wilds of New England, I believe . . . and this is his account. My father was very taken with it. He was inspired by the book to go off camping in the Lake District, muttering, "Our life is frittered away by detail . . . Simplicity, simplicity." He was back within a week seeking out complexity.' She glanced at their escort. 'The solitary life has appeal only for a very particular sort of person.'

He did not rise to her bait but said to Esmé, 'Take it inside, Miss, and buy it, will you?'

Shrugging and uncertain, Esmé did as he asked. She returned moments later with the book in a brown paper bag.

'Good. Now, has either one of you got a pencil eraser?'

'I have one,' said Letty, producing her diary and tiny eraser-tipped pencil.

'Rub out the one-shilling marker. Now, put it in your handbag, Miss Laetitia, go upstairs to the first floor, and ask to see Mr Hilton. He is the buyer of antique volumes. Hand him your card and say you wish to offer this book for sale. It is from your father's library and is surplus to requirements as he has another. Mr Hilton will ask how much you want for it and you will say five pounds. After some well-mannered huffing and puffing on both sides, you will emerge with two pounds and ten shillings.'

Ten minutes later Letty came laughing from the shop holding out three pound notes. She handed one to the old soldier, and the other two to Esmé. 'There! I did well, don't you think? A wonderful return on your investment!'

But Esmé was scandalized. 'This is not right! It is not honest! I shall take it straight back inside!'

The soldier reached out a staying hand but did not touch her. 'Listen to me for a moment, Miss. Who is losing by this? No one. Everyone profits. The book had slipped unnoticed into this unconsidered pile by chance. It should rightly be sold – and no doubt will be before the day is out – to a collector who will recognize its value and be pleased to pay the price Mr Hilton asks, which will be fair and in the region of five pounds. The buyer will be happy with his bargain, the shop will have profited to the tune of two pounds, and the book will no longer be neglected.'

Esmé looked dubiously from one to the other, trying to work out who exactly had been defrauded by their manoeuvres. The soldier watched her struggle with what Letty interpreted with some surprise as tender amusement.

'And twenty shillings will keep this gentleman out of the clutches of the constables for the rest of the month,' said Letty, demonstrating a more basic understanding of her friend's character.

They strolled on, walking together now, a trio of partners in a non-crime. The girls were curious to see where the man had established himself behind the church on Trumpington Street, and entered the graveyard with him through a wrought-iron gate. They were enchanted by the wild garden they found there. Late spring bulbs were flourishing, scrubby, unkempt trees were heavy with blossom, and everywhere ancient headstones leaned companionably together, their inscriptions faded with the years.

Laetitia chose one which looked more secure than most and perched on it. The man invited Esmé to take a seat on a flat tomb and he settled down at the opposite end, looking at the pair quizzically. 'I'm sorry I'm not able to offer you tea,' he told them, 'I gave my housekeeper the day off.'

Letty dismissed his overtures with an impatient gesture. 'Tell us a little about yourself. Who *were* you? How do you come to be in such straits so long after the war? A man of your resourcefulness and address – I would have expected you to be well established. Not leading this somewhat irregular life.'

He scrambled to his feet and stood to attention before her, swaying a little but determined. 'Miss Talbot. I have already thanked you for your kindness in detaching me from the grasp of the constabulary. I do so again. Let that be the end of it. Your thoughtfulness, which does you credit, does not entitle you to pursue the interrogation the police themselves had embarked on. I bid you good day and will now continue with my disrupted sleep.'

'Well spoken, sir!' Letty said cheerfully, not at all abashed by his stiff reprimand. 'I deserved that! But listen, will you? I have a reason for asking these questions – a good reason. I didn't argue with *you* when you told me how to sell the book – extend to me the same courtesy, will you?'

He glared, settling himself back on to the tombstone. But he replied with no more than a touch of truculence: 'I fought in the Great War. I was for four years in Flanders. Twice wounded. I have, as you will have observed, suffered an injury to the left foot.' His chin came up defiantly. 'And, as with many of my fellows, I bear unseen wounds.'

'You are a man of some education . . .' Letty left the sentence hanging between them.

52

He grunted and swept an arm sideways to the ancient wall of Peterhouse College. 'Somewhere in that building you may find a trace, a record of the man I was.'

Letty took a deep breath and came to a decision. 'Would you like to have employment? Or are you quite content to mingle your bones with the long dead? To sit here staring, useless and excluded, at the outer walls of a place where once you were welcomed? Esmé, hand our friend those two pound notes.'

Esmé ferreted about in her purse and did as Letty told her with a breathed: 'Sorry about this . . . she can be very bossy, you know . . .' as she handed him the money.

'I'd like you to use this to smarten yourself up,' Letty told the old soldier. 'Get yourself some clothes. The Salvation Army do a good line in secondhand gents' clothing, I understand, but I'm sure you're better aware of the facilities Cambridge has to offer than I am. I would like you to present yourself here,' she handed over a card, 'at, shall we say, four o'clock this afternoon to attend an interview with my father. There is a position in the household he is seeking to fill. You'll find there's an omnibus service out to Melchester.'

He took the card and glanced at the address. 'Now you know who I am,' Letty persisted. 'May I know *your* name?'

When he hesitated, she insisted: 'So I may inform our butler whom to expect . . .'

'William Gunning,' he said, reluctantly.

'Ah. A good, solid English name,' said Letty. 'Can you drive a motorcar, Mr Gunning?'

He nodded.

'Can you speak French?'

Again he nodded.

'Good. That's settled then.'

'Nothing is settled,' he corrected. 'Tell me, Miss Talbot, something of the nature of the position. Is Sir Richard looking for a chauffeur . . . a groom . . . a steward?'

'All those. Oh, and yes . . . a bodyguard.'

'A *bodyguard*? Is your father's life at risk?'

53

'Oh, no. It is not Sir Richard who is to be the object of your attentions,' she said evasively.

'I must ask – then who exactly *is* the object?'

'I am.'

Without a word, he solemnly handed back the two pound notes.

Chapter Six

A halfhearted game of croquet was in progress on the lawn behind the house when the doorbell rang. Letty checked her watch. Five minutes to four. Although she and Esmé hurried inside, they were too late to catch a glimpse of the visitor being shown into Sir Richard's study. The butler was just closing the door behind him and, though longing to stop and question him, Letty knew better than to interrupt Dawkins in the execution of his duties. His face was inscrutable as usual, giving away no comment on his master's guest. St Michael or Lucifer appearing on the doorstep would have been greeted with the same measure of courtesy, provided he had an appointment.

They loitered nearby, engaged in the self-imposed task of sorting out decaying gum boots in the boot room until, an hour later, Dawkins returned bearing a tray of tea things. The girls looked at each other in surprise as, through the open door, they caught a blast of hearty male laughter.

'That can't be him,' said Esmé. 'Your father's with a *friend*. He didn't come after all and it's your own fault, Laetitia. You insulted him with all that "who *were* you?" and "get yourself smartened up" business. *I'd* have jolly well refused your money, too!'

'Ah, there you are, Miss Laetitia,' said Dawkins, catching sight of them. 'I was confident I'd find you somewhere nearby. Sir Richard asks that you join him directly. And Miss Esmé's presence also is requested.' He opened the door again and announced them.

'Come in, girls!' boomed Sir Richard, leaping to his feet. 'Don't hover over there. Come and join us. Esmé, why don't you pour out some tea? I don't need to present William Gunning, as he is here at your invitation.' His tone was jovial, amused.

Letty gaped in dismay at the man who had risen at their entrance and turned to acknowledge them. She could find no word of welcome that could survive the tide of astonishment rushing through her. This had somehow gone disastrously wrong, and she had most probably ruined forever any chance of gaining permission to take up the job in Burgundy. Her credibility, her judgement, her common sense, were, at a stroke, put in question. And her father was clearly enjoying a joke at her expense.

Esmé was the first to recover from the surprise and, with a whispered, 'Mr Gunning,' and an embarrassed nod, she busied herself with the teacups. Letty went to poke the fire to hide her grim expression.

What could she do? Declare to her father that the man with whom he had spent the last hour was a charlatan, a deceiver, a rogue, and should be ejected summarily? Hardly possible in the circumstances. She would have to find another way of getting rid of the fellow. The man standing by her father's desk could, she thought, have been anyone. He certainly wasn't William Gunning. Or was he? She peered at him again. Tall, spare, and upright, as she had anticipated, when stripped of the blurring outline of the greatcoat, and, yes, grey-haired, but this thick head of neatly barbered hair had clearly been dark and that not so long ago. It seemed out of keeping with the face it framed. Gaunt and weather-beaten certainly, but, freshly shaven and with a neat moustache, that face now revealed a strong bone structure. She had guessed his age, setting his decrepit appearance against the fact that he had taken part in the recent war, as being about fifty, but she now saw that she would have to revise this estimate by about ten years. Surely this man could be no more than forty? She sighed. Far too young to meet her father's requirements. It had all been a waste of time, her time and his.

Through her irritation she felt a twinge of pity for the man and guilt at raising his hopes. The tramp had spent all the money he had in the world, which she remembered to have been one pound, two and sixpence, on bath, barber, and suit. Men's secondhand clothing was easily and cheaply come by but he had chosen well, she thought. The three-piece suit of good Harris tweed in a dark grey blend was well judged for the occasion. The soft-collared white shirt was just formal enough and the tie an odd flourish of scarlet silk. Her father's second requirement: *De aspecto horribile?* Her heart sank. Far from it. William Gunning was far from grotesque. He was failing all the tests. And scuttling all her prospects.

'Shift those dogs off the sofa and sit down, girls. Letty, do leave off! The fire was doing very well by itself. Oh, Esmé, my dear, William might like some shortbread.'

Letty was uneasy at the intimate use of his Christian name, uneasy also to see the haste with which her friend went to ply the stranger with biscuits. The girls settled themselves and waited for the blow to fall.

'Well, I have to say, just for once, one of your ridiculous schemes seems to have been rather well judged, Letty,' Sir Richard said. 'I'll put you out of your misery at once and tell you that we've reached an agreement. William will accompany you to France. He will remain there for the duration of your digging enterprise. We'll hammer out the details all in good time. We've exchanged as much information as is possible in an hour but there must be much more you want to tell him, Letty, so we'll arrange for you to spend some time together to formulate your plans.'

Gunning spoke in his clear voice: 'Is Miss Esmé not to join us on this jaunt, Sir Richard?'

'No, no. Esmé is here for a short holiday only. The two are close friends and have not seen each other for months – Letty's been away in Egypt. No, Esmé returns home to

London next week . . . well, you tell him what you're up to, my dear . . .'

'I am to go up to the University next term, Mr Gunning. University College, London.'

'Ah. My congratulations and best wishes, Miss Esmé. And is Miss Laetitia also to pursue an academic career?'

'Er, no.' Sir Richard broke the girls' embarrassed silence. 'Laetitia *was* up at Cambridge for three years. Bit of a bluestocking, in fact, though you'd never guess it to look at her. But she was, I'm sorry to say, sent down . . . sacked –'

'For bad behaviour,' explained Letty sweetly.

'I see,' said Gunning, nodding his understanding. 'A tattered bluestocking?'

Letty didn't quite like to hear Esmé's suppressed gurgle of laughter. 'My friend has a good deal of reading to do in preparation for her coming course. We won't detain you, Esmé, should you wish to return to your books.'

'And *you* must prepare yourself, Letty,' said Sir Richard. 'Some rather contrapuntal arrangements to be made, which I insist on helping you with. If your project is to go smoothly it must be run with military efficiency. Now, we're envisaging a hostile scenario, I understand. Villains lurking round every corner, innocent young girl at risk . . .' Letty caught the amused glance he exchanged with Gunning. 'I'm thinking that perhaps it would *not* be a good idea if the two of you appeared to know each other. Our notion was that you should travel together as far as Paris. There William will deliver you to your aunt Genevieve, where you will spend a week while he motors on to Fontigny. We can arrange for you to put up in the same guest house. You'll arrive later by train, Letty, as befits a student.'

'And how is Mr Gunning to occupy his days?' asked Letty. 'He surely cannot spend them observing me dig.'

'This is the beauty of it! He will be playing no part. No need for subterfuge or local colour. He will merely be *himself*.'

'I'm sorry, Father, you will have to explain. *Which* of Mr Gunning's selves does he propose to show to the world?'

'William tells me he is a passable artist. Who will look twice at a wandering English clergyman working his way round the French countryside, busy with little pencil sketches, preparing perhaps an illustrated monograph on the ecclesiastical architecture of Upper Burgundy?' Sir Richard roared with laughter at his suggestion. 'Might even get Peregrine to publish it, eh, what, Esmé?'

Gunning's slightly lifted eyebrow involved Letty in a conspiracy she did not wish to acknowledge, silencing her protest. Esmé opened her mouth to speak, considered for a moment, then sipped her tea.

'Clever of you, that, Letty! The retired policeman who was on your shopping list – a deliberately unattainable requirement – might have stuck out like a chapel hat-peg in those surroundings, but a man of the cloth! A pastor! Ah yes, he will have a certain consequence in a country like France, though he be a Protestant. William is prepared, of course, to equip himself with the customary attire – dog collars and so on. I'll make a few phone calls. I may be able to open a few doors, arrange visiting rights, an inter-clergy reception or two. ... Now, he tells me he hasn't driven a car for some years and will need to put in a bit of practice. Why don't you take the Reverend off to the stables, Esmé – you'll find she's an excellent driver, William – and give him a lesson? You may use the second car. It's got a hand gear-change system you may find more convenient. And what about a horse, while you're at it? I hear they're thick on the ground in Burgundy ... Never been myself ... Yes, reacquaint yourself with horses – we keep one or two old hunters out there. Oh, by the way, Letty, William tells me he is able to stay with us here until someone fires the starting pistol ... Esmé, tell Dawkins to have another place laid for dinner, will you, and a room got ready? Right then, off you go and I'll see you all again for sherry. Letty, a moment of your time, please?'

Left alone with her father, Letty was uncharacteristically silent. She wished he were not so obviously enjoying her predicament. He hauled himself to his feet and, scattering dogs as he went, crossed the room to give her a hug. 'Silenced you at last, have I?' he asked, the joviality evaporated and replaced by affectionate concern. 'Now, I've heard from *him*. Why don't *you* speak to me? Why don't you start by telling me where you met this chap?'

'At the church ... St Mary the Less in Trumpington Street,' she replied guardedly.

'Ah? Won't quite do, Letty! Not quite a lie but not quite the truth either, I think. But let me tell you, girl, that you needn't cover up for the man. He told me all. Openly and honestly. He told me how the pair of you rescued him from the clutches of the constabulary and ensured he was solvent. You accompanied him back to the church, curious, no doubt to establish his, um, circumstances.'

'If I'm in the confessional, Daddy, I might as well admit I was not aware that he was a clergyman. I took him for a man of action. He told us he'd served in the war. He walks like a soldier ... he said he'd been wounded and that much certainly is evident. You're a military man – you must have seen it, too? How certain can you be that he was ... is ... a clergyman?'

'Of course I'm sure! Letty, how could you think me so careless? I take no chances with my daughter's safety. Too many vagabonds and rogues roaming the streets these days. Gunning gave me the telephone number of a bishop – a man I happen to know quite well – and invited me to phone him directly. Embarrassing, what! – with the chap there in the room with me! Can you imagine the conversation? "I say, Humphrey, old man, you'll never guess who I've got with me at the moment! ... Yes, sitting right opposite ..." I heard my awful old voice braying on. Though, in the end, it wasn't in the least awkward. Humphrey remembered him well. Told me your Gunning had been missing for years and he feared the worst. He was delighted to hear the chap had surfaced again and insisted on having a word with him there and then. A touching telephonic reunion! Apparently, Letty, your bloke was indeed involved in the war. Saw four years of action. He was a chaplain. An Army chaplain.'

Letty jumped up and began to walk distractedly about the room. 'I'm so sorry, Father! This won't do. I've wasted everyone's time. Can we find some way of sending him away, do you think, without hurting his feelings? Give him a tenner and have him driven back into Cambridge?'

Sir Richard sighed. 'Now what is it? I give you permission – against all my instincts – to follow up your crazy idea, only to find that you've changed your mind? I'm getting pretty fed up with all this!'

'But a *chaplain*, Daddy! I can't go to France with some elderly Woodbine Willie in tow! *I'll* have to look out for *him*! If things should get sticky – not that I'm expecting they will, mind! – what will he do? Whip a prayer book out of his knapsack? Fall on his knees?'

Laetitia had rarely seen her father angry, but she flinched now in dismay at his bellow of rage. His expression was thunderous. 'There speaks the younger generation! Are four years of sacrifice to be so lightly dismissed? Your own half brother paid the ultimate price, Laetitia. I would have expected you at least to show some understanding!' He reined in his emotion and continued in a more controlled tone: 'William Gunning was one of those fighting padres who were right up there with the front line troops! The only difference between those men and the soldiers they served was that they went into battle unarmed. They faced enemy fire shoulder to shoulder with the soldiery: shelling, machine-guns, snipers, but without the comfort of a Lee-Enfield in their hands. The only protection these men had was their faith. Many died. Gunning survived – no one knew quite how, in view of the risks he took. Twice invalided out but each time he went back. Nothing he wouldn't undertake, Humphrey says, from stretcher-bearing to acting as surgeon's assistant. I don't suppose he told you he was awarded the Military Cross? No? Well, he wouldn't, of course. Had to hear about his exploits from Humphrey.'

61

'You must forgive me for being so dismissive – I didn't understand – and please consider that *I* didn't have the advantage of hearing the Bishop's accolade. But, Father, assuming all this is true, it still leaves us with the puzzle of what happened to him. After the war, I mean. *Something* happened to him. Why would a man of his ability and courage – and connections – end up sleeping on a tomb-stone in a deserted Cambridge graveyard?'

'Can't help you there. But I agree – it is a puzzle. Didn't have time to enquire, and somehow I don't think the enquiry would have been a welcome one. The man's got a fine way of diverting the flow of conversation away from certain channels. Still, I've always considered myself a pretty good judge of men and, on first acquaintance, I'd say the one you've presented me with today is a quite out-standing example. But we're to have the pleasure of the man's company for the next week or so and, having got him under my own roof, you can be confident that I shall give him a thorough vetting!'

He gave Letty a mischievous look. 'Of course, a closer acquaintance may produce an unforeseen outcome . . . *He* will have every opportunity to assess *you*, Letty! Could all backfire in an embarrassing way! But – assuming him to be the intrepid adventurer into No-Man's-Land under enemy fire that his reputation indicates – he will not back out now, and you *will* find yourself in France with this man of mys-tery. It'll be up to you to get his story out of him there in Burgundy.'

He looked at Letty a little uncertainly. 'Although if it comes to encouraging confidences, perhaps you'd do better to leave that to Esmé? Yes,' Sir Richard went on, pleased with his insight, 'get little Esmé to draw him out – that would be the way to do it. Good practice for her. She can get to work on him. Tell her William Gunning is to be her first patient!'

Chapter Seven

'Ever heard of something called an Oedipal Complex, Letty?'

Esmé's voice came, straining for a lightly casual tone, from behind a pile of books across the library table. Laetitia, working opposite on an equally impressive pile of ancient history books, didn't welcome the interruption. They had an unspoken rule when working together that they didn't distract each other's attention with comment or even exclamation.

'I've heard of Oedipus. Sad story. Abandoned royal baby grows up, finds his way home, and, all unwitting, kills his father the king and marries his mother. Blinds himself in a fit of self-loathing on becoming aware of his sins. I can see you're reading a psychology text, so it shouldn't be hard to work it out. Just the sort of nonsense that would get Freud into a lather, I should think,' she replied repressively.

'Yes, well, what you may not know is that there exists a complementary condition – an Electra Complex.'

'That's silly,' retorted Laetitia. 'I don't believe Electra suffered in the same way at all. But I can see you're determined to drag me away from the battle of Alésia. And perhaps I could do with a diversion from all the hacking and the slaughter. God! Caesar was a monster! Freud should look into *his* behaviour patterns. Oh, go on! Make your point.'

'According to the myth, Electra tried to have her mother, Clytemnestra, murdered, out of devotion to her father, King Agamemnon.'

'Serve her right, too! I mean, if I remember the story correctly, the queen had been up to all sorts of mischief while Agamemnon was away fighting in Troy. Some chap called Aegisthus intimately involved, I believe. Are you about to reach a conclusion, Esmé?'

'Electra's enterprise has given a name to a theory that girls can hate their mothers, worship their fathers, and suffer from something called "penis-envy".'

'What a strangely perverted idea! You're saying I'm supposed, being female, to envy any male of my acquaintance for his possession of a penis? Well, I've always considered it a useful little gadget to take on a picnic, but there my admiration runs out. You may well not have cast an eye on one yet, Esmé, but let me tell you – they are *not* instantly appealing. You wouldn't want to have one. As for Sir Richard?' Letty was trying not to laugh. 'I'm devoted to the old thing but would never consider him Love's Young Dream. Doesn't it annoy you, Esmé, this bilge you have to read? I mean, couldn't these gentlemen who dare to put such unflattering ideas on paper at least go out and canvass the opinions of a few *females*? Psychology! Are you quite sure you ought to be pursuing such a subject for the next three years? For a discipline they've chosen to call the study of the *mind*, they seem to give undue prominence to the *bodily functions*.'

'You're just rattling on in that silly way to put me off saying what you've guessed I'm going to say!' Esmé complained. 'I'm leaving for London and you're setting off for France tomorrow. It may be some time before I see you again. There's something I feel I ought to warn you of, Letty. I would consider myself less of a friend if I didn't.' She hesitated, then launched into the speech she'd been preparing to give. 'You must admit, Letty, that you've grown up surrounded by elderly gents and you've never shown much interest in men of your own age –'

'Do you mean,' Letty interrupted, 'that I should have welcomed the advances of Felix Dalton when I had the chance? Or what about Christopher Carstairs? John

64

Fortescue? They have expressed an interest. They are one's age. Or – have you seen that new stable lad Father's engaged? Now, that's more like it! No? That's not what you meant, is it, Esmé? I know what you're up to! What you're trying to say is: Keep your hands off William Gunning when you're in France.'

Esmé was astonished and affronted. 'Certainly not! I hadn't supposed William Gunning would let *you* within range. I was thinking rather of the company you seem to seek out – elderly archaeologists and the like. First it was Prof Merriman . . .'

'You've never met Andrew, have you?'

'No, I haven't, but I can imagine. Next it's this Paradee. I fear they may both be father figures following in the wake of poor Daniel.'

Letty sighed with irritation. 'What are you proposing for my condition, Esmé? That some auto-suggestion merchant be called in to identify my complexes and eradicate my inhibitions?'

'Inhibitions, Letty? If only you had some! They might supply a useful brake on life's downward slope.'

Letty rolled her eyes in exasperation. 'This is nonsense! I refuse to be pigeonholed, categorized, or labelled! I won't be a test-case in chapter eleven of your textbook. Save your concern and your theorizing for Gunning. Now, he *does* have problems of a mental nature.'

Seeing Esme's head sink over her books again, Letty persisted: 'You've been out riding with him several times this week. Here am I, all agog to hear your insights – you've had plenty of opportunities to get to the bottom of his problems and you tell me nothing. What on earth do you two talk about? Surely he's communicated *something*?'

'Oh, a good deal. He guessed that my interest in the science of the mind stemmed from my brother's condition. He draws one out, Letty, and it was no time at all before I was telling him about Arthur . . . the nursing home . . . his symptoms. I was carefully calling it "neurasthenia" but Reverend Gunning seems to prefer the soldiers' more blunt expression: "shell-shock". He recognized the symptoms – the panic, the staring eyes, the constant anxiety. I described the awful repetitive gesture Arthur has . . . you know . . . when he clutches at his throat and tries to strangle himself.'

Letty reached over and touched her friend's hand in sympathy. Esmé's three brothers had all come back from the war without a scratch on them, but the youngest, and the one to whom she was the closest, had suffered a mental wound which would not heal. It was the desire to do something to help Arthur and young men like him that had plunged Esmé into a study of psychology.

'And William had something very sensible to say, Letty. He'd come across a condition like it before – attempted self-harming gestures of this kind. A soldier who constantly tore at his own eyes was found to have bayoneted another man in the eyes. One who pounded his abdomen had stuck his bayonet into another's stomach and was unable to withdraw it. Do you suppose Arthur . . .? If we can only get him to remember . . . who knows? If we can discover the cause, we may be able to move on to a cure.'

'It sounds dangerous work to me but it does make rather awful sense, I suppose,' said Letty. 'Gunning seems willing to offer advice and information on others. But am I to believe that he confided nothing of his *own* predicament?'

Esmé shook her head. 'Nothing at all. He hasn't even told me what regiment he was attached to.'

'Oh, I can tell you that! The Northumberland Fusiliers,' said Letty. 'First Battalion. I looked him up. He went off to France with the British Expeditionary Force on the fourteenth of August. And a Reverend Gunning did indeed receive the Military Cross. In fact, Esmé, I've seen the actual medal.'

'But how? He doesn't exactly display it pinned to his breast pocket!'

'I searched his room while he was out riding with you.'

'No! Letty! That is truly gross behaviour!'

'Sensible self-interest,' replied Letty, unperturbed. 'If I'm about to go abroad in his company for four months I want to know everything that is to be known about him. He's charmed Daddy with his manly piety and granite-jawed reserve, that's quite obvious, but *I'm* not so easily impressed.'

'The reassuring exchange of male shibboleths? Don't scorn it, Letty. It's their very effective way of identifying friend and foe in the dark. Men don't have our female sensitivities and insights to light their way! But you're right – Reverend Gunning certainly seems to have made a good impression on your father and that's not a bad thing. Sir Richard is every inch a good officer and a clever strategist. Had you wondered, Letty, if the pair of them are working *together*? Everyone can see that you're still devastated by Daniel's death . . . and those closest to you might even have noticed that you are quite desperate to set off for foreign parts and do your digging. I know you feel you have things to prove after your abominable treatment by those scallywags in Cambridge last year. What better way than to excel in a male-dominated . . . um . . . profession? Two very strong motives for this expedition. Sir Richard has understandably recognized that you're going to circle his head like an angry hornet until you get what you want. He's always indulged you. He's indulging you now – with the connivance of Gunning, I do believe.'

'Must you analyse everything and everyone?' Letty spoke more sharply than she would have wished, disconcerted to have been so clearly read by her friend. 'All right. Try your analytical skills on this, then! The contents of Gunning's room! There were no interesting personal items – just the new clothes and toilet things Daddy had had sent out from Cambridge. All his old gear went on the bonfire. There were no letters, no notes, no telephone numbers. No books, not even a Bible or a Prayer Book. All I could find was the medal in the pocket of his new waistcoat, a rusty old tin of mints, and an epaulette from a German Army uniform hidden amongst his socks.'

'An epaulette?'

'Yes. I examined it. It wasn't torn off but cut off with scissors or a knife. Rather intriguing, I thought. But tell me *your* thoughts – a war trophy of some sort, would you say? I'm sure Malinowski would have the answer . . . what's the name of the South Sea Island tribe that slices off the ears of its enemies slain in combat? Trobriand?'

'You're just being facetious! Can't think why I put up with you. Can you be sure that's all he had? It does speak of a Spartan existence,' said Esmé sadly.

'And a certain Spartan cunning! I went back again the next day, sure that I must have overlooked something and . . . and . . .' Letty burst out laughing. 'The first thing I saw was that on his dressing table he'd laid out the medal, the tin of mints, and the epaulette in a row and added, an inch or so to the right, a plain silver ring. That's all. But the message could not have been more clear: "*You missed this!*"'

'Goodness, how embarrassing!'

'Not at all. But I gathered I was being told there was nothing further to discover.'

'Mmm,' said Esmé thoughtfully. 'Far be it from me to encourage naughtiness of this kind, but . . . had you thought – that might well have been the very moment you should have started to hunt more diligently?'

'I don't know what you mean,' said Letty uncertainly.

'I think you do! William Gunning has been directing you every inch of the way since you set eyes on him! You're a clever girl, Letty, but this man can obviously teach *you* a thing or two.'

'Oh, yes? For instance – how to be penniless and homeless? How to get oneself arrested by the police? Not lessons I would value. Listen, Esmé – this man is my passport into France, no more than that. I don't need to learn from him. If I can satisfy myself that he is who he says he is and that he constitutes no threat or hindrance to my arrangements, that's all I ask. Did you suppose, Esmé, that I would put up for more than a moment with the presence of an elderly, lame vicar trailing after me, wagging a disapproving finger?'

Too late, she noticed the dangerous glare fixing her across the table. Her sweet-tempered friend had once hurled a book at her head and, here to hand, were weapons aplenty. Esmé's fingers twitched on a chunky copy of *The Pilgrim's Progress*, but she restrained herself to say with exaggerated calm and reason: 'Letty, you were ever one to tie a label around someone's neck at first meeting. Mr Gunning is not elderly and, if you bothered to look, you'd see that he isn't all that lame either. Disapproving? Of you? Well, yes . . . certainly that. Who wouldn't be?'

'Well, whoever or whatever the man may be, he does not figure in my plans,' Letty answered airily. 'I shall drive off with him in the back seat with the rest of the luggage, waving a fond farewell to Father, and when we arrive at my aunt's house I shall wave a not-so-fond farewell to Mr Gunning. No – after our safe arrival in Paris, I shall set the Reverend at liberty to do as he pleases and go where he pleases.'

Chapter Eight

'Will you join me in a brandy? Or would that cloud your judgement? We have to come to a decision tonight, you and I, my friend.'

'A brandy would be most welcome.'

The Frenchman's tone was deferential but he braced himself for dispute. A drop or two more of liquid courage might fortify him for the coming clash. He was not deceived by the affable tone. He was being politely warned that a decision had been taken and was about to be announced to him. A decision he was unlikely to condone. He watched as his companion poured out a glass with a steady hand, long fingers holding the decanter delicately, heavy ruby ring flashing with fire from the blaze in the hearth. While he waited, he clutched his cloak closer about his shoulders with a shiver, glad of the fur lining within the stone walls of this bleak room.

'Custos, do you mind if I keep this on? Rather chilly for May, don't you think?'

A polite smile and an impatient gesture encouraged him to get on with the business in hand. He was prompted by a brisk question: 'Do we know by what means she is getting here? Train? Motorcar?'

'We only have information from this side of the Channel but it is exact. Leclerc at SNCF reports a train booking through the Paris office. Her trunk has already been sent ahead.'

'Time enough, then. An irritation we can well do without. I wish no repetition of last year's fiasco. The girl is not to arrive here. We will make sure she ventures no farther than Paris. Plenty of distractions in Paris. People behave recklessly there. Especially tourists. Giddy young girls run off with gigolos, fall off the Eiffel Tower or under a train. The English frequently look the wrong way crossing the road, I'm told. The possibilities are endless but – entertaining though they be – I must not be led astray by them; this is not my area of expertise. I leave the final arrangements to the ingenuity of others. Consider her disappearance authorized.'

The ring flashed again, a blood-red downward flare carrying all the final authority of a Roman emperor's extended left thumb. Custos' hands, the Frenchman thought, always moved with the gestures of an actor: dismissive, encouraging, emphatic, never hesitant. Decisions, once made, were never questioned.

A silence followed.

Custos stirred impatiently and the ring flew out in a very French gesture of amused disbelief. 'You are not happy with this?'

'Not entirely. Forgive me. If I may advise? The girl's a nuisance, I agree, but ought we to ask what is drawing her here? Could it be that she is following information we were unaware she had? Information that escaped our watchers? Has she shared it? I think we should encourage her to reveal the extent of her knowledge and the names of those others who are a party to it. Always a mistake, I believe, to attempt to tear up a weed by its green leaves. Better to insert the tines of a fork at some distance from the stem and exert leverage to ascertain how far the roots are spreading. That way, one may more securely extract the whole.'

'It's too early. I want no hound snuffling her way along this trail. The quarry must remain where it has always been. Undisturbed. Safe. We wait for the time. All will be made clear . . . You are not convinced?'

'Had you thought, Custos,' the Frenchman murmured uneasily, 'that this may *be* the time?'

71

He'd prepared his argument and knew that his words would sound rehearsed – archaic formulae. They always did in this setting. The medieval walls, unsoftened by tapestries, replayed their voices. The attentive eyes of his companion fixed him, accepting – even inviting – dissent, but expecting nothing less than the truth.

He continued awkwardly into a frozen silence. 'The world has changed out of all recognition in the last decade . . . since the war. So many Frenchmen dead . . . the English and German losses also – crippling . . . young men from as far away as India, America, Australia . . . the flower of our armies cut down . . . and more than that – the flower of the nations. The boldest and the best are gone. We are left in the uncertain hands of the second-rate, the hesitant . . .'

'. . . the self-serving and the shirker,' added Custos, with a nod of encouragement.

'Europe has changed, is changing, and the speed of change is accelerating. There are no more certainties. Everywhere there is dissatisfaction, disillusion, and loss of faith. The churches have emptied. The land has been ploughed and harrowed and enriched with the spilt blood of our young men, Custos. It lies ready for the seed. And there are those in the east, godless men, who stand by ready to sow . . . in *our* furrows. I would not like to think we had misjudged the moment. That we had left the fertile earth open to an alien corn.'

His words were being heard with patience and sympathy. Formulaic phrases, an ecclesiastical tone – that was the way to engage the attention of Custos.

'It's not up to us to turn the hands of the clock this way or that. We'd all count ourselves blessed to live through the moment, but you and I, my friend, will not see it. Our job is to hold firm the doors against those who would rush them in a premature assault,' Custos told him.

The expected answer. He nodded acquiescence. This was the point at which he normally ceased to argue, but tonight he persisted. He began again, apologetically, swirling the

72

last few drops of cognac around in his glass. 'I wonder if you have heard today's news from Paris?'

'Go on.'

'The Atlantic has been crossed. By a young American pilot. What he has done, others will now hurry to imitate. The continents no longer seem so far apart, connected as they already are by telephone, telegram, and radio waves.'

His modern words sounded ridiculous bouncing off the ancient walls.

'We were prepared for this. You know that.' There was quiet satisfaction in Custos' reply. 'We have made our arrangements. We will have the rostrum we need.'

'News spreads at the speed of an electric current around the world,' the Frenchman persevered. 'We must be certain that it is *our* news, *our* message that is carried along by it. After two thousand years we have, at last, the means as well as the word. We would be at fault, I think, if we did not at least consider this.'

'So. You would argue that we have the soil – prepared and ready – the seed corn close at hand, the wind to distribute it?'

'Yes, indeed. And one factor only is lacking. I wonder if the time has come to give thought to *la semeuse*? The sower?' He hurried on, avoiding contact with the cynical eyes. 'I have continued to make my monthly trawl through the society pages of the London press and this caught my attention. It's dated the tenth of last month. It seems the wheels of bureaucracy turn even more slowly in England than they do in France. It has taken eight months but the upshot is extremely interesting to us, I believe.'

He took a clipping from the file at his elbow and handed it over.

The response was not immediate and came with unaccustomed indecision. 'Very surprising. And very impressive. Yes, I see where you are leading. I'm wondering whether we could perhaps have anticipated this event? Were there indications? Suggestions that we failed to pick up?'

73

The Frenchman shrugged his shoulders slightly but voiced no criticism. 'And there's something more you should know . . . rather strange. A mere detail, a triviality, but I thought it would amuse you to hear it. You will smile when I tell you the girl has changed her name expressly for this little expedition.'

'Changed her name? Why would she do that?'

'My first thought was that she was sending a message – the first defiant blast on a trumpet, if you like – but common sense tells me it's a mere stratagem. A stratagem embarrassing in its naïveté but reassuring in its amateurish intent. The girl is, of course, aware that her own surname is not unknown in these parts,' he gently reminded Custos. 'She has replaced it with – rather unimaginatively, you will think – her mother's maiden name. And she has selected as her Christian name: Stella.'

He was gratified to see a sudden quiver of the steady hand as it raised the brandy glass.

Chapter Nine

'Something wrong, Stella?' Gunning asked. Without any instruction, he'd driven off the road out of Le Havre and parked the car on the entrance to a woodland track overlooking the Seine winding between rocky banks. She registered with a flash of amusement the fact that he'd remembered to change her name now that they were over the Channel.

'Ten hours at sea on a ferryboat? A day in the close company of a man who never speaks? An uncertain summer ahead of me? What could possibly be wrong? . . . Why are you grinning?'

'Forgive me. I was comparing your reaction with my own when I passed this way thirteen years ago. I could have complained about the twelve hours spent at sea on a troop ship, following on a month in the company of the sweating, swearing soldiery with an uncertain four years ahead of us. If it's any help, I hand you the motto of "The Fighting Fifth", as we were called: *Quo fata vocant.*'

'*Wherever Fate calls.* Hmm . . .' Irritated by his condescension, she bit back a sharp reply. If the man was still abjectly following his wartime motto it might explain why he'd so readily taken up her challenge. Perhaps he'd seen her as his own personal Fate and had drifted after her in his rudderless way. 'Sounds a bit passive to me. I like to engineer my own good fortune. Though I accept your reprimand.'

'And I yours,' he replied politely.

'Just suffering from a touch of cold feet, I suppose – a what-am-I-doing-here feeling. But I didn't realize your regiment set out from Le Havre?' Her voice trailed away in some confusion. 'Father and I deliberately rejected the Dover–Calais crossing, thinking to avoid the Somme and Picardie. We thought it might bring back memories.'

'That was considerate. I had guessed as much. Don't be concerned – my memories of this part of France are pleasant.' He was lapsing into silence again but, gathering himself, continued: 'We were among the first troops to sail for France. A regular infantry force – the First Battalion of the Northumberland Fusiliers. Well trained. Best officers you could wish for. We considered ourselves battle-ready.'

Letty listened, aware that this was the first time he'd confided anything more than name and number since she'd met him. Nodding encouragement, she hoped he would not immediately retreat. She felt – and resented the feeling – that she had to give as much care to approaching William Gunning as she would a dog or horse of uncertain temper. Don't look him in the eye. Adopt an unthreatening posture. Make no sudden movements.

She glanced briefly at him, struck by the contrast between the hesitancy of the man's speech and his now suave exterior. His scarecrow figure had begun to fill out in the month he'd spent with them, and his face, creased and tanned by years in the open air, was now smoother. Her eyes lingered for a moment with guilty curiosity on the line at his throat where the seasoned skin became abruptly white. Like the man himself, she realized. There was a sharp demarcation between the hidden, vulnerable man and the toughened part he was prepared to show the world.

His appearance as houseguest at a dinner party Sir Richard had given the previous week had been a success. It seemed that dinner party conversation, avoiding as it did the personal, the political, the controversial, suited him. He'd listened in a flattering way, replied with flashes of humour, pushed the conversation along, even flirted with the ladies – to all appearances a charming and cultured man.

76

It had been Esmé who'd sensed that he was reaching the end of his resources. With a warning whisper to Laetitia, she'd commandeered Gunning's assistance with the coffee cups when they'd adjourned to the drawing room after dinner. She'd sheltered him from the attention of the rest of the guests who were booming away with increasing conviviality at the other end of the room. Laetitia was already missing Esmé's gentle presence, the buffer between her own impatience and Gunning's awkwardness.

'We disembarked at five in the morning, seasick, hungry, and with a two-hundred-mile walk ahead of us.' He gave an abrupt bark which might have been a suppressed laugh. 'The famous British Expeditionary Force began its glorious adventure following behind a French Boy Scout who'd been sent to guide us to our first camp, six miles away over there through those cornfields.' He nodded towards the east. 'The early morning mist cleared. The sun beat down. We sweltered in our uniforms. It was a dashed hot summer.'

Letty recognized that this was no confidence of an intimate nature – merely the triggering of a memory by a familiar scene. But it was an opening of a kind, one she intended to exploit.

'Why were you so far from the front?' she prompted.

He shrugged. 'Exactly what we all wondered! Something to do with transport arrangements, I expect. They always blamed transport. In the end we were glad of the distance. The march across northern France was just what we needed to toughen up the men and the horses. And it gave us a chance to feel welcomed. Cigars, brandy, wine were thrust at us wherever we appeared. Pretty girls threw flowers at us as though we were already conquerors. Like a medieval knight going in to joust, it was a comfort – no, more than that – an excitement and a validation to have a lady's favour pinned to your lance. It gave us a sense of what we were going into battle for. We got quite fond of the French. We added a further layer to the carapace of patriotism that insulated us from the horrors.' He was silent for a moment, then finished briskly, 'Ten days later we were retreating from Mons to escape – narrowly escape – annihilation.'

She recognized a full stop when she heard one. Esmé would have done better, she knew, but she could not bring herself to pursue him into the gloomy reaches of his thoughts. That would have to do for the moment. She'd chided him for his silence and this awkward outburst was his attempt to respond to her criticism. At least they were moving onwards, if not in step. 'Well, I think we'd better press on, don't you, if we're to be with Aunt Genevieve by this evening? Let's give ourselves a different motto . . . how about – *À l'attaque!'*

'That'll do.' He made to restart the car, then paused. 'Look, Laet – Stella! There's something you ought perhaps to see. Before we go our separate ways and meet up again as strangers in Fontigny . . .'

'Instead of the bosom pals we are now?' she said as he turned to the back seat to fumble in his leather knapsack.

He pulled out two large glossy brochures and handed her one. She took it with recognition and surprise. 'Hansford's? The auction last week? Father went up to London to bid on a bronze statuette . . . this one here on page twelve. He wasn't successful. Some fool put out the word that it was by Degas and it spiralled out of reach. It went for an awful lot of money.'

'Yes, I believe it did. Sir Richard showed me this catalogue before he went. He asked my opinion of the bronze . . . but, Stella, flipping through the pages, something caught my attention. Have a look at page twenty-one.'

She looked with appreciation at the silver chalice encrusted with rubies and emeralds. *Origin unknown, probably French or Italian workmanship of the 16th century. Property of a gentleman* were the slight clues to its provenance.

'Great Heavens! You're a bad influence on Father, William! I hope you didn't encourage him to bid for this instead! It must be worth thousands!'

'So it proved. But what intrigued me was the vagueness of the description. *I* could have told them with much greater precision – late fifteenth century, French, property of the Abbey of Fontigny.'

'And how do you know that?'

'I've seen this chalice's twin, actually *handled* its twin in France, where it forms part of the much depleted treasure of the Benedictine order of monks. The Black Monks of Fontigny. The treasure is not on public display.' He looked aside awkwardly for a moment, then resumed: 'Not many – hardly anyone – would have recognized it. I don't have by heart the contents of the friars' store-cupboard, but it did occur to me that this particular objet d'art was . . . um, displaced. I have no idea how it came to be listed in a sale at one of the three big auction houses of the world or what the identity of the "gentleman" selling – now a very rich gentleman – may be. All I can say is that its twin is locked away in the strongroom of the town we're heading for.'

'Interesting, but no mystery. I expect it's the same chalice. I dare say the monks have fallen on hard times like everyone else, following the war, and have discreetly sold it off in a foreign capital to avoid a scandal.'

'My first thought. But my second was to make a telephone call to someone I know in France.' Again, Letty caught his uncertainty. 'Their chalice is still where it ought to be. My curiosity was aroused. I asked Sir Richard when he went to the auction to see if he could lay hands on any recent catalogues of sales by the big houses in London, Paris, and New York. He brought a bundle back home with him and we had a pleasant evening rooting through them.'

He'd spent almost every evening in the library, she remembered resentfully, many of them in her father's company.

'And did it turn up anything interesting, your jolly treasure hunt?'

He handed her the second catalogue. 'New York. Six months ago. Page forty. Two items. Tell me what you make of those.'

Letty looked, and admired in silence. Since he didn't help her with a commentary she began hesitantly, 'If you're offering to put one of these in my Christmas stocking, I'll say thank you very much but I'll find it hard to choose between them. *A Madonna. Twelfth Century, Burgundian. Carved wood image, eighteen inches high*, it says. Reminds me of something I've seen before . . . It's made of black wood – that's unusual, isn't it?' As he made no attempt to encourage her, she blundered on. 'Ebony? Or black-painted hardwood? The lady's wearing a crown so she's quite obviously meant to be the Queen of Heaven.' She smiled. 'Though the model for this piece was not regal. I like her country-girl's face. Lovely! But then, below – what's this? *A Book of Hours. Fifteenth Century.* And they claim it's from the hand of the Master of Mary of Burgundy.'

The illustration glowed on the page. A woman in a bright blue medieval dress sat quietly reading by an arched window surrounded by a trompe l'oeil border. On a gold background, pink and white daisies were scattered at random and, delicately painted, a transparent dragonfly had settled on them, believing them real. 'I've seen this before,' she said in some excitement. 'In the Bodleian, I think, in Oxford.'

'Not this very book. But one from the same workshop.'

'Were you able to trace these items further?'

'It's difficult. These auction houses are nothing if not discreet. Sir Richard made some enquiries, called in a few favours but, even so, we made little progress. The closest we could get was the discovery that they had all at one time passed through the hands of the same dealer. In Switzerland. End of trail, I'm afraid.'

'I ask you again, William: what are you telling me?'

'You're determined to play the detective, Laetitia. Make what you will of it. I'm merely handing you information which may prove to be interesting . . . nothing more than that.'

'I'm supposed to infer that these objects may have the same geographical source? That they all originated in, or at least passed through, Burgundy at some time?'

'Of course, it may be a distracting piece of nonsense but – just in case! . . .' He took the catalogues from her hands, got out of the car, and pushed them deep into the centre of a log pile stacked by the side of the track. 'Useful kindling for someone next winter.'

'You're a careful man,' she remarked.

'I seem to survive,' he replied grimly.

'It might help, Stella, if you were to tell me,' he went on after a few moments' silence, 'exactly what your godfather was doing in Burgundy. I had understood from Sir Richard that he was employed by the British Museum.'

'He was. He was out on loan, you might say. Charles Paradee had approached the director and asked if he could recommend someone to assist him. Every dig needs such an expert and Daniel welcomed the chance to travel. The American team are exploring and revealing the extent of the original abbey. But Daniel wasn't actually digging in the foundations himself . . . he was a medievalist and linguist. He was there on hand to put finds in their context, identify, research, and catalogue any written material. Anything from Roman gravestone inscriptions to the dockets of Napoleon's scrap merchants. He was mainly concerned with the translation of medieval documents in Latin, of course. He worked on the translation of texts, too, secular and religious, when they came up. He was busy with a new translation of the *Lais de Marie de France* . . .'

She heard her own voice accounting her godfather's many skills in disjointed phrases. It occurred to her that she'd never before needed to explain the man or his brilliance to anyone. Everyone in her large circle was aware of Daniel Thorndon. Praising him in conversation with a stranger or just doing him justice was proving as embarrassing as praising oneself.

Gunning seemed to pick up the reason for her hesitation. 'He sounds a remarkable man.'

Good Lord – now he was encouraging *her* to talk. She smiled and went on more freely. 'He certainly was. The development of languages was his fascination – from

Sanskrit onwards. He taught me Latin and Greek and made sure I went to a school which encouraged intellectual curiosity as well as cold showers and lacrosse. Are you thinking,' she said, bluntly, 'that these medieval treasures you've just waved under my nose belong in France and may have been illegally sold abroad? And that my god-father was somehow aware of this?'

'I wouldn't voice such a suspicion without a great deal more evidence. I just thought it was interesting and that you ought to be alerted. I know you didn't preserve any of his letters, but can you recall any details of his work or his life in France which seem significant in the light of his killing? Perhaps something in his earlier correspondence, before he became aware that he was under surveillance?'

'You're really taking your job seriously, William.' She said it gently.

He turned to her in some surprise. 'Why would I not? I'm being – and for the first time in my life – well paid! And this is, I believe, a very serious situation you're plunging into with such insouciance, a situation which provoked the murder of a good man on account of something he knew, something he was about to discover or reveal to the world. A man, from all accounts, who could well – in the days when I had friends – have been my friend.'

She was moved to touch his hand and say quietly, 'Daniel would have agreed, I know.' She added lightly, 'But cheer up! Now you've got *me*.'

She decided to interpret his gusty sigh as a welcome touch of playfulness.

'I have been holding something back,' she confessed. 'It's not much, probably nothing. Tell me what you think.' She leaned over into the dickey seat and opened her Gladstone bag. 'Here, look at this.'

He examined the book she handed him. 'An English publication: *The Ecclesiastical Architecture of France.*'

'It was in a box amongst Daniel's effects, returned to us from Burgundy. I thought it might be just what you needed to use on this expedition. Turn to page forty-one, will you?'

He did as she asked. 'It's a section on Fontigny-Sainte-Reine . . . but more precisely, the church – not the abbey – the Église de la Sainte-Madeleine.' He frowned. 'Is this significant?'

Letty sighed. 'Perhaps. Perhaps not. The book just fell open at that page because he'd left a marker in it. It occurred to me that it might give us . . . me . . . a clue as to what had been occupying his mind at the last. Daddy says they found it on his desk when they cleared up his things.'

'I know this church,' he told her. 'Not intimately, but I visited it once for a service. As described here – squat and solid twelfth century, Romanesque style with a belfry. And a surprisingly lovely fresco. Of the patron saint, of course. Mary Magdalene.'

'You know this area well?' she ventured to ask.

'Not very well. I passed through it some years ago. After the war.' His reply was, as she had come to anticipate, evasive, reluctantly given. He took the guidebook from her hands. 'Look, if you don't mind, Stella, I'll keep this. It's just the sort of thing a wandering English vicar would have in his pocket anyway.'

She nodded her consent.

He leaned across to put the book away in the glove box and continued with his questioning. 'Tell me what Daniel did outside his working hours. Did he tell you how he spent his leisure?'

She frowned. 'It's a small country town. The opportunities for pleasure-seeking are few, I should imagine.' And, wriggling impatiently: 'Look, shouldn't we be getting on?'

He made no move to start the car, so she added, 'He did say he'd become friendly with a local family . . . an elderly couple . . . what was their name? Daumier . . . Dulac? His new friend was an antiquarian like him, and the two old buffers had taken to spending their evenings together poring over ancient manuscripts. If ever I meet them, I'll thank M. and Mme Daumier for the comfort and companionship they brought to Daniel's last months.'

'That's all you have to report?'

Was that disappointment in his tone? No, it was impatience.

Feeling herself under interrogation, Laetitia replied coldly, 'I'm not obliged to report anything to you, Mr Gunning. If you're fancying yourself as a Dr Watson figure in my life, you can forget it!' She decided to be firm. 'Listen. When we arrive in Burgundy we will be two English guests using the same guest house, but we will not *know* each other. In the exceedingly remote possibility of my life being threatened I will try to alert you, so that you may start praying, but that's as far as it goes. You are not to shadow me, get under my feet, or in any way annoy me. Is that clear?'

He turned a stern gaze on her and for the first time she became aware that his eyes were blue. Why would she have noticed? They were eyes that normally received more than they gave out. But at this moment they were crackling with the chill of a February sky over the frozen fens.

'I take my pay and my orders from your father, Miss Stella. I will deliver you safely and I will return you in pristine condition back home to Cambridge at the end of your four months' self-indulgence. And may I make it quite clear that I will do whatever is necessary – whether it meets with your approval or not – to bring about that happy outcome. An outcome to which I look forward with not a little eagerness.'

Laetitia swallowed and dragged her eyes from the cold blaze to stare ahead through the windscreen. Any riposte to his biting cynicism would have sounded petty. She pointed a finger in the direction of Paris.

'You may drive on, Gunning,' she said coolly.

Chapter Ten

The watcher in the Église de la Sainte-Madeleine sat motionless, a darker shadow amongst the deepening shadows on the south side of the nave. Large-brimmed hat, long black robe, head bowed over his rosary, it would have been easy to mistake him for one of the many ecclesiastics who came and went during the day. But his eyes, which flicked constantly towards the apse, were not lost in adoration of the Lord or even admiration for the medieval frescoes. They were narrowed in irritation and were focused on the back of an iron-grey head, it too bowed in contemplation.

What in hell was he up to, this Englishman? He'd been in place at the east end of the church for an hour or more and his follower, not a man readily seduced by church architecture, was growing impatient. Whatever was going on in front of the altar, it wasn't prayer. His target's head was constantly on the move, looking up and then immediately looking down. Oh, Lord! The fellow was at it again! Sketching. The watcher shifted his position slightly. This could take hours. A vicar *and* an artist. The watcher wondered how much of his time he should spend on this innocent before reporting back.

He swallowed a yawn. He'd wasted a week observing the man. The most tedious week of his life. Still, Don Juan himself would have been pushed to find opportunities for mischief in this part of the world. An English vicar wouldn't know where to start. They all headed straight for the fleshpots of the Côte d'Azur anyway. He'd give it ten minutes, no more, then slip out for a beer.

The watcher's eyes rose and lingered furtively as they always did on the image of the patron saint of the church painted in glowing colours on the wall opposite.

Harlot!

He'd never understood why such a woman should be venerated above all others here. There were so many more deserving saints to choose from. By no means an incisive or informed critic of art, he tried to account for his revolted fascination. The red dress with its sumptuous folds, the flowing yellow hair, the adoring sea grey eyes – all these were to be expected in a depiction of the Magdalene. But there was something different about this one, more disturbing. He couldn't quite put his finger on it.

Still no move from the Englishman. The watcher rose to his feet and genuflected automatically, but then slid abruptly back into his seat again at the entry into the church of another visitor. A woman. Young and lovely. English, too, judging by her clothes and looks. His heart-beat quickened. He was about to witness a rendezvous. This was more like it!

The blonde girl put down a travelling bag at the back of the church and moved slowly down the aisle, head raised, guidebook in hand, pausing to take in details of the decoration, quite obviously a tourist. Hardly worth his attention, but she was certainly easier on the eye than the curé.

Suddenly she became aware of the other visitor still busily sketching away with his back to her. She froze and, with a sigh of annoyance, turned on her heel and walked silently from the church. The watcher smiled. That was the English for you – they'd run a mile to avoid the company of a foreigner on holiday. They'd run two miles to avoid the company of a compatriot. Decidedly not an assignation then.

He slipped out of the building. The girl was much more interesting than the vicar. He'd follow her for a bit. He knew how to justify a change of target. Lugging her heavy bag, she made her way across the square to the Café de la Paix. A bit of luck at last. He seated himself at a table on the terrace, from where he had a clear view of both the girl and the door of the church, and ordered a cold beer. She took her time choosing a table and ordering a drink and the waiter hurried off to get it.

All foreigners passing through came in for surveillance. Occasionally for action a little more decisive. It was to be hoped neither of these two foreigners raised any lethal suspicions. The watcher fingered the heavy cross dangling from his neck.

If ordered, he'd do it without question or comment, of course, but all the same – a man of God . . . a pretty young girl – He had a sudden tug of doubt. What nonsense! He must be letting the robes he was wearing influence him.

Fantasies flooded his brain, fantasies where he got close enough to the girl to kill her. Close enough to smell the scent of her smooth skin, her sudden rush of fear, the flaring of her eyes as they opened wide to take in their last terrifying image, her helpless wriggling. Though this girl's wriggling might not be all that helpless. He peered at her in a professional way under the brim of his hat. She was as tall as he was, and well built. Confident-looking. Better taken from behind. Through the folds of his robe he touched the reassuring handle of the weapon in his belt, calculating distances and angles. At least she'd be easy to track – that golden head would stand out against any background. Apart, perhaps, from a cornfield. A ripe cornfield in August. For a confusing moment the image of the Magdalene flashed into his mind, challenging and disturbing him. He crunched his rosary in his palm and put some coins on the table, preparing to leave.

Too late! He'd left it too late. To his consternation, she looked straight at him and smiled. At *him*? She raised her eyebrows in . . . what? Greeting? Recognition? He cast a furtive look over his shoulder to check whether she'd spotted someone behind him. No one else in range. He tilted his head forward, hiding his face under his hat.

Not to be put off, the wretched girl got up and moved towards him.

'*Mon père, excusez-moi de vous déranger,*' she said, and went on to ask directions to the rue Lamartine.

He couldn't have been more wrong. It seemed the girl was French. She spoke with the speed and confidence of a Parisian. He couldn't be drawn into a conversation. He put a finger over his lips and, with the other hand, signed to her that she should take the road on the left at the far end of the square. She thanked him and apologized again for disturbing him, as if taking him for a member of a silent order. With another smile, she returned to the *citron pressé* which had just appeared at her table.

An hour spent in careful survey can save a week's work.

Remembering Andrew Merriman's words, Letty sat back and stared about her, eager to absorb the character of the pretty town. She sipped her lemon drink and looked around as a tourist might, shading her eyes to look upwards first of all at the commanding height of the spire of the abbey. The remaining structure, bulked about it, was very obviously truncated – no more than fragments of the extensive ecclesiastical buildings that had been put up in the tenth century. In its day, Fontigny abbey must have rivalled Cluny or Vézelay in grandeur. She cursed the vandal hand of Napoleon.

Relieved to have spotted William Gunning in the church before it became necessary to acknowledge his presence, she'd been struck by his careful planning and the whole-hearted way he'd apparently plunged into his role. But it had been a mistake on her part, perhaps, to have approached the man in black for directions. Probably no lasting harm done. She hadn't got a clear look at his face, but she had the impression that he'd been shocked out of all proportion to her mundane enquiry. What could have triggered the over-reaction? Not her appearance. Her beige travelling suit and white blouse were deliberately

88

chosen to raise no eyebrows, even in deepest conservative France.

She watched the priest's retreating back as he shuffled slowly off towards the church. Returning to say a few Hail Marys? To ask forgiveness for wicked thoughts? She didn't think so. She lingered on, enjoying the sudden rush of people on to the square. School was turning out. Mothers and children chirruped together as they made their way home. The door of the *boulangerie* opposite swung open constantly, releasing tantalizing wafts of newly baked bread. Small boys sent, still wearing their grey school pinafores, to buy the family baguettes for the evening meal, paused to take a bite from one nubbly end before scooting off on their way home. In the market square, the last stallholder to pack up and move away, a grand-motherly figure with a face the colour and texture of a walnut shell, doled out leftover strawberries to passing children. Letty smiled with satisfaction. It didn't take her long to feel at home again in her mother's country.

Small-town France. Yes, that was Fontigny-Sainte-Reine all right. Green hills rose up on all sides, protective or suffocating, depending on your point of view. The bound-aries were clearly marked out as, no doubt, were the lives of the people who lived within this sheltered bowl. And Stella St Clair was going to stand out like a sore thumb among them. Letty shrugged. She wasn't there to hide herself.

The time spent with her mother's family south of Paris had been blissful. A great deal of riding in the forest and good conversation. Flirting even, with the parade of eli-gible young Frenchmen her aunt had laid on. And: 'Burgundy? But why? Oh, no, my dear! You can't possibly! But it's the back of beyond! Whom will you meet? What will you do all day? Dig? Dig! Are you mad? No – we're all going down to Cap Ferrat next week. Do come! Your trunk has arrived – we'll simply re-direct it. Now – let me tell you who'll be there ... There'll be crowds of young things of your age ... all the cousins ... oh – and do you remember that young man you got fond of in Brittany five years ago . . .'

And, of course, Tante Genevieve was quite right. She was mad to have embarked on this nonsense. She'd been tempted to go off with the family. Her father, she knew, had calculated as much. But, in the end, she decided she couldn't run the risk of being fished, struggling, out of the Mediterranean by an irate William Gunning, determined to earn his five pounds a week. Her very own parfit, not-so-gentil knyght. Gunning would have tracked her down, she thought with a shudder.

Letty lifted the lion's head knocker and gave two sharp raps, an anxious eye on the crumbling masonry of the façade of number 42 rue Lamartine. She took a step back in case she'd dislodged a loose piece of plaster and looked upwards at the tottering building. Fourteenth century, possibly earlier, she guessed, with the glamorous Romanesque arch to the ground floor that most of the ancient houses in this street had, announcing an earlier use as a shop of some sort. The house next door had even pre-served its ancient stall-board. Preserved? Just failed to remove it, probably. There were few indications of delib-erate preservation in this tumbledown part of the town.

Daniel must have adored it.

The heavy door creaked open and a smiling woman wiping her hands on a pinafore flung it wide in welcome and then seized her bag. 'Mademoiselle St Clair? Come in! Come in! I am Constance Huleux. You arrive a little early, I think? You catch me dressed like a kitchen maid! Will you have a cup of tea before I show you to your room? We have many English guests, mademoiselle – I can assure you that the tea will be good.' She called over her shoulder: 'Marie-Louise! Tea in the guests' parlour! At once!'

Unlike the disregarded exterior, the inside of the house was as neat as a pin, polished to perfection and lightly scented with lavender. From the back quarters crept a delicious smell of cooking. Letty followed Mme Huleux into a parlour overlooking the street, though she could barely make out the street through the cascades of geraniums and thick net curtains. The room was comfortably furnished with a sofa and matching chairs that would not have disgraced Versailles. There were tables scattered about and, along one wall, crowded bookshelves. The sober shapes of dictionaries and works of reference were jostled by the jaunty yellow spines of French novels; there was a good admixture of English books, mainly popular thrillers and detective mysteries of the kind left behind, generously or carelessly, for the enjoyment of other readers. A good-sized desk was provided with ink and a blotter and bore a neat stack of letters. Residents' mail, Letty guessed.

'This is the guests' room.' Mme Huleux gestured about her with satisfaction. 'Your own room, you will see, is very adequate for space but we find that the sort of visitors we have like to gather together in the evening for conversation or games or even work. We invite you to make use of this room whenever you please, mademoiselle.'

They chatted with increasing confidence about the journey and Letty's first impressions of Fontigny while they waited for the tea. Mme Huleux mentioned several times her relief that her new guest spoke such good French. 'If only some of the others would take the trouble,' she muttered, rolling her eyes to the ceiling. 'But you will meet your fellow guests for dinner this evening. Seven o'clock sharp. We keep early hours in the country, you'll find. Just the family in the house at the moment. My old husband is out in the back garden choosing a pair of rabbits for tomorrow's meal, and Marie-Louise you'll see in a moment ... Ah! Here she is!'

Not the maid, after all, but the daughter of the house, Marie-Louise Huleux entered bearing a tray of blue-and-white flowered china and an enormous teapot. A slight and pretty woman in her late twenties, she had an angular, strong-featured face whose gravity was lightened by a

91

cloud of frizzy, rich brown hair cut fashionably short. By scissors expertly wielded, Letty guessed, in Paris rather than the High Street in Fontigny. Her eyes were the dramatic dark brown shade the French called *marron* and she wore no trace of make-up.

Marie-Louise smiled shyly and shook Letty's hand, murmuring politely. She took shelter behind the ritual gestures of the tea tray.

Letty pursued her. 'And are you a working woman, Mademoiselle Huleux?' she asked, sure of her answer and so risking no offence. The smart blue serge dress and good shoes and the general air of watchful intelligence were indication enough that this girl didn't spend her days peering out from behind those net curtains.

'Please call me Marie-Louise,' she replied with a warm smile. 'Or Malou, if you prefer. And, yes, I am. I'm a teacher. I'm in charge of the oldest class at the primary school.'

'You must call me Stella.'

'And, of course, Malou helps me with the organization of this place in the holidays,' added her mother. 'Since the excavations started over at the abbey two years ago we've had a constant flow of visitors, one after another. Most of them are American and English.'

'Delightful guests,' commented Marie-Louise quietly. 'We have with us at the moment two young Americans, gentlemen, both working for M. Paradee. Philip and Patrick. Those are their Christian names – they have surnames but they never use them. Such attractive informality, don't you think? And we have an Englishman. A priest!'

'No, that's misleading, Malou.' Her mother hurried to correct and enlarge. 'He's not a curé, mademoiselle. He's a Protestant vicar. Quite different. English vicars are not celibate – they are allowed to marry, is that not so, Mademoiselle Stella?' She threw an impish look at her daughter, who decided the moment had come to give her total attention to the refilling of the pot.

Suddenly Marie-Louise looked up, face flushed from bending over the steaming hot water jug, and smiled at Letty. 'An odd concept for Frenchwomen to absorb, perhaps! But, on the understanding that this is so, one really must ask oneself why such a man as M. Gunning has remained unmarried.'

Letty could have supplied a thousand reasons.

'I can't wait to meet him!' she said politely.

'How old do you suppose he is, Maman? Forty? Perhaps. But charming and so good-looking! I can tell you, Stella, that your compatriot – for every moment he spends in this sad country of spinsters and widows – is at risk! Though you are not to tell him so. We would not like to see the vicar pack his bags and flee.'

'Do you know this man, mademoiselle?' Mme Huleux's shining round face was alert with innocent interest. She suffered, apparently, from the common misconception that all foreigners must be acquainted with their own countrymen.

'I'm sorry, you'll have to tell me his name again . . . I didn't quite catch it,' said Letty. 'William Gunning, you say?' She thought, then shook her head. 'It's a distinctive name; I would have remembered it had I ever heard it before, I think. No. I've never met him.'

The easy conversation wound to its natural close, which coincided with the emptying of the teapot, and Mme Huleux rose to her feet. 'And now – if I may leave you down here for a moment or two – there are some finishing touches to your room which would have been attended to had you arrived on time – or better still – late! You will learn, mademoiselle, that I am always chasing my tail! Malou! The flowers! Did you remember to . . .?'

'In the sink. I'll get them, Maman!'

They swept from the room and clattered upstairs.

Letty strolled to the window and tugged at the net curtain. It rattled aside on its metal pole and she peered out into the street. A man was approaching from the town centre. William Gunning. She tweaked the curtain back and waited anxiously for him to enter. He greeted her politely and went straight to the bureau to pick up his letters.

'I'm about to be shown to my room,' she told him urgently. 'I'll be brief. William, you're being followed.'

'Ah, yes. Today he chose to wear a black robe and funny hat. I was alarmed to see you approach him head-on.'

'You saw . . .?'

'Of course,' he interrupted, softly. 'Who watches the watcher? I do! You're to keep out of that man's way.'

'Don't be theatrical. He looks a bit sinister but I don't think he can be dangerous. He made sure I didn't see his face but his hands gave him away. Gnarled! One broken thumb – right hand. Not the hands of a priest – I'd have said a farmer . . . a countryman of some sort. He was much too meek and flummoxed even to reply to my simple question. Tried to make out he was a Trappist or something to avoid speaking to me. I had noticed he'd used his voice to order a beer from the waiter though. Idiot!'

'Meek, you say? He carries a pistol.'

'A pistol? In Fontigny? I find that hard to believe. And how would you know? Does he take it out and twirl it round his trigger finger like Tom Mix?'

Gunning snorted with irritation, turned hurriedly, and made to leave the room. As he tried to pass her he caught his left foot under a rug, lost his balance, and would have fallen over if Letty hadn't instinctively reached for him, holding him firmly for a moment before setting him straight on his feet. 'So sorry, William! Your poor leg! One forgets . . . you manage so well . . .' She murmured embarrassed reassurances.

Gunning seemed to have no time for apologies. 'It's hardly a Colt revolver. It's the size of a Browning . . . slightly longer in the barrel perhaps – a Luger? Could be.'

With the impression of his hard body clutched against her side still troubling her, she sighed. 'Ah! I see. You lurched into him, doing your "I'm only a poor one-legged cripple" routine? Thanks for the demonstration! Next time, I'll let you fall!'

'It can be surprisingly successful,' Gunning said dryly. 'If I groped at the Queen, she'd feel sorry for me and apologize.'

'Well, every job has its challenges,' said Letty thoughtfully, 'and I'd say hugging the man in black earns you a gold star. You're saying you got close enough to detect a bulge on his hip?'

'Yes. A pistol-sized bulge. Or a seriously bad case of arthritis. We – the early morning service starts at six o'clock but is not generally well attended and the atmosphere is somewhat bleak ...' The door opened and Marie-Louise came in. '. . . You would do better, would she not, mademoiselle?' he continued smoothly, switching to French, 'to attend the evening Mass.'

'Oh, yes,' Marie-Louise agreed. 'The singing is so much more impressive. With a full choir. Mr Gunning, I see you have introduced yourself to our guest?'

He smiled and nodded and put his letters away in a pocket. 'And I'll see you both again at suppertime.' He sniffed the air stagily. 'Thought I caught a whiff of boeuf bourguignon as I came through the hall? The cooking here, you'll find, Miss ... um ... St Clair? ... is nonpareil!'

Humming cheerfully – Letty thought she caught a snatch of 'Onward, Christian Soldiers' – he went upstairs.

'Well, Stella?' asked Marie-Louise earnestly. 'What do you think of our vicar?'

Chapter Eleven

Letty thought her own hearing was acute but she hadn't been aware of Marie-Louise's silent approach until Gunning had abruptly changed tack. She wondered what the Frenchwoman would have made of an impromptu reply to her question: *A man with the senses of a semi-feral cat . . . a man in whom the thin shell of urbanity is stretched tight over goodness only knows what writhing tensions. A serpent's egg.*

'Charming!' she said, instead. 'Quite charming! As far as I can judge on two minutes' acquaintance. He was a bit put out to find me here . . . though he must have been expecting me? He seemed to know my name.'

Marie-Louise nodded, rather disappointed with her response, Letty judged.

'And good-looking – as you said.' Ah, yes, that was what Mademoiselle wanted to hear! 'A characterful face and rather distinguished. But a touch ascetic, don't you think? His idea of welcoming me to Fontigny was to recite the days and times of the church services!' She managed a disparaging giggle.

'When what you were dying to know was who's appearing at the Music Hall and where the casino is to be found?'

Letty was pleased to hear the slight touch of asperity that accompanied the other woman's bland smile. 'Well, of course,' she agreed lightly, picking up her bag.

* * *

96

Her room was on the second floor overlooking the street. The furnishings were simple but she had everything she needed to spend a comfortable season here and, with the rigours of an English boarding school not a distant memory, it was a delight. Who wouldn't gladly have swapped a faded print of 'The Light of the World' for a gentle Watteau landscape, thin cold linoleum for an Aubusson rug on polished oak floorboards? She noted with approval the creaking armoire, the dressing table and chair, all old and country-made. The bed looked comfortable, its sheets draped with a counterpane of pink-patterned toile de Jouy.

A black vase filled with a bountiful arrangement of white florist's blooms spoke of Marie-Louise's attentions. Letty acknowledged them with warmth. 'How elegant! How modern! A touch of the Crillon in la rue Lamartine!'

As she spoke, she heard what might have been interpreted as condescension in her tone and blushed.

But Marie-Louise, she was relieved to see, accepted it as a compliment and smiled her pleasure. 'And the latest novels.' Letty hurried on with genuine enthusiasm, pointing to a row of books on the bedside table, one or two still with uncut pages. 'But where do you do your shopping, Marie-Louise?'

'I go to Paris with Maman once a year, but mostly I manage to go to Lyon on my day off. It's a wonderful city and has everything I need to affirm my sanity! Cafés, cinema, libraries – even bookshops! The bus route to Lyon is my lifeline.'

'What a wonderful selection,' said Letty, fingering the books. 'I say, may I? You didn't buy these just for me, did you? You did!'

'Of course. Though if you should choose to leave them behind when you go – I should enjoy reading them. Some I've already read.'

'*Le Rouge et le Noir* ... one of my favourites. And *La Femme Cachée*. The latest Colette? How lovely! And here's one in English I shall definitely re-read – *The Beautiful and Damned*. Is Scott Fitzgerald much read in France?'

97

'Oh, yes, but the translations lag behind the English publications. Perhaps you will be able to help me with some of the passages? But I'd like you to come and see the bathroom now, Stella. You will share this with me. We are the only people on this floor. My parents have their quarters at the back of the house on the floor below and the third floor is occupied entirely by the gentlemen guests.'

So – the sexes were conveniently segregated by floor. A good arrangement. Letty would not have been amused to bump into a dressing-gowned Gunning groping his way to his early morning ablutions.

With a reminder that pillows were to be found in the wardrobe, Marie-Louise left her to spend a happy ten minutes unpacking her trunk, which stood waiting for her. She took a hasty bath, calculating, by the increasing intensity of the clattering of dishes and musical burbling from below, that dinner must be imminent. Doubting that such a household would dress for dinner, she put on a demure frock in blue linen and, just in case it looked too uncaring, added a single string of pearls.

She appeared five minutes before seven in the guests' parlour to find Gunning in conversation with a portly white-haired man neatly dressed in suit, stiff collar, and tie. This was obviously her host, the elderly officer of gendarmerie. Capitaine Huleux's eyes sparkled with warm approval as they were introduced and the ritual exchange of polite compliments was made. Moments later, a clamour on the stairs heralded the arrival into the room of the two young Americans.

Letty's first thought on seeing their broad handsome faces was, *Well, Esmé at least would approve! Both in their early twenties!*

Philip, slightly the older, was dark, deep-voiced, and, she would have guessed, the more reflective of the two; Patrick had springing red hair and the mobile, responsive features that go with it. Both were wearing clothes her father would have dismissed as 'outdoorsy': corduroy suits, soft-collared shirts, and loosely tied ties. The two young Americans made Gunning in his dark outfit and white dog collar look even more English and old-fashioned.

They introduced themselves to Letty, managing with impeccable manners to involve the vicar and the policeman in their conversation. '. . . Well, we're glad to have you aboard, Miss Stella. You arrive just in time! Start of the season and everyone's going a little crazy! It's getting hectic around here – but then that suits us.'

'I'd say Paradee's got a good thing going with this setup,' Patrick was saying with an enveloping gesture round the room. 'Put your key staff all together in the same place and what happens? They work in the trenches all day, then come back here and what do they do? Continue working! Overtime! Ever know an archaeologist who was prepared to shut up if there was someone else around to listen to him? Excuse me, I should also say *her* now. Paradee gets twice the work out of us. And now there are four in the gang!'

'Four?' Letty looked around the room for the missing musketeer.

'There's Patrick and me, and now you and the Reverend here.'

'The Reverend?' She couldn't quite keep the astonishment and disapproval out of her voice. 'I'm sorry – I hadn't taken you for an archaeologist, Mr Gunning.'

He smiled condescendingly. 'Then your common sense has not let you down, Miss St Clair. Indeed, I am not an archaeologist.'

'But he does do the most amazingly accurate drawings!' Philip interrupted, perhaps in an attempt to counteract the fit of English self-deprecation which would surely have followed. 'Paradee snuck up behind him one day and discovered he was sketching a profile of the trench we were working on. The proportion and perspective and the way he has of suggesting materials and structure with a few pencil strokes impressed Paradee no end. He'd been doing the records himself up till then. We keep photographic

99

evidence, of course, but there's nothing like an accurate sketch for recording a profile.'

'Sir Flinders Petrie would applaud your sentiments,' murmured Letty, not wanting to hear what she was sure was coming.

'Upshot is – the vic's on the payroll!' announced Patrick.

'Drawing architectual features is what I really do best,' said Gunning modestly. 'Stones, earth, ruins – anything that stays still and doesn't try to engage me in conversation. Never ask me to produce a portrait.'

'I wouldn't dream of it,' said Letty. 'I'm sure you wouldn't have the time. You must find it demanding, Reverend Gunning – serving two masters. The Lord and Paradee?'

'It's okay, Stella,' said Philip with a sharp glance from one to the other. Sensing the antagonism between them, he went on lightly, 'There's no contest! The Lord has signed his exeat for a month or two – what did you call it, Reverend? – a sabbatical? Just as well – Paradee doesn't like to have folk around him suffering from split allegiance.'

To Letty's relief, Mme Huleux popped her head round the door to announce that dinner was ready.

They ate with the family at a long mock-Gothic table. The cooking, as Gunning had predicted, was excellent, the best that the French provinces had to offer. A creamy leek soup was followed by the boeuf bourguignon whose aroma had been tantalizing them for the last hour. Local red wine – 'From my cousin's vineyard . . .' – was poured with a liberal hand by Capitaine Huleux from an earthenware pitcher and the conversation grew louder and more animated. A platter of cheeses Letty had never encountered before circulated once or twice and the meal drew to a triumphant close with crème caramel and a dish of wild strawberries.

Letty had noticed that the general conversation had divided into two or three topics around the table. The

100

American boys, though with many an attempt to change the subject, always came back with guilty pleasure to a discussion of archaeology. They were fanatics both, and she had worked alongside many like them. One of their attractions for her was that they scarcely noticed that she was female. No allowances were made in this world; none were expected.

She was closely questioned by Philip on her experiences the previous summer when she'd been invited with her father to take part in the opening up of a prehistoric barrow, the property of a large landowner in the West Country. It had been his idea to carve his way through the site in the old-fashioned way, using labour from the estate, the whole process staged for the entertainment of his houseguests as they stood by, sipping champagne, nibbling quails' eggs, and exclaiming with wonder.

The boys hissed their disapproval of these goings-on.

'Can you imagine!' Letty told them. 'The fellow was recently returned from Lord Carnavon's scintillating display in the Valley of the Kings. I don't know how it is with you Yanks but quite a number of people one knows are King Tut crazy.' She ignored Gunning's shudder at her descent into what he would no doubt consider flapper talk. 'And his lordship of the Barrows rather fancied himself in a starring entrepreneurial role in British treasure hunting . . . I won't call it archaeology! But don't worry,' she reassured them. 'This story has a happy ending! As soon as Father got wind of the performance he hit the ceiling! Called up his old friend Andrew Merriman . . .' The boys raised their eyebrows in acknowledgement of the name but did not interrupt. '. . . who gave the lord a very bad time. But Andrew's a gent and rather than ruin a chap's sport he arranged to bring a hastily assembled team of professionals, including students –'

'Which is how you got in on the act?'

They were leading her to talk about her experiences, assessing her in their cool way. She had expected no less.

'That's right! . . . and show them how to do it properly. I'm sure the guests would all much rather have uncovered a hoard of gold and silver and a skeleton or two instead of the beaker pottery we did find – but precious metals were not on offer that weekend. No Roman coin or silver cup for them to take home as a souvenir, but at least they went back having learned something useful. And one or two were impressed enough to follow it up.'

Gunning was holding his own in French with the occasional shriek of laughter from Mme Huleux and murmured encouragement and correction from Marie-Louise. Capitaine Huleux was quietly watching everyone and Letty was reminded that he was a police captain. Letty was conscious that Daniel had shared meals at this table with most of these people. She wondered if they remembered him and what they could tell her about his last days, but there was no way she could ever ask. Her father had tried the frontal, straightforward approach and had not been successful. Her way was the only way left: silently collecting information, listening, putting herself as far as possible into the situation Daniel had occupied, thinking as he had thought. But now she was landed with the impediment of a sketching vicar sharing her trench. She sighed.

No one, it seemed, wanted to leave the convivial table. Tiny china cups of coffee had been refilled twice and they could no longer put off the moment of rising with polite compliments to Mme Huleux.

'Hey! It's not late. Seems a shame to go to bed or crowd into the parlour . . . why don't we top the evening off with a brandy at the café? Have you tasted the local marc, Stella?' Patrick suggested. 'Phil? Reverend? How about it?'

'Oh, I say . . . thanks very much but it's not actually my sort of thing, you know . . .' Gunning began to stammer and back away.

'It's quite all right, Mr Gunning,' said Letty with an encouraging smile. 'God's off watch, remember. And I'm sure Mr Paradee wouldn't mind. This is France, where even the monks drink beer.'

'And brew stuff you've never even heard of!' said Patrick. 'What's that firewater they make at the monastery up in the hills? It's green and sticky and made of herbs . . . supposed to make you live forever.'

'*La Dame Verte,*' supplied Marie-Louise. 'Do try it, Stella. It's quite delicious. But don't believe the stories. It has *shortened* quite a few local lives! Though I believe you have to drink rather a lot of it to achieve that effect. My father finds it works wonders for his cough.'

'Let's sit out here on the terrace,' said Phil, helping her into a seat at the Café de la Paix. 'The interior gets a bit steamy and it seems to be kind of reserved for the local folk. Good that you brought your wrap, Stella – it can get a little chilly in the evenings. Here's the waiter . . . Monsieur! . . . ah . . . Now, is that "green ladies" all around? Stella? Sir?'

'Um . . . er . . . I'd rather have a plain brandy if you wouldn't mind,' said Gunning, looking about him uncomfortably.

The café had changed its character completely since the afternoon. No longer a quiet spot where a tourist might sip a lemonade or a mother and child indulge in an ice-cream served up in a silver dish, it was ablaze with light, crowded with people and, somewhere in a back room, a gramophone was playing: Mistinguett, throatily vowing eternal servitude to '*mon homme*'. Letty glanced at the other clients surreptitiously, then more boldly as she recognized that they were all quite openly staring at her. A mixture of young and old, they came and went with much hand-shaking and kissing. Finding no room in the smoky interior, a group of three lads chose to sprawl at a nearby table, shouted an order for beer, lit up yellow cigarettes, and took out a pack of cards. They were joined moments later by a fourth.

Letty's eyes lingered on the fourth. He was probably no more than sixteen, she judged, thin and white-faced and perfectly ordinary-looking. It was his furtive movements that had caught her attention. The boy was checking the crowd, though foreigners seemed to hold no interest for him and his eyes slid past their table. He placed himself, she noticed, with his back to the café, facing the square. Not at ease.

Letty followed the line of his nervous gaze but could see nothing alarming. She found she was looking, and looking with appreciation, at a charming stone building across the square, a building discreetly lit and having an elegant escutcheon over the door.

'Ah, that's the Lion d'Or,' said Phil. 'The local auberge . . . hotel . . . restaurant . . . whatever you like to call it.' He traced its roofline with a forefinger. 'That marked the north wall of the original abbey. We're digging over there, to the left of it. Farther down the road, to the right, you can see the Stud – the "Haras" – in the same stones. Built by Napoleon using material from the abbey he was demolishing. He pulled down the finest church in Christendom to build a stable!' He shook his head in disgust.

'And if you look closely at some of the houses in town, you'll see they've got a little extra decoration,' said Patrick. 'Carved friezes, statues in niches, all taken from the abbey. Stolen? Rescued? Who's to say?'

'Ah, yes,' said Gunning knowingly, 'we experienced the same sort of thing in the English Reformation. Much of beauty destroyed, but a surprising amount of things simply vanished . . . Altars smashed, but does anyone know what really happened to the gold or silver communion vessels that had rested on them? Interesting things turn up in English churchwardens' attics from time to time . . .' His voice trailed away and he looked casually from one politely interested face to the other and, leaning closer, confided, 'And it's not always the vicar who gets first refusal . . . though in my last parish, where the church had suffered badly from the attentions of Cromwell's foot-soldiers, I was offered . . . ah – here come our drinks, I think.'

As the waiter came through the door carrying their drinks, he was jostled with unusual rudeness by an elderly man hurrying away from the café. Deftly, the tray and its cargo were whisked out of harm's way and placed with a flourish on their table. They raised their glasses and Phil proposed a toast to 'successful digging'.

'You should have tried this, Mr Gunning,' said Letty appreciatively after one sip of the violently green and viscous drink. 'It's a bit like Chartreuse ... but sweeter ... very herby and ... ooh – rather fiery as it goes down.'

Conversation was no problem. The Americans were ready talkers and entertaining, and seemed to understand that Gunning was more than happy to remain on the fringes; they treated him with the affectionate deference appropriate to a well-liked uncle. Letty began to relax and enjoy the company. She listened to the laughter around her, increasing in volume as the sky grew dark; she was entertained by the raucous squawking of jackdaws squabbling over the best roosting holes in the stonework. She hummed along with the tune when, Mistinguett having spiralled to a melancholy close, a man strolled from the bar playing an accordion. His selection from *The Vagabond King* seemed to be more in tune with the crowd's mood and everyone seemed to know at least the choruses.

The convivial atmosphere was suddenly shattered by the arrival on to the square of a rider. She noticed the horse before the man. It was a tall black stallion and it was being urged along at far too fast a pace over the cobbles. It slithered showily to a halt in front of the café and danced about, fretting, while its master flung the reins around the branch of a plane tree.

The accordion wheezed a last note, glasses were set down, and conversations ceased in mid-sentence. The crowd held its breath, all eyes on the dark figure striding towards the terrace.

'Oh, great Heavens,' whispered Patrick. 'Come on! Drink up! We should move on.'

No one else appeared ready to do this.

'Who *is* this man?' Letty asked, intrigued.

'Edmond d'Aubec, Comte de Brancy.'

105

Letty stared, like everyone else, at the outlandish figure, who stalked closer, sweeping the café with a hunter's eyes. He wore a black riding coat and black trousers tucked into shining boots, and approached with such swagger she almost expected to make out a sword belt around his waist. In his right hand he held a riding crop.

Suddenly sighting his prey, he stopped and slapped the palm of his left hand with his crop in triumph.

'Gadzooks!' muttered Gunning, laughter bubbling.

'Zounds!' said Letty, catching his eye. 'Or should I say: "*Sacré bleu!*"? We're caught up in a Dumas novel, Reverend!'

A second later her amusement at the performance turned to dismay, then to horror as the stranger, with a violent gesture, knocked over a table, spilling cards and drinks to the ground, the more easily to get at the white-faced boy. The lad looked pathetic, rigid as he was with fear and mesmerized into complete stillness by the approaching threat. With a string of oaths, the man brought down his crop on the boy's shoulder with vicious energy, raised it, and slashed again. The victim cowered backwards but made no attempt to run away. His friends, flinching with each whistling cut, bowed their heads and made no move to come to his aid. No voice was raised in protest. No hand attempted to stay the flailing crop.

Letty's was the voice that broke the silence: 'Stop him!' she yelled. 'For goodness' sake won't someone stop that lunatic?'

Chapter Twelve

No one responded.

With a cry of exasperation, Letty picked up her half-drunk liqueur and was across the terrace. She sank her fingers into the rider's shoulder and tugged. When, distracted and impatient, he turned to shake her off, she flung the sticky liquid straight into his eyes. The glass fell from her slippery fingers and crashed at his feet.

His look of astonishment was all she could have hoped for. The exclamation that followed it was of the crudest. She took a step backwards, repelled, in spite of herself, by the savagery etched in every line of the man's body and features. Abruptly, she was pushed sideways out of his range and William Gunning's gaunt frame stepped between her and the attacker. Gunning gave no warning, issued no challenge. The only sound he made was a satisfying crunch as his left fist connected with the count's jawbone.

'Ladies present,' Gunning said calmly as the count staggered backwards. 'In England we don't use the language of the stableyard to greet a lady, and I expect it's much the same in France. Not quite sure what your problem is, but this is a pretty disgraceful display of private passion in a very public place. Quite spoiled everyone's evening. Suggest you apologize, whoever you are, and bugger off!'

Receiving no response but an incredulous gurgle from his dazed and blinking adversary, he changed to French and added in tones audible to everyone, 'If you'd like to take this further, I daresay the management has a backyard we could use for fisticuffs. I have no quarrel with *you* but I'd say this lad could do with a champion. Will a weedy Englishman fit the bill, my boy?' He addressed his question with a smile to the paralysed youth.

Snorting disgust, the count pulled himself together. With another curse, he shouldered his way past the two unyielding forms of Gunning and Phil, who, fists clenched, had moved swiftly up in support. Weaving his way unsteadily over the cobbles to his horse, he mounted and spurred it away with a recklessness that made Letty wince.

Before the hoofbeats had died away, waiters were scurrying amongst them, righting tables, sweeping up shards, refilling glasses, and joking nervously with the clientele. The injured boy staggered quietly away from the scene, supported by his friends; the accordionist picked up his instrument and launched into a polka.

Phil, concerned and embarrassed, took Gunning's arm and led him back to the table. A waiter hurried to set down a double brandy in front of the older man with a murmured: 'Are you all right, *mon père?'*

'Thank you, yes. It's nothing,' Gunning murmured, massaging his hand. And, with a smile for the two Americans: 'Not as resilient or potent as it once was, I'm afraid, but my left hook has helped me to many a victory in school boxing championships. I have a very long reach. The only quality I have in common with Jess Willard. People find they can't get near me.'

Patrick groaned. 'No reach is gonna be long enough to keep the count at bay. Now we're all in trouble! Paradee won't like this! He won't like it one bit.'

'Oh, come on, now!' said Letty in disbelief. 'What concern can it possibly be of Mr Paradee's? And I'd really like to know exactly who that cartoon character was. Why doesn't someone ring the police? Or even look a little outraged? That would be a start!'

'Waste of time,' said Patrick glumly. 'Outraging the populace is the count's favourite sport. Edmond d'Aubec owns the château just out of town and most of the land around here.'

'Probably owns the chair you're sitting on,' remarked Phil. 'Biggest employer in the region. There are folks in this café who won't appreciate your making their guy look like a monkey. They won't be applauding your little side-show. Here, he's owed allegiance.' He glanced around him discreetly.

'But not respect!' said Letty. 'Surely not respect, if he goes around behaving in that unbalanced way? I thought the French had got rid of their overbearing aristocracy in 1789?'

'As far as d'Aubec's concerned, there might as well never have been a Revolution. God knows how a family of parasitic bandits like the d'Aubecs ever survived the guillotine, but they did. And they go on lording it over the peasantry with impunity.'

'You're joking,' said Letty aghast. 'You're telling me that an atavistic throwback like that can barge in here dressed up like the Black Pirate and whack away at anyone he chooses? Someone should tell him what century the rest of us are living in!'

The Americans exchanged amused glances. Phil shrugged. 'He knows what century we're living in, Letty. His family not only survived the Revolution, they prospered. There have been ups and downs in their fortunes, but the present count is extremely rich and powerful – even Paradee can dig only where d'Aubec gives him permission, and as far as doing a little archaeological prospecting's concerned – forget it! Frustrating! D'Aubec and Paradee don't exactly get along.'

'In fact,' said Patrick uncomfortably, 'we're all under orders to avoid him. The boss is going to hit the roof when he hears what just happened. And you two,' he paused, uncertainly eyeing Letty and Gunning, 'are likely to come in for some unwanted attention when d'Aubec finds out who put a stop to his sporting activities this evening.'

'I expect he's boiling up the oil as we speak,' said Letty, 'or adjusting his thumbscrews. Oh, come off it!'

'I mean there'll be explaining to do . . .'

'Leave it to us,' said Phil, kindly.

'Do you think he got a look at you, Stella?' Patrick wondered. 'Before you blurred his vision?'

'Yes, as a matter of fact, I think he did. I'd swear his expression changed. He gave me a rather odd look. But I don't care if he *does* remember me. I shall remember *him* all right, if we ever meet again,' she promised.

Letty was downstairs in the dining room early the next morning sipping from a bowl of black coffee and regretting the previous night's double liqueur when the men joined her. Gunning looked pale but well groomed, the Americans as ebullient as on the previous evening. Marie-Louise had already left for school and Mme Huleux was in attendance. Just as they were rising from the table, the door-knocker echoed through the house. Mme Huleux hurried to answer and, after a brief conversation with someone on the doorstep, she returned, in some excitement, with a bunch of creamy pink roses in one hand and a silver-wrapped box in the other.

To Letty's surprise she thrust both items at her with a delighted giggle. 'For you, mademoiselle.'

'For me? What is this? Who on earth would send me flowers here? And great heavens! I know these roses – they're *Souvenir de la Malmaison*!' Puzzled, she buried her nose in the roses, enjoying their rich scent.

'*Souvenir de la* what? Is that something special?' asked Patrick.

'*Malmaison*. Oh, yes, they're special. They're named after the Empress Josephine's château, where she grew them. These were her favourite roses . . .' Silently she suppressed the thought: *And they're* my *favourite too.*

'And delivered at . . . what's the time? . . . at half past seven on a working morning in Fontigny?' Phil's question

110

echoed everyone's astonishment. Four pairs of eyes willed her to open the box on the spot and satisfy their curiosity.

'I don't know anyone in Fontigny. Could they be from Mr Paradee, do you think? To mark my first day's work? Is that the sort of gesture he would make?'

'He didn't send *me* roses,' grumbled Gunning.

She tore off the silver wrappings to reveal a bottle of champagne – very expensive champagne, she noticed. A further tag around its neck carried a message in elegant and spidery French handwriting:

Brancy le Château.

My dear Miss St Clair,

A thousand pardons for my intrusion into your evening. You were constrained to waste your drink on me, so at least let me repay you. I will meet you for dinner at the Hotel du Lion d'Or this evening. At 8.00 p.m.

Edmond d'Aubec.

'Well?' four voices asked in chorus.

Letty had turned pale.

'What is it, Stella?' Gunning asked quietly.

'Thumbscrews,' she answered. 'I believe it's the first twist of the thumbscrews.'

She detached the tag and gave it to Phil, who took a swift look and passed it on to Patrick. They both burst out laughing and showed it to Gunning and Madame Huleux.

'I guess he didn't get a long enough look at you last night!'

'Seems to want another eyeful! What'll you throw next time, Stella? Cognac? Or champagne?'

Mme Huleux, however, was impressed. The roses were put in water, the champagne was whisked away to the cool of the cellar. Something about her response made Letty say firmly, 'I shall be dining here tonight, madame. I wouldn't like to miss your rabbit stew.' She found she was irritated by the polite assurance that it was a simple casserole and one guest more or less wouldn't make the slightest difference should Mademoiselle happen to change her mind.

A low whistle from Phil brought her attention back to the note, which he still held in his hand. 'Say! Would you look at this here,' he said with an exaggerated drawl. 'Stella, you didn't look on the back. The count must be really smitten with you! You rate wine, roses, and dinner – but not only that! Look, you've got a pretty picture too! Hadn't realized d'Aubec fancied himself an artist, but this is kind of good.' He held it up for everyone to see. 'It's a pack of dogs – well, three dogs. They're all the same – black ones – and they're stepping out, all wearing gold collars. Now, what the heck is that about?'

For a moment, Letty couldn't move. Her heart was thumping; her voice was stuck in her throat.

'Say, are you okay, Stella?'

She snatched the card from Phil and took it to the window. With her back to the company she pretended to study it, hiding her confusion. 'I've no idea what it's about,' she said. 'But yes, it's very intriguing. Now, what can he be up to?'

'May I?' said Gunning, strolling over and holding out a hand for the card. He began to laugh. 'Ah, yes, I thought it sounded familiar. Surely this is a reference to an old English nursery rhyme? How does it go? . . .

>'The three black dogs of the Queen,
>The blackest you've ever seen,
>Ebony, Jet and Pitch,
>As black as the blackest witch . . .

'You're going to have to help me out, Miss St Clair! You're much nearer the age of nursery rhyme than I am!'

She guessed, cynically, that he could probably have spun

out the nonsense for several more verses, but she picked
up his challenge to return to normality:

> *'Their collars, I'm told,*
> *Were all of pure gold, . . . um . . .*
> *You couldn't tell which was which,'*

she finished with a rush.

The Americans stared from one to the other, uncomfortable with this display of English eccentricity. 'But, altern-
atively, it could be a reference to the *French* folktale *Les trois
chiens noirs de Chinon*, don't you think?'

'Oh, yeah? And if that's a French folktale, I'm the
Gingerbread Man,' said Phil genially, holding out her
jacket.

'Well, it adds another charge to the count's sheet,' said
Letty dismissively. 'To Grievous Bodily Harm and
Exhibitionism you can now add Infantilism. He really
should be put away in a place of safety.'

There was no time even to flash a look of gratitude to
Gunning. Phil was herding them out of the door.

'Save it for Paradee, Stella. You're ready? Don't want to
be late on your first day. Come on now!'

Chapter Thirteen

The church bell was tolling eight when they ducked through an archway and entered a courtyard crowded with freshly watered flower boxes.

'That's Mr Paradee's private residence,' Phil explained, pointing to the left-hand side of the medieval stone building. 'And over here's where the boss has his office ... workroom ... control centre.'

The boys lined up at the carved wooden door of Paradee's office and banged the knocker. Letty was impressed to see them unconsciously smooth down their hair and adjust their collars as they waited. What sort of martinet could their employer be? And would she pass muster herself? She'd put on an outfit that clearly announced her intention of stepping straight into a trench, trowel in hand. She was telling the world that she was not the kind of woman who would teeter on the edge of an excavation shouting out instructions and keeping her shoes and fingers clean. Freshly pressed but well worn, her khaki trousers, matching shirt, and laced desert boots had been unremarkable in Egypt but, strangely, here in France, she'd noticed a few startled looks as she ran along the street with the boys. Too bad – if the *fellahin* could accept her, so could the French.

The door swung back, opened by the director himself.

'Stella St Clair, sir,' murmured the boys respectfully, and they slipped away around the corner, leaving her face-to-face with the talented archaeologist Daniel had written of in admiring terms.

114

And her letter to Esmé that evening, she decided, would be full of fascinating detail. Esmé would expect it. An impressive man. Yes, she would say – impressive. Taller than herself by an inch or two, slim and active-looking. Light brown hair worn rather long, and narrowed brown eyes in a weathered face which seemed moulded thinly over a well-shaped skull. This was a face destined for distinction in later years. But for now, Letty thought, a severe face when his smile of welcome faded. And it seemed to her that it faded more quickly than might have been expected. A calloused hand took hers in a formal handshake. A man who evidently still did his share of trench work, then. With his well-cut tweed Norfolk jacket, linen shirt, and Charvet scarf knotted at the neck, Charles Paradee presented, all in all, an entirely proper appearance for a site director. Letty thought she might omit to mention in her letter that he was, as her friend had annoyingly predicted, somewhat elderly. About forty? Disappointing perhaps, but unsurprising. This was the age by which a man might count on having risen to a position of esteem in the archaeological world.

She was less confident of the impression she was making on him. Had the first, hastily disguised reaction been one of astonishment? Or could it have been disapproval? His moment of consternation over, he began to speak and to speak volubly: 'Come in, Miss St Clair . . . Stella. We're all glad you could get here – we'd worried we'd be starting the season short-handed. I've read your recommendations and you're far too well qualified for the job you're going to do but – what the heck! – if you're willing to do it, I'm not going to complain.'

He went on talking as he led her through to his office. She took a swift look around and approved the ordered efficiency of the large room. Neatly labelled filing cabinets and storage drawers covered two walls. A third displayed large-scale detailed maps of the area and a montage of photographs, some taken from the air. In the centre stood a large table and it was to this Paradee directed her attention.

115

Her first reaction to what she saw there was one of admiration, her second one of speculation. The three-dimensional model of Fontigny and the surrounding countryside was beautiful and carefully crafted, the work of expert hands. It was showy, it was not strictly necessary, and it must have cost a good deal of money. She could imagine the tuttutting such a flourish would have raised from her mentor, the parsimonious and perpetually cash-strapped Andrew Merriman. The aerial photography underpinning the project was at the leading edge of archae-ological research and represented a considerable invest-ment of funds. She guessed this display was calculated to dazzle the eye of whoever was behind the enterprise: *See how impressively I'm spending your money!* Someone in this enterprise had more money than sense, she concluded. But the model was seductive, she had to admit.

All the details were there: the tiny river curling away through wooded slopes, ranks of vines patterning the hillsides, and, in the very centre, the snail-shell cluster of houses that was Fontigny and at the heart, a superb minia-ture abbey.

Paradee stood by, noting her appreciation. He answered the questions she put to him as she walked around it, look-ing and learning. They fell silent for a moment, in total rap-port as they contemplated this ancient part of France spread out before them, rich and welcoming, fought over and lived in from the most ancient civilizations that wandered through, hunting and fishing, on to the early farmers, the horse-breeding Celts, the Gauls killed or enslaved by the settling Romans, and then the Middle Ages rising in triumph from the welter of the Dark Ages.

Paradee was explaining that he was hoping to make further progress in tracking and revealing traces of the original abbey so that a definitive floor plan could be drawn up.

'But with all these layers of civilization,' said Letty hes-itantly, 'I'd guess the abbey itself was constructed over the ruins of earlier buildings?'

'That's so,' he said with an encouraging nod for her in-sight. 'We know an earlier church existed here before the monks arrived with their stonemasons and their grand designs. We're finding traces. And, of course, there are written records of such a church – it too was dedicated to Mary Magdalene, like the present one in the square. We have no clear idea yet just how far back it goes, but we'll get there.'

'Back to Roman times?' she offered. 'A shrine to Mithras, god of the soldiery? I know people tended to build time after time on a spot considered hallowed in the region.'

'Roman!' Paradee exclaimed, in gentle reprimand. 'Oh, the glamour of the Romans! Why are they always the ones that women get excited about? I don't hear them sighing with anticipation at the idea of digging up a ... a ... Visigoth!'

'You're not to take me for a romantic treasure-hunter, Mr Paradee!' Letty was stung to a sharp reply by the fear of being categorized with the rest of her sex. 'I'm no admirer of Schliemann and his methods. But a civilization that left so many treasures, so much literature, that gave us our legends, our language, and our laws – surely I can be excused for finding it relevant and fascinating? I'll dig up a boring, moustachioed old Visigoth, if that's what's on offer, with all due care and attention and profound respect for his culture. I'll record and tabulate his remains to the inch and publish a learned paper on it if required, but I'll not deny that it's the people I can sympathize with and feel I know that spark my deeper interest.'

'You speak deprecatingly of Schliemann – surely you admire the work he did at Troy and Mycenae?'

A sly question. Letty was keenly aware that this overtly companionable conversation was, in reality, an interview.

'Schliemann! What man hasn't admired his attack and energy, envied the way the gods appear to have smiled on his enterprise? What woman hasn't pictured herself decked out in the gold and jewels of Helen of Troy? Like everyone, I've revelled in the buccaneering way he revealed to us a Homeric past. But . . . well, I've talked with men – scholars – who have serious reservations concerning Mr Schliemann's methods, even his honesty. One of his own countrymen described him bluntly, and possibly slanderously, as a "swindler and con man". Another has suggested, more judiciously, that "he who hideth can find". I've been trained to ask questions and take nothing at face value. So – my admiration is qualified.'

'You know the story of Schliemann's unearthing of the gold Mask of Agamemnon?'

Letty nodded. '"Today I have gazed on the face of Agamemnon," he said in his telegram to the King of Greece. What a moment!'

'Yes, something like that – but, did you realize that's exactly what he meant? He'd seen the *face* of the old warrior? The story goes that the metal had preserved the part of the body that it covered and, the instant Schliemann lifted the mask from the earth, he saw below the actual features, thirty-two perfect teeth, half-closed eyes, moustache, and all. He bent and kissed it but the face disintegrated into dust at his touch. He was left holding no more than the gold death mask.'

'Hail and farewell!' said Letty. 'No, I hadn't heard that story. And I'm not sure I believe it – though it's certainly entertaining. Can you be certain of this?'

He smiled an acknowledgement of her scepticism but persisted: 'I have a question for you. Imagine yourself in that grave shaft. You uncover the mask. At your elbow is an ancient deity. She . . . something tells me it would be *she* . . . makes you an offer. She gives you a magical choice. You can keep either the face of the Achaean warrior himself, preserved for posterity, or the golden image. Which would you choose?'

'Oh, the face, of course.' Letty had not hesitated. She enquired innocently, 'Have I passed the test?'

He laughed. 'You made the female choice. But you're very direct. A Merriman disciple, of course. Stands out a mile! It's that blend of scientific rigour and romantic

118

enthusiasm he teaches. Merriman! There are rumours about the good professor. Tell me – are the stories we hear about his exploits true?'

Letty had learned that archaeologists revelled in a hint of scandal, usually about their fellows, and she'd been asked the same thing a hundred times. Andrew Merriman, as her father had hinted, was a man who attracted gossip, most of it undeserved. She decided to tease Paradee a little for his indiscretion and murmured in reply, 'Oh, yes. I've heard those stories. I grew very close to Andrew in the desert – miles from civilization and living in tents as we were, it is quite inevitable that a certain intimacy will develop – and I can tell you . . . his technique is amazing and the reports of his stamina are not exaggerated.'

There was a stunned silence while Paradee digested this. Letty chided herself for falling into his trap. Encouraged by his friendly enthusiasm, she had been lured into a premature assumption of confidence. Now he would mark her down as an untrustworthy female tittle-tattle. She belatedly remembered that she was not speaking to one of her Bohemian friends who would appreciate and respond lightly to saucy innuendo of this kind. No, she had gone too far, and she hurried to finish, not with the knowing air of conspiracy she normally used when repaying the indelicate question, but with a show of girlish innocence. 'The skill with which the professor handles a trowel is superb, and, do you know, he digs for twelve hours a day and then spends two more hours writing up the day's report! And is quite deaf to Lady Merriman's complaints and dire warnings concerning his health. Andrew's in wonderful health for his age. He declares the hot dry climate keeps his arthritis at bay. But you were about to speak of Roman remains, I think?'

'Ah. Yes. Romans. Well, we're encountering traces of them – and of earlier civilizations.' Relieved by the change of tack, Paradee moved along the board and pointed to the excavation site. 'We're technically digging to reveal and define the eleventh-century abbey, but . . . well, if our spade should slip and go a little deeper ... or wider ... who knows what we might find? A forum, a theatre, a villa, a mosaic floor, a hoard of coins? Any of these would be frosting on the archaeological cake.'

'Though in revealing them, you'd be destroying the traces of the original abbey?'

He frowned. 'Archaeology is destruction of a sort. You know that. No way around it.'

'And Roman remains would guarantee wide interest and financial support?' she suggested.

His face creased in a very pleasant way into a grin. 'Straight to the heart of our problem, Stella!' he said, again approving her perception. 'Funding is vital, of course. We're all seeking our own Lord Carnarvon. And, you're right – in this game money follows glory.' His mouth narrowed in – distaste? determination? 'We're concerned to reveal the language we can learn from the layers of earth we uncover ... the broken lug of a pot, a dark patch of charcoal staining, a glittering gold coin, a dull halfpenny – they all have their equal and exact place in the context of a dig. They are our grammar. But it's not always immediately comprehensible or attractive to the general public.'

'A general public that enjoys screaming headlines of the *Revenge of the Pharaoh! Fabulous Treasure Revealed in Egyptian Desert, Ten Archaeologists Die Hideously, Victims of an Ancient Curse!* type?'

'You've got it! Certainly beats *Further Six Feet of Monastery Wall Uncovered in Deepest France. All Excavators Healthy and Well.'*

She turned again to the model. 'And where, Mr Paradee ... very well, Charles ... given a clear area, would you have placed your villa, had you been a colonizing Roman?'

'It wouldn't have been exactly clear even in the first century. As a colonizing Roman, let's say a soldier being pensioned off with a parcel of land here in the Burgundy hills, I'd have thanked the gods and the emperor for their generosity and I'd have set about clearing my land of indigenous and, no doubt, unfriendly tribesmen. Probably some of my old army buddies would have come along to help me. Anyway, I'd have been pleased with what I found here. Good river providing links to Provence, which was already Romanized, and beyond to the sea. Good rolling land that would produce better wine than the old vineyards back home, as well as grain and fruit. Plenty of wood and easily worked local stone for building. Game in the forest, fish in the river. No shortage of Celtic slaves to do the hard labour. Time, at last, to marry, perhaps the daughter of a good friend back home, perhaps a local woman ... time to settle down and raise a family. Sons to continue the line ...'

Into Letty's mind flashed, unwelcome, the memory of the aggressive stranger of the previous evening. She remembered his dark looks, his springing black hair, his aquiline nose, its majesty somewhat reduced by the trail of green liquid dripping from the tip. Did Edmond d'Aubec trace his aristocratic bloodline back through the centuries to some energetic and prolific Roman settler now no longer even a race memory?

Paradee was talking on with enthusiasm. 'There. That's where I'd have settled,' he said, pointing. 'It's perfect. It has everything – a high promontory of a site ... easily defensible ... commands a view down two valleys. Fresh water and grazing.'

'But there *is* a building there,' said Letty, leaning over the model. 'It's a castle, isn't it? Thirteenth century, by the look of it.' She took in the tiny but detailed keep surrounded by a double curtain wall; she could even make out a formal garden in the courtyard.

'That's right. Thirteenth century and still impregnable, I'm afraid,' said Paradee. 'We've tried. What wouldn't I give to be able to do a little digging around up there! But that's Brancy le Château, ancient seat of the Counts of Brancy. They were almost as rich and powerful as the Black Monks of Fontigny for centuries, but they've weathered somewhat better than the monks. The castle is more or less intact and remains the stronghold of the latest in the line,

121

who lives there with his old hag of a mother and a small army of retainers. Edmond d'Aubec.'

'D'Aubec? Ah, yes . . . I believe I may have caught a glimpse of him last night.'

Paradee allowed her half-truth to hang in the air. 'So I heard. Now listen, Stella – you keep away from that man. You're part of my team now and my team has strict orders to stay clear of him. D'Aubec's trouble.'

'He's an arrogant bully and a very suitable subject for a study by Herr Freud,' she countered lightly.

'He's not a man you can dismiss like that. His cavalier style may seem outrageous and from another age, but this is no worn-out aristocrat pathetically hanging on to the shreds of his pedigree. He's got the clout to back up his pretensions. He's got a lot of money – not an inherited fortune, but new money, money he's made himself. He's a businessman with a finger in every pie in Burgundy – and beyond. And he's in my way.'

Letty was startled by the vehemence in his words, the intense dislike he made no attempt to conceal. Sensing this, Paradee grinned apologetically but seemed unwilling to abandon his warnings. 'And something else, Stella – just in case you were thinking I'm being overly concerned . . . d'Aubec has a certain reputation . . . um . . .' He floundered and seemed unsure how or, indeed, whether, to continue.

'Let me guess,' she said, helping him through his confusion. 'This being the land of the troubadours, I should not be at all surprised to hear that the man shows an interest in the Art of Courtly Love. Am I right?'

'Nothing *courtly* about it,' he replied, 'not the way he plays the game. Exercising his *droit de seigneur* is more his style.'

'Crikey!' Letty said unguardedly. 'Who needs to dig a trench to turn up fossils in this neck of the backwoods? The fossils parade about the streets for all to see!' She began to shake with laughter.

'For goodness' sake! You'll have to pay closer attention than this!' he said stiffly, angered by her wilful mis-

122

understanding. 'Maybe I should have known better than to take on a woman ... If I'm honest, Miss St Clair, I should admit that, after receiving your testimonials, your warm letters of recommendation from the highest quarters, I was expecting someone ... well ... more on the lines of Gertrude Stubbs ... an embryo Ada Hepplewhite ... a budding Isadora Bell ... You know – a Daughter of Empire with a bullwhip in one hand and a Bible in the other. Instead of which I get ...' Her raised eyebrow confirmed his suspicion that he was making matters worse. 'Okay, I'll spell it out. A girl who looks like you do, arriving in this town, is a surefire target for this reprobate. You'll be a challenge to d'Aubec. You've landed on his turf and he'll see you as all the more tempting a trophy because you're working for me – a man he dislikes. Now do you understand?'

She nodded. She understood. And she was repelled by the thought that she might be seen as no more than a lioness to be fought over by two warring lions stalking the same territory.

'I want a promise from you,' Paradee continued. 'You must consider yourself under my protection for the duration of your stay here in Burgundy ... You won't be surprised to hear that certain assurances were sought by your mentor, Professor Merriman ... No, don't frown like that, young lady! Perfectly proper in the circumstances – I would have expected nothing less ... And I intend not to let him down! I want to hear you say you'll go nowhere near this man.'

He waited for her reply.

Letty's thoughts were grim. Rebellious. Any child who'd read her *Fascinating Animals of the World* knew that, when it came to hunting skills and killing power, it was the lioness who was the more effective. While the lazy lions shook out their manes, roared, and posed about impressively on rocks disputing territory, the lioness, with a weary sigh, would shoot off into the bush in pursuit of the next kill.

But the face she turned toward Paradee was alight with humour and honesty. Her voice, to his ears, was innocent, warm, and deferential: 'Thank you, Charles, for speaking so openly. I really do appreciate and welcome your concern. And, of course, I'll pay careful heed to all that you say.'

Chapter Fourteen

Gunning was in the parlour, book open in front of him at the desk, when Letty slipped in at the end of the working day. 'Good Lord!' he said, faintly, at the sight of her. 'What *have* you been up to? Taking out a contract on the Augean stables? You look frightful. Don't you think you should take your boots off at least – this is rather a good carpet.'

She found she welcomed the sound of his dry voice. 'Yes, William,' she said dutifully, and sat on the floor to unlace her boots. 'Aren't you going to ask me how I got on? This *was* my first day . . .'

He sighed, put a finger on his page to mark his place, and turned to her with an interested smile. 'Tell me, my dear, how did you enjoy your first day? Did you learn anything? Did you make any nice friends?'

She was eager to share her excitement with someone – anyone – and Gunning would have to do. Taking his questions at face value, she tried to catch his genuine attention. 'We uncovered a Roman drainage system,' she said. 'Problem was, when we tried to dismantle it – it gushed into life! It poured suds – very modern suds, lavender-scented – into the trench. The good townsfolk of Fontigny are still using the system! Paradee wants you to come down and make a sketch tomorrow.'

'What on earth did you do about it?'

'What do you expect? We called in the local plumber and had it put back again.'

Gunning chortled. 'You summoned the *plumbarius*! The

worker in lead. I wonder if he knows his name's the same after more than two millennia?'

'Yes, he did, as a matter of fact. And he had some disparaging remarks to make about the skills of our assembled company. But now, William, I've got less than two hours to turn myself from sewer rat into siren. Listen. Paradee had already heard about our little altercation last night when I met him this morning. He would seem to have an effective information service in place.'

'Telephone,' said Gunning. 'It's called the telephone. There's a public one in the post office and old Huleux has one somewhere about the place. I've heard it ring.'

Letty ignored him. 'He's a clever man and ambitious, I'd say. And he runs a tight ship. He could strut the deck with Admiral Collingwood! "Yessir, nosir, three bags full, sir," I'd guess are the words he most likes to hear. His staff seem very loyal. He's the kind of man who inspires loyalty, I'd say. Our new boss is a good-looking man – for his age – don't you think?'

'Is he? Pretty average, I'd have thought,' said Gunning, eyes straying back to his book. 'If I were kind I'd give him the name of a good barber.'

'Huh! A Mr S. Todd, care of The House of Correction, Cambridge, would that be? For a down-and-out you don't half give yourself airs, William!'

He closed his book with a bang and, flushing with shame at her careless remark, Letty stuck out her chin and waited, ready to accept his justified reprimand.

But he smiled. 'True enough. It's many a year since the gentlemen at Trumpers had the honour of wantoning with my locks. Black as a raven's wing they were in those days.'

'Sorry, Reverend! I'm truly sorry. Was that a lesson in turning the other cheek you just gave me?'

'No. Your moral education is outside my remit. Thank Heavens! It was not specified in my employment contract with Sir Richard. "Return sound in wind and limb" was the extent of his requirement, I remember. And now, if I may have your cooperation in satisfying his caring

126

concern ...? And risking a further knuckle-rapping for interfering ... Did you notice, I wonder, that yon sharp-eyed Philip was not in the least taken in by your rubbish in the matter of the count's little present to you this morning? And he took a very long look at that drawing.'

'It wasn't mentioned again,' said Letty uncertainly. 'But Paradee made me promise not to have any contact with the count.'

'Ah. And yet you're planning to flout orders on your first day? You'll be in for a keelhauling tomorrow, then. Anyway, I stand with your boss on this. From all I hear, that young Edmond is not a suitable playmate for you. There'll be tears before bedtime. Stay at home tonight.' Momentarily doubtful of his authority to speak to her in this way, he added: 'I'm sure your father would expect me to hand you some good advice at this point and here it is – stay at home and play an exciting game of backgammon with the vicar.'

'How can you say that? You saw as clearly as I did what that drawing meant! It was a direct and very personal slap in the face! D'Aubec was flinging down a challenge I can't ignore.'

He sighed. 'Yes, I do see that. Bit of a mystery there and one ought to try to get to the bottom of it. I thought you'd insist on going. Ah, well ... I shall be on hand.'

'What! You'll be sitting in the hotel, watching me eat my dinner? Your presence will cramp my usual dashing style somewhat.'

'No. But I shall be in the environs. If you've not left the Lion d'Or by ten o'clock I shall come in and give your new friend the benefit of my right hook this time, wherever he is and whatever he's doing. Clear?'

'Clear. Environs? You're not thinking of spending the evening in the café, are you?'

'I've not been wasting my time here. I've been reconnoitring – digging in. In fact, I've set up a fox-hole. When I arrived, I sought out the local priest and introduced myself. Luckily Father Anselme is a genial fellow and we have much in common. I'm invited to spend all my evenings at the vicarage if I wish. He has a good library and a reputation as a local historian. I'm helping him to improve his English. If ever you should need me and I'm not at home, you should go to the priest's house in the rue Tellier. It's only a few strides from the square. I shall spend a convivial hour or so with my confrère and then stroll across to the hotel to make certain you've come away. Intact!'

'Well, don't leave it too late, will you? I've had a completely exhausting day and I shall most likely nod off and collapse into my pudding.'

'In such stimulating company? I doubt it! Ten o'clock, then! Off you go!' he finished firmly, and turned back to his book.

Letty stood in front of the cheval mirror in her room. Bathed and scented, hair washed and towelled dry, she'd slipped on the one evening dress she'd packed as an afterthought for France. The Lion d'Or looked rather smart and she thought the simple black silk sleeveless dress would be perfect. Silk stockings, strapped shoes, and a light cashmere wrap completed the outfit. No, one more thing. Defiantly she put down the pearls she had been about to choose and picked up the plain gold necklace she usually wore, a modern design from Asprey's, a twenty-first birthday present from her father. She smiled at the effect. Well, that at least ought to start a conversation.

The Huleux family had accepted her excuses, exchanging knowing glances. Marie-Louise had hurried to iron her dress; Capitaine Huleux had even volunteered to leave his dinner before the dessert to escort her down to the hotel. In the understanding that this was a very thoughtful way of stamping the occasion with the seal of his respectability, she thanked him gracefully for his offer and accepted it.

He gave her his arm as they set off together, an unlikely pair, to walk the short distance to the hotel, greeting several friends and neighbours along the way. On leaving her at the door to the hotel, Huleux informed her that she was not to hesitate to telephone to let him know when he should come to collect her. His crisp voice was directed as much to the maître d'hôtel, who stood smiling a welcome, as to herself. Letty squeezed the old officer's arm in silent acknowledgement of the air of propriety he was conjuring up. She hurried to confirm that she wouldn't be late and that the Reverend Gunning was standing by to assume escort duties.

'Mademoiselle St Clair? Please come this way. The count is expecting you.'

With an uncomfortable feeling that a net was closing around her, she followed the maître d'hôtel down a carpeted corridor to the dining room. It was with a rush of pleasure and relief that she turned the corner and caught sight of the dining room. Nothing could have been further from her worst imaginings of a gloomily lit, red plush seduction scene. Chandeliers twinkled reflections off polished silver; starched white cloths gleamed on tables lit by candles around which nestled small posies of pink flowers. The places were almost all occupied by elegantly dressed diners. Plain white walls were studded at intervals with large dull paintings of Burgundian scenes and, at the far end of the long room, she caught sight of a portrait of a very handsome fellow in nineteenth-century dress, a face and figure she'd seen before: Lamartine, the Romantic poet, born hereabouts.

Another dark, romantic figure rose from the table below the portrait and stood waiting, motionless, while the maître d'hôtel led Letty between the tables, running the gauntlet of enquiring gazes. Thirty pairs of eyes watched as the count took her hand and kissed it, conversations resumed as he handed her into her seat opposite.

'Ah,' he murmured, mouth twitching with amusement, 'what have we? How would you express it? "A Talbot, passant, sable, collared or." Heraldically correct, Miss, er, St Clair.'

His eyes ran mischievously over her black dress and gold necklace.

'I'm relieved to see that your vision at least is unimpaired by last night's episode,' she said coldly, in English, as he had addressed her in her own language.

'I am desolated you should have seen me in such a bad light at our first meeting. I would have liked to have made a better impression.'

'You made an impression on that boy you were beating. He will bear the scars for some time.'

He replied stiffly, 'I had my reasons. Believe me, I had my reasons.'

Rapiers were temporarily sheathed when the waiter advanced to show d'Aubec a bottle of wine chilling in a silver ice bucket and then to pour out a glass for each. As the silence spread between them, she despaired of coaxing from the count the information she was sure he had. In other circumstances she would have been flattered to be dining with such a man. The intrigued glances cast surreptitiously in his direction by several ladies in the room were indication enough, had she not trusted her own judgement, that her companion was attractive.

He was younger than she had at first assumed, and she now guessed that he must be less than thirty. She had been misled by his decisive manner and frowning brow. His thick, silky hair was tidily brushed across his forehead, his strong-boned face was dark-complexioned and flawless, though she was gratified to see that the firm jaw was marred by a purple bruise. When he glanced aside to make a comment to the waiter she stared, fascinated, at the sharp profile of his nose. He became aware of her scrutiny.

'I trust it meets with your approval?' he asked, turning to her.

'Oh, yes. Quite divine! Full of flinty character and just exactly what I appreciate.' She waited for his look of incredulity and then added slyly: 'A local wine?'

He smiled. 'I had feared it might be a little dry for your taste. But – yes – it is from my own vineyard.'

'You appear to be well informed as to my taste, monsieur. The roses you sent this morning were most appealing.'

'And I'm sure you will enjoy the *fruits de mer*,' he said as the first course was served.

Letty ate her shellfish in silence. She was rapidly tiring of this cat-and-mouse game. As it was cleared away she asked sweetly, 'Well, I wonder what you're going to surprise me with next? Since I am not to be consulted as to the menu, wonder is all I may do.'

'No surprises,' he said. 'We're to have breast of duck and with it we'll drink a bottle of Gevrey Chambertin.'

There was no possibility of a mistake, no possibility of coincidence. This was the wine and the dish she'd always chosen as their first meal whenever she had come to France with her father and Daniel. This man knew her. Not only her identity but her habits and preferences, and he could have learned them only from Daniel. But what link could there be between two such uncongenial men? And how could she get the handsome menace sitting opposite to tell her? Outwardly, his behaviour was perfectly correct, charming even, and she realized with some resentment that the smiling attention he paid to her every response was a deliberate show. She had no doubt that the whole town was aware of the part she'd played in the farce the previous evening, and no doubt that the town's grandees were now noting that all was well. The pretty stranger who'd insulted the local lord was accepting his hospitality. And this show of dignity reinstated was, it seemed, the sole object of his invitation.

She chose a chocolate mousse from the trolley while d'Aubec waved away the shining display of fruit tarts, sorbets, and gâteaux, content with a slice of hard mountain cheese. The coffee arrived and, despairing at the opportunity rapidly wasting away, she leaned towards him. 'Very well. You've demonstrated that you know who I am.

I'm impressed and intrigued. But was this farce necessary? Couldn't you just have sent me a note?'

'Oh, it was quite necessary,' he said confidently. 'As is the next demonstration.

'Stella, my darling! What a charming suggestion! How can I resist?' he exclaimed in French and, reaching across, seized her by both ears, and kissed her on the end of her nose.

Eyes were turned on them from every corner of the room; wine spilled over as a distracted waiter allowed his surprise to overcome his professional attention. Hot with embarrassment, Letty stared straight ahead, avoiding the amused and indulgent stares of the citizenry. Enough was enough. Letty came to a decision. She flung down her napkin and rose to her feet. The maître d'hôtel, taking this as a signal that the meal was over, hurried forward and placed a large, clanking key in front of d'Aubec. 'Your room key, monsieur. Your usual. Number ten overlooking the abbey.' He eased back Letty's chair and d'Aubec stood and smoothly came to offer his arm.

Refusing it with a brusque gesture, she stalked ahead, eager now to make her way outside, shake him off, and flee back to the rue Lamartine. And if Gunning was lurking outside, well, just for once, she'd be relieved – no, delighted – that he was there. And what was that hocus-pocus with the key? The man lived only three miles away. Why would he be planning to stay here? She shivered. Surely he couldn't . . .? Of course not. Her doubts were allayed by the comforting presence of the friendly recep-tionist murmuring her polite phrases. 'I hope you have enjoyed your meal, mademoiselle? Would you like perhaps to visit the ladies' room? It is just on the first floor. If you'll follow me?'

Letty spent some time in the sanctuary of the cool room planning her next move as she ran a comb through her hair. She checked her watch. Half past nine. Would Gunning be in place yet? Better to waste a few more min-utes to be certain. And it wouldn't do any harm to leave d'Aubec loitering by the door. She hitched up her stockings and straightened the seams. She combed her hair again. The tapestried chair looked uncomfortable but she sat down on it and began to file her nails. This was ridiculous. Skulking in a powder room was demeaning and silly. What had she to fear? The explosive energy, vicious bad temper, cunning, and evil reputation of her host? Well, that would do for a start. She decided to excuse her cowardice.

But this was a very public place. She was surrounded by ordinary people, spending a happy evening. Nothing untoward could happen in such a civilized setting. Snatching up her bag, she opened the door and stepped into the corridor.

And stepped into total darkness. Cursing the French lighting system, she began to grope her way along the wall, hoping she would find the stairs before she fell down them. Her mutterings were silenced by a large hard hand closing over her mouth. Another powerful hand on her waist spun her around, then propelled her forward, struggling, and in seconds she was pushed into a bedroom. The shutters were closed, discreet lights on. A tray on a table by the door held champagne and glasses. The bed was turned down. The air was thick with the scent of roses. Twisting round, she saw Edmond d'Aubec deftly lock the door and thrust the key into his pocket.

Chapter Fifteen

'I was beginning to think you'd shinned down the drain-pipe,' he said cheerfully.

She selected her weapon. Icy calm would do well. Screaming and hysterics and pounding on the door would draw attention to a situation she'd rather not advertise, and this thought was followed by the practical consideration that the staff here were undoubtedly on the count's payroll.

'"Number ten, overlooking the abbey?" "Your usual, sir?" How disappointingly predictable! How laughably Gothick!' She looked around the room with exaggerated distaste. 'Good Lord! I've strayed on to the set of a Feydeau farce!'

To her surprise he grinned. '*Heart's Desire Hotel*, perhaps? That's my favourite!'

'I prefer *The One That Got Away*,' she replied. 'Now – I'm not familiar with this script – tell me, through which of these doors am I meant to exit? Right? Left?'

'*Heroine sinks gracefully on to small gilt chair, centre stage*,' he said, and moved one of a pair forward. He settled on the other and waited until she responded by perching uncomfortably opposite him. 'No need to be afraid of me, Laetitia . . . I may call you Laetitia, Miss Talbot? I apologize for tonight's charade, but circumstances are propelling us together. Forgive my games but – consider this, will you? – you have questions to ask me, no? How else was I to contrive a meeting with you? If I'd invited you to come to my house . . .?'

134

'I'd have refused. Naturally.'

'If I'd come calling on you at the rue Lamartine with a bunch of roses?'

'I would not have been at home.'

'And that leathery old boss of yours would never allow me to approach you while you are under his eye doing your digging.' He glanced with curiosity at her hands. 'Tell me, Lactitia, can you really enjoy that? Scrabbling around in the dirt? Amongst all those worms and old bones?'

Encountering a gimlet glare he hurried on: 'But *here* . . .' He waved a hand around the room in satisfaction. '. . . we may exchange information and confidences in secrecy and comfort, and if anyone cares to speculate, it will be supposed only that we are seeing each other for the most understandable and excusable of motives.'

It was a moment before his meaning dawned on her. Shock and disgust shook her but it was rage, a killing rage, that took her over, coursing through her, strengthening her limbs. She looked around for a weapon. A poker would do . . . a champagne bottle?

'Ice pick?' he suggested, again following her thought. *'Nobleman found dead with ice pick in heart.'*

'I will go for a bigger target,' she snapped. 'The head will do.'

He grinned. 'Hear what I have to say and if you're still feeling murderous, I'll let you choose the weapons *and* take the first swing. I'm so sorry, Laetitia! I fear I have offended you. And I failed to make allowances for your English manners.' He took the key from his pocket and handed it to her. 'The least I can do is release you at once. Perhaps I may depend on *you* to engineer an opportunity to exchange our information? If you wish, of course. At some later date . . . and at a place of *your* choosing?'

He rose, made a swift and formal bow of dismissal, and started for the door.

'Oh, wait a moment!' she said resentfully. 'Sit down and talk to me. But . . .' She looked at her wristwatch. 'I must

135

ask you to be brief. My escort is even now crossing the square to collect me at ten.'

'Ah! The sporting vicar?'

'Not your concern. But since you seem prepared to talk some sense at last – how did you discover my identity? You must have thought yourself very clever, sending me a drawing of my own coat of arms?'

He smiled, pleased with himself. 'Three hounds – talbots you call them in England, I understand? – black as sable, passant, collared or, as you said. The crest appeared on the letter headings printed on the writing paper you used to communicate with your godfather. I asked Daniel to explain it once. He talked of you a good deal, Laetitia. I feel I know you. He even showed me a photograph of you.' He put a hand in his pocket and drew out a crumpled photograph. 'In fact . . . very strange request, I thought . . . at the time . . . on the last evening we were together, Daniel gave me this and told me to watch out for you. I recognized you last night in the brief glimpse I had before you covered my eyes in that disgusting muck. I say, Laetitia, were you *really* going to drink that rotgut?'

'Your last evening? What are you saying? You *knew* Daniel? You? Well, clearly, I have to suppose that you did, but – how? Why?'

His reply took her aback.

'I did not, unfortunately, know him for long, but I considered him an exceptional man – and my good friend. We met at the stables, soon after his arrival in Fontigny. I keep some of my horses there in the season. I met him poking about, obviously enjoying the sight of so many wonderful horses under one roof, and we started to talk. As he appeared to be a keen horseman, I invited him to come to my home, and that was the beginning of our friendship. We had much in common besides a love of horses. I care very much about my roots, Laetitia; I know a good deal about Burgundy and particularly my own corner of it. I know its history from yesterday back to the time before man. At Brancy I have an extensive library,

136

including many ancient documents which I thought would interest Daniel. I was not wrong! After his day's work with the Americans he would come and spend an hour or two on most evenings in my library, joining me for a talk and a brandy before returning to town. Weekends, also, he was spending time at Brancy. He was working. Translating, researching, and codifying the contents of my library.'

Letty was startled to realize that she was listening to the man Daniel had mentioned in one or two of his letters. Not Daumier but d'Aubec. Assuming, as she had, that the antiquarian described was of her godfather's generation, a kindly old dodderer, she had not made the connection with this all too vigorous young man.

'He got on very well with my mama, too,' d'Aubec was saying. 'Astonishing! She's old and snobbish and can be very bad-tempered, but Maman looked forward to his visits. He wasn't impressed by her nonsense – deference did not come naturally to Daniel! He made her laugh and they enjoyed a good gossip. Last summer, I had to go to Africa to work with the Moroccan government on the breeding of a new half-Arab strain. Of course, I gave full visiting rights to your godfather, who'd reached a pivotal stage in the decipherment of some papers he was working on – he promised me a surprise on my return.'

He fell silent for a moment and Letty said nothing, aware of what was coming next. 'The news of his murder was not the surprise either of us had anticipated. I got back to Fontigny two days after he died.' He gave her a tight smile and looked her in the eyes before continuing with emphasis: 'Two days, Laetitia. All times and dates checked and verified by the Police Judiciaire. You may contact the officer in charge if you wish: an inspector called Laval. And – no – I have no influence over the Lyon cops – Laval is not in my pay . . . In fact, he rather hates me! Nevertheless, I gave the authorities every assistance, of course, in their enquiries, but by then the trail had begun to cool. Laetitia, I have never believed that Daniel was killed by a street robber. A ridiculous notion and I said as much!' He added

137

more calmly: 'I have influence in this town that stretches beyond that of the local gendarmerie; someone would have come to me with the name of his killer the moment I returned, had it been a homebred malefactor. My friend was killed because he was on the edge of a discovery that others wanted to keep quiet. Of that I'm certain.'

'Who else would have known about his work, other than yourself and your mother?' She could not keep suspicion from her voice.

'Paradee.' The name burst from him. 'Or any of his crew. Any of Daniel's fellow guests in the rue Lamartine. I wasn't the only friend your godfather made in this town. Many people knew and liked him. The curé of la Sainte-Madeleine was a good friend. Daniel dined regularly with the mayor and his family. The director of the Haras . . . I could go on . . . If you've come here looking for his murderer, there must be more names on your list of suspects than mine. Though I must concede,' he added gravely, 'that Edmond, Comte de Brancy, most probably figures at the head of it.'

'And there he stays until I know better,' she said crisply.

He asked his next question with uncharacteristic hesitancy. 'Laetitia, did he, I wonder, communicate anything of this to you before his death? Perhaps if we were to share our information, we would arrive at a solution more quickly? Did he write to you in that last month?'

Letty took a moment to weigh her options and judged that she might gain more information than she gave away. She took the postcard from her bag and handed it to him. 'It's nothing. Just a jolly greeting. I was away in Egypt that autumn and winter and if he did send anything apart from this it must have got lost.'

He examined the card carefully. 'As you say . . . perfectly ordinary.' And then, with sudden interest: 'Who is this lady . . . this Uffington? I don't know her. Daniel never spoke of her.'

So that much was confirmed. The lady remained mysterious and unconnected with Fontigny. Letty took back the card. 'Oh, one of his old friends, a lover perhaps, pass-

138

ing through on her way down to the casinos, I suppose. You can't have known everything there was to know about Daniel. Rather a goer in his youth! But it's two minutes to ten, monsieur. I must thank you for a remarkable evening and let myself out.'

He smiled and took the key from her, making for the door. 'I'll hand you over to your pugilistic Reverend ... your *preux chevalier*, then.'

'Thank you.' Pausing in the doorway, she turned and cast her eyes over the room she was leaving, lingering over the luxuriously decadent scene. 'Champagne ... crystal glasses ... roses ... a feather counterpane ...' Her voice held a tantalizing trace of regret. 'Seems a pity to waste all this. Tell you what – why don't you ring for a serving wench?'

As she groped her way down the unlit stairs to the door, a cold trickle of fear chilled her back and she hugged her shawl close about her. Daniel had always kept that photograph in his wallet. Had it still been there when the wallet had been taken from his body as he lay dying? Taken and kept by his killer?

A tall shape detached itself from the trunk of a plane tree and hurried to her side.

'Heavens, girl! You're shaking! What's he done? Is the lout still in there? I'll tear his head off!'

She seized Gunning by the arm and sidestepped to put herself between him and the open door of the Lion d'Or, alarmed to feel the tension in his muscles, to see the combative glint in his eye. 'It's all right, William. Calm down! No harm done. Truly. A few surprises, though. Much to tell you. Shall we walk home?'

Unusually, he offered his arm and, unusually, she took it.

Chapter Sixteen

Was there a cooling in the previous day's warm cama-
raderie to be felt in the trench the following morning? Letty
decided there was. Though on the surface perfectly polite,
the three diggers she was working with, one local and two
Parisian students, were avoiding conversation with her.
Replies to questions came in monosyllables; eyes skittered
sideways when she addressed a remark to them. She
gathered that the news of her evening spent with the count
had spread and, as d'Aubec had anticipated, a link of the
most dubious kind had been forged between them. No skin
off Laetitia Talbot's nose, of course, but the Stella she was
fast becoming was distressed and aggrieved.

Phil and Patrick, on the other hand, behaved with their
normal joking friendship and, sensing the problem, did
their best to rectify it. 'So – Cinderella was back early from
the ball last night? Prince Charming failed to impress,
I guess?' Phil asked in a carrying voice. The pair had been
sitting in the Huleux' parlour when she got back and
knew very well that her evening had been short and
miserable.

'I'll say! I've spent less tedious evenings playing snakes-
and-ladders with my deaf aunt Daisy. I didn't wait around
for the pumpkin – I dashed for home at nine-thirty.' She
was grateful for the opportunity so kindly thrown her to
retrieve her reputation.

For the rest of the day she kept her head down, worked
hard, shared information, and consulted the other diggers
in an unemphatic way. When the time came to clean up

and put away the equipment, friendly relations seemed to have been restored. Paradee had not put in an appearance. When she enquired about his absence, Phil told her cheerfully enough, 'You've got a day's respite, Stella. He set off early for Lyon in the site van. He goes every month to make his report to the Church authorities and pick up supplies.' The well-trained group seemed to get along very well without him.

Gunning had arrived at the trench towards the end of the day's steady dig to sketch his record, and he timed his departure for a careful minute or two after her own. His long strides brought him level with her as they reached the old church of Mary Magdalene.

'Step inside for a moment, Stella. There's never anyone about at this time of day and I notice my shadow seems to have been called off.'

She followed him to a side aisle where he stood to admire a fresco. It was painted on the plastered wall of the nave and was lit by the warm radiance of the late afternoon sun streaming through the lead-paned windows.

'Page forty-one?' she asked, watching him take Daniel's guidebook from his pocket. 'Are you about to show me page forty-one?'

He nodded. 'Tell me what you make of this.'

Challenged again by the feeling that she was under male scrutiny, she replied briefly. 'Fresco. Contemporary with the rest of the church fabric, I suppose. Look in your book. It's a much better authority than I am.' She sighed and, led on by his silence and one slightly raised eyebrow, began again: 'We're looking at a depiction of the patron saint of the church. It's Mary Magdalene. Identifiable by her appearance and the presence of the usual accompanying icons – there's the skull . . . there on the left . . . and under her arm that highly decorated pot represents the unguent jar she used to anoint the Lord's feet . . . And down here on the ground at her feet is a rather charmless bit of earthenware – large and rounded – something in the nature of a funerary urn, I'd have thought. There's nothing special

141

here . . . lots of churches in this area have chosen her as their patron . . . even the cathedral at Vezelay is dedicated to her. And she's popular in Provence, too – *worshipped* there, you'd say. They have a ceremony on the coast each year at Les Saintes Maries de la Mer where they parade a black statue through the town and walk it into the sea. It's supposed to represent Sarah, the servant who accompanied the three Marys. She's much revered by the Gypsy tribes who come from all over Europe each year in May to take part in the ceremony. Have you seen it?'

He shook his head.

'Well, according to the folktale, Mary Magdalene, Mary Salomé, the mother of James and John, Mary Jacobé, Jesus' aunt, and their servant Sarah sailed across the Mediterranean after the death of Christ and ended up in Provence.'

She paused for a moment and added, 'I've seen her skull.'

'You've seen whose skull?'

Pleased to have startled him, she explained. 'Mary's! An ancient skull was found in the mountains of the Sainte-Baume, where Mary is said to have led the life of a healer and holy woman. They claimed that it was that of Mary herself. They dress it up in a rather improbable blonde wig and display it in procession about the streets on her saint's day. I was there with my family five years ago. Tante Genevieve said the skull was a fake but I must say it looked convincingly old to me. It had the brownish yellow colour of tobacco-stained teeth. Rather gruesome. Especially when you compare it with this picture of her – so young and lovely.'

They stared at the alluring fresco in silence, enchanted by the slight shift in angle of the declining sun whose rays had now reached the stained glass of the western window and shone through, dappling the saint's pale features with a glow of amber and rose.

'Oh, Lord!' whispered Letty. 'She's coming alive! Do you see it, William? Tell me – I expect this is the sort of thing vicars know – why is she always shown with flowing fair hair and a red dress? Is this a medieval convention?'

'I think so. And both attributes false. Entirely mistaken.'

'Mistaken? The red dress, surely, is an indication of her loose nature? The colour signals her status – identifies her as the prostitute that she was.'

'That was the intention. But Daniel was wrong in this – the lady was no prostitute.'

'But ... but ... I could quote chapter and verse that –'

'And all misrepresentations. There is just one word in the Gospels that gives rise to the stories: *harmartolos*, in Saint Luke. It doesn't mean "prostitute", as people have said – the Greeks had quite a different word for that. It means "outside the law", and Jewish law, at that. It could refer to other less reprehensible types of behaviour, like failing to pay your taxes. It could even be a comment on her foreignness. A further problem is that there was no town of Magdala in Galilee after which she could have been named, though there was a Magdolum just over the border in Egypt. At all events, we can assume from the brief references in the Gospels that Mary Magdalene was an independent woman – in those days women were always referred to in the context of their relationship with a man ... Miriam: mother, sister, daughter of ... But the Magdalene stands alone. She must also have been wealthy. The unguent with which she anointed Christ was spikenard. Imported from India. Much used by temple priestesses ...' He paused. 'Worth a working man's wages for a year.'

Letty was sorting through the mixed bag of knowledge she had been left by girls' school Divinity Class and yawned-through sermons in the local church. She acknowledged that she was on shaky ground and in the presence of an expert.

'But why mistranslate? Carelessness or deliberate intent, do you think?'

'Deliberately done, I'd say. Pope Gregory cast the first stone in the sixth century. He declared Magdalene to be a

143

sinful woman, quoting the mistranslation from Luke, and calling up the evidence of the perfume pot to strengthen his argument. Only a professional harlot, the Pope surmised, would have been in possession of such an expensive substance and he could well imagine – and he proceeded to rather fervidly conjure up – the erotic uses to which it might have been put by such a woman. Part of the age-old male struggle to keep women in their rightful place. It suited the early Church and the medieval clergy to dismiss her as a harlot whom they could despise and hold up as an awful warning and – a *reformed* harlot, one who repented and owed her rehabilitation to Christ – all the better! Repentance is always to be applauded.'

'Mmm ... The sort of thing that goes down well in certain quarters in women's colleges, too. But I like this lady,' said Letty, eyes still on the fresco. 'She doesn't look repentant, does she? And can you explain the hair? If she came from the Holy Land or Egypt, she would have been dark-haired, wouldn't she?'

'Undoubtedly. And here's another possibly deliberate mistranslation of her name: in ancient Hebrew it can be taken to mean "wavy fair hair" – and, of course, the symbol in the Middle Ages for a harlot was uncoiffed, flowing golden hair. Combine that with the story of a woman drying Christ's feet with her hair and there you are – a damning convergence.'

'Well! So you're saying that the original, living Magdalene – assuming her to have, indeed, once lived – was a dark-eyed, dark-haired, modest Semitic girl of untarnished reputation and some consequence?'

He smiled and shook his head. 'Won't quite do, either. I think the lady was a firebrand,' he said, 'whatever her appearance. In the male-dominated society of the day – and even Christ speaks dismissively of his own mother at times – Magdalene stands out. She was intelligent, determined, and resourceful. Praise is not exactly heaped on her by the men who wrote the Gospels – you wouldn't expect it in that society – but anyone can deduce her quality

144

purely from her behaviour and her reported words. And if her critics, some might say her enemies, who recorded events weren't able to conceal her abilities, she must have been a remarkable woman. I've always been intrigued by her.'

'She does shine through,' said Letty slowly, 'though never in the fire-and-brimstone sermons your profession delivers from the pulpit. Have you ever heard a vicar preach about her courage – the way she stood at the foot of the Cross with Mary and John when everyone else had run away? That's the bit that always impressed me. What about all those tough fishermen? Where were they? In hiding. And who was first on the scene at the tomb? Who rousted out the disciples and opened their eyes to the significance of what was happening? Magdalene.'

He gave Letty a glance, a glance in which surprise was mingled with calculation. 'There are those who would say, particularly amongst *German* Bible scholars – and with very good evidence at their disposal – that Magdalene was more influential than Peter himself. That she was the Apostle of Apostles.'

'William, where on earth do you come by your information?' She looked at him doubtfully, and as he made no reply she turned her attention again to the fresco. 'That's an astonishing claim.' She stared with fresh eyes at the portrait. 'And yet I have a feeling that whoever was responsible for this picture might well have agreed with you . . . I know what's different about this one! Sorry! I've been a bit slow on the uptake, William. Let's sit down for a moment . . . ease your leg a bit – and my back. Give me a chance to absorb all this.'

'So you've seen it at last?'

'Yes. In all the other portraits, she's shown on her knees, looking upwards and sideways to the heavens with a beseeching look on her face. Like this . . .' She affected a pious pose. 'But not here. Here, she's looking straight at the camera, you could say. Is that a challenge or a question in her expression? It's disconcerting, anyway. William! That's what Daniel saw! He saw a girl who, whatever else she may be, is quite definitely *not* a saint. A girl with all the conscious seduction of a Botticelli girl – an Aphrodite, a Persephone . . . a goddess, anyway, with the power to do good or evil at her whim.'

'Anything else you notice?'

'You really want me to plod on? Very well . . . The countryside. The scenery. It's here. It's Burgundy. But you'd expect that. The artist was probably home-bred and familiar with no other. But it's very precise, isn't it? It's not an idealized picture of Arcady. The outline of those hills on either side of her . . . that abrupt slope over there . . . the way that wooded valley curves down . . . is that a spring leaping from her right forefinger? I think it is. And those sheaves of corn at her feet? It's an actual scene familiar to some medieval artist. He's claiming her. Planting her firmly in the soil of Burgundy.'

'I think so, too. I was so intrigued by the artist's view of the horizon I made a copy of it.' He searched in his pocket and handed her a folded sheet of paper. 'Over the centuries, forests and fields change their shape, encroach on each other's territory, but I'd say the range of hills we see here has stayed more or less the same over the centuries.'

'May I keep this?'

'Of course. Perhaps one day in a far corner of the county you'll look up and see this very formation. My new friend the parish priest tells me Provence doesn't have exclusive rights to this saint. There have always been folktales which stress that her body was carried north from Provence and buried here in Burgundy.'

'Perhaps here? In Fontigny Sainte-Reine,' murmured Letty. 'I had assumed the Holy Queen title referred to Mary the mother of Christ, but it could, I suppose, be honouring the Magdalene?'

'I suppose it's possible,' he said indulgently.

She sighed. 'Daniel would have known. You know, William, it's at times like this that I really miss my god-father.'

146

He grimaced. 'Well, "now you've got me", as someone once said. Not a completely satisfactory arrangement for either of us, I'll agree, and, compared with Daniel's certainties, my hesitations and supposings must be very irritating. I'm sorry.'

'I'm not unsympathetic, and I didn't mean to be rude. And Doubting Thomas is my favourite saint. I've often wondered why he isn't the patron saint of scientists – "Prove it!"' She grinned. 'I always back the wrong side. I support the underdog, the reprobate, the sinner. I know I'd have an easier conversation with Thomas or the Magdalene than with any of the other biblical cast of characters. "Subversive" is the label they gave me at Cambridge. I'm not good company for a Man of God, you'll find.'

He rose, smiling, to his feet and offered his hand. 'I've had worse. You should hear what they had to say about the Lord down in the destitutes' shelter. But that's enough saints for one day. And, I'll tell you what, Letty, a very unsaintly feeling is taking the place of all this intellectual curiosity – I'm hungry. And I know we've got *ris de veau* this evening.'

'Really? Shall I like that?'

Paradee had just returned from his overnight stay in Lyon, the engine of his old Citroën still steaming, and was waiting for them on site when Letty arrived for her third day's work. Tactfully, the boys melted away, moving off in the direction of the supplies store to start getting out the equipment. The director of the dig was stern when he greeted her but Paradee was not, she thought, quite in a sacking mood.

'I hear you had a productive day, yesterday? Well done. I haven't had time to check the work myself yet but I will. Everything okay, Stella? *Everything?*'

The emphasis was unmistakable. Concisely she told him that she had been unable to avoid meeting the count but

147

had spent very little time in his company and, after a mutually disagreeable experience, had returned home and played poker with the boys and the vicar. Paradee's eyes narrowed in disbelief and he seemed uncertain as to how to deal with her. Finally his expression melted into one of humour. '"Of course not, Charles ... Anything you say, Charles,"' he mocked, in imitation of her butter-wouldn't-melt-in-the-mouth lie. 'Hmm ... you know I will never believe another word you say, Stella? Seeing d'Aubec was pure disobedience, and if I were paying you a wage I'd darned well dock you a day's pay. As I'm not, I'm left a bit short of suitable punishments so we'll have to let it go.' He scrubbed the soil with his boot, in thought, and then asked her, 'I trust the villain was on his best behaviour?'

'I have no complaint,' she said, 'except that he wasted my evening.'

'Ah? You weren't exactly swept away by his charms, then? He has the reputation of being a charmer.'

'He wasn't practising his skills on *me*. Merely attempting to make a public restitution for his display of bad behaviour the previous night. I don't think we exchanged a civil word the whole evening. And I never did find out what I really wanted to know.'

'Yes? Which was ...?'

'Why he was beating that poor boy.'

'He wouldn't want to discuss that. The boy is one of his stable lads, I hear, so d'Aubec probably thinks he has the right. Now, if you're ready, you can get to work.' He looked at his watch. 'Where on earth is everyone? Patrick! Phil! Fabrice! Perhaps I should go out and get myself a riding crop,' he grumbled. 'That's the way to get attention around here!'

A concerned Phil hurried over to them with bad news: the trench that they had been working on the previous week had collapsed. 'We didn't shore it – didn't see the need. It's not particularly friable soil and it's not that deep. Should have been okay, but there's just a pile of rubble and soil in there,' he reported, dismayed. 'Right at the point where the corner of the colonnade was turning. There's a half hour of digging to be done before I can get on with the reveal.'

They all trooped over to have a look. 'The tarpaulin?' said Paradee, in a voice laced with suspicion.

'Over there. Neatly folded. I thought I'd put it in place before we packed up,' said Phil. He exchanged a concerned look with Paradee. 'In fact, I know I did. The warning markers are all, as you see, where they should be.'

'Any sign of interference? I hope to goodness we're not looking at a recurrence of last year's trouble.' Paradee turned to Letty. 'When we first got started here and folk didn't understand what in blazes we were up to, digging around in the square, some of them resented our presence . . . a child crawled under a tarpaulin and scared himself silly . . . and there was a little sabotage as a result. No problems since then. The curé, bless him, had a few words in the right ears. And we're meticulous about public safety. We put up barricades . . . I even employ a night watchman. So where was *he* last night?'

'In his shelter in the main square,' said Phil, 'where he always is. I had a word with him before he left. Nothing to report, apparently. This alley is way off his sight line. But judging by the empty brandy bottle in his shelter, he might well not have noticed a great deal, sir.'

Paradee sighed. 'Drunk again? Well, it's the last time he pulls that trick. Tell him to see me when he reports for duty tonight.'

'Of course. Look, I'll get in there and move this mess.' Phil's shoulders slumped at the prospect. 'Barrow it away and see if I can find out what caused the collapse.'

Paradee was turning to Letty with a question or an order when she spoke quickly: 'Shall I help him? We could take an end each?' She heard herself volunteering for this boring task and was not eager to examine her motives for offering. With nothing to feel guilty about, nothing to atone for, perhaps she simply wanted to impress Paradee? She chose to think her motive was to repay Phil for his kindness the day before.

'Well, I reckon that would be a kind act.' Paradee rewarded her with a broad smile. 'I'll stop by and take over in a minute when I've dropped off my bags.' He peered resentfully at the crumbling earth filling the trench and the gaping hole in the side from which it had slipped. 'What a waste of time! Look, you two – keep an eye open, will you? Not quite sure what for, but . . . well, there's something wrong here . . . Looks to me as if there's far too much soil down there for an accidental slippage. And it's been churned up. Some fool's been messing around.'

Phil leapt into the trench and took up the shovel lying ready by the pile. Letty, similarly equipped, jumped down and started at the other end. Someone obligingly wheeled barrows to the side of the trench and they began, good-humouredly, to clear up.

Letty had filled a barrow with earth from her end when the rhythm of her swing broke. She stopped digging and uttered a gasp of surprise. She looked up and hailed a passing student. 'Léon! Lend me your trowel for a minute, will you?'

Paradee, strolling towards them, heard her exclamation and saw that Letty was looking intently at something buried at her knee level. She had exchanged her spade for a trowel to remove earth more delicately from the object she had her eye on: the unmistakable sequence of gestures an archaeologist will pick up and interpret as a find in the offing. He quickened his stride.

'Stella?' he said eagerly. And asked the inevitable question: 'What've we got?'

She looked up at him. 'Feet,' she said. 'We've got feet.'

Chapter Seventeen

Suddenly the sky above her head was almost blotted out by faces lining the trench, startled, eager, curious faces.

'Get another spade and help, will someone?' Letty said urgently, beginning to dig again. 'It's not ancient. It's not a skeleton. It's a body – a man. He's wearing size eight boots.'

'Get the girl out of there!' Paradee's voice rapped out, concerned and decisive. She impatiently dashed aside the hands that reached down to her. 'No! Charles, come down and help me.'

The director lowered himself into the hole. In a moment he was grasping her arm, moving her gently aside, picking up the shovel, and attacking the layers of earth above the body. He threw up instructions with every shovelful of earth. 'Léon, run for the doctor. Alain, fetch the police – report an accident. Keep digging! He may not be dead, whoever this is. Fabrice – see if you can find the curé.'

'Well, if ever I'm caught in a landslide at the bottom of a trench,' Letty decided, fighting down a touch of hysteria, 'I'll count myself very lucky if there just happen to be six trained archaeologists on hand.'

Phil made inroads from the other side and in minutes the body had been dug free. They stood looking down with pity and fascination at the young man revealed. He was lying on his side in a foetal position, which reminded her sickeningly of Iron Age burials she had seen. He was caked in earth, and was ominously still. The leather jacket he was wearing was a size too large for the skinny body and much scuffed. The fists were clenched in a pathetic show of retaliation. Paradee bent over him and listened for a heartbeat. Then he pulled back the jacket sleeve to check for a pulse. Paradee glanced up at the anxious faces and slowly shook his head, stricken. 'He's dead. Poor feller – he's been dead for some time, I'd say. Hours rather than days, probably.'

Letty was standing rigid with shock, glad that all eyes were riveted on the dead man. She hoped that anyone taking notice of her – which seemed unlikely – would dismiss her pale face and staring eyes as no more than the girlish reaction to a grisly discovery. When she could find her voice, she said, 'I know who this is. And so do you, Phil.' Phil nodded, clearly shaken. 'It's the young man d'Aubec was beating two nights ago. His groom, I think you said. As for time . . .' She pointed to the wrist Paradee had revealed when he pulled up the sleeve. 'Look! His watch has been smashed. It may tell us at what hour he died, don't you think?'

Before he could stop her, she had knelt by the body and with quick fingers unfastened the watch and, after a glance, held it out to Paradee.

He took it gingerly and peered at the face. 'It says twelve-thirty. Half past midnight, do you think? Last night? The night before?' he said, then recollecting himself, 'For goodness' sake, Stella! Why d'you *do* that? We should leave everything as we found it. This may be the scene of a crime.'

'Oh, gosh! Yes, you're right, Charles. I'll put it back. Though it does tell us he was messing about here after dark. Long after the team had packed up. What was he doing? Looking for something?'

'Having a pee?' suggested someone above. 'Vomiting? Drunk? Lost his balance and fell in?'

'No . . . er . . . physical evidence of the evacuation of bodily fluids immediately visible,' said Paradee delicately. 'And his clothing is all intact and buttoned up. And are we to suppose that the side of the trench obligingly fell in on

152

top of him? Hmm . . . Look – let's leave this speculation to the police when they get here, okay?'

Letty noticed that his eyes were taking in every detail. He was doing a good job of hiding his distress under a layer of calm authority, until he instinctively rubbed his damp forehead with a hand, leaving a smear of earth which suddenly made him look harassed and vulnerable. She took a handkerchief from her pocket and with a muttered 'Let's posh you up a bit for the officers of the Law, shall we?' she managed to repair the damage.

'Just in time,' Paradee said with a shaky grin. 'Here comes the gendarmerie, fastening up its trousers and putting on its képi! Listen! Everyone not directly involved with the unearthing, go back to work. We're going to lose enough man hours over this anyway – let's pull back what we can. Stella and Phil, stay here, will you? The rest, stop gaping around and make yourselves scarce.'

He turned to greet the one gendarme. 'Sorry to trouble you in the middle of breakfast, Pierre, but we seem to have a body in our trench. A local man, we think. Not long dead.'

The policeman took one look and, deciding his sphere of responsibility did not encompass the scene in the trench, he sent at once for Capitaine Huleux. The nearest detective on duty was with the Police Judiciaire some miles away in Lyon, but Huleux would take charge for now.

They sat disconsolately in a row on the edge of the trench, the gendarme shooing away a few inquisitive children who tried to get near. He allowed the stately figure of the local priest through, and all watched in respectful silence as he lowered himself nimbly enough, buoyed up by his black soutane, into the depth of the trench. Ceremonial gestures and words followed until finally he accepted a heave upwards back on to street level. Courteously he introduced himself as Father Anselme, confirming the dead boy was known to him though he had scarcely seen him in recent years. The priest's pale, angular face reflected their own sadness and puzzlement. 'Very little I can do, I'm afraid. It rests now with a higher authority. Higher even than that of the good doctor,' he remarked, catching sight of Dr Macé hurrying to the scene.

Elegant in his consulting room attire, Macé scrambled fussily down to the body using a ladder hastily provided. 'It's Fabien Morel's son – Paul!' he shouted up. 'And he's dead.' He turned the body over on to its back, revealing the sharp features Letty remembered. Did she imagine it or was the face still frozen in the same grimace of fear?

The doctor moved the limbs about and shone a torch into the eyes. 'Dead no more than twelve hours, probably less.' He took out a fresh white handkerchief and gently dusted the dirt from the boy's face. 'And there's the reason he's dead, I'd say.' He pointed to a wound on the right side of the forehead. 'Not much blood. Death must have been very swift in coming. They'll have more to say when they get him to the morgue in Lyon. Guillaume! Thank God you're here!' he said, breaking off to exchange greetings with Huleux. 'Crack on the skull and here's what caused it, shouldn't wonder. No – don't step on it! There – that rock . . . piece of carved stone . . . whatever it is. Trace of blood on it and I think you'll find the three-cornered shape corresponds with the profile of the wound. Did he fall on to it? Or did it rise up and hit him? Well, that's for you to work out, old friend!'

The twinkling bonhomie she had grown to expect from Capitaine Huleux had disappeared, to be replaced by a chill efficiency. Suddenly she was 'Mademoiselle St Clair' and Paradee was 'Professeur' and they were being told to hold themselves ready, as the discoverers of the corpse, for interrogation. The headquarters of the Police Judiciaire had been alerted by telephone and officers might be expected to put in an appearance within the hour. But in the meantime there were certain formalities he could get out of the way to facilitate matters.

'I think we all recognize Paul,' he said, crossing himself, 'but I'll check his identity card.' He opened the jacket and slipped a hand into the inside pocket.

The black leather wallet took his attention for a moment before he opened it. 'Here's his card and a few francs. Yes, I confirm that this is Paul Morel and we should now alert his father.'

He held the wallet carefully by the edges, giving it a long look before putting it back in the pocket. 'And now, if Mademoiselle and the gentlemen would be so good as to . . .' They retreated to the town hall where Huleux took possession of one of the public rooms and called for a tray of coffee to be brought from the café. He produced a notebook and began to take down their story.

The long day wore on. Officials came and went; Letty repeated her account several times and heard Phil and Paradee saying exactly the same things. All those closely involved with the discovery had their fingerprints recorded. The boy's father, who seemed vaguely familiar to Letty, made a brief appearance and stared, silent and dry-eyed, at his dead son before being escorted away from the scene.

The Lyon contingent of the Police Judiciaire leapt, smartly suited in navy uniforms, from a squad car and liaised with Huleux. Paradee's team were required to go once again through their testimony by a young inspector with unsmiling, chiselled features and equally chiselled moustache. Letty handed over her passport for identification and watched as the officer who introduced himself to her as 'Inspector Laval' checked her details, made careful notes, and paused to give her a long stare.

'You have had a distressing experience, Mademoiselle St Clair,' he said, a touch of sympathy in his voice, as he closed her passport. 'Would you mind if I keep this for a while?' And, noting her reluctance, he added, 'Just our routine.' The sudden smile that accompanied his remark was dazzling and reassuring. He gestured to a pile of other such documents on his desk. 'Quite normal. We would not wish a witness to make off without our knowledge before our enquiries are finished.' Finally, with the police satisfied, all the witnesses were told they were free to go provided they could hold themselves ready for further interview if called on.

Paradee made his own dismissal. 'Go home, Stella. Clean up. Rest up. Phil and I'll deal with the mess here.'

She was relieved to be sent away. She wanted to order her thoughts, sort through her suspicions, and – she had to admit it – share them with Gunning.

He was working in the parlour, surrounded by books and maps, when she got back.

'I thought you'd come and put me out of my suspense if I waited long enough,' he told her. 'It's been pretty turbulent here with old Guillaume dashing in and out. All this police activity – anything to do with you, by any chance?'

'I'll say!' She grimaced and launched into an account of the morning's find.

When she got to the end of her story, he asked one question: 'Are you going to tell me why you took the boy's watch off?'

'It wasn't his watch. It was my godfather's watch. I recognized it straight away. It was quite an old but distinctive Patek Philippe. I took it off ostensibly to show to Paradee and, on handing it over to him, I had a chance to see Daniel's initials engraved on the back.'

'Are you thinking this groom, this Paul Morel, acquired it as a result of his participation in your godfather's murder?'

'No. I don't. Because I had a look at the boy's wrist as well. No earth on his arm – under the watch strap he had the evenly tanned skin of someone who works outdoors all seasons and who never normally wears a watch. If he'd been sporting that one for any length of time before he died or was thrown into the trench, there'd have been a paler band of skin in evidence. I think it was put on to him or on to his body just before he was buried there.'

'And the wallet?' said Gunning sharply.

'Also Daniel's. Again probably meant to incriminate the boy.'

'And who would wish to do that but . . .?'

156

'... but the actual killer – and we both know who that is! – d'Aubec! He must have realized showing me the photograph was a terrible giveaway of his involvement and this was his way of diverting attention.'

'I thought he told you he was in Morocco at the time Daniel was killed? Pretty jolly difficult to stage a murder even by proxy if you've been out of the country for some time, I'd have thought? I'm sure d'Aubec's up to his ears in guilt of the nastiest kind, but I don't think we can pin Daniel's death on him. He'd have been tossing on the Mediterranean at the time in question.'

Letty glowered. 'I shall see what I can do. The police will put two and two together – Huleux definitely reacted to the sight of the wallet. They'll probably check it for finger-prints. If d'Aubec's dabs are on there, they'll clear up an old murder case!'

'But they'll be left with a fresh one on their hands: the groom. Paradee – any of the team – would have been able to arrange the show at the trench, but then so would any-one in town. We know nothing of the lad's social circum-stances. He might have died as a result of an affair of the heart, an unpaid debt ... who knows? That part of the dig is tucked away down the Allée du Parc, isn't it?'

Letty nodded. 'You can't see it from the main square and there's no lighting. Once you'd lured or forced him down there it wouldn't have been difficult to dispose of him. Poor lad. He was so skinny and so young, William. Hardly more than a child! They say he was only sixteen. And so frightened. You remember his terrified face at the café? And this time he was cornered, alone, down a dark alley where there was no wandering Knight Templar to come to his aid with a left hook.'

At last the horror of her discovery, contained for so many hours, spilled over. Her voice faltered, her eyes filled with tears.

'I really must take you up on your casual reference to the Templars,' he said briskly, passing her a handkerchief. 'They never "wandered" anywhere! You are confusing

157

them with the feckless fools who trailed about after King Arthur. The Templar Knights moved purposefully in tightly organized squadrons from A to B, cutting a swathe through whoever got in their way. Warrior monks who fought with perfect discipline and loyalty to the death.'

Letty knew that he could call on only two means of dealing with the threat of her tears: he could clamp her in a tight and embarrassed Englishman's hug, muttering, 'There, there!' or he could pretend he hadn't noticed and trail a more acceptable topic before her. He'd thankfully opted for the second.

'Are you suggesting that my hero, Lancelot, would never have made the grade?'

'With vows of poverty, chastity, and obedience and an enforced neat haircut? He'd have failed on all counts.'

'Templars don't sound much fun to me. What did they do on Saturday nights between battles?'

'Ah. They were allowed to have a little fun if they wished. They were allowed to whittle tent pegs. Rule 317.'

'Good Lord! You've been checking the small print! Thinking of signing on, William? Poverty, chastity, obedience, and a short haircut, eh? How do you measure up?'

He grinned, happy that the crisis was over. 'I'd fail on two of those.'

'I'm all right, William, you can stop clowning.' She sniffed and dabbed at her eyes. 'But tell me why you mentioned Paradee just now? He's been away in Lyon and didn't get back until this morning. The site van was still panting and he was in place, striding about, firing off orders when I arrived. He knew the trench was there and open, but he also knew it was about to be worked on today. Not much point in Paradee killing off a stable lad and hiding his body exactly where it's going to be found in a few hours, is there?'

'And the whole town knew about the trenches. I think, Letty, that someone calculated that this poor young man would be unearthed and very soon. He was never intended to be hidden. Whoever put him into that trench was

158

probably watching, having timed your arrival at the trench to the second.'

Letty was silent for a moment, trying to recall who and where, presences and absences at the trench-side. She remembered the line of faces leaning over the trench, summoned by her cry of distress. Was one of those faces more than usually interested in the discovery? Concern, curiosity, dismay, horror: all these emotions had been on display and none had appeared out of place.

'But why go to the trouble of covering him with earth?'

'That's the bit I don't like, Letty. It's more than an effective, clinical killing. It begins to feel like a . . . a . . . staged, and rather nasty, pre-prepared shock for the discoverers. By someone who doesn't admire archaeologists, perhaps? Or one in particular?'

'If you're saying that someone intended that *I* should find the body, that's nonsense. It was Phil's job. He'd already started. He'd got a thankless task on his hands – just dull digging. I offered to help him.'

'Mmm. And if you had *not* volunteered your assistance, would it have seemed at all unnatural if Paradee had – perhaps in a waggish manner – suggested that you should? Helped you into the trench with a gracious hand?'

'It would have been exactly what I expected,' she admitted. 'Because that's the sort of man he is. He would have asked me to take the other end without a second thought, because that's why he employs me. And he knows I don't expect favours. But there's a lot of implications there! That Paradee set this whole thing up? Barmy idea! What would he have to gain? It's been the most awful nuisance for him. He's lost a lot of digging hours and got into very bad odour with the town. It didn't take long for the rumour to get around that Paul Morel had tripped over a rope and fallen headfirst into an open trench and killed himself. Just what Paradee wanted to avoid. And what am I to make of your suggestion that young Paul may have been killed for some motive not associated with him? Not killed because he was Paul Morel, but as a sacrifice offered

159

up. His body merely a useful vehicle to provide false evidence of guilt planted on it? Chills the blood! Or perhaps he was laid out, the unwitting means of disconcerting a bunch of foreign archaeologists? No. I can accept none of that.'

'If you could,' Gunning said carefully, 'and if you were the normal, thoughtful, sensitive English girl people might suppose you to be, you'd be having a fit of the vapours and checking your return ticket to England, Home, and Beauty right now. And perhaps that's really what's behind this death? Someone close to you or to Paradee – or both – is making a very strong statement, and the language it's expressed in is – murder. You should leave at once, Letty. Let me take you home.'

Chapter Eighteen

Letty dreamed that night. She was fleeing astride a great white horse across the downs. An unseen horror followed her, hooves booming over the chalk, gaining on her with every stride, louder, darker, acrid breath assailing her nostrils. Her horse surged under her, equally terrified, straining every muscle to escape. Her head drooped on his heaving neck, face lashed by his stinging mane, and she felt herself sliding off, bare legs unable to grip his silken back until she hit the turf with a bump and a scream, right in the path of the pursuing horror which closed on her, hooves plunging, fire darting from the nameless dark creature astride his black beast.

She woke, sweating, from her dream to find that the hoofbeats were real. Horses were going by in the street. She hastily flung on her dressing gown and rushed over to the window. Opening the half-closed shutters, she smiled down with delight. It was barely dawn as she gazed over the rooftops of Fontigny, and the inky blue sky had just enough light to throw the abbey into silhouette. And under her balcony, in the cobbled street below, clattered a long file of horses from the Haras. They had been out on early morning exercise and were returning to their stable, each one ridden by a young uniformed soldier. The sleek thoroughbreds and saddle horses mingled with the heavier cobs and Percherons, these heavy horses moving with surprising grace, worthy mounts for any medieval knight. A dappled grey Percheron passed with long supple strides, his shining coat remembering his Arab origins. Carried away by a rush of admiration, she leaned out over the balcony and waved, calling out a shy greeting.

At her voice, the riders looked up, and the sight of a silk-clad, fair-haired girl produced an instinctive gesture. Hands flew to hips, backs straightened, and heads tilted, throwing a proud glance her way as they clattered by, in the timeless way that horsemen through the centuries have reacted to an admiring gaze from a pretty girl at an upstairs window.

She was returning to her rumpled and unappealing bed, kicking aside the pile of yesterday's dirty clothes, when she heard a light tap on the door, which immediately creaked open. A concerned face peered round.

'Stella! Are you all right? I thought I heard you calling out?'

'Oh, Marie-Louise! You're awake too? I was having a nightmare, that's all. It's gone now.'

'Poor thing! After the day you had, I'm not surprised! Look – I've just been down to make a pot of tisane. Would you like a cup? It's vervain, fresh from the garden, with the dew on it – it'll calm your nerves.' She hesitated slightly before suggesting, 'Come into my room and I'll pour you one.'

Rather wishing she could feel more grateful for the kindness, but lured by the idea of a pale green and fragrant tea easing her dry throat, Letty followed her into her bedroom.

'I hope I didn't disturb you? I often creep about the house at this hour.' Marie-Louise looked at her clock. 'Five-thirty. I like to wake early and have an hour to myself! There's precious little time in the rest of the day between the demands of the school and the demands of my mother. Will you sit down?'

Letty perched on a small chair and watched as Marie-Louise poured the tisane into a china mug with all the aplomb of a duchess at a tea party. She was wearing a cream satin dressing gown tied up with a black sash, perfectly complementing the decoration of her room. Letty looked about her in surprise. Marie-Louise had, it seemed, been much impressed by the exhibition two years ago of

162

Arts Décoratifs. Quite out of step with the rest of the house, where the Middle Ages lingered on in the fabric unchallenged, she had gone her own way and transformed the ancient structure. And she had begun by covering over the beams to lower and smooth out the ceiling, creating a space she had then filled with simple pattern and dramatic colour. The matching black wood furniture, spare, elegant, and clearly expensive, must have come from some *ébénisterie* on the Right Bank; a mulberry silk cover hung smoothly over a bed which appeared never to have been slept in. The sculptured white elegance of lilies accented perfectly the modern and minimal décor and lightly scented the air.

Aware of the contrast with the dishevelled, post-nightmare image she must herself be presenting, Letty tugged at her dressing gown and smoothed down her hair. Marie-Louise, noticing her embarrassment, looked tactfully aside, and Letty was struck by a surprising resemblance. She'd seen something very like this girl's features somewhere before and the sudden tilt of the face and the half-closing of the eyes had made it clear. At the end of March she'd attended the premiere of Fritz Lang's film *Metropolis*. She hadn't enjoyed the film much but she'd been taken with the programme cover. The face of a girl, its cold and expressionless whiteness betrayed by a sensuous red mouth, had, with closed eyes, gazed internally at who knew what appalling vision. A vision hinted at, perhaps, by the sleek black machine-tooled helmet she wore?

The brief illusion faded when Marie-Louise spoke again, in a voice warm with sympathy. 'I heard all about the incident at the trench from Rolande at the café. Everyone's talking about it. Poor Stella! What a dreadful discovery to make!'

'Oh, I'm all right,' Letty replied. 'But I feel so very sorry for the young man. I can't imagine the circumstances that led him to such a death!'

'Oh, *I* can,' said Marie-Louise, frankly. 'Dozens of circumstances. Paul Morel was a village boy. He was notorious

163

hereabouts . . . a *voyou* of the worst kind. Such a trial to his father, who has worked on the count's estates all his life. A loyal servant. A good man. But the son was completely out of hand. There are many in Fontigny who will not be mourning him.'

'The count himself being one of them?'

Marie-Louise smiled. 'You are quick to blame him? You have taken a dislike to our local lord, I think. Look, Stella, you must make up your own mind, of course, about Edmond d'Aubec, but he may not be the ogre you take him for.' And, in response to Letty's snort of cynicism: 'Who has told you these bad things about him? Paradee! The American. Well, there you are! Those two men hate each other and have no good words either for the other. But most people who know d'Aubec have reason to be grateful to the man . . . I myself have personal experience of his generosity. Indeed, the count is very good to our school and to the whole community. You will find many to praise his concern for their welfare.

'I'd better declare,' she added with a hesitancy that warned Letty to expect a revelation of some sort, 'that my political leanings, such as they are, are to the left. *You* would call me a "socialist", and it goes against the grain to admit that this aristocrat is generally well regarded in the region. But d'Aubec is. He is not an absentee landlord – one of those who live in Paris and turn up on their estates briefly for the shooting. No. He lives his life here. He employs – and pays generously! – many local people. I would, of course, prefer that his privileges and property were returned to the community but . . .' – Marie-Louise shrugged – 'he does well with what he has and he loves and protects his native land.'

'You forget that I saw him in action myself the other night. Bully of the worst kind! I dread to think what would have happened if Reverend Gunning hadn't stepped in to put a stop to his activities!'

Marie-Louise's eyes sparkled with amusement, but she was not about to join Letty in her condemnation. 'Ah, yes!

I heard that our surprising *pasteur* has skills we had no idea of! William is a most intriguing man, is he not, Stella?'

'He is indeed,' Letty said, and, holding out her cup for more tisane, decided to plunge into the confidences-in-the-dorm session that the French girl seemed to be craving. 'Tell you what, Marie-Louise, why don't you do the man an immense favour and run away to Paris with him? Ensnare him! You'd make a lovely couple.'

Marie-Louise gave a derisory laugh. 'You think so? I would certainly love to get away from this stifling little town, and the vicar would be a most agreeable companion.' She moved to the window and flung back the curtain. 'Come and look!'

Letty looked out at the dawn breaking on a peaceful garden and understood. She saw an orderly garden enclosed on all sides. Vegetables stood to attention in neat rows; espaliered peach trees struggled, crucified, on a south-facing wall; and, contained in their hutch, rabbits grew fat awaiting their fate. Beyond, a flush of ochre in the sky outlined a sweep of dark blue sheltering hills – sheltering or restraining, a symbolic barrier. The yearning in Marie-Louise's eyes saddened Letty. She suddenly saw the young woman's room for what it was – no more than a medieval cell papered over with the pickings of glossy magazine illustrations – and she caught the blast of an almost out-of-control despair.

'What does the future hold for you, Marie-Louise?' she asked quietly. 'I had understood that the world had opened up for women in France?'

'Oh, yes. Of necessity women took the places of men away at war. Four years' carnage advanced our cause more effectively than forty years of suffragism! And next autumn women in my profession are to be awarded a salary equal to that of the men.' Her words were bland, though her tone was bitter.

'Well, that's better than you could expect in England. Though, like us, you have not yet been given the power to vote, I think? It annoys me to a murderous pitch that since

I am under the age of thirty and own no property I may not vote, though any cottager in the village may do so, however ill-informed, so long as he be male. And most of the opportunities women had snatched at during the war years when men were pleased enough to look the other way have been dashed away with the return of men to civilian employment. So, if it's new horizons you're seeking, you may have to look farther than England. Other countries? You'd like to travel farther than Paris, perhaps, with this agreeable companion?'

Marie-Louise nodded and closed the curtain.

'You and the vicar – you're both intelligent and sensitive people,' Letty continued, as further comment seemed to be expected. 'I don't see why you shouldn't hit it off. I mean, a rip-roaring, eye-crossing love affair would be wonderful but, really, Abelard and Héloïse are the exception, aren't they? We can't all wait about for Fate to serve up an experience like that. I'm quite resigned to never finding my own knight in shining armour, my own Lancelot. In fact, I'm coming to the conclusion that hen-headed old Guinevere didn't know when she was on to a good thing. If King Arthur pops his head above the parapet I shall raise my bid card!'

Marie-Louise smiled. 'That's a very modern view. I would have expected something more . . .' She flushed: 'Stella . . . I wonder if you ever . . .?'

Oh, Lord! thought Letty. *Now we're in for a hot squashy corner! Can I bear this before breakfast?* But she at once felt guilty at her selfishness. This sort of intimacy was obviously a new experience for a single daughter, who had never been away to school and benefited from the very particular educational possibilities of girls' dormitories after lights-out. 'Have I ever been in love? Is that what you're wondering?'

Marie-Louise nodded.

'About fifty times. I started with the usual crushes on my boy cousins, the Head Girl, the gym mistress, even my piano tutor came in for a bit of attention, predictably . . . but I can tell you that nothing compares with the knee-

166

trembling surge of emotion you feel when you fall in love for the first time.'

Marie-Louise was listening intently to this nonsense, eyes gleaming with anticipation.

'Hang on a tick! I'll show you a picture of my first love . . . if that would be of any interest?'

Letty hurried to her room. She pulled open the bottom drawer of the chest where she'd tucked away a pile of comforting reminders of home: photographs of her ten-year-old self with mother and father, herself with a changing series of large black dogs, one of Letty arm in arm with a friend's brother (always willing to masquerade as a boyfriend), a five-year diary, an old May Ball programme, and – there it was – the exercise book she was looking for. She returned and handed it to Marie-Louise.

'But what is this?' Marie-Louise trailed a finger over the pattern painted in primary colours on the cover. And then, with distaste: 'Is this some book of magic, perhaps?'

Letty burst out laughing. 'No! Not at all! It's perfectly innocent, and there's nothing in there to offend the sensibilities of a good Roman Catholic girl.'

'But these symbols? What are they? Red Indian? These words *Kibbo Kift,* are they Indian? No . . . but it's pagan of some kind, I'm sure . . . And this star? And two Latin words: *Stella Maris* . . . Three moons and . . . ah, I recognize this sign – a cross with a sort of loop at the top – it's the ancient Egyptian ankh, isn't it?' She was holding the book as though she had just fished it out of the gutter.

'Yes,' said Letty, 'I took it to be symbolic of Isis. *I* decorated the book myself. When I was sixteen. It's my diary of a fortnight spent in summer camp. The organizers of the camp encouraged us all to design our own personal emblems and even invent our own clan names. Our leader was called White Fox, I remember. My name being "Stella", the star – well, it made it rather easy for me. I did a bit of research and discovered that Stella Maris – such a pretty phrase – meant "Star of the Sea" and was a reference to the bright star Sirius, worshipped by sailors when it rose out of the eastern Mediterranean. It was the symbol of the mother goddess Isis, whom they worshipped. They believed that her appearance over the horizon would lead them to good fortune. Rather glamorous, I thought; this is for me! I pursued my goddess through the pages of Frazer's book on mythology and added the moons and that border of ears of corn which are also attributes of hers. And I set it all out on this green background.'

'Green? Wouldn't dark blue have been more dramatic, more aesthetically pleasing?'

'Probably. But green is significant. Isis had many names: Mistress of Mysteries, Corn Goddess ... but I especially liked Creator of Green Things, Green Goddess.'

'I see,' said Marie-Louise, clearly mystified. 'I think I see. Decidedly pagan! You English! You were an *éclaireur* ... a Boy Scout then?'

'Oh, no!' Letty grinned. 'Certain things in common, I suppose, but this was a very special camp – open to both sexes and all ages. It was run by an organization called the Kibbo Kift.' She pointed to the words on the cover. 'It's not Red Indian – it's old English dialect and it means "a proof of strength". It's an association of like-minded people: boys, girls, men, women, all pacifists, all intensely inter- ested in the preservation of Englishness, fitness of mind and body, the learning of handcrafts, the appreciation of nature, the regeneration of urban man and woman through the open-air life. And it has wider ambitions – nothing less than to be the human instrument that will create a new world civilization.'

Marie-Louise gasped. 'A cult! It all sounds dangerous to me! And especially dangerous when it springs from the empire-building souls of the Anglo-Saxon race. There is a movement like this in Germany – the *Wandervogel* – intense young people set on developing physical perfection, dis- cipline, and nationalistic fervour. Poor France! Is my coun- try to be trapped between two ambitious, muscle-flexing races? You fought each other on French soil ten years ago. How long will it be before you re-discover your shared roots? There are those who have always maintained that the English have far more in common with – and more sympathy for – the Germans than they ever had with the French. Your royal family have German cousins, do they not?'

Letty was taken aback by the girl's passion and at a loss as to how to counter what some might consider her well-judged apprehension. She hurried to reassure her. 'No, no. You misunderstand! It's all jolly sing-songs round the campfire, reef knots, and treasure hunts. I can't speak for the ... *Wandervogel*, did you say? ... but I can tell you there's no political and certainly no religious aspect to the English movement at all. It has some very famous and admirable men and women on its advisory panel: H.G. Wells, Julian Huxley, D.H. Lawrence, Rabindranath Tagore. None of them would be associated with anything remotely suspect. It's grown in popularity and there are thousands of members scattered all over England.'

'And this is what you fell in love with? A movement of nationalistic woodland folk aiming for world domination?'

'Gracious, no! I loathe camping and cocoa and wood-whittling! I'd have done a bunk after the first day, but I fell with a bang for the leader of the movement! Complete, trembling, gasping passion! Just look inside the front cover at the photograph I stuck in there.'

Marie-Louise sighed and opened up the garish book. She looked and was silent for quite a long time.

'That handsome fellow is "White Fox". He was twenty-six when he formed the Kindred and I was present at one of his first camps. He's a man of amazingly strong charisma, tall, athletic, inspiring, with the hypnotic powers of a Svengali! Do you wonder that my knees trembled?'

'But this man is a dark angel,' said Marie-Louise. 'He is Lucifer before the fall.' She went on staring at the strong features, the bold eyes glittering and partially hidden by a black Saxon hood. 'My poor Stella! Being exposed to the force of a man like this at sixteen! It could have ruined you for life!'

'I'm not so easily ruined! I think of it as a sort of immunization,' said Letty practically. 'After an injection of Lucifer Attraction, nothing much can touch me henceforth.'

'I wonder if it's occurred to you, Stella, that the count – d'Aubec – is cast in much the same mould?' Marie-Louise suggested hesitantly.

'Yes. Of course, I had seen the resemblance. Physically at any rate they are, as you've noticed, strikingly similar. But the presence, the personality . . .' She sighed. 'No two men could be more *un*like. No, Reverend Gunning is more like the White Fox in character . . . unyielding, demanding, self-sacrificing, on the side of the angels . . . if he believes in angels. And I understand him to have been a Boy Scout in his youth.'

'I'm not sure *that* would recommend him to a French girl!' Marie-Louise smiled. 'It's clear to me that you have little time for the man but – can you not think of *anything* it would please a woman to hear about Mr Gunning?'

'As I said, I think he'd make a wonderful travelling companion for you. He's full of information on a range of interesting topics and he drives well.'

'But . . . Stella . . .' She hesitated and bit her lip, searching for words, unaccustomed to exchanging confidences of this kind.

'But you can't be certain that he's interested in *you*?' supplied Letty.

'Yes, that. But more than that . . .' She coloured and looked away and suddenly Letty understood.

'Oh, you mean, you can't be sure that he takes an interest – an amatory interest – in females at all? Do you know, I really have no idea. I can usually tell but I have to say, in his case, I just don't know for certain. Only one thing to do, isn't there? Now, had you thought you might . . .?'

They laughed together in eager conspiracy and Letty wondered what would be the reaction of the austere Gunning, lying asleep in the room above their heads, if he could have heard some of the scurrilous schemes they were devising in an effort to test out his sexuality.

Poor Marie-Louise, though, she decided as she made her way back to her own room, was in for a disappointment. Letty had told an easy lie. It was perfectly obvious to someone of her experience. Neutered tom. That was what, in her innocence, Marie-Louise had to deal with.

Chapter Nineteen

Letty was not aware that Paradee had been standing a few feet away from her, watching her work. He approached and inspected the length of foundation she had neatly revealed with trowel and stiff brush, then moved on to check the contents of her finds tray. A smile broke through at the sight of her anxious face and he hurried to reassure her. 'Relax, Stella. That's just fine! You've done a lot this morning. Glad to see that yesterday's nastiness hasn't put you off your game. Keep this up for a few more hours and I'll think you've deserved some time off. Report to my office at four o'clock, will you? Oh – go home and change first. Into something comfortable.' He called after her, 'And put your boots on!'

At four, in clean shirt and trousers, she banged on the knocker and entered on hearing his shout. 'Come in!' he invited, and proceeded to sweep charts and pens to one side, clearing a space on his desk. 'You look as though you could do with a drink.' He shot ice cubes into two glasses and filled them with a swish of water from a dark green bottle, added a slice of lemon, and handed her one.

'Well, now,' he went on, sipping his drink, 'how would you like to come for a ride? It's high time you got a look at the surrounding country – so far you've only seen it on a plaster model.'

Letty looked at his humorous, inviting face and thought there was nothing she would enjoy more after her hot day bent double in the confines of a trench. 'But what will I do for a horse?'

'You ask that in Fontigny?' He was laughing at her. 'The cream of the country's horses are just around the corner, the director of the Haras is my good friend, and I have a key to the stables,' he said, flourishing it. 'What are we waiting for?'

Minutes later they were letting themselves into the stables by a side door. As it swung to behind them, shutting out the noises of the town square, Stella's eyes adjusted to the gloom, her ears to the soft familiar sounds of the stable and her nose to the well-remembered smells. In delight she wandered along the beaten earth track between the stalls, reading the name of each stallion on the board above his head. She paused occasionally to run her hand over a silky rump or fondle an inquisitive nose turned in her direction. She quivered with anticipation when she realized just what was being offered by this confident American – a ride on one of these horses, lined up in their stalls; horses of different sizes and breeds and colours but all with one thing in common: an impeccable pedigree.

'Careful now! Keep your distance from that animal!' warned Paradee as Letty approached a large Arab, gleaming from nose to lashing tail.

'Carnaval,' she murmured, reading his name. 'Lovely creature! Well-bred but rather evil-tempered, I should guess,' she added, keeping well away from the waltzing hooves, the thrashing head, and the angry white eye.

'You've got it!' said Paradee. 'Like horse, like master! That brute belongs to Edmond d'Aubec. With any luck they'll kill each other one day. But don't worry – I'm not about to offer you anything to freeze the blood! No! I'm on good terms with the director, but not so good I'm allowed to make free with the flower of his flock. Come on!'

He strode ahead, leading her out into the sunshine of the courtyard. Gardeners were sweeping gravel and watering flower beds, and grooms were fetching and carrying for the horses, but there in the middle stood a groom patiently holding by the heads, ready saddled, two impressive animals.

173

'The bay is mine and the other is yours. His name's Goliathe.'

Letty lost her heart at once to Goliathe. He was rich brown, with an unusual gunmetal sheen. Four white socks gave him a jaunty air and he stamped about, impatient to be off. Moments later they were clattering down the street, past her own window and, very abruptly it seemed, out into open countryside. They rode uphill for some time, until, reaching the crest of the hill above Fontigny, they eased off and looked back at the town, now shrinking to the proportions of the scale model she had inspected on her first day. They dismounted, hitched the horses to the branch of an oak tree, and stood, grateful for its shade, enjoying the loneliness of the landscape.

Paradee was an easy companion who showed none of the English compulsion to keep up a steady polite chatter. As on their first meeting, she felt herself moving at his speed, sharing his enthusiasms, his equal. And this man had been her godfather's friend. She felt a stab of guilt when she remembered she was deceiving him. Why not confide in him? Ask his help?

'What in blazes?'

He stiffened abruptly and, raising his head, looked over her shoulder and down the hill. A rider mounted on a great black horse was cantering easily up the slope towards them.

'Well, Edmond d'Aubec can certainly ride,' Letty muttered. 'He and that murderous horse of his were made for each other.' And, though angered by the unwished-for intrusion, the horse-lover in her wondered at the change she saw in the stallion now moving gracefully and obediently. On and up they came, and passed by the oak tree with never a word. D'Aubec suddenly reined Carnaval back to a walk and appeared to loiter about fifty yards away from them.

'Well, I'll be darned! What *is* he up to? Is he waiting for me to challenge him? I think, Stella, I'd better stroll over and tell him we've admired his profile and now what we'd really appreciate is a view of his rear elevation.'

174

Oh Lord! The lions were shaking their manes! Concerned to sabotage any such confrontation, Letty spoke sharply. 'No, Charles. You're to do no such thing! He's just trying to provoke you. Ignore him.' She was uneasy at the quiet anger her boss was showing. 'I've no idea why he would be shadowing us like this. I resent it, but I advise against meeting him head-on here out in the wilds – precisely because that seems to be exactly what he's after.'

Paradee was prepared, even relieved perhaps, to listen to her.

'I've found out for myself that – as you warned me – he's a dangerous and unpredictable man. Perhaps even a killer,' she finished.

He was not alarmed by her thought, but considered it and agreed. 'It's possible. We're still waiting to hear about that boy in the trench. And there is more, Stella. I ought to have warned you about this earlier . . . before you took the job . . . but it didn't seem at the time to have anything to do with us . . . the dig, I mean . . .'

She could only look at him in silent puzzlement at his hesitations, though she thought she knew what was coming.

'Seems Fontigny isn't the tranquil backwater we've all assumed it to be, and you ought to know it. There was a killing last year very close by, in the centre, again – at night. One of our team – a linguist, antiquarian, and all-round good egg, as you'd say – was stabbed to death and robbed. Daniel Thorndon. You'd have liked him. We all did. He was working with us – lent to us by the British Museum.'

Calmly she asked, 'Did this man – Mr Thorndon – have any connection with our shadow over there? Is that what you're trying to tell me?'

'Certainly is. I thought they were friendly. Thorndon – Daniel – had taken to visiting the château at weekends. He seemed to have the entrée whenever he chose. They had a lot in common, he said. Seemed like a pretty warm relationship from what I could gather, but he didn't discuss his personal life much with the team.' He cleared his throat.

'Look, I didn't interfere, though now I wish I had. Perhaps I could have warned him off, raised his suspicions at least. And why?' Paradee shuffled uncomfortably. 'Because, well, I thought – here's an opening, a crack in the defences.'

'You sent this Mr Thorndon in as a spy? You used him as a cat's paw? Is that what you're saying?' Letty couldn't keep back the sharp comment full of distress and accusation.

'No! No! I didn't *send*! No chance of directing old Daniel to do anything he didn't want to do. He was about as open to influence as you are! Seems to be an English trait . . . smile agreeably, say "Yes, of course you're right, Director," then go straight off and do the opposite. But it did occur to me that this was our best chance of finding out what the possibilities of the castle site were. I can't imagine a more experienced eye being cast over it short of getting in there myself.'

'And did he have much of value to tell you, your discreet informant?'

Paradee shook his head. 'You'd need to have known the feller to understand why I couldn't even ask! It would have been "prying, don't you know", and English gents don't talk about their friends behind their backs. Oh, he spoke of the layout of the building, the age, the architectural features . . . but told me nothing I didn't already know from the aerial photos.'

'Are you putting into my head the idea that perhaps the death of this Englishman may be connected with the boy in the trench? And that both deaths are linked to the count?'

'Yes,' he replied bluntly. 'And I'm giving you the chance to hang up your trowel and retreat back to London. There's something evil swirling about in this oh-so-peaceful little burg. I don't like the feel of it. I wouldn't want you caught up in it. I have a duty towards a young and vulnerable girl in my employ. I hold myself *in loco parentis*.'

'Lord! I hope not!' said Letty. 'Look, I have absorbed the information and the warning. But I think you're making a bit of a leap there. Shall we wait and see what the police come up with and have this conversation again?'

'Okay, but I'm more concerned that this little display,' he waved an arm in d'Aubec's direction, 'is something to do with you. I know we ambled up here, but he arrived pretty soon after us. He must have had someone alert him, don't you think? Someone hanging around the stables? But he wouldn't have had *me* followed. It's you he's hunting. Now, look, Stella, does he have any hold over you? If I'm out of line here, you must tell me.'

'He has no hold over me. I don't know him. I don't want to know him. I have no idea why he should be shadowing us like this. I wish he'd go away!'

'Well, that's clear enough,' said Paradee, laughing. 'Come on, let's mount up and ride. I have some more wonders to show you, and these I don't mind d'Aubec witnessing. Two archaeologists together – we shouldn't have too much trouble boring the pants off his lordship.'

They swung along together, easy companions, finding much to admire in the countryside until, abruptly, Letty reined in Goliathe and exclaimed, pointing at a rock formation in the distance.

'What's that over there? It looks like an enormous cliff. You'd expect to see the sea at the base of it instead of a valley rolling away.'

'That's the Rock of Solutré. Sinister place! At the foot of that overhang they found the skeletons of thousands of horses. It's thought that Stone Age hunters herded wild horses up the slope of the cliff, driving them to their death over the top. Horses smell fear. What a scene it must have been, but what a simple way of restocking the larder.'

Letty shivered at the thought of the wild despair – the shouts, the screams of the horses, the snap of bones, and the smell of blood in that primitive abattoir. 'I think we've gone far enough,' she said. 'We'd better turn for home now if I'm going to be in time for supper. The lodgings you found for me are wonderful, but the Huleux are very

177

particular. Mealtimes are sacrosanct. Not even the vicar dares wander in late.'

The countryside in the slanting sun had taken on a menacing note, echoed by the dark figure which, as they moved off, left the shelter of a tree and continued to trail them, just out of earshot, until they regained the town. Back in the stable courtyard, Paradee dismounted and turned to give a gallant but unnecessary hand to Letty. Before she could accept it, he was tapped lightly on the shoulder. He turned around to confront a pleasantly smiling Edmond d'Aubec, lowering his riding crop and saying apologetically but firmly, 'No need to put Goliathe to bed just yet. I think Miss St Clair has further need of him.' Greeting Letty with the same charming smile, he said invitingly but formally, 'My dear, there is, at my château, someone you have been longing to meet again. You remember your old friend Lady Uffington? She is staying with us now. My mother has asked me to bid you to supper. Good old Goliathe is well named – he is far from used up and won't object to a further five kilometres. Good-bye, Paradee. We must not keep her ladyship waiting. Come, Miss St Clair!'

He walked off and in seconds had swung into the saddle and clattered out of the yard.

Eager though she was to track down the mysterious lady mentioned on Daniel's final postcard, she'd been about to refuse this peremptory summons, and turned to Paradee for support. It came in a torrent. 'What the hell! . . . Stella, get off that horse! There's not a chance I will allow you to ride off with that rogue!'

He put a firm hand on the bridle and prevented the horse from moving forward.

She looked from Paradee to the retreating back of d'Aubec, undecided but keeping her seat in the saddle. When she could make Paradee listen to her, she spoke calmly. Such a nuisance but Lady Uffington was an old and very dear friend of the family . . . but more than that . . . perhaps Paradee was aware that Lady Uffington was also the patroness of Professor Merriman? She improvised, now determined on her course. Andrew had rather thought the old nuisance might be passing through on her way from one watering hole to the next, going south for the summer, and Letty had promised him to meet her if the opportunity arose. And here it was arising. It would not be wise to decline contact with such an influential and wealthy woman. Letty's light stress on the word 'wealthy' produced a gleam of understanding at last.

And anyway, she added, seeing his fingers relax their grip, wasn't this just the opportunity they'd been hoping for? As a guest, she could take in details of the château with an archaeologist's eye and report back tomorrow morning. With d'Aubec's mother, the countess, and old Lady Uffington both present she would be perfectly adequately chaperoned.

His hand dropped to his side and he grinned. 'You English! You'd take tea with the Devil if he sent you a correctly worded invitation. I can see you're determined to chase down this rich old biddy, but you're not leaving without a further warning . . .'

He raged on, assuaging his guilt and unease, and Letty listened dutifully, understanding his concern and glad of it. Finally, she turned Goliathe. A gentle kick was the only urging the horse needed to set off in pursuit of Carnaval.

As she passed under the arch into the road she heard Paradee's voice shouting after her, 'Take care! Don't trust him! Or his mother!'

Chapter Twenty

Curiosity clashed with irritation as she cantered along behind d'Aubec. He knew she would follow. He'd attempted no persuasion and had avoided any confrontation with Paradee simply by ignoring him. It had appeared to be her choice to accept his invitation. But she wouldn't give him the satisfaction of her willing company, and she controlled Goliathe's speed enough to keep him a good fifty metres behind d'Aubec until, at last, they rounded a spur in the road and came within sight of his stronghold.

The threatening bulk of the thirteenth-century defensive walls towered over her, warning her off, and it took all her pride and obstinacy to keep her on the track winding through the guardian ranks of vines marching upwards to the moat's edge and its bridge. She rode over, expecting to hear at any moment the clang of a portcullis descending, into the jaws of the imposing entrance.

Once through the curtain wall, Letty reined in to gaze at Brancy le Château sleeping in the June sunshine. Her first impression was of how kindly time had dealt with the great building; how gently the ochre wash, faded to milky whiteness where the sun struck and darkening to amber under the eaves, was dappled by reflections from the moat, how the formal march of tall windows across the front was softened by the cracked and faded blue of their shutters, some discreetly closed and speaking of coolness within and some hospitably open on a tall interior. She took in the swelling corner turrets, their arrogant purpose contradicted by the fairy-tale peaked roofs. As she watched, the impression of mighty but comforting informality was completed by a flight of fat white pigeons, which circled the blue sky and settled prettily on the cascade of rosy tiles among the ranks of round dormers that climbed the roof.

At least the house welcomes me, she thought, heartened. The perfect proportions had concealed the great size of the château. Within the entrance door, with its shell pediment, lay an inner courtyard – neatly bisected to sunlight and shadow by the declining sun – and beyond that a rising jumble of roofs and chimneys; of turrets and battlements reaching up to the sky and back into a turbulent past.

D'Aubec had already handed his horse to the care of a dark and unsmiling man, and he gestured to Letty to do the same. 'Jules, see to the horses!' And off he strode across the gravelled courtyard.

Letty gave Goliathe into the care of the groom, thanking him as she did so and venturing to add, 'Monsieur Jules, I noticed that Carnaval has a loose shoe on his near hind.'

The groom looked surprised to be addressed by a guest and in such an open English manner, but gravely acknowledged the information and the brilliant smile which had accompanied it.

She joined d'Aubec, who had paused to watch the exchange. 'How's your courage holding out, Miss Talbot? Ready for an assault on the inner sanctum?'

'Why should I not be? I see no hostile hordes repelling invaders. If I had a suspicious mind, I would say I was expected. Shall we proceed to the second act of your charade, d'Aubec? After you.'

She hurried after him through a wide door to the coolness of an entrance hall and the sweep of an ascending stair, and passed under the detached regard of a marble ancestor in a curled periwig to a pair of high doors and an airy room.

'The summer salon,' he announced.

Faded green panelling, an intensely patterned inlaid floor, a curtain that stirred in the wind, and, in a tapestried chair by the window that gave on to a broad terrace, an

181

elegant woman wearing a blue silk tea gown. She sat listening to the last notes of a Strauss waltz swirling to a finish as they entered and Letty had time, before she became aware of them, to take in the once beautiful face, the hair, dark as d'Aubec's but now streaked with iron grey, and a frame of a delicacy amounting to fragility.

On catching sight of them, a young man stepped to the phonograph, flipped back the arm and removed the record, and stood quietly by, watching Letty. A manservant? His gaze was rather bold, she thought.

Edmond's mother rose and hurried forward to greet her. She spoke very fast in an oddly accented English.

'Laetitia, dear Laetitia! What a joy to meet you at last! And you are every bit as bonny as your godfather told me. Your poor godfather! We were desolated to hear of Daniel's death. He had become a great friend of mine also, and I shared many an evening with him when he came over to work on those documents, full of dust, in the library. He was here the evening he died, did you know that? And such a happy evening we had passed! With Edmond away, I had Daniel all to myself. We played a game or two of *belote*, we listened to the gramophone ...' Her voice dropped to an almost inaudible murmur as she remembered: 'We danced a tango ... He was a very good dancer, Daniel.' She fell silent.

Letty was witnessing a tangle of emotions and was struck by the sly thought: *Tango, eh?* Could it be that she was looking at the dashing Daniel's last conquest? Recovering, the countess raised her chin and confessed. 'If I had only insisted on his spending the night here he might not have been attacked!' She grasped Letty's hands tightly to convey her concern. 'But I ramble on. Let me introduce Constantine.'

The dark young man stepped forward and briefly bowed his head. Not a manservant, then.

'Constantine is my son's secretary and right hand. Without Constantine there would be no sanity in this household.'

Letty smiled a greeting and murmured, 'Monsieur Constantine, I'm delighted to meet you,' receiving a cool: 'Mademoiselle,' in response.

But Letty could not deny the warmth of the twinkling lady before her and hid a smile when, without pausing for breath, the countess addressed her son: 'But, Edmond, you great lout, what do you do standing there, staring? Go, fetch the champagne! We must celebrate Laetitia's arrival.' D'Aubec flashed a smile so full of affection and humour at his mother that Letty was taken aback.

'My son speaks excellent English, do you not find, mademoiselle? He had the benefit of a Scottish governess. We are so hoping you will stay and have a simple supper with us,' the countess went on when d'Aubec, accompanied by Constantine, had left the room. 'No, no! You are not to concern yourself that you are dressed for the outdoors,' she hurried on, interpreting correctly Letty's dismayed glance at her trousers and boots. 'This is a horse-worshipping house, as you will find. My son has stolen you shamelessly from your evening pursuits and we are pleased to take you as we find you. Think of this as a "come-as-you-are" party! You are in good company – my son, you will have noticed, looks and smells like a groom.'

Letty cast an inquisitive eye over Edmond as he came back carrying a tray of champagne. Yes, the rough shirt, the cord trousers were unexceptional and reassuring; they softened the impact of the sharp, aristocratic features. As they clinked glasses and drank each other's health, Letty judged the time had come to enquire after her mysterious friend, Lady Uffington. When she did so, a look passed between mother and son, and both fell into an uncomfortable silence.

Edmond was the first to speak. 'Yes, of course, as you can see – she is not here . . .'

Seeing Letty's eyes narrow in suspicion, he added hurriedly, 'But she is not far away. Mother, we will have supper in about an hour if that is convenient? Laetitia,

183

come with me.' Taking her by the elbow, he steered her out of the room.

Everything on their journey through the château spoke of ease and elegance, strongly underpinned by affluence. Darkly gleaming paintings and rich tapestries cladding the panelled walls were echoed in the glowing colours of Persian rugs scattered the length of the oak floors. Open doors gave enticing views of other rooms – a library, a music room, a billiard room, and here, towards the rear of the house, a strong smell of strawberry jam accompanied by a peal of laughter and the clatter of cutlery announced the kitchen. They emerged into a courtyard bathed in warm evening light.

The exterior was equally lovingly cared for. Raked gravel was surrounded by formal flower beds, densely planted with bright early summer flowers, and in the centre of each bed, a nursery-rhyme rose tree. In spite of herself she was delighting in the scene unfolding before her as they moved on, crossing a wide stretch of trimmed grass shaded by chestnut trees. Under their spreading branches and revealed by degrees lay the low, golden stone stable court-yard and its wings, stretching forward in welcome, the whole neat, clean, and tidy, redolent of an ancient, solid, and homely efficiency.

As they approached, the clank of pails and stamp of hooves was momentarily drowned by the wheezing clatter of machinery and a muted bell softly sounded the half hour. It was towards this building that Letty was being resolutely steered by her silent guide.

He's crazy! she thought. *He invites me to meet a lady I'll swear I've never heard of and takes me to the stables to do it.* Out loud she said, 'Lady Uffington I assume to be some kind of a horse enthusiast, as she is to be found lingering in the stables at the aperitif hour?'

'Oh, yes,' came the laconic reply, 'you could certainly say that.'

184

Coming to a halt in front of the entrance, d'Aubec pointed upwards and directed her gaze to the wall over the arch. The focal point of any stable building in France, this was where, traditionally, the owner would have installed a carving, often a statue, of a horse. Letty was not disappointed, though she was puzzled. Here was no flamboyant, rearing stallion, mane flowing artistically in the breeze, but, in this place of honour, was fixed a simple stone shield, carved and coloured.

'If you are your father's daughter you should be able to interpret the heraldry with no difficulty, though I can help you out if you wish. Tell me, Laetitia, what do you see?'

Stung by his cheerful insolence she focused all her attention on the carving and, finding it a rather simple, if unusual, device she recited without hesitation – 'Vert, a horse courant, argent, bearing a seated lady, affrontée, of the same.' Against a green background, a rather crudely drawn silver-white horse was caught in mid-stride, running with rangy legs whilst on his back there perched, with a sideways seat and smiling down at the onlooker, a lady with flowing hair, she too drawn in silver-white.

And then the significance of what she was looking at hit her. The shape of the horse carrying the rider was very familiar. She had passed such a figure several times in England carved in the chalk on the side of the Berkshire downs near the village of – 'Uffington!' Letty cried out. 'The White Horse of Uffington! But this one has a lady on his back! I've never seen such a thing before.'

'And can you tell me, I wonder, what she's doing here in Burgundy?' said d'Aubec thoughtfully. 'So far from home?'

'Lady Uffington! Of course! How do you do, your ladyship? Well, there you are and here am I! Now we've finally met – what am I supposed to do next?'

'I was right then.' D'Aubec smiled. 'I've never seen the horse on the hill in Berkshire, but I remembered an illustration from a book on Celtic art. I'm sure this is what your godfather was referring to in his note and where he meant us to start our search.'

Us . . . our search? wondered Letty. She decided to hold her peace for the moment as she could do no searching on her own account on d'Aubec's land. '"The old girl can still show you young 'uns a thing or two,"' she quoted instead, remembering Daniel's note. 'But how on earth do we follow her example?'

'I've no idea yet,' admitted Edmond. 'I was rather hoping a bright little English archaeologist would be able to work out the next step.'

'Don't count on it – I have no further inside knowledge on this,' she said doubtfully. 'I'm supposed to follow her, but she's not pointing in any direction, is she? She's just staring down in an impersonal way at whoever passes through the archway. Is there anything behind the carving? Have you . . .?'

'I have. There's nothing. Just solid wall and then the stables. The building you see here was put up in the early nineteenth century when the château was being restored after the, er, unpleasantness. It is tucked up against the western defensive wall – rather clever use of a relatively small space. I should imagine that, on completion, someone found this plaque somewhere about the place – it's obviously much older than the stables – and they preserved it by installing it here over the arch of the new building. I fear that our lady up there is no more than a distraction – an anachronism, an architectural flourish if you like.'

Letty looked up again at the indifferent stone eyes and wondered.

'It is, as you must guess, my family's insignia, the paternal d'Aubec, that is. The green background is obviously our own Burgundian hills and the horse was a symbol of the region even before horse-breeding Celtic warriors settled here. But the lady? Who could she be?'

'Any one of several,' said Letty, gathering her thoughts. 'She could be the Virgin Mary, of course. She's not uncommonly found in European heraldry, though you would scarcely find such a thing any more in Protestant England.

186

Whoever she is, I think your lady with the flowing fair hair is not a visitor. I think she's at home here, and I think she goes far back in time. You mentioned the Celts just now ... magnificent horsemen, and they were thick on the ground hereabouts from about the fifth century before Christ. They weren't merely the savage, nomadic headhunters most people suppose, you know. They had a strong artistic tradition and their metalwork was outstandingly sophisticated and beautiful. They had a strong, if bloodthirsty, religion too, with a pantheon of gods and goddesses. One of these was the horse goddess, Epona.'

She fell silent. D'Aubec listened intently, nodding agreement. He didn't seem to mind being lectured, watching her with a slight smile and the indulgent attention of an adult hearing a child read. Provoked, she picked up her theme again, 'Yes, I think we might be looking at a representation of Epona ... an ancient memory going back through your family and beyond even your Roman ancestors to the fair-haired Celts. A fine lady on a white horse ... Perhaps she was worshipped here over two thousand years ago?'

'I should like to think so.' D'Aubec spoke with enthusiasm, then shook his head regretfully. 'But I know every stone of this château and every square metre of hilltop and I can't think of any traces of a civilization older than the thirteenth-century fortifications. There may have been earlier layers, but the building works of the Middle Ages have quite obliterated them.'

'No – there are always traces ... One could ...'

'And I don't,' he warned, 'intend to invite a marauding crew of American archaeologists to bring in their spades and dig up my back garden. Even if their assault is fronted by the most attractive figurehead,' he added. 'My mother would be horrified at the thought of their big boots stamping through her strawberry beds. Which reminds me that we have strawberries for supper and we're only halfway through our tour. Come, Laetitia, would you care to see my horses?'

Letty followed him through the arched door into the warm gloom of the stable. As her eyes became accustomed to the low light she made out a long array of stalls for near on forty horses. Half of the stalls were occupied, and by animals the equal of those she'd seen at the National Stud. Two of them were familiar to her – Carnaval and Goliathe had already been unsaddled and rubbed down, and were now feeding. Letty stiffened as she noticed Goliathe, apparently bedded down for the night, and Edmond said in reassuring tones, 'Don't worry about him. Someone will have rung the Stud to say he's spending the night here. By the time we've had supper it will be too dark to ride him back – he's not fitted with lights, you know.'

Another trap like the one at the Lion d'Or opened up in front of Letty and she said swiftly, 'Goliathe may be spending the night as your guest but I'd rather not, if you don't mind.'

'Of course,' came the courteous reply. 'I have arranged that Jules will drive you back whenever you wish.'

Turning her attention back to the horses in an attempt to recover her dignity, she appreciated the perfect order, the litter of fresh straw, the winking brasswork. A familiar object fixed to the wall above the stalls caught her eye. 'So you have these in Burgundy too?' She pointed upwards. 'That's a corn dolly, isn't it?'

Obligingly he reached up and took the straw figure from the wall, shaking off the dust. 'We call this the Corn Maiden. At harvest time the last clump of wheat to be reaped is brought home and plaited into this rather unconvincing representation of what I've always supposed to be an ancient harvest goddess of some sort. The farm girls like to dress her up in ribbons and bows, as you see. The Maiden ensures fertility for the coming year – there'll be abundant crops, the herds will increase, and there'll be babies in the cradles before the next harvest time. It's a tradition I wouldn't care to break!' He put the figure back on the hook. 'And there she stays until her year's up.'

'What happens to her at the end of her time?'

'Oh, she's torn apart and fed to the horses. Minus the ribbons, of course.'

'It seems a mean reward for her year's service.'

'Seems to work – I have a lot of luck with my breeding mares.'

'But not with this one, evidently.' Letty's words were hushed, her voice full of pity. Coming at last to the end of the line, in a loose box, she was confronted with a sight which made her cry out with surprise and distress. No silken hindquarters here; instead, a lacklustre grey rear, a drooping head, and four bandaged legs. A bucket nearby was half full of stained waste and the clean smell of iodine cut through the pervading smell of horses.

'An accident?' she asked.

'Not exactly,' he replied curtly, and made to move on.

'But what, then?' Letty persisted. 'What happened to this poor creature?'

'This is Dido,' he said, making the introduction with a wide gesture. The horse lifted her head and shuffled forward to nuzzle his outstretched hand. 'She's North African – a young broodmare . . . is . . . or was . . . my best horse. But . . .' His eyes focused over her shoulder and he went on rapidly in a monotone. 'Last month she was with foal for the first time. I was away from home but intending to be back in time for the birth; I had her put safely to graze in an upper pasture. I had taken into my employ – reluctantly – the son of one of my outdoor staff.'

'Reluctantly?'

'Yes. The lad was a well-known tearaway. But for the sake of his father, who's worked for me for years, I gave the boy a chance. He went into apprenticeship with Jules, in the stables, though he made it quite clear from the start that he had no time for anything that didn't have an engine and wheels. The other day, looking for easy jobs for him to do, Jules asked him to find Dido and bring her in from the pasture as the time for her confinement was getting close. A boring task. The lad decided to liven it up a bit and save his legs by rounding up the mare on a motorbike. I keep a

Moto Guzzi in the garage. Too much of a temptation, I'm afraid. He started it up and rode to the pasture, entered the field, and tried to corner her, still aboard the machine.'

Letty could guess at the disastrous ending.

'Of course, she was terrified and bolted. She'd never been close to an engine before. She tried to escape from the field by jumping a ditch and a hedge topped with barbed wire. Old barbed wire. I thought it had all been removed. She nearly made it. Her legs were badly cut, as you see.'

'And the foal?'

'She lost the foal. Will never have more. People keep telling me – pityingly – that I should have her put down . . . she'll never amount to anything . . . but . . . ' He broke off to stroke the soft nose.

'You got fond of her?'

He nodded and prepared to move on.

'What happened to Paul Morel?' she asked, in dread of his answer.

'He drove off and disappeared. Reported the incident to no one. He left her struggling, entangled in the wire. If Jules hadn't got worried and checked on the boy, she'd have died where she lay.'

'But you caught up with him when you got back? In the café the other night.' She remembered the purposeful stride which took him straight to the boy's table. 'How did you know he was there?'

He gave her a steady look, a defiant look. 'His father told me. He was there, in the café that night. He left and tele-phoned me from the auberge.'

She had a sudden memory of an elderly man pushing his way anxiously past the waiter bringing them their drinks.

'The punishment was expected. He thinks his son got off lightly. A public chastisement to cancel the family dis-honour. But no arrest, no accusation, no long-drawn-out court case, no shameful references in the newspapers. Not even much pain. Did you not notice the lad was wearing a leather jacket? I can assure you there were no marks on

190

his body when it was found two days later. By you, I understand?'

Unwilling to hear argument, recrimination, or accusation, he turned and walked back towards the château.

Letty followed across the courtyard, thoughtful and with a hundred questions still to ask him, one of them, perhaps: By what authority had the results of the autopsy been made known to him already?

He had waited for her just inside the door.

'And no, I didn't finish the boy off. But I shall find out who did.' He sighed. 'Now, we have a few minutes before dinner to take a look at the library. This is where your godfather was to be found every evening for the last few weeks of his life. I've had his things left as they were – the books he was consulting, the notebooks he was using. The police contingent stirred them up a bit, I gather, hunting for clues of some sort or another, but mostly they're as he left them that night. You, who understood his working methods, may well be able to find an answer to our mystery here.'

He led the way down a panelled corridor hung with the portraits of long-dead Counts of Brancy, and Letty was intrigued to note the familiar nose repeating itself down the centuries. She was looking with curiosity for the luckless generation which had suffered the revolution of 1789, but so seamless was the continuation she almost missed it. She had to turn and go back a few paces before she was sure that she was looking at d'Aubec the Survivor. She identified him by the style of the dress worn by his wife. In the foreground of an out-of-doors bucolic scene, sat, large, blonde, and smiling, la Comtesse, wearing the puff-sleeved, gauzy muslin gown of the First Empire, its low-necked bodice barely equal to the task of containing her rounded bosom. In her lap she held a woven cornucopia overflowing with autumn fruits and ears of corn. A superfluous piece of symbolism, Letty thought, counting,

191

wide-eyed, the line of small d'Aubecs disappearing into the depths of the perspective.

She became aware that the present count was standing behind her. 'Eleven,' he said. 'They had eleven children eventually. And, unbelievably, they all survived. And the lady herself lived to be eighty, though she grew extremely plump.'

'She doesn't look very French,' Letty said, nodding towards the countess.

'No. She was English. When times got hard for Hippolyte, he fled across the Channel like many of his compatriots. But, unlike most of that ne'er-do-well bunch, he was clever and hardworking and he knew whom to please. He made a fortune for himself in London, married Charlotte, herself an heiress, and the two of them, in more settled times, came back to France and re-possessed the family estates.'

He moved on down the line to the last group of pictures, obviously the work of the same artist. The first was evidently a wedding portrait of his mother and father. The countess, clearly recognizable and spectacular in her belle époque froufrous, stood proudly holding the arm of a handsome man in army dress uniform. Letty couldn't work out his rank but from the weight of gold frogging in evidence it seemed to have been a high one.

'My parents were cousins of some sort,' said the count vaguely. 'My mother was a d'Aubec by name also, before she married.'

'A military family?'

'Oh, yes. Down the generations. We were always able to offer up a soldier. Though it didn't always work out as planned.' He smiled and drew her attention to the last two portraits. 'This distinguished fellow is my uncle Auguste. My father's younger brother.'

Letty looked and admired. A painting done some years ago, she assumed, as the recognizably d'Aubec features were youthful and dark.

'He's grey now and somewhat worn down by the effort

192

of helping to raise me as well as his own two children, but still a handsome old devil. Not sure I should introduce you, Letty.'

'You're fond of your uncle?'

'Oh, yes. He's the driving force of the family company. If I'm the figurehead, Auguste is the engine. And this,' he said, moving on to the last portrait, 'is the man who should be standing here now. The last soldier. My older brother. Guy. Became count on my father's death. All Guy ever wanted to do was farm the land but when the bugle sounded, off he had to go. Ypres. He didn't survive Ypres. And as for me – too young in 1914 to be accepted, I was straining at the leash. My mother held me back as long as she could. The heir and the spare. The younger son came in useful on this occasion.'

His dismissive tone barely concealed his bitterness. Looking at his sharp, aggressive profile, Letty could only imagine the havoc he would have wreaked on a battlefield.

'I see no portrait of the present count?'

'No. All in good time. An engagement portrait, I think. But perhaps it would be thoughtful to allow my fiancée to choose her own style and moment?'

'Always a good idea.' She moved away, unwilling to show a deeper interest in the count's domestic arrangements.

And then they were standing before the great oak door of the library. It opened on an interior smelling of beeswax and lavender. The walls were entirely covered in bookshelves holding ranks of leather-bound books, and a vast polished table occupied the centre of the room. All was immaculately neat apart from one end of the table. Letty thought she recognized her godfather's untidy nesting habits. The table was piled high with books, most with bookmarks protruding, and sheets of paper, some of which had spilled on to the floor. A paper bin overflowed with screwed-up pieces of discarded notes and sweet wrappers.

No promise of supper could have held her back from an instinctive step forward to see for perhaps the last time her

193

godfather's handiwork, the familiar scrawl laced with crossings-out and exclamation marks.

'Some of the books he was working on are very ancient, you understand, handwritten and decorated by the monks of Fontigny. Precious and delicate,' warned d'Aubec, gently slapping the covetous fingers she reached out towards them. 'Go and wash your hands. There's a cloak-room next door.'

'The monks?' said Letty when she returned. 'Why are they then in your possession? Why aren't they in the abbey?'

He smiled. 'Don't concern yourself. My rapacious ancestors didn't steal them. This was a sort of summer place of residence for certain of the monks throughout the Middle Ages. They used to come up here to get away from the heat and doubtless filth and plague of the town each summer, and their distraction consisted, as far as we are able to judge, of creating books, some – unusually – not on religious subjects. The illustrations are quite wonderful. They were probably done as a gift for the count, their host.'

At his consenting nod, Letty took from the pile a heavy, leather-backed volume which fitted easily into her hand and began to leaf reverently through it. A Book of Hours. The black Gothic text on a page she selected at random was surrounded by a richly painted tapestry of Burgundian life: cornflowers of dazzling blue, white daisies dedicated to Athena and Diana the virgin and moon goddess, a purple iris, emblem of royalty, and shy heartsease, the source of love potions. And, in the margin, just alighted, a fly. A fly so realistically rendered that, her throat tightening with emotion, Letty, in mime, flicked at it with her forefinger, hearing in her imagination the approving laughter of a long-dead artist. She was silent, no words adequate to carry the impressions of ancient and rare beauty in her hands.

'Well, there you are. Do you think, Letty, that if you came here each evening after your work, you could go through all this? I've no idea how long it will take.' He paused and continued in a firmer tone, 'In a fortnight's time Maman and I have to go to Lyon for several days – the annual meeting of my family company – but I am free until then to spend my evenings here with you. Do you think in two weeks, together we might be able to trace this so important discovery your godfather was excited about? Will you try?'

'Oh, Edmond, I will.' She smiled in delight, her eyes not moving from the books. 'Nothing would please me more.'

Chapter Twenty-One

The curtained darkness of the town was reprimand enough for her late return; Letty had no wish to add a ticking-off from Gunning. She asked the silent Jules to set her down at the entrance to the rue Lamartine and approached the front door quietly, hoping that it would have been left unlocked. It eased open at her touch and she crept into the hallway, slipped off her boots, and made for the stairs.

Before she could reach them, however, the parlour door opened and Gunning's imperious forefinger beckoned her inside. She went to stand, defiant and rebellious, watching impatiently as he closed the door and placed himself in front of it, arms behind his back, the expression of a severe but understanding schoolmaster on his face. 'No need to creep about. No one is aware of your assignations. It's Madame's birthday and the family have all gone off to celebrate at the Lion d'Or. With thirteen courses much anticipated, they won't, I think, be back until after midnight. The boys are still out at the café, so I can raise my voice.' He proceeded to do just that. 'Where in Heaven's name have you been, you selfish idiot? I've been sitting here all evening imagining you dead in a ditch! Well? Account for yourself!' he thundered.

Though she was wincing with dismay, Letty recognized the desperate tones and language of a parent worried out of his wits, and bit back an angry response. She employed a device which had often proved successful in the past: distraction.

'Goddess hunting! That's what I've been doing. So glad you waited up! Top shelf, William!' She pointed to the rows of reference books. 'I think I saw a book on Celtic mythology up there and I know there's a copy of *The Golden Bough*. Get them down, will you? If you're not too tired, that is? I've really no right to be keeping you up! No? Very well . . . let's look up someone whose acquaintance I made this evening – Lady Uffington, otherwise known as Epona.'

Gunning was, as she had expected, immediately drawn in despite his show of anxiety. Growling unconvincingly, he settled down with her at the table, a pile of heavy books between them. Feeling his still-unresolved tension, she reached over, impulsively put an arm around his shoulders, and dropped a light kiss on his cheek. 'There! You're the third man I've kissed in earnest in six hours,' she lied. 'That's good going even for me.'

'And you're bidding fair to be the first girl I've smacked in thirty years! Explain yourself!'

'Well, I wonder if you were aware that it was Paradee who asked me if –'

'You were last seen heading for the hills with the boss. He returned hours later by himself in pensive mood. Having pushed you off the cliff of Solutré? Can't say I'd blame him, but it would have been good not to have been kept in suspense. Carry on.'

'Very pleasant ride. It helped to get the area in focus. We must do it one day, William. I kept an eye open for Magdalene's perspective but I didn't see it. No hanky-panky with my handsome American escort, I regret to say, was on offer either, because we were chaperoned through-out by d'Aubec from a distance of a few yards. But when we got back to the stables . . .'

Gunning's expression of deepening astonishment was all she hoped for as her story unfolded. 'And Paradee let him whisk you off like that? He simply stood by and watched you ride away with a man we know to be violent and poss-ibly a murderer?'

197

'Not easily, no. He tried hard to stop me, but . . . well . . . you know what I'm like when I've got the bit between my teeth.'

Gunning glowered. 'It's not good enough, Letty. Amounts to dereliction of duty. I shall take this up with Paradee.'

'You will not! This isn't the 1890s. I can look after myself. Please don't start fouling up my relationship with Paradee, William. We get on well. We've been watching each other and I think we both like what we see. Daniel admired him and so do I.'

She hurried on with her account of the château, not setting out to emphasize the glamour of the ancient setting or the richness of the furnishings, but hearing the awe in her voice as she spoke – and sensing Gunning's mounting scorn.

'And whom do we see surrounded by these Louis Seize chiffoniers, these Boulle cabinets? The inhabitants of this so civilized establishment? Not, then, the Count and Countess Dracula we had supposed?'

'Oh, come off it, William! I can't say they're normal, everyday folk, but d'Aubec and his mother were very welcoming and friendly.'

'It would be interesting to know the source of their apparent wealth. Were you able to form any impressions?'

'Yes, in fact, I was. I knew you'd see I haven't been wasting my time once you'd got off your high horse and calmed down. As Paradee said – "the count's got his fingers in every pie in Burgundy". Estate sources, rents, farm revenue, vineyards all providing but, equally, his outgoings must be enormous. That's an expensive place to run. He keeps a large staff – servants everywhere you look and a male secretary of a superior sort. D'Aubec maintains a generous stable, and he and his mother appear to have expensive tastes – cars . . . jewellery . . . and the old girl was sporting the very last tea-leaf in tea gowns. Lanvin, I'd say. They don't stint themselves! I'd guess there's some other strand to his finances. And I couldn't help noticing . . .'

'Do go on, Letty. I'm aware of your keen eye for detail.'

'There was a newspaper on the telephone table in the library. D'Aubec left me alone when he went to check whether supper was ready. It was a copy of the London *Times* and it was open and folded. Folded as you do when you're intending to spend some time reading the contents. Anyway, I took a closer look. It was open at the business pages. He'd been studying the stocks and shares reports. There were circles around the shares he was interested in and there was a telephone number scribbled in the margin. I copied it down.'

She took a notebook from her pocket and read out a series of numbers. Gunning solemnly recorded them in his own notebook.

'That's a London number. City exchange, predictably. Look, Letty, if you don't mind I'll do a bit of investigating of my own. In my life before the war – I know you first saw me as a down-and-out and I'm sure that's how you'll always see me . . . but . . .'

'William, I won't say I know who you are, but I know where you were born, who your parents were, where you were educated. You've noticed that prying comes naturally to me. Start from there.'

'Well, you can imagine, then, that should I choose to reanimate them, I have contacts in some high and influential places in London. And the telephone is a wonderful instrument. Tomorrow I shall get the car out and drive to Lyon. From there I can make a few calls which I can be certain will go undetected. But do carry on with your account. I find the d'Aubecs most intriguing.'

'I didn't perhaps stress sufficiently how *friendly* they both were. His mother is charming. I liked her. She does her best to present that son of hers as halfway civilized . . . excuses his overbearing manners by making fun of them. And he seems genuinely fond of her. And they spoke warmly of Daniel. William, he was still there! Or traces of him. D'Aubec had left all his things right there in the library where Daniel had been working on them. He said he was intending to get around to examining them himself.'

'Really? How very odd!' said Gunning. 'I've never met the maid who would be prepared to polish around clutter of that kind every day for *eight months*!'

'It is a bit strange.' Letty shivered. 'Almost as though they were expecting someone . . . *me*, do you think? It was so . . . so . . . intimate, so trusting and unremarkable. Daniel was obviously *at home* there, William. I think that's what d'Aubec wanted me to understand. And I'll tell you something else! To all appearances, the wastepaper basket hadn't been emptied. Look . . .' She scrabbled in her pocket. 'It was in what you might call the top stratum. It's his last chocolate bar wrapper. I stole it!'

Where she had expected derision there was a slow, sympathetic smile. 'I don't blame you. It's the little personal things we need to keep by us. Memories. Is this all you have of Daniel – apart from the postcard?'

'Oh, William! You didn't know? Didn't my father mention it?' She was suddenly uncomfortable in the face of Gunning's asceticism and uncertain whether to continue. It was no business of his, after all. '. . . And I didn't know for certain until some weeks ago when the Probate Court finally pronounced. I have quite a substantial souvenir of Daniel. Astonishing. We'd always assumed he was comfortably off but not rich – he was ever a modest spender. What we didn't realize – because he never spoke of it – was that some years before his death he'd inherited large sums from two old bachelor uncles. Even Pa was kept in the dark about that. Daniel didn't allow his change in circumstances to affect his life; he just carried on as he always had, living for his work. We'd always known he looked on us as his family – whenever he came back from foreign parts, it was *our* home he came to – but he did have cousins . . . a nephew or two . . . We just assumed, as far as we ever thought about it, that his estate would be divided between them. But he willed everything to me. Many thousands of pounds but with instructions that I was not to inherit before my twenty-fifth birthday. So, in a couple of years' time, I'm going to be a rich woman. Undeserved and unearned, I *know*,' she hurried to stress, 'so you needn't feel you have to point it out.'

'Oh, my good Lord!' Gunning's jaw sagged in mock horror. 'This is terrible news! Every rogue with a mention in Debrett will be alerted. Squadrons of penniless younger sons will be buzzing in like wasps to a mulberry in summer. You'd better employ me on a permanent basis to shoot them down. And don't, for goodness' sake, let d'Aubec get a scent of this – he's acquisitive and still a bachelor.'

'You won't be reassured, then, to hear that his family has a history of marrying English heiresses!' She laughed to see the concern in his expression. 'No – I exaggerate. Just one, in fact. And that was a long time ago. I hardly need you to alert me to the dangers when there's the Awful Warning of Countess Charlotte plastered all over the château walls! But, don't worry, William, you can stop growling and come off watch – I gather he has, in his aristocratic French way, a long-standing engagement to be married.' Frowning, she added, 'They seem to emulate the royal dynasties of Egypt – you know – one of those families that prefer to marry close relatives.'

'No wonder they're a bit strange. About time for a bit of fresh blood, perhaps? You're *not* to go volunteering your services!'

He listened intently as she took up the tale of her tour of the château, but it was her encounter with the lady emblazoned on the d'Aubec coat of arms that was of greatest interest.

'Ah! The lady Daniel's card told you to follow? Fair hair, you say? White horse? Seated sideways? Was there a hound following her? There usually is.'

They leafed through the books, on the trail of Epona. 'Goddess of Horses,' said Gunning, running a finger down a page. 'But much more. She was the Celtic expression of the Mother Goddess. She's often portrayed carrying a sheaf of corn or a cornucopia. Earth Goddess, Corn Goddess,

201

Moon Goddess . . . seems to have been one of the harder-working members of the pantheon. Areas of responsibility: trees, crops, all living creatures, with specific interest in horses. Oh . . . and no rest for the virtuous – she was required to take an interest in the underworld in her time off, which I suppose was the winter. And as if that wasn't enough to keep a girl busy, here's the author handing her yet another role – Mistress of . . .'

'Mysteries! The Enchantress! William, I know this lady already! I met her some years ago when she was going by a different name.'

'Demeter? Ceres? The Romans obviously recognized this goddess, so important to their Celtic enemy, as one of their kind and voted her straight into their own club. Very open-minded and welcoming, the Romans, when it came to absorbing foreign gods. Hedged their bets, placated the local community . . . and Epona had the advantage of echoing their own deep love of horses. She was worshipped by the cavalry units of the legions based in this region. In fact, looking at the references in these books, she was particularly strong on the ground in this area. If we were to plot the mentions of shrines and statues on a map of Burgundy from, let's say, Alésia in the north down to Lyon, the concentration would be very evident.'

'No, William. I was thinking of a goddess more ancient even than Demeter.' A prickle of excitement ran along her spine.

'Ah! I think I can guess where you're going with this. And I know someone who can help you. You met him briefly the other day. The priest of St Mary Magdalene. Father Anselme's a considerable scholar and I think he may well have the knowledge we need to guide us through the labyrinth I see stretching out before us. Don't be alarmed by his presence – he's quite intimidating on first acquaintance. But he's very agreeable and unusually open-minded.'

Gunning hesitated for a moment and then confided: 'If he feels he can trust you, he may well introduce you to the lady you're chasing after. That other Mistress of Mysteries: the Green Goddess – Egyptian Isis.'

Paradee's reaction when she went to see him the next morning was far more rewarding. 'No! You don't say! D'Aubec's given you the keys to the château? You're kidding!' He couldn't disguise his excitement. 'So his defences have finally been penetrated!'

'Well, he's left a side door open,' she said, feeling she'd over-steered and ought to dampen down his enthusiasm. 'It may not be as straightforward as it looks. We'll see.'

Quick as ever to pick up her mood, Paradee frowned and said seriously, 'Of course, Stella – you're right to be cautious. And you know I don't like the idea of you getting too close to that rascal. Ask anyone in town – they'll tell you he's a ruthless horseman, employer, and ... yes ... I have to say it, lover. He's had affairs with some pretty fancy ladies hereabouts, and none of them has lasted longer than a season.' He took a deep breath and Letty felt his turmoil and indecision. Finally he said quietly, 'No. It's not worth the risk. I want you to stay away from there. And I'll make that an order if you like.'

But he'd gone on to ask her about her impressions of the château, about the layout, the staff, and even the quality of the furnishings and objets d'art. He listened intently to Letty's descriptions of some of the precious things she had noticed, commenting with a hard edge to his voice, 'You'd expect some outstanding décor, after all. Antiques dealing is one of his activities – he didn't tell you that? No. Hardly dinner table conversation. You wouldn't know, then, that he owns boutiques in London and New York? He's always at the salerooms. Unrivalled opportunities for acquiring and disposing of valuable artefacts. I wonder how many of them are legally his to be traded?'

He hesitated for a moment, then, coming to a decision: 'You know, the Police Judiciaire take a keen interest in what they call the *trafic de biens culturels*. There's a law, which they enforce pretty strictly, forbidding the sale of objects of a cultural value or national importance out of the country.'

Letty remembered the auction house catalogues Gunning had shown her on their arrival in France. And here was Paradee voicing suspicions she could with some certainty have confirmed. Someone was getting valuable items out of the country by a devious route and making a good deal of profit in the process.

Paradee was snorting with derision, 'And don't you think that's a bit ironical when you consider the piratical depredations that stocked their Louvre museum! That bunch in Lyon are all too ready to hassle *me* ... forever breathing down my neck, asking impertinent questions, checking the logs, quoting the latest regulations. They seem to think that because I'm digging in French soil I must be turning up all kinds of items of interest to foreign antiquarians. Now, Stella, what was the name of that smart young cop from Lyon? The one who impressed you with his investigative routine ... and his moustache. What was his name ...?'

'The chap who still has our passports? I think his name was Laval.'

'Yes, Laval, that's it.' He gave a nasty grin. 'Right then, Laval – it's time for us to have a little talk. Time to point the finger at one of your own!'

Chapter Twenty-Two

She met Gunning, face still lined with dust from his drive back from Lyon, on the doorstep of the priest's imposing Romanesque house in the rue Tellier. The door swung open before they could speak and they were welcomed into a cool interior by the priest himself. Father Anselme swept ahead of them, elegant in his black cassock, shouting for tea to be brought to the drawing room. As she settled into an armchair by a log fire smouldering lethargically in the hearth, Letty looked around and decided with approval that she had never seen anything calling itself a drawing room that contained so many books. They were stacked on shelves, on the floor, even piled high on a desk under the window. Gunning seemed very much at home here. He automatically cleared papers and books from a tea table and set it ready by her chair. The room smelled agreeably of leather, toast, wood smoke, and a scent she thought she recognized, tracking it down eventually to an ancient hound of indeterminate breed who advanced on her, wagging disarmingly, to nuzzle her hand.

'Oh, push him away, mademoiselle,' advised the priest. 'Borvo! Behave yourself! His problem is that he loves to meet strangers and is not in the least aware that he has become old, smelly, and unattractive. But William tells me – and he has told me much about you – that you live surrounded by dogs and horses in England? You must feel quite at home in Burgundy!'

They talked agreeably on generalities until the tray of tea things arrived carried in by the housekeeper but, with her disappearance, Father Anselme embarked at once on a consideration of the puzzle of Lady Uffington. He had known Daniel well enough to give serious attention to his final message and appeared unsurprised by it.

'But of course! This was his deep interest and one which I shared on a professional as well as a personal level. We often spoke of it. Before he died, his – dare I call it obsession? – was becoming overpowering. I was concerned. But Daniel's mood was not oppressed – rather excited and elated. I had no idea he had communicated his thoughts to you, mademoiselle.'

'As Mr Gunning has probably told you, there was little to communicate. Just a vague feeling of anxiety and danger, and suggestions that I might find two goddess figures in the vicinity interesting. I daresay I've over-interpreted what he had to say. He was always one to encourage me to ask questions, follow a trail to the end. But in this case, I'm beginning to think I've allowed my godfather's enthusiasms and his weakness for intrigue to run away with me and drop me off in a cul-de-sac. I can't imagine what I think I'm doing here wasting your time!'

'Don't trouble yourself! You're speaking to a very receptive audience, mademoiselle! Well, now you are here, you might as well pursue what is, in fact, a fascinating subject a little further. Let me assure you – Daniel is not the only person to fall victim to the lure of these ladies. I think you're wondering what the connection between them can be? Mary Magdalene? The Celtic Goddess of Horses? And I would add for your attention: Mary the Mother. I'm sure you'd think a Roman Catholic priest remiss if he did not bring Our Holy Lady into the conversation! There is a thread connecting them and Daniel is, I believe, indeed presenting you with one end of it and challenging you to follow where it leads. It would not surprise me to discover that I am myself built in as one of the steps along the way! Or cast as an unlikely Ariadne, handing you a ball of magical thread to guide you to the centre of the labyrinth.

206

I cannot take you to the end of the road but perhaps I can start you off?'

He walked to the mantelpiece and lifted a pile of envelopes, hunting about and blowing away dust. 'Here we are! My paperweight. Take this in your hand, mademoiselle. It will explain much.'

Letty held out her hand for the small black carving he was offering her. Four inches tall, no more, the figure was seated, narrow-waisted, full-bosomed, and smiling, and on her left knee she tenderly held a small child. The two men were silent, waiting for her comment.

'Um ... basalt? Is this dark stone – basalt?'

Anselme nodded.

She pressed on. 'It's very old. I've been shown figures like this in Egypt. Four thousand years old possibly, I'm told.'

Again an encouraging nod.

'It's the mother goddess Isis and she's nursing her son Horus. I've seen paintings of her in tombs in Egypt. She's always shown holding the looped cross and she's easily recognizable in the pictures by her red dress. If one were to disregard the distinctive headpiece she's wearing ...' She put a thumb gently over the solar disc between two spreading horns '... she could be the Virgin Mary ... or any Mother Goddess. Demeter, Cybele ... A truly ancient image. At any rate, she's pagan. Are you sure you ... Aren't you concerned that someone might be alarmed to see such an object holding down your papers, Father?'

The priest laughed. 'I have no intention of giving her up! She's very special! She was given to me, on his deathbed, by an old parishioner of mine. I'm not quite sure how she fetched up here in France – though many of these images turn up in remote country churches as well as in glittering cathedrals. Probably brought back by Crusaders. Some say their appearance in this country coincides with the return of the Templars from the Holy Land.' He glanced at Gunning, who grunted in agreement. 'I must say, when this was pressed into my hand I was somewhat alarmed.

But my parishioner reassured me: "Father," he said, "it's all right! Don't you fret! I've had her blessed at Lourdes. She's one of us now." And you don't frighten me with the use of the word "pagan", Miss! It's from the Latin *paganus* – a countryman. And I am proud to confess myself a countryman. Though, in less enlightened times, I suppose I might have risked interrogation and perhaps the stake as a heretic for my interest in mythology.'

His cheerful openness was disarming.

'I come from a country town west of Paris. From Chartres, where there was built the most beautiful Gothic cathedral in the world – do you know it?'

'Oh, yes! I've visited twice. Marched around by my aunt, who lives not far away. I have seen the statue of the "black virgin of the pillar" and the "subterranean virgin" and, the loveliest of all, I think, the "blue virgin" of the stained glass window. Are these connected?'

'I think so. Perhaps you didn't know that the hill on which the cathedral is built was the cult centre of a Celtic tribe? The Carnutes. It is from their name that we get the word "Chartres". The hard *c* tended with time to be worn down into a softer sound: "ch."'

'Like *caballus* – a horse – changing to *cheval*, you mean?'

'Exactly. According to tradition, the priests of the Carnutes held that spot to be their holy place. *Nemeton* in their language, a sacred grove. Not a temple but a holy space open to the sky, a space where they worshipped their deity, who was most likely the Mother Goddess. The *Virgo Paritura*, she who is about to give birth. Such a site underpins Notre Dame in Paris also. In this Holy of Holies they would be facing the east – for the Celts faced the rising sun – in front was life; behind them, to the west, was death. *Our* Christian churches are designed also for the congregations to look to the east, it is said because that's the direction in which lies the Holy Land, but the traditional alignment is inherited from a much older culture.

'The Celts had many gods but they all represented no more, I believe, than aspects of the unifying force of creation and renewal. Countrymen, you see – *pagani*. They understood and celebrated the elemental forces of nature. And do you know what underlies that vast symphony in stone at Chartres? Deep below the cathedral there still lies the holy well of the Celts. Water is a vital element of the holiness – the *numen* – of these sites. And it is said that there was once, on an altar by the well, a statue, a very ancient statue carved from black stone, perhaps like the one you hold in your hand, and it was venerated there. It disappeared . . . long ago . . . but I believe it is the memory of it that lingers on in the depictions of the black virgins. There are many in this part of France and in the south also.'

'But why are they black?' Letty asked. 'Is that significant? There seems to be a quite deliberate attempt to colour them or choose a dark wood to represent the virgin.'

'No more than artistic tradition. The small carving you have there is of basalt, as you say, a very black rock and one difficult to work, which, of course, makes it all the more precious – the harder the rock, the more enduring the image. And then – if your inclination is to esotericism – you could argue that the very darkness of the virgin is a promise that, like the dark phase of the moon, she will bring forth light.' He smiled, shrugging apologetically for his philosophical proposition.

'So – trailing after the goddess, through Gothic and Celtic cultures, we are taken back to the time of the ancient Egyptian civilization?' She handed back with some regret the small figure which felt so comfortable in her hand.

'No. Older even than that,' said the priest with a smile. 'The journey back into mankind's artistic – and possibly religious – past is quite dizzying! The very first carvings ever made by his hand were of female fertility figures, the Paleolithic Mother Goddess. Mostly of stone, sometimes of mammoth ivory, they began to appear fifty thousand years ago all over Europe and through to Turkey. In the Dordogne there's a particularly fine rock carving – the Goddess of Laussel. Now, I'm afraid I can't offer you one such to hold, but . . .'

209

He passed her a copy of an archaeological report and she opened it at the marked page.

'Daniel was most impressed by this carving.'

Letty studied the photograph. It was of a naked and heavily pregnant woman with pendulous breasts. The face had been obliterated so it was impossible to guess her mood, though Letty would have gathered from the flaunting way she carried her body that it would have been one of pride and fulfilment. Her left hand was poised protectively over her swollen belly while, with her right, she triumphantly brandished an object which might well have been a cornucopia. The image of d'Aubec's English ancestor came at once to mind and Letty smiled at the resemblance between two women separated by twenty thousand years.

'This crescent shape?' she asked, pointing to the object the woman held. 'Is it a horn of plenty?'

'A bison's horn, perhaps. It may represent the moon. In the Stone Age the phases of the moon were vital for time-keeping – for agriculture, for hunting, for the regeneration of the tribe, in fact. In its simple way, this carving makes a timeless statement. When the first artists discovered their skills they used them to portray the most vital, most precious aspect of their existence: rebirth, renewal. And the source of this to a primitive society was the female principle. A concept more readily understood by a Catholic, I think, than an English Protestant.'

'Daniel wasn't, I suppose, contemplating a conversion to Catholicism, was he, Father?' she asked uncertainly.

'As far as I know, he remained to the end an interested and enquiring agnostic,' said the priest. 'He did not appear to me to have the bump of religiosity. He would pursue the Madonna with the same enthusiasm as Celtic Epona without ever feeling the need to sink to his knees before either. If Daniel ever sought the Divine on a personal level, I'd say he turned his searchlight on himself. He believed that the Spirit, the Creator, was to be found in each of us. A divine internal spark? And that was sufficient for him. Such men are exceptional. Most men and women need to see and feel *outward* symbols of their faith. And if it's solidly carved in granite or cast in gold, so much the better. And what image speaks to them so directly as the nurturing mother or the suffering son?' He waved a hand to a painting nestling between bookcases. A medieval oil painting, a Pietà, showed Mary the Mother, Mater Dolorosa, distraught, weeping, but still finding the strength to cradle the tormented body of her dead son on her lap.

'Our experiences of life are so vastly different, but there is one thing all creatures have in common – we've all had a mother. For most, she remains to the end the most fundamental influence on our lives. After all, Christ himself learned his language, his attitudes, his stories, his compassion, and his strength from his mother. From Mary. His words, his stories, were *her* words, *her* stories, learned at her knee. I believe there is no stronger force for good or evil in this world than a mother's words.'

He turned to Gunning. 'Your four years of working amongst the dying must have given you insights into man's relationship with his Maker? In extremis, a man's faith reveals itself in its raw state, unvarnished by ritual?'

'Yes, indeed. Though I don't despise ritual – good old Sunday school! It put hymns remembered from childhood on to men's lips when nothing else would come.' His face clouded. 'One of the most terrible sights I've seen was, in fact, one of great beauty and one which stirred my soul to its roots. One summer morning, I watched as a company of Welsh infantry marched by on their way up the line to the trenches. They were singing and, Father, if you've never heard Welshmen sing, you've missed one of life's acutest pleasures. They were singing a hymn. 'Guide Me, O Thou Great Redeemer'. We all just stood entranced, listening until they were far into the distance. Until the last moment, when their song was obliterated by the obscene crash of the German artillery they ran straight into. Their Great Redeemer was apparently deaf to the pleas of angel voices that morning.'

211

'Celtic voices,' the priest corrected quietly. 'The Welsh are a Celtic race, are they not? I'm glad to hear they survive in some part of your land.'

'It's the Anglo-Saxon you hear most often, unfortunately,' said Gunning, breaking away from his dark thoughts. 'Disappointingly, half the men whose last words I heard died cursing. Though you're right: many men died calling out for their mothers. With their last breath they'd beg me to write to their mothers. "Tell her I died bravely. Tell her I didn't suffer. Tell her I love her." It became routine. I remember automatically asking a sergeant dying of a stomach wound what he would like me to tell his mother. "My mother, Padre?" he gasped in surprise. Then, "Tell the old bat I'm slinging my hook and the only good thing about *that* is that where I'm going I'm not likely to bump into *her* again." But he was the exception.'

'But I think you're right, Father,' Letty ventured an opinion, 'when you say most people need some image external to themselves to help them understand . . . painting, sculpture . . . rosary beads . . . a cross. One of the most telling events early in the war involved a sighting of the Virgin. Or was it an angel? At Mons. The Angel of Mons. We were all thrilled and awed and – yes – heartened by the appearance. Thousands of our troops, vastly outnumbered by the German forces, claim to have witnessed an appearance in the sky, a holy presence, a female presence, whom they believed to be on their side and, indeed, inspired by this, they went on to fight bravely and many escaped the net.'

Gunning gave a sharp laugh. 'I was at Mons,' he said, 'during the reported incidents. At the defence of Mariette Bridge on the canal. I was continually watching the sky for enemy aircraft. One German plane crashed in flames, that's all. I saw nothing unusual. Nor did any soldier I met. But, do you know, this is the first time I've admitted that? The story ran through the army and the whole of Britain like wildfire – thanks to the newspapers and the radio – and was unthinkingly accepted, to such an extent that anyone denying that it happened would have been denounced as unpatriotic.'

'But so many claim –' Letty began to remonstrate.

'Mass hysteria,' said Gunning firmly. 'Self-deception on the most enormous scale. One loose observation, a misinterpreted comment, a newsman standing by to pick up and run with the idea – that's all you'd need. Those men had had little sleep and no food for thirty-six hours. It was a hot Sunday. But the only religious activity was in the square of the village of Cuesnes. Right there in the middle of what had become a battlefield, the church bells suddenly rang out; people dressed in their Sunday best flooded into church, held a service, and went back to their homes. Then all hell broke loose.

'I saw many disturbing sights that day, but nothing supernatural. Nor did any man I spoke to. No – I believe someone told the nation what it desperately needed to hear. "We may be outnumbered three to one, we may be retreating but, look – God's on our side." If you send the message all over the country on the filmed news reports, within days you have a country hypnotized by a lie it *wants* to believe to be the truth. And this sickness communicates itself faster than the flu germ – which it much resembles! We've hardly begun to understand the power of the human mind and its weakness for self-delusion. And the possibilities for directing minds en masse towards some preordained end are frightening.'

'But some consequences are beneficent, surely?' the priest challenged. 'What do you have to say about the appearance of Our Lady at Lourdes? And the many other sightings this century alone which have brought healing and relief and an affirmation of faith for thousands?'

'My judgement would be the same,' said Gunning. 'Hysteria. Delusion. If I had to trace my antipathy to its source, I believe it would come down to the attempt to claim ownership of the deity by a particular sect. Why should the Virgin be witnessed exclusively by Catholics? Why is Yahweh's voice only audible to Jews? Allah's to

Muslims? I'm disturbed by those groups of humanity who claim special preference for themselves, who make a god in their own image and then believe he will champion them above all others. The only thing in the war that raised my spirits was the very English response to the Germans who had hung out a banner asserting that God was on their side – *Gott mit Uns*. In no time our lads had put up their own sign – *We got mittens too!* Stupid, irreverent, but sane.'

Letty was absorbed by the exchanges, but well aware that she was the third wheel on the bicycle. She lost track of time and was surprised when the priest gently reminded her of her appointment at the château. Gunning escorted her to the door, muttering hurriedly as they passed along the corridor. Mainly injunctions to behave herself and avoid confrontations of any kind, which were heard with patience.

'No time now to tell you what I found out from London,' he said, opening the door and looking out into the street. 'Very disturbing! Ah – here comes your conveyance ... if I dare call a Hispano-Suiza a conveyance!' He stared in astonishment as the huge car throbbed its way gingerly down the narrow street. 'And your chauffeur – just look at him! Hat, gloves, insignia, the full regalia. Who *is* that?'

'Jules. Jules le Lugubre!' Letty laughed. 'He's really in charge of the stables but he's been poshed up to fetch me. William ... do you get the impression I'm being *paraded*?'

'He forgot the marching band. This time,' said Gunning, tight-lipped with disapproval.

Jules braked abruptly on catching sight of her on the priest's doorstep, and got out to open the door. Anxiously, Gunning grabbed her hand and held it tightly. 'Listen, Letty! You're to treat your new friend with the same scepticism you seem to reserve for me. Question everything! And remember the Angel of Mons!'

214

Chapter Twenty-Three

'No, really, Charles! There's nothing more to report. We spent the evening in the library translating Old French, classifying and codifying medieval books. I met some of the household. He has a smart young man working for him as a secretary and steward combined, and an elderly housekeeper who really runs the place.'

'Resident?'

'Yes. Both.'

'Tell me something more about this smart young man, Stella. How you seem to collect them!'

'Oh, I won't be adding *his* name to my list of conquests! I think he rather hates me for taking up his master's time. He's called Constantine. He's a few years older than d'Aubec. Saturnine good looks, you might say. But there's something a bit creepy about him, I thought. You know how plants go when you start them in a cellar and forget about them? It doesn't matter how much sunshine you give them when you bring them out, how they strengthen up – they go on being pale and unnatural. But Constantine seems to have influence with the boss and the respect and, yes, affection of the old girl.'

The unwelcome questioning was cut short by Phil, who knocked and entered Paradee's office hurriedly. He looked anxiously from one to the other. 'Excuse me, sir, but the police are here. They want to see Stella at the Town Hall. Right away.'

* * *

She was shown into the room they had previously used for interviewing. The same young inspector with the impeccable good manners and the impeccable moustache invited her to take a seat opposite.

'Inspector Laval,' he reminded her. 'I retained your passport, mademoiselle, and now I wish to return it to you. You were also kind enough to provide us with a sample of your fingerprints when last we met.'

She nodded.

'So we were able to identify the thumb and forefinger of prints belonging to you on the strap of the wristwatch worn by the unfortunate boy.'

'Golly! Did you really? Well, that is truly amazing! Can you pick up prints as clearly as that? From a bit of old leather?'

His reply was stiff. 'You may not be aware, mademoiselle, mesmerized as are all the English by the glamorous reputation of Scotland Yard, that it was here in Lyon that the first police laboratory was created. We are capable of forensic detection at least the equal of anything you can supply in London. And yes, it is not difficult, particularly when the fingers of the interesting party are sweaty or greasy as were yours, mademoiselle.'

'But I told you I'd handled it in front of witnesses – and why!'

'I have your statement,' he said, tapping a file. His voice took on a confidential tone: 'It had seemed to me a little strange that you should lay hands on a corpse to remove the watch from its wrist. Most young ladies would naturally recoil from contact with dead flesh caked in dirt . . . in fact, I do believe it would take an overpowering motivation to undertake such a disagreeable task. It occurs to me that perhaps the watch itself was of special interest?'

He left a pause for her comment but she remained silent.

'A special watch indeed . . . didn't you think?' he continued. 'Not the type a groom would be wearing. Especially a groom whose initials were P.M. and not D.M.T. You noticed the engraving? Of course.'

216

His eyes were dancing with ill-concealed humour. 'Shall I reveal, mademoiselle, that this watch was known to me also? Along with the wallet found on the body – likewise, not Morel's property. Last autumn, my department investigated a crime committed here in Fontigny. A British academic was stabbed to death ... you are aware of the circumstances, perhaps?'

'I have heard it spoken of. The unfortunate gentleman was staying at the Huleux house.'

'The victim's name was Daniel Thorndon. He was robbed of his watch and wallet. Now, this is where names become interesting. The French forces of law and order were held to account – pursued, indeed – with some vigour by an English gentleman, a friend of the dead man. I noted his name.' Laval flipped over a page in his notebook and read out: 'Sir Richard Talbot.'

He produced from a file Letty's passport and opened it up, studying the front page with affected interest. 'So, when I find I have in front of me a Miss Laetitia Stella St Clair Talbot ... Not, in fact, a hockey team but a single charming young lady ...' He passed it back to her. '... I begin to make connections. I draw lines which lead back from a newly arrived English archaeologist to a man who was murdered last year. Would you like me to go on?'

She opened innocent eyes to the inspector. 'I think I'd better come clean. Tell me – are you able to assure me you'll keep what I have to tell you to yourself if you possibly can?'

He spread his hands in a wide gesture. 'Look on this as the Confessional, mademoiselle. Why not?'

'Now, what have we?' he said, checking his notes. 'The watch and wallet of the godfather of Miss Laetitia Talbot (names one and four on your passport) disappeared last year in mysterious and criminal circumstances. Their whereabouts remained obscure until Miss Stella St Clair

217

(names two and three) dug the body of the current wearer from a trench.'

She started to get to her feet. 'Well, now that's all cleared up, may I go?'

'No. I have two further things to say. First: the question of Professor Thorndon's murder has not been shelved. And the possibly linked death of young Morel also remains undetermined but not ignored. I can guess what you're up to. Please hear me when I say – leave this to the police. The Police Judiciaire have a high reputation throughout Europe, though perhaps in England they would hardly know about such things.'

'Clemenceau's Tigers?' She smiled. 'Oh, we've heard of you!'

'Not so much a tiger perhaps.' He returned her smile. 'Hound. I keep my nose to the scent until I get my man. Or woman.'

Letty believed him. 'And your second point, Inspector?'

He placed a small paper evidence bag on the desk in front of her. 'Your professional help. Tell me what you make of that.'

She opened the bag and shook the gleaming contents into her hand. 'Good Lord! Where *did* you come by this?' And, with a sudden rush of doubt: 'Why are you showing this to me? I'm sure my director, Mr Paradee, could give you a much more authoritative opinion than can I.'

'I had understood your boss to be a medievalist,' the inspector replied mildly.

'Oh, he has a very broad base,' she said, loyally. 'His perspective is quite wide enough to encompass anything of interest or value that the soil of Burgundy may throw up. I would show it to Paradee. He'll tell you what you want to know.'

'I rather particularly wish *you* to give me your opinion, mademoiselle.'

'Very well. No guarantees on accuracy, you understand. It's an aureus. A gold coin of the Roman era, which means it's just about pure gold and must weigh about eight grams. The Emperor on the obverse, facing to the right, has very recognizable features. It's our chubby old friend Lucius Domitius Ahenobarbus. Nero, that is. You can make out the letters around his head – *Nero Caesar Augustus.* (That'll be names four, five, and six.)'

A fleeting smile encouraged her to plunge on.

'He started calling himself "Augustus" in AD 54, so that gives us the earliest possible date for this. It could have been struck at Lyon – there was an important coin manufactory there. I'm looking for the letters PLG on the reverse – *Pecunia Lugdunum,* "Lyon Mint" – but of course they aren't there. It's too early. On the back we've got a depiction of a ferocious bearded old chap with thunderbolt and sceptre, and his description is *Iuppiter Custos* – that's Jupiter, and *Custos,* his second name, means the Guardian.'

She handed the coin back to him. 'I confess – that was an easy one!' she said. 'Believe me – I wouldn't have rushed to answer had the coin been from a later reign . . . let's say of Maximus Horribilis Gothicus. But you're a Lyon man. You're aware of the city's Roman roots. As a policeman you are the guardian of your heritage. You'd think me naïve if I didn't guess you know all this?'

He smiled in acknowledgement. 'I know all that. But what I don't know, mademoiselle, is what our poor young Paul Morel was doing with it clutched in his dead hand.'

'Is there anyone in town who *doesn't* know who you are, Letty?' Gunning asked, wincing.

'I doubt it. Wretched passport! Why do we have to have them? I leave it in my chest of drawers under my socks so I expect if old Huleux is any good at his job at all he'll have checked up on me. I feel a complete fool! Ah, well . . . I shall just say I'm here working under my *professional* name. Why not? Lots of women have . . . George Eliot, Currer Bell . . .'

'Mata Hari?'

'Yes. That sort of thing.'

'And you weren't able to put the inspector out of his misery?'

'I think I was very helpful. I gave him a crash course on stratigraphic sections, recording techniques, and the chronological sequences indicated by remnants of ceramic artefacts. He was fascinated.'

'Oh, I expect he was just enjoying the sound of your voice, Letty.'

'He was interested enough to ask me to draw a cross-section of what he called "the trench in question" and point out whereabouts a gold coin from AD 54 might have lodged itself.'

'I know that section. Barren, isn't it? Not even any pot-sherds down there – no sign of habitation.'

'Yes. I told him that, wherever the lad found that coin, it was most likely not down the Allée du Parc. And then Laval asked me something really rather odd. He produced a tracing, a plan of the diggings and the foundations revealed so far – I think I recognized *your* handiwork, William – and asked me to plot the expected outline of the remaining walls.'

'And you were able to do that?'

'Yes, of course. Any fool could. Any fool with an inkling of the concept of symmetry . . .' She sighed. 'I think my disdainful friend was suggesting that this digging is all a piece of nonsense . . . why bother to dig at vast expense and to the general inconvenience of the community when it's quite obvious what's under the ground and where? I'm sure he was implying that leaving six-foot-deep holes about the place is an open incitement to the concealing of fresh corpses. Or else,' she added thoughtfully, 'he was trailing before me the notion that Paradee's operation could be a distraction, a flummery . . . a cover for something else. Laval really doesn't like Paradee much, you know.'

'I'd say he'd made a point about the symmetry, wouldn't you? No more surprises down there, I'd have thought.'

'I'd say there's always a point to what that clever young man says. The inspector told me to ring him up if I had anything I wanted to discuss. I thought he was as smart as a whip and charming with it.'

'Then I'm sure you'll be able to think of some urgent matter requiring his attention.'

Letty passed her arm companionably through his. 'Look, let's not go straight home, William. Why don't we take a detour into the hills? I always have a feeling someone may be listening or watching in town. And in the rue Lamartine.'

'Know what you mean. And have you noticed, Letty, that the house is never quite still at night? Whenever I wake in the small hours I seem to hear a door closing. At the risk of sounding like a gossiping girl – tell me, Letty, what do you make of Marie-Louise? You seem to have hit it off.'

At last! Here was the opportunity Letty had been waiting for. 'I like her,' she said warmly. 'I think she's an unusual girl. Clever, pretty, ambitious. Quite wasted on this town. But I'd have thought you'd have formed your own opinions by now, William. She doesn't exactly flee at your approach! I've been intrigued to see her interest in you developing.'

He stopped walking and turned to her in surprise. 'Interest in *me*? Oh, no. How could you have so misunderstood?'

'Well, at any rate, um, you know that you're always very welcome to make use of the motorcar, don't you, William?' she said awkwardly, and plunged on, fearing she was only making matters worse. 'It needn't be Marie-Louise you take out for a spin ... the mayor's second daughter is really very attractive – had you noticed? And her father's doing very well for himself. The local builder. He's just put up a rather splendid extension to the family home. Everyone seems to know you, William. I think you should consider settling down here.'

He seemed confused and unwilling to take the discussion further, compelling Letty to fall silent, hunting about for a change of subject.

221

'You were going to deliver a dreadful warning about my new friend at the château, William,' she reminded him.

He seemed relieved to take up the topic. 'Interesting! Fascinating, in fact. It took all day and I'm afraid I've worked up an enormous telephone bill for your father, but I managed it. I phoned a chap I was at school with and set out my problem. He knew various others in the City who each seemed to have a snapshot of our count and his activities. My friend pieced them all together and was himself astounded by his findings when he rang me back some hours later. Had you any idea, Letty, that d'Aubec is reputed to be a financial genius? Though some would have it that the count is under the tight control of a secretary . . .'

'Constantine – the man I told you about. Tight-lipped, as are they all – apart from the mother. Polite enough but wary. He doesn't much welcome my invasion, I think. I can't give an opinion of his abilities but he seems bright and he's certainly pretty thick with the count.'

'Well, whoever is responsible – the family firm has already made a fortune. My friend was full of information. Men as successful as d'Aubec soon begin to rouse interest. Experts shadow their every move, trying to analyse their technique. But, apparently, he moves in strange ways, wriggles along routes no one else is inclined to follow. And he doesn't just play the stock market – he buys up companies or acquires a controlling interest in the ones that take his fancy. My friend thinks he's spotted a trend, a pattern to all this activity. Bit of a puzzle.'

He took from his pocket a copy of an American newspaper. '*New York Times*, April 1927. This is an example of the sort of thing that has d'Aubec frothing at the mouth with excitement. He's reported to be making enquiries about the technique described here. I was lucky enough to find a copy of the newspaper in the library in Lyon and I stole it. Tell me what you make of it.'

Letty perched on a fence by the side of the road and began to read. 'This is a joke, surely?' She checked the date of the newspaper. 'Not April the first. But I can't believe this. Can you, William? Are we to understand that two months ago the president of the American Telephone and Telegraph Company not only sat at a telephone in New York and talked to Herbert Hoover in Washington two hundred miles away but,' she paused and looked at Gunning in astonishment, 'that he *saw* him speaking? He *watched* Hoover on a screen two and a half inches square? Not a film. An image transferred, like the sound, down a wire? By a series of electrical impulses. Good Lord! Whatever next?'

'I do believe it. And the American reactions to such a facility are nothing if not entertaining, if you read on. Mrs Hoover's comments are interesting. She can't see it catching on, apparently. Who would want to be seen by the party they were phoning? Why – a lady might be caught in her curlers!'

Letty looked at him steadily. 'The question *I'd* be asking, if I hadn't already dismissed this as magic . . . a Leonardo fantasy . . . a chapter from Jules Verne . . . is: If you took the camera – and there must be one at the other end? – up in a plane and ranged it over a battlefield, could you transmit the images to a commander below or two hundred miles away? And if so, how much of an advantage would *that* give?'

'Enormous. And if the camera and, indeed, the plane itself were owned, designed, and produced by a particular company? If the activities – whatever they are – of the people concerned were reported by a press owned by that same company? Newsreels shown in every town, courtesy of the company? My astute friend in London summed up d'Aubec's interests as communications, technical innovations, transport – the acquisition of power.'

'Power? But that is ultimately achieved through politics. Are we to expect d'Aubec to have himself elected into government . . . made a *député*? I really don't see him as a plodding conscientious representative of the people.'

'Oh, no. A *député*'s position is too near the bottom of the ladder and too time-consuming to be of interest to him. But he doesn't completely disregard political influence – he has several *députés* in his pocket.'

Letty snorted with disbelief. 'This is really all rather silly speculation, William. I only need to hear he has a controlling interest in the Dubosq armaments factory and I'll suspect he's out to conquer the world!' She began to laugh. 'A modern-day Alexander?'

Gunning did not join in her laughter. His expression was solemn. 'Dubosq *and* Armstrong's.'

Chapter Twenty-Four

The late afternoons brought relief from the heat and the labour and, after a shower and a change of clothes, Letty would wait for the arrival of Jules. She began to enjoy their journeys to the château, firmly seating herself in front next to the old groom and talking to him about the horses and his master. His discretion forbade him to gossip, but through the formality of his replies to her questions came a sense of deep admiration and loyalty for the family he served. And, she would have said, judging by his few remarks, he showed a particular devotion to the old count ess whom he called 'Madame Mère'.

More conversation followed as she was shown into the sitting room to take English tea with d'Aubec's mother. Here she scarcely needed to broach the subject of her interest – the mother was only too garrulously forthcoming on her son. Within a week Letty knew what had been the first words uttered by the infant Edmond – predictably, a command; she could have pointed out the gash in the gilded frame of a wall mirror where he had crashed his pedal-car; she could have judged his academic record – patchy. But she found that any questions she innocently put concerning Edmond's more recent exploits were deftly set aside, though always with a light touch of humour.

Each time she passed the portrait of Charlotte she paused, head on one side, interrogating the English count ess. She sighed. She could interpret the other woman's expression as nothing other than one of blissful happiness.

The teatime confidences would be cut short by the sound of boots along the corridor. The now familiar features would appear at the door and, excusing herself to the indulgently smiling countess, Letty would follow him to the library.

Side by side and working with perfect accord, they had devised a method of tracking their way through the books and papers which seemed to have been of greatest interest to her godfather. Most of the scripts were in Latin, which Letty understood better than d'Aubec; some were in an ancient form of French in the Burgundian dialect, which he was able to translate. She had found, to her surprise, that the count was a good listener and eager learner and he quickly caught on to Daniel's system of note-taking and commentary.

Scrupulously, Letty made d'Aubec account for everything in which he was conscious of her godfather showing an interest. Together they examined the plans of the château Edmond remembered him calling for, though these were only available for the nineteenth-century stable block, the chapel erected at the same time, and the twentieth-century improvements including the remodelling of the gardens.

But it was a delight in the study of the pages of the books, crackling with old age, which increasingly began to absorb Letty. And d'Aubec seemed to find himself captured by her enthusiasm. In unspoken agreement, they found themselves drawn to the long-dead monks' renderings of folk stories. D'Aubec had read out with obvious enjoyment some of the passages of bloodthirsty boasting of warriors from these hills, warriors who detailed with unholy relish the killings and ritual beheadings of the enemy – usually the dreaded Germani tribe – carried out during their cattle raids and tribal wars.

But there were softer passages of a lyrical beauty which caught his eye and, one evening, he had exclaimed and pushed a passage in front of her. Eager to share it, he had leaned close and murmured the lines which had so moved him.

'Listen, Laetitia! I've found a piece about a faery lady – it's a striking description!

> *Tall and straight as a spear, she stood in her green gown.*
> *She raised her arms which were white as the first snowfall*
> *and loosened her red-gold hair.*
> *It tumbled over her breasts, pure as swans, and fell about*
> *her knees.*
> *Her eyes were the blue of the cornflower*
> *And her cheeks held the blush of the foxglove.'*

Letty had covered her own pink cheeks with her hands and studied the improper text with exaggerated attention. His voice had been low and charged with an emotion and a wonder which had taken her by surprise. She glanced swiftly at his vivid face and tried to reconcile the image with that of the manipulative financier Gunning had sketched for her. She found she could not.

'It's lovely. An amazing piece to find here . . . I've come across something very like it somewhere . . . But, Edmond, can you imagine the effect on the poor old monks, celibate as they were, committing such profane thoughts to paper? Who were these men? Do you know anything about them?'

'Some came from other parts of Europe – Italy, Spain . . . some of them joined the order at an early age, no more than very young boys. They signed on for a settled life in turbulent times – to learn a trade – for devotional reasons – who knows? Many were country lads from these parts. They'd be taught to read and write and speak Latin according to their ability. Perhaps the Seigneur of the day directed them to write down these secular pieces to coincide with his own interests – and repay him for the summer's lodgings?'

Letty laughed. 'Are we saying that a distant d'Aubec was the first European publisher?'

'French publisher, perhaps. I'm certain the Romans beat him to it.'

* * *

By the end of the first week, Letty noticed that the pile of dictionaries she had stacked between her and d'Aubec had been dismantled. Other token barriers, artificially set up, had melted away: she was calling him by his Christian name and talking easily to him as she would to a trusted colleague. As the end of each day arrived she would drowsily rejoin Jules for the journey back to town, happy, excited, and looking forward no further than the next meeting. And steeling herself for the inevitable encounter with Gunning, who always seemed, no matter how cleverly she attempted to avoid him, to be there, in her way, frowning his displeasure, perpetually dissatisfied with her revelations.

On her thirteenth evening Letty hurried to the château's drawing room. She entered to find the countess looking anxiously through the open window and no sign of Edmond.

'Ah! Laetitia! Come! Hold my hand and help me watch! They are an hour late and already I am quite certain that my Edmond is dead! I hate it when he uses that infernal machine!'

Mystified, Letty joined her at the window.

'He's gone off to Lyon with his secretary in the Hispano-Suiza. They are on the road at this moment. At least I hope they are on the road . . . they may already be lying dead at the foot of some precipice . . . These big cars are most unsuitable for our country lanes.'

Sensing that the countess's concern was, though excessive, genuinely felt, Letty talked reassuringly of the sterling qualities of the motorcar – its reliability and strength; she mentioned the skill and resource of the two motorists. This produced a sceptical shrug, but at least she agreed to leave her post at the window when Letty briskly noted that tea had been laid for them.

'Ah, yes, my dear, pour some tea and entertain me. Take a mother's mind off her scurrilous son. Tell me how your search, your mysterious quest, is going. For nearly two weeks you and Edmond have been shut up together in the

library. Working, you say.' The countess arched her eyebrows in mischief. 'Laughing, chattering, and having a
happy time, *I'd* say. Have you found what you're looking
for yet? Have you uncovered the missing pay packets of
Caesar's army? The bones of Mary Magdalene? Surely you
have made a discovery of some sort?'

'As a matter of fact, madame, I rather think we have,'
Letty replied carefully. She considered for a moment, then
decided to confide: 'Though something neither of us
expected to find. In fact, I think that later this evening we
should have something very special to tell you.'

'At last! Are you telling me you've seen the light? Well,
thank goodness for that! I was beginning to think you'd
never get there and I was seriously considering banging
your two stupid heads together. I was despairing that poor
Daniel's scheme – our scheme – would have come to
nothing.'

'*Your* scheme, madame?' Letty asked, bewildered.

'Yes! Shall I now confess? We devised it together! Oh, it
began as no more than the self-indulgent imaginings of
two fond old parents – you know . . . "Wouldn't it be
wonderful if . . ." and then I realized that with Daniel the
fancies were taking on a more purposeful tone. Had he
then already begun to fear for his life? To tell you the truth,
Laetitia, I had thought that perhaps he was ill and was
preparing, as we elderly do, for an efficient leave-taking.
Setting his house in order, doing what he could to influence the one dearest to him. And now, at last, it seems to
have produced results. Daniel would have been so
relieved.'

Deeply puzzled, Letty decided to listen on to the countess's ravings and hope to make some sense of them. Perhaps Paradee had it right and the old girl was indeed mad.

'He knew your character, Letty. He knew coercion,
suggestion, or even recommendation was likely to send
you skittering off in the opposite direction!'

Letty frowned, disconcerted by this accurate reading of
her character and uncertain where it was leading.

229

'Daniel *lured* you here! To us! You could never resist a puzzle, he said, and he was right. He didn't warn me that you could be so *unseeing*, though, and would fail to recognize a treasure when you had it in your grasp. But, in the end, he has succeeded. Both his aims are fulfilled.'

'Both his aims?' Letty echoed faintly. 'I have no idea of what aims you speak, madame. He never expressed them to *me*.'

The countess's expression was one of teasing disbelief. 'Well, his *first* intent, which perhaps you pretend to have already forgotten about, is that he should provide for your financial security by means of his will. Yes – he confided his arrangements to me. You are a lucky girl, my dear, and were much loved. But that was the easier part and involved no more than the effort of signing a piece of paper in his lawyer's office. The *second* was more of a problem. I know he wanted to ensure your *happiness* . . .' She sighed. 'Now, *can* any interfering old relation presume to do that for a modern young girl? Daniel was determined to try! I think at the end, with time running out, he took the only action available to him. And what he proposed was so blindingly obvious! My dear, you are still showing me a puzzled face! I hadn't taken you for a coy girl . . .?' She paused, allowing time for a show of enlightenment that did not come. 'You push me to spell it out? Very well! He saw your future *here*, Letty, with us. With Edmond.'

Confused and lost for words, Letty could only exclaim: 'My future? Here? With Edmond? But what you suggest is impossible!'

The countess appeared puzzled by her outburst. 'Are you quite sure of that? Would Edmond say the same, I wonder, if I asked him? I know my own son! And it's blindingly obvious to everyone! It's even spoken of in the scullery and the stables! And with warm approval, I may say! Laetitia, the boy's in love with you. Please don't pretend you haven't noticed!' Her face crinkled with a smile of maternal indulgence. 'My son has many good qualities – many – but patience and an interest in academic research

230

are not among them. It takes a very particular kind of allure to chain him to a pile of dusty old books in a library every evening for a fortnight! I would never have thought it possible! I have not, of course, put this before him yet ... I would not wish to meddle ...'

She caught Letty's cynical look and burst out laughing.

'You speak of meddling?' Letty could not disguise her anger. 'If I understand you rightly, I have never heard of a more blatant piece of meddling than this by Daniel! The old villain!' she said, venting her rage on him when good manners would not allow her to direct it at her equally culpable host. 'How dared he? By what right did he think he could play God in my life?'

The countess wagged a finger at her, knowingly. 'Just exactly what he predicted would be your reaction! But you ask by what right ...' For a moment her confidence deserted her and she went on slowly, feeling her way: 'My dear, I may have misunderstood, over-interpreted a relationship gleaned solely from Daniel's perspective, and I know you will correct me if I have this wrong ... People correct me with increasing frequency these days ...' she added with a wry smile. 'But it was evident to me that he assumed a much greater role in your life than the traditional one of godparent – you know, remembering your birthday, supplying you with a white prayer book for your confirmation ...'

Disturbed by Letty's truculent silence and momentarily at a loss for words herself, the old lady went to fiddle with an arrangement of lilies on a table, hiding her face from Laetitia. When she turned to her again, she had achieved the level of control she sought; her normally expressive features had been wiped clean of animation. She had steeled herself, Letty guessed, to speak a truth the reception of which could only be uncertain. A truth which might even be unwelcome. Letty had seen the same expression on the face of her admired headmistress: *This pains me more than it pains you, my dear, but you know I have no alternative but to ...*'

She waited, puzzled and alarmed, to hear the countess's pronouncement.

'Laetitia, my friend Daniel regarded you with the affection of a father for his only child.'

The simple sentence whistled over and landed with the shattering effect of a whizbang.

The countess waited for Letty's response.

In her uncertainty and with an increasing feeling of dread, Letty cobbled together a reply of sorts: 'Well, of course ... yes ... he would be likely to, wouldn't he? Daniel was a bachelor. He was much in my life when I was a child. My father was posted abroad with his regiment for long periods and my mother never accompanied him – her health was never wonderful and she hated hot climates. My earliest memories are of Daniel coming through the door with his arms full of presents ...' Her voice petered out as she struggled to understand, to steady the feeling that the ground was opening under her feet.

There had flashed into her mind a long-forgotten memory. She must have been very young because she'd been playing with a doll, sitting on the window seat looking out down the drive. She'd seen his car driving up and had shouted eagerly, 'Daddy! Daddy's here!' Her mother had turned pale and dropped her sewing, while Letty charged to the door and flung herself at Daniel when he entered. Of course, the misunderstandings of a solitary child were easily explained and the relationships were subsequently untangled to everyone's satisfaction. She had never referred to the incident again and she did not do so now. None of the countess's business.

'It must have been very confusing for you, my dear. What damage we adults, we parents, unconsciously do with the good intention of sparing the children the truth.'

'Well, no actually,' Letty lied. 'I had two fathers and loved them both. When my mother died they were both distraught. Daniel and Sir Richard were always good friends and her death brought them even closer. Daniel moved in and lived with us, sharing the thankless task of keeping me on the rails.'

'I had guessed as much,' said the countess. 'So – what more natural than that this caring man should, to the last, have your welfare in the forefront of his mind? Daniel loved it here – the château, the estate . . . and I'm certain he had an affection for Edmond. They had disagreements, of course – you'd expect it of two such opinionated men and my son can be quite unpalatable at times, I know it. But I believe their friendship and admiration for each other ran deep. They shared the same values.'

Thoughts whirling out of control, Letty was relieved to hear the growling of a powerful engine as the big car swung into view and braked on the gravelled sweep in front of the château. D'Aubec stepped out and strode, laughing, towards them, his secretary Constantine following, carrying a briefcase. Expensive suit, white shirt, and silk tie pulled casually to one side, Edmond was hardly recognizable in his business clothes. He came in through the French window, dismissed Constantine with a few crisp instructions, then hugged the countess, his eyes seeking out Laetitia over the top of his mother's head.

'I know, Maman – you were imagining me dead by the roadside. It was a long meeting and I ought to have spent the night in Lyon but – too much to do here. I wanted to get back.'

'You look tired, darling. How did it go, your business with André?'

'You know André! But it went well! Yes, I really think – well! Dashed frustrating for most of the time and I had to concede on quantity, but the sum we agreed on looks acceptable. More than acceptable!'

Letty was glad to remain silently in the background, lost in her own turmoil, while they discussed the details of the business deal. Mother and son laughed together in a self-congratulatory way.

'You'll soon have those rose diamonds, Maman!'

Like a pair of pirates, Letty thought, *gloating over their loot! How many more jewels does the countess need*? and she busied herself with the teapot, suddenly out of place in their company. In an instant the goodwill and – yes – friendship they had built up over the past weeks had dissolved.

After tea Edmond excused himself and Letty started off for the library. In the quiet room she had the time she needed to order her thoughts and adjust her expression before d'Aubec appeared. Now in box-cloth trousers and soft shirt, he looked much more like the man she had grown close to over the last days. 'That's better! I was a bit overawed when you looked as though you meant business!'

He used her sudden warmth towards him to lean over and kiss her cheek lightly before settling at the table. More disturbed than she was ready to admit, Letty fell silent, unexpectedly sad that the closeness that had developed between them was about to be cut short. Had he any suspicion of his mother's insane schemes? Catching her speculative glance, he grinned and winked, fidgeted in his pocket, and held out his hand across the table.

'I wasn't so busy in Lyon I didn't have time to do a bit of shopping! I had you in my mind all the time, and, I regret to say, a goofy grin on my face. Disastrous! André must have wondered what was wrong with me. I let him get away with far too low a price. But I bought you a present. Something you'll like!'

Letty tensed, then held out her right hand, preparing an embarrassed refusal. But no jeweller's box with winking diamond ring or pearl necklace was on offer. She stared in surprise at the cellophane-wrapped confectioner's package.

'Nougat! With almonds! From Montélimar! My favourite. Oh, thank you, Edmond.'

Well, this answered her question. The count was not a man to do his wooing with a lump of nougat. She began to suspect that young Edmond had no idea of the fate being proposed for him.

*   *   *

234

It was seven o'clock and the day still brilliant when she closed the last of the notebooks. 'Well, there we are. It's finished. Just one puzzle remaining, I think. One document I can't account for: this one from 1810 or thereabouts. Any idea what it means? Does it mean anything? It seems to be sketches and a summary of works to be carried out here at the château . . . after the return of the family from exile in England. Part of the statement of re-possession, I would expect. Rather grand plans for the stable building and the chapel . . . very specific . . . drawn up by an architect, I'd say, judging from the phrasing. And, here at the bottom, in flowing script – in a different hand from the bureaucratic one that drew up the body of the document, I think – there's a sentence that doesn't fit with the foregoing specification.' She pointed it out.

'Looks like a doodle,' said Edmond, intrigued. 'You know . . . boring meeting . . . "Let's all look at note twenty-seven subsection eight, shall we? Can the architect please elucidate . . ." Yawn, yawn. Scribble, scribble. Impressive handwriting, though. Could it be a quotation? Seems to be in old French – the spelling's old even for the nineteenth century.'

'Daniel seems to have thought the same,' said Letty. 'Look here, I've found another sheet in his handwriting where he seems to have been working out a translation. Surely this is a commentary, don't you think?' She read out a sentence: '"With the Lady of Ancient Days lie the worldly belongings of our Holy Queen."'

'"Holy Queen"? Well, that will be "Notre Dame" – Our Lady, the Virgin Mary, patron saint of the abbey, and her "worldly belongings" . . .? Check the French. It does say "belongings", does it? Not "remains"? *Les biens temporels.* Hmm . . . yes . . . well, only Our Lady would, by extension, be regarded as the guardian of the abbey treasure – that could be regarded as "earthly" all right.' Edmond tried to keep a rising excitement out of his voice. 'But don't forget that the town is called Fontigny Sainte-Reine – "Holy Queen" – another and probably much earlier reference to Mary.'

'Wait a moment, Edmond. Abbey treasure, did you say?'

'Ah. Just another of our Burgundian tales. According to tradition, the citizens didn't just sit about waiting for the arrival of Napoleon's wrecking crews. The precious and movable elements of the abbey's riches disappeared. It had been the wealthiest monastic establishment in Europe – its abbots lived like princes and were often criticized for their fondness for precious objects and high living. By the sixteenth century, though, the abbey was already in decline, and I really doubt there was much left to pillage by the end of the eighteenth.

'But who knows what the attics and cellars of the town conceal? Pieces do pop out from cover every once in a while. There's a well-known local story that there are quantities of gold and silver work hidden away somewhere in the vicinity. There isn't a child in the town who hasn't dug, in hope, in his father's back garden. But who's this other guardian – the "Lady of Ancient Days"?' he said. 'Never heard of her! Seems to bring us round full circle to our useless old friend Lady Uffington.'

'Not useless, perhaps. Remember my godfather was writing that postcard to *me*. I think he was simply directing me here – to the house of d'Aubec. The goddess on horseback is – you say – your coat of arms. Heraldically, she represents *you* . . . your possessions . . . all this. Daniel seems to have been directing me to Brancy.' She paused and, hoping to needle him into an admission of some sort, added: 'I can't imagine why.'

'No. Irritating, I agree. I do wonder why Daniel couldn't just have written *me* a note and left it on the mantelpiece,' said d'Aubec testily. '"Edmond, old boy, welcome back from Morocco. Now, go and dig in the stables where I've chalked a cross on the floor . . ." Something of that sort.'

'Yes, of course,' said Letty. 'But he clearly thought leaving notes around the place a dangerous procedure or he would have done that. I'd guess he had his doubts about the staff here. Have you been *infiltrated*, I wonder, Edmond?' she asked in a teasing voice, hoping to conceal

236

her thoughts. If her godfather had gone to this trouble, perhaps he couldn't trust d'Aubec himself to do the right thing by his discovery? It was through *her* he intended to involve the academic world, the solid and impeccably respectable world of the London and Paris museums. And she thought she knew exactly whom to contact when she could get back to London.

The time had come to tell d'Aubec the truth.

'Edmond, there *is* a treasure here. It's not the obvious kind . . . jewels secreted in the cellar for centuries and that sort of thing. And we're not going to be led to the Holy Grail, a piece of the true cross, or any of the other legendary things buried hereabouts. But what we have here in our hands makes my head spin! It's very, very important. Unique. And much more valuable than any cache of Roman gold!'

Chapter Twenty-Five

'What can you mean?'

'These,' she said simply. 'The books themselves. You've read through some of them without, I think, quite recognizing them for what they are. The pile over there – the prayer books and Books of Hours alone – are worth a fortune but it's these here, the folio vellum manuscripts, that are uniquely valuable. I can hardly believe what I have in my hands!'

'The folk stories? Delightful, I agree,' he said, uncertain and not quite able to catch her mood.

'Oh, these are more than folk stories, Edmond! History, philosophy, theology, and magic, and I think I know the source. And it's the source that's making me shake with excitement! Have you heard of the stories of the Celts handed down through Welsh and Irish manuscripts? *The White Book of Rhydderch* . . . the poets of Munster . . . we even know some of their names. They had a rich mythology pre-dating Christianity, and so important was it to these people that it was preserved and passed on orally, to be finally – thank God! – written down by those literate Christian monks who clung to existence in a hostile environment. Perched on sea-swept cliffs, islands in the Atlantic . . . at the mercy of Viking raiders . . .' D'Aubec was smiling at her enthusiasm, but she pressed on. 'They took the trouble to record the stories. They must, most of them, have grown up listening to them, hearing them as we hear nursery rhymes. The earliest of the Irish sagas hark back to a time when their god-like ancestors were in possession of the island. They called them the *Tuatha Dé Danaan* – the tribes of the Goddess Danae.'

'Danae? Should I have heard of her?'

'One of the ancient names for the Mother Goddess.'

'And what has this to do with the monks of Fontigny?'

'The same scene. The monks could write. It's as simple as that. The Welsh and Irish culture was preserved, though sketchily, and is available to us, but it's always been thought that no trace remained of the Celts of old Gaul. And that is a tremendous loss, as this country was the centre of their culture, according to scholars, including Father Anselme.'

'Culture, you say? But weren't the Celts a warrior society – bands of barbarians – and not too concerned with the finer qualities of life? The classical writers are silent on the more civilized aspects of their society, aren't they?'

'Of course. They did what victors always do – they undervalued the opposition and edited out of their accounts any reference to creativity and culture. Though they do stress the courage and fighting skills of the enemies of Rome. They were afraid of these huge, fair, tattooed men who charged naked into battle. And these warriors harried the classical world mercilessly; they got as far south as Delphi and sacked Rome itself. No wonder they became stereotypical bogeymen for the classical writers. But they had, we're beginning to discover, a very fine side to their nature. Their metal-working shows an artistic flair far more impressive than that of the classical world to some eyes – certainly to mine. They had a high culture of religious belief and a developed literature. We don't know exactly where their origins are, but the foundations of their society may well have been laid two thousand years BC. They pre-date the Romans.'

'Does Caesar have a view?'

'He certainly does! A rather close-up view. He killed a million of them. He confronted Vercingetorix of the Aedui tribe in pitched battle at Alésia not so far from here, and he could well have lost. But he too prefers to restrict his comments to the Celts' behaviour on the battlefield. The more formidable he makes them appear, the greater his own achievement, of course. He does, however, mention their religion, and is one of our main sources of information on the druids, who controlled the lives of the Celtic tribes. We know tantalizingly little about these gentlemen.'

'The druids? Their priesthood, you mean?'

'More than that. They were the practitioners of the religion, certainly, but much else. They were the lawgivers, the doctors, the bards, the intellectual force of the society. It took twenty years of learning to become a druid. Children would be sent away for training, to acquire the ancient lore and the facility to recite it. Yes, recite. The essence of their culture was passed down by word of mouth. Not a word was written, and that's a puzzle because the druids did understand Greek and could probably have committed their history and literature and science to vellum or papyrus.'

'What secrets must have been lost!'

'We can only guess and regret. In Ireland, there were storytellers, the *filíd*, who, it's said, originated in Gaul, and they were a sort of light through the Dark Ages, a bridge, I suppose, between the Celts and the medieval society. They had an immense repertoire – there's a record in an eighth century text of one of these *filíd* who was employed by the king of Ulster to recite stories and poems by the fireside in winter, and he was able to keep up the flow from the feast of Samhain to the feast of Beltane. That's six months! A lot of stories!'

D'Aubec reached for one of the large leather-backed books and opened it with more than his usual deference. 'And you're telling me that the Gallo-Celtic stories may have been preserved, by word of mouth, over the centuries and lasted until they were finally heard and committed to paper, well, calf-skin, by men who could write and illuminate and who were encouraged to do this by . . . well, who knows? And I've been struggling to read them!' He began to shake with laughter. 'I'd like to think it was some remote

240

ancestor of mine who was responsible but that's probably a romantic idea. Am I holding in my hands something approaching the importance of Homer's *Iliad*, do you suppose? Good Lord! No wonder Daniel was getting so agitated! But what exactly do we do now?' He frowned a warning. 'They're not going off to London! Don't think it!'

'No,' Letty agreed. 'But they must be preserved and translated. There are experts in Paris – I bet you already know some of their names – who would faint with excitement at the idea of getting their hands on them.'

'Laetitia, will you stay on here?' His tone was formal. 'I agree that these books must be published, the knowledge made public. Come and work here full-time on the books. Finish what Daniel started.'

'Heavens, no! I'm just an enthusiastic amateur. And I've been staggering along, following Daniel's notes. My own knowledge wouldn't take me to the end of the first page! You must entrust them to a professional. You don't want me!'

'But I do want you, Miss Talbot. And you know how spoilt I am – I always get what I want.' He spoke lightly then added, more seriously, 'But I do understand what you're saying. I'll keep them safe until I can get someone down from Paris.'

It was still early and Letty would very willingly have gone on talking and speculating about the texts, reading and exchanging ideas, but d'Aubec was beginning to pack up his things and tidy up the piles of books. Sensing her disappointment, he looked at her speculatively for a moment then said, 'Why don't we just leave all this? It's a wonderful evening and I've kept you cruelly cooped up here for nearly two weeks. Let's have some fresh air. Come to the stables – there's something I want you to see! Something very special!'

Chapter Twenty-Six

He led the way out to the stables and down the long line of stalls until they arrived at Dido's loose box. The mare snorted gently and slathered his hands with an affectionate and trusting tongue. 'There!' he said. 'All the dressings are off. She's healed beautifully and is longing to have some exercise again. Will you ride her to the top of the coach road? I'll come with you on old Hannibal. He won't mind going slowly.' Letty was introduced to Hannibal, a blue roan, going over a bit and distinctly past mark of mouth but a noble and friendly animal. D'Aubec called for the chief stable lad, Marcel, who, unusually, was standing in earshot, and told him to saddle up the horses. And then: 'Is all in order?' he asked, mysteriously. Marcel gave a conspiratorial nod, grinned at Letty, then went off to see to the horses.

'What are you two up to?' she asked suspiciously.

'Preparing another surprise for you! Impossible to offer this one gift-wrapped but I think you'll be impressed.'

Edmond took her hands lightly in his and smiled down at her. The dark eyes were full of boyish mischief. Irresistible. She found herself responding with an eager anticipation she couldn't quite disguise with feeble protests: 'Not sure I like surprises . . . nougat quite enough for one day, surely . . .'

'You're to have a small reward for the hours of work you've done on my books. Very small. Tiny!' The smile broadened to a grin. 'Now – men ask themselves this all the time: What do you give a girl who has everything?

Well, quite obviously – more of what she likes. Come and see!'

He walked ahead of her to a small room near the entrance, a groom's quarters, she would have guessed, and opened the door an inch at a time, peering inside. Having spun out the suspense, he flung the door fully open.

'Here they are!'

For a moment Letty was speechless, enthralled by the group in the straw that covered the floor. Six large pups were jumping and wriggling, snuffling and annoying beyond reason the mother dog. One little chap headed at once for the open door and almost squeezed through before being scooped up by d'Aubec. The mother gave a warning growl and he went to place it with a soothing word back at her side.

'I've never seen anything like them before. What are they? Mongrels?' Letty asked.

'Certainly not! And you're lucky to see them at all! The breed very nearly died out in the war. They're *Bergers de Picardie*. Herd dogs. Very ancient. Your heroes, the Celts, bred them.'

Letty tiptoed through the scrambling puppies over to the bitch and introduced herself, talking in a crooning voice and gently offering her hand under the woolly chin. As this was received graciously, she caressed the upright ears, admiring the large black nose and bright eyes watchful behind the tousled mop of face hair. The brindled grey coat, when she was allowed to stroke it, was rough and deep. A dog that would survive well the harsh Burgundy winters.

'As you see, they're ready to go out to their new owners,' said d'Aubec. 'Poor Bella's had quite enough of them!'

'You've managed to find good homes for them?'

'It's never difficult. Local farmers clamour for them. Five out of the six you see here will be collected tomorrow.'

'You're keeping one back for yourself?'

'No. I want *you* to have it, Laetitia. A gift. Choose whichever one you like.'

Letty tried to control her rush of pleasure. 'A charming idea, Edmond, but I couldn't possibly ...' But her eyes were already running over the swarm of silky-coated puppies, admiring and assessing.

'Nonsense! And I'll bet I can guess which one you'll choose.' He waited for her to commit herself to a choice but as she still resisted, shaking her head, he pressed her further: 'That dark one over there? Yes, he's the one!'

'No! You're wrong! I'd have the intrepid little escaper who got between your feet when you opened the door. Anyone who can see a chance of tripping *you* up gets my vote!' She leaned into the scrum of puppies and picked up the one she had her eye on. 'Fawn with a white front,' she observed. 'Ouch! And with very sharp teeth! Strong and spirited. This will be a good dog, Edmond. I'd keep this one, if I were you.'

'So be it. I'll inform Marcel. Are you going to name him?'

Letty shook her head and d'Aubec's smile faded. Naming a dog was the first sign of acceptance and he recognized her gesture for the decisive refusal it was. 'Then *I* shall give him one. Let's call him "Dagobert" – a good Burgundian name. But, Letty, I mean you to have him. On one condition: that he stays here. This is a breed that works hard in the fields but it's highly intelligent, it loves human company, and becomes devoted to its master and its mistress. A herd dog, remember – it doesn't like to see its humans straying off. You should be aware! Now you've got acquainted ... this dog will know you next time you come ... You can give him back to Bella, who's growing anxious, and we'll get on with our ride. I see the horses are ready.'

The sun was glowing richly on the hills ahead of them as they first walked, then with Dido gaining confidence, trotted down the slope away from the château and began the steady descent to the valley beyond. A wonderful evening and, in other circumstances, Laetitia would have

244

felt herself completely in tune with it, blessed to be here in this corner of France which she acknowledged was weaving her into its enchantment. Critically she asked herself how much of the excitement she was feeling was due to the countryside and how much to her companion: a man who alarmed but attracted her, a man whom she despaired of ever truly knowing, distorted as his image continually was in her eyes by Daniel's shadowy, necromancing presence.

And d'Aubec's mother had sabotaged, with her over-hasty revelations, what was to be her last evening with Edmond, her last chance properly to understand him. Should she be influenced by the extraordinary claim with all the undercurrent of insinuation and deceit? Laetitia needed time to delve back into her own past, searching her memory for badly understood childhood impressions; she needed time to uncover and face something she had always known and ignored. Something uncomfortable. But, in a contrary way, she found she wanted to seek d'Aubec's assurance that he knew nothing of Daniel's alleged plans for her. She wanted to hear his gasp of surprise when she told him, and his hot denial that he was involved in the deception. She wanted to hear his incredulous laughter warning her that his poor old mother was surely on the rocks and breaking up fast, and Letty was to smile and humour her. No harm meant. Just the romantic imaginings of an elderly lady.

She glanced sideways at him to find that he was watching her, warm and concerned. She instinctively returned his smile and her heart gave a warning thump. Oh, Lord! What had happened to the immunity she had boasted of to Marie-Louise? The defences she had assured Paradee she had? Had she heard a single one of Gunning's warnings? She wouldn't be the first woman to have fallen for a rogue, but surely that could never happen to someone with her common sense and awareness?

She urged herself to take the thoughtful, adult approach and put her feelings for Edmond d'Aubec under a microscope. And what she saw there was: friendship – certainly;

admiration – yes, but qualified; physical attraction – undeniable; love? There she stopped. An unconscious twitch on the reins communicated itself to the horse, its reaction reflecting her own uncertainty. Love? How could she know? What was her yardstick, where her co-ordinates? She rejected as unhelpful guides both the emotion she had felt for the White Fox of her early years and the almost cerebral awakening at the touch of her scientist. She mistrusted even more the state of being in love as portrayed in novels. She'd met lady novelists. Her problem would not have arisen in an earlier age – if a marriage with the dark lord had been arranged for her in feudal times, she'd have counted herself lucky to be his fair lady. Ah, well . . . Edmond d'Aubec would never take her heart by frontal assault, she thought whimsically, picturing him all too easily in armour and plumed helmet. But perhaps he knew of other, more stealthy ways of approach. She grinned at the intriguing idea.

'Something amusing you, Talbot?' He poked her in the ribs with his riding crop.

'No . . . I was just thinking about . . . fortifications. There's a wonderful view of your château from here. I was trying to trace the line of the original walls and work out whether there may have been room for a Celtic *oppidum* on the flat top. Something on the lines of Bibracte, perhaps? I think, you know, there would have been space enough for a small town, and you're right on an ancient trade route from the tin mines of Cornwall down to Marseilles. And, have you ever noticed? . . . it's more obvious from up there now the wheat's fully grown . . . that there are field markings down here in the valley. Small – half- to five-acre Celtic field outlines, I'd say . . .'

He reined Hannibal to a halt with a groan. 'Will you take your nose off the historical scent for a while? I brought you up here to get away from all that. I would have been proud to take you out to dinner in town tonight, to show you off. And you've certainly earned it, but I think you would have refused to be seen in my company.'

246

'Edmond, how can you be so unaware? Everyone knows I've been coming here to see you almost every evening since I arrived in Fontigny. What do you suppose they think I'm doing here? Teaching your mother needlepoint? It's just as well I have an alternative identity to hide behind – I'm afraid my reputation was shot to pieces the first evening I spent with you. I expect you've ruined many?'

'Ruined? Some women have been honoured and delighted to have been observed in my company!'

'And why have you never married one of these grateful ladies? I'd have thought a fellow as dynastically minded as you, would, by now, have been busy ensuring that the line would continue. I'm amazed that you haven't a whole troupe of little d'Aubecs walking behind you learning how to swagger!'

He looked frostily at her. 'None of my "grateful ladies", as you so unkindly call them, would have been suitable for me. But you're quite right. As a matter of fact you touch, in your usual insensitive way, on an issue of pressing importance to me. Many people are of the opinion that I should marry.' He thought seriously for a moment then added, 'I'm twenty-eight years old and I've led an interesting life; yes, I could well settle down now. In fact, Laetitia, I think of it more and more often. My mother is weary of helping me to run such a grand establishment – she would be delighted to hand over her châtelaine's keys. She has probably confided her concerns to you? The house needs a mistress, children racing down the corridors as I used to do with my cousins, ponies in the stables again . . .'

Letty began to bite her lips, casting about for emollient phrases of rejection.

'Well . . . the next time I ask Gabrielle to marry me, I'm confident that she'll say yes.'

'Gabrielle?' said Laetitia. 'Who's Gabrielle?'

'My cousin. I think I may have mentioned her? The family have been trying to marry us off for years,' he said with a dismissive shrug. 'I told you I had to go to Lyon tomorrow. We shall be staying at my uncle's house, and my cousins François and Gabrielle will be there. We always have a sort of Family Annual General Meeting at this time of year. We own a lot of property between us, we have many commercial interests, and there are important affairs to be decided. You remind me of my duties at a good moment, Laetitia. Yes, perhaps this year I will add an extra item to the agenda ... The Question of the Dynastic Succession,' he said, and, kicking up Hannibal, he moved on.

'Wait! Edmond! I think Dido's gone far enough!' she called after him.

'Dido is doing very well and enjoying the ride,' he called back. 'Can I say the same for you? How are your spirits, Laetitia?'

'Never higher!' she shouted back, and set off after him.

They worked their way along a twisting old green trackway which she thought was taking them back, in a loop, towards the outcrop of the château. The huge mound, bristling with military fortifications, was visible from every angle in this countryside, and whenever she looked up it seemed her eye was challenged by its imposing presence. They emerged once again into the sunshine before he stopped. 'We'll get off here!' he announced, dismounting, and taking the horses by the bridle, he led them off the path and through a stand of stunted oak trees.

'Where are we going?'

'To a favourite place of mine. I discovered it when I was a child and I come back often when I'm feeling sad or angry. It has a calming atmosphere which always does me good. Perhaps it will work its magic on you, Laetitia. I am not a total insensitive – I do notice that you have been pre-occupied this evening ... anxious ... not yourself. I would like to think you are distressed at the idea of my leaving you behind for a few days.' His sudden grin defused the sharp remark that came to mind.

A few yards farther, bursting through a clump of fra-grant juniper bushes, they came upon a small glade. It was a circular space of close-cropped, springy turf, surrounded

248

by short-growing oak trees and dotted with yellow stonecrop and pink rock roses. The side farthest from them was closed off by a low cliff of red-gold rock, and from the rock jetted a spurt of pure spring water which gurgled into a stone trough and spilled over back through the rocks and underground again.

The horses made for this at once. When they'd had their fill Edmond led them off and hitched them to a branch. Turning back into the clearing, he stopped at the sight of Laetitia, who had been drawn straight to the spring and was playing with the water, drinking from cupped hands and cooling her hot brow then raising full hands and gasping as the water ran down her arms.

He watched her in silence for a moment, seeing her silhouetted against the dying sun, hair the colour of the rock and arms gleaming. She turned, all hostile feelings dissolved away by the magic of the glade, and saw him staring at her.

'I love your special place, Edmond! It's a holy place. I can feel it.'

'And you are its spirit, Laetitia. It recognizes you,' he said softly, and began to move towards her.

The last melancholy note of a thrush died away and did not come again. The air was still with the expectant hush of an audience just silenced by three warning raps. At last the sun dipped below the surrounding hills and Letty shivered. Not quite sure how she had allowed herself to be led so smoothly into this remote and Celtic scene, she was starkly aware of his intentions. Aware also of her own treacherous thought – Why not walk towards him? She judged the space between them. Four steps would take her into his arms and into his life for a little longer, perhaps forever. The water which had trickled down her body in a cooling shower now clung, hot, to her skin; her breathing was unsteady, the dark man filling her horizon no longer a threat but a desired object. Hers if she chose him. She was aware of a rush of power through her limbs, a playful confidence. He moved again towards her, arms reaching out,

and she saw him afresh, clearly, the distorting mist of suspicion melted away: a suppliant, loving and beloved.

Three steps.

A piercing whicker of fear from the white mare ripped
through the silence, speaking to her directly. Startled, Letty
turned to see her tugging at her halter, eyes rolling in
terror, hooves waltzing.

'It's getting dark, Edmond. There's something out there
spooking Dido, I think. I'll lead her back over the next bit,
it's rather rough for her.'

She started towards the horses but her arm was seized
as she attempted to pass him. 'Never mind the bloody
horse! You're perfectly well aware of what I'm offering and
what I want in return,' he muttered in her ear, holding her
close. 'Aware of, and, I would have said, eager for. But I
see I've misjudged the moment and perhaps even the place
– dammit! And I risk exposing myself to a rejection. You
know me well enough by now to understand that my pride
will not countenance a rebuff!'

'You're quite wrong, Edmond – I don't understand what
you're saying. You have nothing to offer me and I have
nothing to give you. In fact, I'll tell you straight – you and
the countess between you have thrown me into total confusion. You tell me you are to marry this . . . Gabrielle? Well
– you'd better confide in your mother, then. She appears
not to be aware of your plans. Indeed, she has schemes of
her own, to marry you off to me in a medieval way! A little
project dreamed up, she tells me, by herself and Daniel. It's
all for our own good, apparently. And it's confidently
expected that we will be very happy.'

Instead of releasing her, his grip tightened. 'Oh, no!
Damn it! I specifically asked her not to . . .' His voice trailed
away in confusion.

'You *knew* this? You stand there, a stranger, claiming to
know more about me than I know myself ? Are you colluding with your mother . . . with my godfather . . . in this?
I hadn't taken you for anyone's puppet, Edmond.'

'I think for myself. I act in my own interests!' he

exploded, clearly rattled. 'My mother – your fathers, my cousins, the whole boiling – they can all go to hell! We don't need to listen to anyone, Laetitia! Who cares what anyone else thinks, wants, advises, requires, or expects? I'm fed up with being told what I may and may not do! I know very well what I want and soon you'll know what you want and it will be the same thing. Why are you laughing?'

'I was just thinking that your grove doesn't seem to be working its magic this evening. It's rather eerily exaggerating the differences between us, driving us farther apart. I'm increasingly tearful and petulant and you are shaping up to be the insensitive brute I'd always suspected you to be.'

He was instantly contrite. He sighed and moved a lock of damp hair gently from her face. 'Forgive me. It's not easy . . . Making a proposal that you think is bound to be rejected . . . well . . . it leaves a fellow a bit exposed, you know. Not used to that. But I'm not the clod you describe. I concede that all this,' he waved a hand at the surrounding countryside, 'is intimidating. Scares me sometimes,' he lied unconvincingly. 'But you're right. Not quite ourselves this evening, either of us, are we? And perhaps it's too late to retrieve your goodwill. But I don't give up. Ever. And I have more patience than you give me credit for. Laetitia – there's something I want you to do for me.'

Feeling her begin to shiver in the night air, he took off his jacket and put it around her shoulders. Holding her firmly by the upper arms he bent his head to look her in the eye. 'I want you, while we're away, to assume my mother's duties of châtelaine here. The run of the house, the bunch of keys – literally! – all the trappings. A room will be prepared for you and the staff left behind will be told to take their orders from you. You will have to come up to visit your dog, anyway.'

He smiled to see her mystification. 'I am, of course, showing myself to be exactly what you have suspected: manipulative, scheming, and thoroughly selfish. I want you to have the time, unencumbered by my presence, wagging like a spaniel at your heels the whole while, to fall in love with the house, with my possessions, with the spirit of the place. You already love me, Laetitia,' he said with a grin that acknowledged and mocked his own over-confidence. 'It shouldn't be difficult to . . .'

But she wasn't listening.

'Laetitia, what's wrong?'

All her attention was fixed over his shoulder. Alarmed, he whirled around, ready to confront whoever had invaded their glade. 'That bloody priest! If that's him, slinking about in the underbrush, I'll . . .'

The horses were restive but d'Aubec could detect no human presence.

'Have you seen a ghost?' he asked, bewildered.

She pulled her startled gaze back from the horizon. 'No, Edmond. Not a ghost. A saint, perhaps . . . or a goddess,' she murmured.

He nodded, understanding. 'Ah! That'll be Domina Luci! The Lady of the Grove, the tutelary deity in these parts. She'd be likely to surface to take a look at a rival!'

'A rival? For your attentions, d'Aubec? Are you then her devoted acolyte?'

'But of course,' he answered with mock gravity. 'I worship at her altar. The Lady would always expect me to present the human object of my affections for her inspection. I think she'll approve of you.'

The ride back was completed in silence, Letty's emotions an uncomfortable mixture of regret and relief. When they entered the château she walked a pace behind him, lagging back as they went along what she had come to think of as 'the portrait corridor'.

'Getting to know them?' He waited for her to catch up, smiling approval. 'I shall, of course, quiz you on all their names and dates the moment you accept to join their ranks. You'd better do your homework.'

'I was wondering why they almost all had their portraits painted outdoors? And with the same backdrop? Unusual, isn't it?'

'Just showing off the family estate from the best angle, I assume. What about your English artists: Reynolds? Gainsborough? Weren't their subjects shown in bosky dells or set against wide acres?'

'Yes, you're probably right.' She wandered along the row, making contact with each of the counts and his family. 'Poor chaps! Oh – lucky chaps, I know, to have their wealth and position, but what turbulent times they lived through. So many in uniform – it seems they never were at peace. I wonder how many of them died at peace in their beds?'

She could not imagine what it was in her innocent remark that triggered his odd reaction. His face darkened and he went silently to stand by his brother's picture at the end of the line. 'The uniforms end with this one,' he said. 'The last sacrifice.' He stretched out a hand and pointed back down the line. 'Look at the last two centuries. War, nothing but war. Struggles against almost all our European neighbours . . . the Revolution . . . the German invasion of 1870 . . . the German invasion of 1914. Millions dead. A constant haemorrhaging of French blood. Why?' His eyes appealed to her to supply a reason. 'Tell me why, Laetitia.'

Throughout her life Letty had been subjected to rigorous questioning by men who thought they knew the answer and who waited with varying degrees of patience for her to chant their views back to them. She was a skilful player, but she was suddenly tired of the game. 'Do you want my diplomatic answer or my honest one?' she asked.

'Both,' he said, surprising her.

'Well, I could say, tediously, that the casualties were incurred as a result of interstate disputes arising from national, religious, economic, or demographic pressures. Or, I could say that men have slaughtered each other for the usual male reasons: an inborn urge to kill their fellow man to establish superiority, natural aggression, arrogance, land-grabbing greed, and blood-lust.'

253

She thought she must certainly have offended a man who, she judged, was guilty himself of most of these dire charges, but Edmond was looking at her with humour and approval.

'A proponent of the Darwinian evolutionary theory, Miss Talbot?'

'But of course. And these ancestors of yours bear witness to the truth of it. They owed their existence to a long – and blind – struggle for survival. They are a part of slowly evolving natural history, a sequence, a progression. Natural selection has occurred over aeons and,' she pointed an accusing finger at him, '*you*, Edmond, are the culmination of all this struggle, this bloodletting and – let's not ignore the female role in all this – selective breeding.'

She had expected him to stalk off down the corridor, dismayed by her rudeness, but instead he chuckled and slipped an arm companionably around her waist. 'Laetitia, my love, I see at last you're understanding me!' He looked again at his brother. 'I've made a vow to him. No more. Never again, Guy.' He repeated the phrase quietly. 'Never again.'

Laetitia did not wish to cut across his thoughts and remained silent. But he looked at her quizzically, expecting a response. 'No more war, do you mean? Can anyone ever be certain of that?' she asked tentatively.

'Oh, yes! I can be certain. France will never again be weak. Never unprepared. Never be sent reeling by the first blow.'

Embarrassed by his vehemence, she said with an attempt at lightness, 'Gosh, for a moment, I thought Napoleon had joined us.'

'He would not be welcome here. I would have no use for his vainglorious self-interest.'

'Are you expecting a blow, Edmond? Hostility from some quarter towards your country?'

'*Our* country, Laetitia. It's *your* native land too. I don't forget that your mother was French.' The clasp about her waist grew tighter.

254

'But we've fought the war to end war, Edmond. It's over. Let it go.'

'A delusion! War will come again.'

'*L'étendard sanglant est levé?* But whose bloodied standard do you see opposing you in your nightmares, Edmond? Germany's? Surely not? They suffered more than anyone. The country is destitute, bled white by the reparation they are still paying to France, hardly able to live through the peace, let alone another war.'

He shook his head. 'There are forces at work already. For some years now they have been quietly planning, gaining ground, seeking financial backing from abroad, recruiting support from disaffected and mindless riffraff at home.'

'But who would encourage or finance an aggressive German faction? I can't imagine . . .'

Her naïveté seemed to amuse him. 'International banks, the Ford Motor Corporation, Dutch Oil, certain elements of the Anglo-Saxon business world, American senators, English aristocrats . . . Do you want me to name names? They would be known to you. They would make you gasp.'

'This is nonsense!'

'Sadly, it is not. I have clear evidence of this, and a thick file on the activities of the troublemaker at the centre of it all, a nasty little Austrian layabout, a nobody, who yet seems to have the knack of conjuring gold from deep pockets. You are half English and half French, Laetitia, and well placed to understand me when I say that we French must never trust the Anglo-Saxon world. They feel they have much more in common with their Germanic cousins than they have with the French. The British royal family are, after all, in reality exactly that – cousins of the Kaiser, are they not? The United States is heavily populated with German immigrants. France is threatened from two sides.'

Marie-Louise's words had been similar. Had Letty's blend of French and English blood blurred her political vision? Would the day ever come when she would have to decide where her allegiance lay?

'Are you proposing that something should be, could be, done to prepare for this threat you envisage?'

'Should be done, could be done, and I'm doing it,' he said with quiet satisfaction.

'I can't imagine what a single man, however active and influential, might achieve. The French are too tired to fight again,' she objected. 'Materially, they are at a low ebb, and morally, they are exhausted. I don't believe they would rally to the standard of a d'Aubec, however rampant.'

He smiled. 'No. You're right. But I understand my countrymen and the standard that I have in mind every Frenchman will honour and rise to.'

'Well, knowing the French, I think you'll need something pretty persuasive to get them going,' she said lightly, disturbed by his dark mood. 'I would offer to tear off my sleeve as a favour and attach it, as in days of old, to the tip of your lance, but I think your scenario calls for something more alluring than that?'

'Yes, it does. I have in mind something utterly compelling and bewitching.' He paused, then added quietly, 'And female.'

Perhaps regretting his outburst, he tucked her arm under his and hurried her along to the library. There she was disconsolately stacking away teacups and putting the books in order, listening out for the dinner gong, when Edmond's urgent tones broke through as though he had read her thoughts. 'No – let's leave the books just where they are. I'd like you to feel you can come and visit them while I'm away. The bait in my trap, you might say! If you're not coming for *me*, then my books, my horses, and your dog might just prove attraction enough.'

She was moved by his ingenuous good humour and with a rush of affection towards him, unthinkingly went to plant a friendly farewell kiss on his cheek. A swift manoeuvre on his part neatly diverted the kiss to his lips.

In the distance a gong sounded.

'Look – we won't say good-bye, Laetitia,' he murmured. 'We're in the middle of a kiss – you're to remember that when I see you again. Today's Wednesday. I shall travel back next Monday. Promise me that while I'm away you'll do what I suggested?' He held her at arm's length and studied her face. 'Tell me that you'll come and, well, just be here? Be seen. Clank the keys about a bit? You could get to know the staff . . . the housekeeper is very prepared to be your friend . . . exercise the horses – Dido is well enough to be put out in the pasture now, and you could take her for a gentle stroll in the evenings. I want, in the middle of a boring meeting, to be able to think of you here, surrounded by my things – missing me!'

'Jules won't be here – he's driving Maman. She won't entrust herself to the skills of me or Constantine! But I'm leaving Marcel and three lads in and about the stables. One of them can drive and you can use the Citroën. I'll tell everyone that you are to come and go as you please. I make only one stipulation.' He grinned. 'That you don't invite your buccaneering boss to cross the drawbridge. Paradee must come nowhere near my property! And the same goes for your vicar friend – he's persona non grata, too. My staff have orders to eject them on sight. Understood?'

'Of course. But you needn't be so bossy, Edmond. And I don't much care to hear you dismissing my friends with such unconsidered derision. Charles Paradee is a man I like and admire, and he's one of the most talented archaeologists I've ever met. He has my loyalty and my regard, and I do believe I'd follow him anywhere. In an archaeological context, that is,' she added, blushing at the instinctive warmth of her riposte. 'And the vicar . . .' For a moment she was lost for words. 'Well, he's a vicar. Perfectly trustworthy. A gentleman. Neither one would welcome an invitation to join me in an assault on your privacy . . .'

He gave her a look of exaggerated disbelief which provoked her to say firmly: 'They would both refuse, as do I. I'm sure I shan't have the time to come and visit. I'm very touched that you should ask me to, but no, I'll be too busy with the dig. I haven't been giving it my full attention lately and we're just about to expose the foundations of a side chapel no one realized existed. It's getting very interesting . . .' she added lamely.

'Well, I shall come and pull you out of your trench the minute I get back,' he said easily, quite obviously not believing a word. 'Come along, then – suppertime. And on the way to the dining room you'd better work on a convincing reason for rejecting me – if indeed you have? Maman will not be pleased. I noticed she had had champagne put on ice. Could it have been something you let slip, Laetitia my love?'

Laetitia had no idea whether he was teasing.

Chapter Twenty-Seven

'But, my poor girl! Why didn't you come to me straight-away with this?' said Gunning the next day. They were sitting whispering together in a pew at the back of the empty church of Mary Magdalene. 'I was only playing backgammon with old Huleux – I would have come at once had you called. Your new friend's clearly barmy, wouldn't you say?'

'I do wonder what else we are to think of a man who sees himself as a reincarnated Jeanne d'Arc! Frightening!'

'Yes, distressing enough, but . . .' He stirred impatiently. 'But we were prepared to discover some power complex of the sort. It's not *that* that disturbs me. It's the blatant manipulation of *you*, Letty. This stuff and nonsense about their plans for your future.'

'An annoying bit of well-meant interference. It's the sort of thing parents do all the time. And, in theory, on paper, so to speak, it's not all that mad an idea. We're a jolly good match! Surely even you can see that? Anyway, I can shrug off parental manoeuvrings. No, William, it's the countess's barely stated implications that upset me. She was leading me by subtle hints to reconsider my relationship with Daniel. She planted in my mind the idea that he might actually be my real father.'

'Good grief!' Gunning was shocked and took a few moments silently to digest the information. 'But if you understood her properly, this amounts to a quite disgrace-ful piece of calumny against those concerned, doesn't it? What is she implying about your mother . . . Sir Richard . . .

to say nothing of Daniel himself? I'm amazed that you can tell me of it with so little emotion.'

'With one sentence, she turns my mother into a slut, my father into a cuckold, and Daniel into a Casanova who'd betray his best friend. Emotion, you say? Just wait until I've thought this through! Just wait until I know the truth! Then you'll see an outpouring of emotion!'

The words were bold but Gunning was not deceived.

'Well, I never expected to see it.'

'See what?'

'Your Achilles' heel. Your sensitive spot. A girl who can incapacitate a count, challenge the Cambridge Constabulary, get the better of Sir Richard Talbot, that redoubtable leader of men – your *father* –' he said with emphasis, 'it's rather surprising that the half-suggestion of a dotty old lady should derail you. You can't allow yourself to be swayed by the word of a stranger who sees every advantage in exploiting you. Go straight to Capitaine Huleux and ask if you may use his telephone. Ring up Sir Richard and seek reassurances.'

'"Seek reassurances"? That's easily said! How do I frame my question? "I say, er, Daddy, could you possibly confirm that you are, in fact, my father? A certain suggestion has been put to me out here in Burgundy that you have been deceiving me and concealing my parentage all these years . . . and it is further asserted that the guilty party is your best friend." I can't do it, William.'

'And there you are! When you rehearse the situation like that, it takes on its proper ludicrous character. I can't imagine why you did not immediately dismiss the scurrilous proposition.'

'One thing held me back: a memory. William, it's a *convincing* account. And there's the problem. Daniel did pay me a lot of attention as a child and everyone knew it. But not everyone knew – as I did –' She gave him a speculative look, then, deciding to make an awkward confidence, finished with a rush, '. . . that he was in love with my mother.'

'Good Lord! But however did you . . .?'

260

'Listening at doors, behind sofas ... creeping up on people when they didn't expect it ... you'll recognize a persistent trait, I think? I believe that with childish intuition I had always known, but in later years he talked of his affection openly with my father when they were together. Sir Richard was aware of his feelings and they'd arrived at the stage, after my mother's death, when they could talk about it if not with humour, with an indulgent tenderness. Her death, I'd say, brought them closer. They shared a huge loss.'

'I can just about believe all this, but it's no evidence that Daniel was your father,' Gunning said firmly. 'Do you mind, Letty, if we examine the proposition a little more closely, check the facts of this bold assertion?'

'I wouldn't expect anything less,' she said. 'Never the emotional response from you, William!'

'If it were true that Daniel was your father it wouldn't be at all unusual, Letty. I mean, in the circles in which your family moves in London ... enlightened ... would that be the word?'

'Oh, you're too polite, William! "Bohemian" is the word you're trying to avoid. Progressive, modern, dissolute, freethinking? Take your pick. They'd all do, without necessarily being accurate. And I'm not unaware of the "arrangements" that are frequently made in families at this level of London society. I could tell you stories that'd scorch your ears! And can one ever really know one's parents and what they are capable of? I feel I know the truth in my bones and my blood – literally – but without evidence I cannot possibly conjure up so far from home, I don't have the strength to take on these people.'

'And perhaps, for the moment, there's an even more urgent question we must ask ourselves: What tricks is the countess playing with you, Letty? This is a strange cruelty, isn't it? What can these people hope to gain?'

'Well – me for a start! Edmond's proposed marriage. At least I think he's proposed marriage. It wasn't perfectly clear,' she finished awkwardly.

261

'Evidently. But why *you*? This is a man who could have his pick of the foremost families of France – or abroad. You're going to be wealthy, but on a world scale you'd hardly figure. There are richer and prettier girls by the dozen in . . .' He thought for a moment. 'In America. He could do better. No, there must be some other unlikely reason.'

'Apart from my wit and allure? William, you might at least allow that he's fallen in love with me. His mother seems to think he has.'

'I suppose that might be an answer,' he said doubtfully. 'I have other suspicions. Esmé would have a technical explanation for their behaviour! I think she'd say that this was a calculated piece of manipulation. Think, Letty: away from your home, disoriented, far from friends and family and any emotional support – they're not aware you have me on tap, of course – sad at the loss of someone dear to you, the earth suddenly shifts under your feet at her revelation. Dizzily, you reach out for someone to steady you and – lo! – here, arms outstretched and waiting, is handsome young d'Aubec, a suitor chosen for you by the man who could perhaps be your father. The man who had your best interests at heart. The man you could trust to choose someone in his own image – handsome, dashing, sharing your interests. It's a strong brew, Letty! I'm impressed that you were hardheaded enough to resist.'

'The head was never targeted, William,' she said wistfully. 'They were aiming for the heart.'

Something in her tone alarmed him. Hearing a distinct sniffle and detecting a small sound which might well, if not checked at once, develop into a sob, he reached for his handkerchief. 'Are you all right, Letty?'

'No. I'm putting on a good show but – you said it, William – a bit dizzy . . . earth shifting a little . . . could do with a hug . . .'

She shuffled closer and, uncertainly, he placed his arms around her, patting her back. She stayed for a few moments in the frozen circle of his awkward embrace, her

262

cheek resting lightly on his tweed jacket, regretting her faux pas and waiting for the earliest moment she could, without offence, pull away and end his embarrassment. 'Well, their machinations have had a delayed reaction – they've pushed me into a pair of waiting arms, though not the intended ones,' she said, attempting feebly to explain her neediness.

'Yes,' he agreed. 'Wrong arms. Sorry about that.'

After a moment, he asked carefully, 'Have you told me everything?'

'Not yet. No. I have one more revelation . . . something rather startling happened to me in that grove . . . I've never felt anything like it before . . . but I thought first of all I'd let you wrestle with the problem of d'Aubec's delusions of grandeur, now the evidence is in.'

'You dismiss the man too lightly.'

'But his theory of impending attack from Germany is a clear indication of what Esmé would call paranoia, don't you think? I mean – it's a bit far-fetched, isn't it? The League of Nations would never countenance such an attempt. My father insists that the real threat – if threat there be – is from farther east, from Russia.'

'It disturbs me to say the man's fears are not as outrageous as you may think. The sinister movement he mentions exists, Letty. It grows. It bides its time. It looks to the future and indoctrinates its young. And, believe me – this is no innocent Kibbo Kift! It's a deeply unpleasant and infectious variety of nationalistic fervour. It seeks alliances. It marches under the banner of what they call National Socialism, and before you ask – yes, it's true that it has some appeal for certain sections of the British hierarchy. Oh, not for the Man in the Street!' He smiled. 'The man standing in the soup queue or the market or walking behind the plough would say the expected: "That's the bloody Hun for you! 'Ere we go again!" And he will shuffle forward when called on, part of a new generation, to do his duty.'

Letty was pale with anxiety. 'A new generation, William? We are not ten years yet from the end of the war. Are

263

you implying that the next batch of sacrificial victims are, as we speak, singing patriotic songs round their campfires?' The warning words of Marie-Louise again came back to her.

'Exactly that. It's brutally easy to calculate the date of the next outbreak from the age of the participants.'

'You think someone's put a big red circle round market day?'

'I wouldn't be surprised. And I don't think d'Aubec will be taken by surprise, either. Allow for the natural immediate postwar increase in births and add on, say, eighteen years . . . Wait until the harvest's in and declare war.'

'So we should mark 1938 as an important year in our forward planning diaries? That's in eleven years' time!' Her laugh was fuelled by derision but even to her ears it sounded nervous. 'How can any country possibly build up an armed force in that time?'

'They are halfway there. Thanks to United States backing, the Wehrmacht is already a force to be reckoned with . . . Storm trooper squadrons strut through Munich, and Britain looks the other way.'

'Every movement needs a leader . . .' she said speculatively.

'No shortage of applicants for that position. Some of them even manage to avoid assassination by rival factions. There's a – to my mind – sinister society, rich, influential, and with aristocratic pretensions that calls itself the Thule Society – after the ancient word for "Iceland". They're very keen on mythology and pagan ideals, and they base their philosophy on the theory that the Aryan race – which they seem to have invented – is a super race, descended from the gods, and will eventually conquer in Europe. And the world. They have devised a banner . . . Here, let me show you . . .'

He took his drawing pad from his pocket and she watched him sketch a four-limbed cross, rounded to fit into a circle. A dagger plunged downwards from the cross and was encircled with foliage that might have been oak leaves.

'Oh, I know this. It's runic ... no, probably older ...
Hindu? It's supposed to bring good luck. My aunt has it
embroidered in beadwork on her spectacles case.'

'A swastika. Yes. And this same emblem has been taken
up by another group – the Socialist Workers' Party, they
call themselves ... the National Socialists I mentioned just
now. And they have in their numbers a rising star. Name
of Hitler. An Austrian rabble-rouser who seems to have
the whole of Bavaria eating out of his hand. He'll be the
menace d'Aubec mentioned. Now he's taken the cross
and straightened out the limbs for his flag. It's black on a
white circle, and the whole set on a blood-red ground. Very
striking.'

'And do people follow him?'

'Oh, yes. In floods. They're more than willing to listen to
someone who's telling them what they want to know – that
the German people are God's chosen Aryan race, and
despite the present setback, they will prevail. It's their
destiny.'

'William, I've been meaning to ask ... I think I understand how you've formed your opinions – but where on
earth do you get your information?'

'Sleeping on park benches being something of an isolat-
ing situation, you mean?' he asked.

She nodded.

'In those circumstances – destitution, I mean, of course –
a man seeks out warmth and shelter. And if one is not too
offensively feral this may be found in libraries. You will
possibly not be aware of the increasingly generous provi-
sion for the working man in our country. Books – and seriously improving books – are available for the ranks of
earnest self-educators who frequent these places, but also
newspapers and journals. Over this last bit I've kept warm
and dry and widened my perspective on the world. Where
else may one find *The Times* rubbing shoulders with the
Daily Worker? It's better than a club.'

'Nothing you've read appears to have cheered you in
any way. You speak of nothing but gloom and doom.'

265

'I'm afraid I have this in common with d'Aubec – I fear for the future. But my fear is unfocused and unseizable. He, at least, has identified a threat and is taking bold steps to counter it. He, at least, we know to have the power to back up his aspirations. Whatever they may be.'

'You're as mad as he is, William!'

'Perhaps it helps me to understand him. Bear in mind, will you, the disquieting things we've discovered about his financial and political dealings. He's made an effective springboard for himself. Oh, not overtly, like his thuggish neighbour to the east, but, in its quiet way, much more impressive. D'Aubec or someone in his outfit,' he said thoughtfully, 'is an intelligent strategist.'

'And that would be all very well if these tensions could be decided by single combat,' said Letty. 'My money would be on d'Aubec against all comers. But if there were to be another war in Europe, it would come down to men and women, nations fighting each other on battlefields. And nothing will persuade me that the French or the English would be ready to shed more blood so soon after the last lot. We'd be contemplating a generation of women who lost fathers, husbands, and sons. The leaders and their standards may be in place but they should look over their shoulders. No one will be following them.'

'And yet d'Aubec is blazingly confident. He's got *something*, Letty . . . something we're unaware of.'

Letty was struck by an unwelcome thought. 'Some sort of secret weapon, do you mean? William, do you suppose Daniel had trodden the same path – had found out what Edmond was up to . . . what he'd got hold of?' She sighed in exasperation. 'This is barmy! What are we expecting him to be concealing up there? A Big Bertha trained on Germany? I've got to know that fortress well and I don't believe there's space to hide so much as a pea-shooter. It's so ordered and civilized, William.'

'Well, whatever it is – and I'm sure it's more subtle than a cannon under a tarpaulin – perhaps d'Aubec had even confided in Daniel; they were quite close, I think?'

266

'He's begun to open up to me in the same way. It's lonely work being a megalomaniac, the secret saviour of your country in waiting. It must be a relief to have a sympathetic ear, someone to reassure you that you're not crazy. *Is* he deluded, do you suppose? I mean, one man, William – however energetic and influential – how could he possibly galvanize a weary country?'

'It's happened before. And d'Aubec starts from a much higher base than, let's say, Napoleon. He was a lowly artillery officer, a Corsican, and not even regarded as truly French by most, surviving in a country devastated by years of war and internal slaughter when he burst through. Yet in no time at all he was master of Europe.'

'Not all of Europe. That awkward little island across the Channel refused to be impressed by the Emperor.'

'Imagine what he might have accomplished had we been his ally! If he'd done what medieval monarchs did and made a diplomatic marriage with, say, an English princess, assuming there to have been a selection available at the time? An Anglo-French coalition would have dominated Europe for decades. There would never have been a Waterloo . . . never a Great War.'

'Oh, Lord! Do you think he sees *me* playing a part in his schemes? A Marianne figure with breastplate and flag . . . *Allons enfants de la patrie* and all that?'

'Isn't it Britannia who has the breastplate? Marianne, I'm certain, is much more sketchily clad in a Gallic sort of way. But, yes! I'd say you were carefully chosen. Not royal, but I don't believe that counts for much these days. You have the advantage of being young and intelligent, rich in your own right, well-connected, half English, and bi-lingual. And that's your attraction for d'Aubec – you lend him credibility. I'd say you had all the characteristics he required to complete his plans. And it would be your cap-tivating features we'd be seeing on the front pages of news-papers and magazines, in all the newsreels. I'm afraid you'd put the Prince of Wales's nose out of joint. Who wouldn't rather look at you – smiling and confident – than at his soulful spaniel's face?'

'You fail to notice that Edmond and I would make a lovely couple!' said Letty. '"He so dark, she so fair, both so fashionable, and don't they do a lovely Charleston?"'

'There's that, I suppose. But tell me about this banner – this standard, did you say? – behind which he confidently expects his countrymen to rally.'

'There's no more. I told you everything he said.'

'Pity he was so reticent. This is the most intriguing thing he told you. Let's consider what he gave away . . . what was it? Something with a troubadourish flavour . . . "more alluring than your sleeve on the end of his lance"?'

'Gabrielle's knickers, do you think?' Letty shrugged, then she blushed. 'Oh, I'm sorry, William. Whispering together like this in a pew – it takes me back to subversive gossip in the dorm. All he would say was: "compelling, bewitching, and female".'

'Mm . . . Definitely the knickers, then,' said Gunning morosely. 'And speaking of displaced drawers – the revelation you've been storing up to shock me with? Carry on, if you must, though I warn you – nothing you can say will surprise me. Don't expect it.'

Frozen with outrage, Letty rose stiffly and went to stand in front of the fresco of Mary Magdalene. After a few moments he joined her, melting with contrition. 'Don't interrupt,' she said coldly. 'I'm saying a prayer to someone who understands what it is to be wrongly accused, judged, reviled . . . I'm begging the saint to give me the strength not to . . . not to . . .'

'Put another kink in my nose?' Gunning suggested. 'I promise not to duck if you want to take aim. I'm sorry.'

She ignored him, keeping her eyes on the painting, sensing his mortification at his unguarded remark. The voice of reason that always sabotaged her more frivolous flights of fancy now reminded her that the man had been out of society for many years and had lost the knack of censoring his thoughts. 'In fact, to tell the truth, William, your fears were very nearly confirmed. It was a pretty close-run thing. I blame that spring! It's a real hazard. They ought to post a warning. *Get wet at your peril!'*

He looked puzzled and waited for her to explain.

'D'Aubec's secret spring – it has a strange effect on the unwary. I dabbled about in it . . . got thoroughly wet, in fact, and . . . well, I know I have a vivid imagination and perhaps it was unwise of me to attempt it . . .'

'Letty!'

'Most odd. I felt about ten feet tall when I came out of the spray, immensely powerful, and . . . um . . . not quite sure I have the vocabulary . . . carnally confident, if you understand me. Like her!' She pointed to the knowing, painted face.

Gunning was making an effort not to laugh. 'Lucky old d'Aubec,' he snorted. 'But what on earth went wrong for him?'

'It was this same lady who saved me from a fate which was certainly preferable to death and might well have proved very interesting. Just at the *moment critique* my attention was distracted by the horse, who decided to kick up a fuss, and, with the sun just below the horizon, I saw, silhouetted with extraordinary clarity, exactly the shape of those hills there painted in the background. And, William, at that moment of realization, I was standing with my back to a spring which jets out of the limestone rock-face – just like the one here by Mary's forefinger!'

'Good Lord! Well, I can see that that would put a girl off her stride. Did you raise the matter with d'Aubec by any chance?'

'Oh, yes. I said, "Unhand me, sir, and pray take a moment to analyse the geological profile of those hills on the horizon." I pretended I'd seen an apparition in the trees – a saint or a goddess.'

'And you thought that more convincing than an interest in earth sciences?'

'It had the advantage of being the truth! I had clearly in my head the image of this fresco at the time! And perhaps

I did sound convincing, because d'Aubec didn't question it. In fact he said something offhand about himself – claimed to worship the goddess of the grove or something very like that. Joking, you know, but it got us through an awkward moment.'

'Can you find it again? This grove?'

'Oh, yes. Give me your map and I'll show you.'

She took the dog-eared map he handed her and, turning it this way and that, finally pointed. He took a pencil from his pocket and drew a circle around the spot.

'Nothing marked here. Not even the spring. Perhaps the cartographers were discouraged from visiting? Did you realize, Laetitia, just how close this is to the outcrop of rock the château sits on?'

'Well, of course! It does loom over one. We took a circuitous route, as flat as is possible in this part of the world, so as not to strain poor old Dido's legs. It follows one of those old green trackways. Not much evidence of recent use. Rather overgrown.'

'I'd like to take a look. They've all gone off to Lyon, you say?'

'Yes. He's expecting to be away for four days. The countess's luggage was lined up in the hall last night. Two suitcases and four hatboxes. I walked to work early this morning,' she said, 'and watched them go by. Just to be certain.'

Gunning looked at his watch. 'No chess engagement for me this evening – Anselme's gone away on holiday. And there are three more hours of daylight at least. I'm going over there. We'd better slip out of here separately.'

'Take the car, William. You can drive it within half a mile of the greenway. And why not pause for a second on the bend just beyond the Haras?'

When Gunning slowed for the bend ten minutes later, he was not surprised to see Letty leaping nimbly into the passenger seat.

270

Chapter Twenty-Eight

They approached the spring, hot from their walk down the overgrown lane, and fell at once into the silence that the grove seemed to impose. Gunning tramped about, scanning the horizon and absorbing the atmosphere. He made a few quick sketches in his book. Finally he joined Letty, who had settled down on the turf to watch him, arms clutching her knees.

'I see what you mean, Letty. A superstitious type, which I'm not, might well describe it as spooky . . . haunted. Though some would say: holy. And you didn't mistake the outline of the hills. I'd say this was a place of some significance to the people who've lived around here for generations. Have you noticed that it's a circular space, smaller than an arena, bigger than a threshing floor, perhaps, which is where the earliest attempts at what you might call drama were made. And the acoustic qualities are amazing. We've both of us lowered our voices instinctively to a whisper. Can you imagine what it would sound like if we spoke in an actor's voice? Well, let's put it to the test, shall we?'

To Letty's astonishment, he jumped to his feet and began to recite. His priestly baritone boomed out across the open space, reciting, to her greater horror, lines from a pagan incantation from Swinburne.

> 'I have lived long enough, having seen one thing, that love hath an end;
> Goddess and maiden and queen, be near me now and befriend.

Thou art more than the day or the morrow, the seasons that
*   laugh or that weep.*
For these give joy and sorrow; but thou, Proserpina, sleep.'

Satisfied, he sat down again. 'Very good! Not quite
Epidaurus but all the same – very good!'

'Proserpina? Daughter of Demeter? Is that the goddess
whose presence you feel?'

'Yes. Somewhere out there,' he said, waving a hand
towards the screen of stunted oaks and bushes, 'there's a
sympathetic, though mischievous, young presence, don't
you think? How did Milton describe the result of the
Zephyr's meeting with Aurora? The love child of the summer breeze and the dawn, as he met her once a-maying . . .

> *'There on beds of violets blue,*
> *And fresh-blown roses washed in dew*
> *Filled her with thee, a daughter fair,*
> *So buxom, blithe, and debonair.*

'She's probably intrigued to welcome you to the grove,
Letty – her mirror image, in human form.'

'What? Buxom? Like a barmaid? Not sure that's very
flattering.'

'Old English meaning, stupid! "Meek and kindly." And
"blithe" is the Old English for, er, "meek and kindly".'

'And "debonair"? Don't tell me!'

'Ah, now that's Old French for "meek and kindly".'

'Rot!'

'All the same, it's a phrase I find suits you. "Buxom,
blithe, and debonair."' He savoured it once more.

From anyone else Letty would have judged this heavy
flirting. But from the vicar? With a rush of relief she recalled that men of Gunning's background frequently made
a parade of their classical education, and this orchestra-
shaped place was just the setting that would incite them to
a show of oratory. She remembered her father in the
Roman amphitheatre at Orange walking firmly to centre

272

stage and entertaining the startled tourists with a blast of Aeschylus – the messenger's eyewitness account of the sea battle of Salamis, from *The Persians*. She'd hidden behind her guidebook, blushing with embarrassment, pretending to have no acquaintance with this show-off.

'. . . and the location's intriguing, don't you think?' Gunning was chattering on. 'It's sheltered by the bluff from the prevailing winds, which gives it that quality of stillness – have you noticed that not a leaf is stirring? – but it's not overshadowed, so it enjoys and retains the heat of the sun. And where we are now – in late June – that's pretty unbearable! . . . I say, do you mind?'

He took off his jacket, unclipped his starched collar and threw it down on the turf, unbuttoned his shirt, and groaned with relief.

'Oh, for goodness' sake, William! Why don't you go and cool off in the spring? That's what it's there for.'

He got to his feet, shrugged off his shirt, and made towards the spring. After a couple of steps he turned and grinned at her. 'How did it go? "Ten feet tall and a rush of heat to the loins?" You sure you want to risk this?'

She listened without turning her head to his yelps of delight. He was splashing about for a very long time, she thought, but she had no intention of interrupting his activities with a nannyish call. After ten minutes he returned, invigorated and dripping wet, and sat down by her side.

'Did you find the goddess?' she asked.

'Yes, she was at home. She sends her regards. She was pleased to see me and complimented me on the removal of my moustache.'

'Moustache?' Letty peered at him. 'Oh, yes. So you have! Shaved it off, I mean. Yes, an improvement, I agree. Didn't much care for the Douglas Fairbanks look. Here, put your shirt on, William, or you'll catch your death! You're cold to the bones and shivering. You were a long time in the water. What were you doing?'

'Oh, poking about. I found that someone's been doing a bit of minor engineering. Nothing much . . . a stone

273

channel has been fitted into the head of the spring – to make it jet out in a more dramatic fashion from the rock face, I suppose. And pushed down the side of the channel, and still dry, was this.'

He dragged a small shining object from his back pocket and held it out to her. As she studied it in stunned silence, he talked on. 'Have you ever thrown a coin into a fountain? For good luck? Old Celtic custom. The Celts often placed spells, requests, invocations to their gods in holy places like this, especially where there's water present in some dramatic form. Carved on stone, bits of slate, even sheets of lead. You know the sort of thing: "How about a bit of help with the rheumatism? Don't let me die in childbirth like my two sisters. May all the ewes produce twins this year."' He looked at her steadily. '"This is the image of my chosen one. Let her love me"?'

Letty stared at the photograph in its silver frame.

'I'd say the chap was deadly serious, wouldn't you, Letty? As though his personal charms and his vast estates were not enough to do the trick, d'Aubec's calling up a little divine intervention. He means to have you for his nefarious purposes.'

'Don't be so pompous! It wouldn't have occurred to you that he might just be a young lad in love?' She took the photograph from him. 'This is very touching. A *human* side of d'Aubec? He was trying out his new camera . . . he's got one of those tiny Leicas . . . He asked me to stand in the courtyard where the light was good – I'd no idea I was about to be offered up to the goddess. What a cheek!' Her wondering smile belied her words.

'Well, it clears one thing up. He put you to stand in front of the stables, dead centre, I'd guess. But if you'll stop staring at yourself for a moment and look at the extremes of the photo. There – on either side of the building. Do you see the hills?'

She glanced up at the bulk of the mound behind them. 'The stables are right there. In line with us.'

'Yes. If you were to demolish them, you'd see the same contour we're looking at now. More or less. Not quite. From down here, can you see the river that passes between the two hills on the left? No, you can't. But it's there on the fresco all right. I think this place is right for direction but wrong for elevation. The place where we were intended to be standing, the viewpoint, is no longer visible. It's up there, obscured by the stable block.'

'Just what Epona's been telling us all along.'

'Interesting. But nothing further we can do about it this evening, I think.'

Gunning settled back on the grass at her side, put his arms under his head, and closed his eyes with a sigh of satisfaction. Free from his sceptical and censorious glare, she dared to study his face, relaxed for the first time – in her company at least – his mouth narrowed in a half-smile. She reached over and gently ran a finger over his top lip. With its bristling defence removed, the skin below was smooth and she noticed now, evenly tanned like the rest of his face. He must have shaved it off on their arrival in France.

'I'm sorry I didn't notice, William. And Domina Luci was right – it does suit you!'

His half-smile became a full one. He turned his head and gently bit her finger.

She snatched back her hand, surprised by her own over-intimate gesture, and wondered whether she should apologize. A contented wuffling sound from deep in his throat suggested that perhaps this was not necessary, and she took up again her covert inspection. Had she missed other obvious changes? Mme Huleux's cooking had continued the good work begun in Cambridge, and his skin-and-bone frame, though it would never be robust, was now slender and elegant.

'Keep your hands and your lecherous thoughts off the Goddess's Chosen One, Talbot,' he advised. 'She might fly into a jealous rage and turn you into something small and disgusting. I don't want to have to take you back to Sir Richard in a cardboard box.'

Letty laughed. 'What risks I run! This is a dashed dangerous place!' She picked up his clerical collar and handed it to him. 'Here, put this back on. I could never lay wanton hands on a man having this to protect his virtue. It's just as well you're a Man of God, William, now you're getting so handsome.'

He half opened his eyes and looked at her in amusement. 'But I'm no such thing, Letty. Hadn't you realized?'

'What? Not handsome? Oh, come on – you're too modest –'

'No! I'm not a Man of God.'

Chapter Twenty-Nine

For a moment she was silent, trying to gauge his mood. Serious or playful? Flirtatious or menacing?

'Well, I've witnessed you blaspheming, drinking, left-hooking a lord, making lewd comments to an innocent young girl – me, of course! – and communing with a pagan goddess, so, yes, I suppose I have to take your declaration seriously. Tell me – how long has this been going on? And did you confide your faithless condition to my father when he interviewed you?'

'No. He never questioned it. So I didn't raise the matter.'

'Then I add deception to my list. Oh, and gluttony!'

'Add what you like. My charge sheet is already full. And full with much more serious sins than any you can come up with.' His voice had lost its lightness and she heard again the tormented Gunning of their early days.

On impulse, she took hold of his hand and spoke quietly. 'What happened to you, William?'

He turned away, unable to speak.

Letty ventured her best guess: 'Many men lost their faith on the battlefield. You are not alone.'

Into his continued silence: 'Throw off the shroud of the war, William! It blankets your senses. It suffocates you,' she said. Esmé would have condemned the edge of impatience in her voice.

He still could not respond.

She tried again, a more direct challenge: 'Did you kill a man, William? The epaulette from a German uniform that you carry around with you – I had wondered. Just the kind of dreadful memento a sensitive man might take away from the battlefield to torment himself with evermore.'

At last a glance towards her. 'No. I killed no one. The man who wore it is alive and well. He is my dearest, perhaps my only, friend.'

She did not interrupt this halting beginning. Instinctively, she closed her eyes like a child preparing to hear a story.

'I answered a call for help . . .' He paused and started again. 'A call which I ought to have ignored. It was November. Last of the battles of the Somme. It had been raining for a month and we were attempting to advance over clay soil south of the Ancre River. I went out with a stretcher party. Some of our chaps had gone out in a raid over No-Man's-Land to the nearest German positions to grab a prisoner or two . . . we badly needed to wring some information out of them about the timing of the next assault . . . We had no idea they were mounting the same sort of operation from their side. What a mess. The two groups clashed horribly in No-Man's-Land. Those who could retreat did, but there were several men, including officers in possession of valuable information, left wounded in the middle. Dangerous to leave them to the opposition. Off we went, two stretcher parties and me in support, an hour or two before dawn to sweep them up. The last clue we'd had about position was the glare of the Very lights the Boche had sent up when it all broke loose. There was a half-moon, but covered by scudding clouds and not much use to us.

'Skirting our way around the water-filled shell holes, I heard a voice calling for help. In German. I started towards it. "Leave it off, Padre!" I was told. "Not one of our lads." I went anyway. Letty, do you know what "Anzac Soup" is?'

'Yes, I do. A shell hole filled with water, mud, dead horses . . . probably worse.'

'The voice was coming from such a stinking pit. A German officer, judging by the peaked field cap, was stuck, up to his armpits and sinking. In a flash of moonlight he identified my outline and called to me in English. "I say, old man, would you mind awfully extending a hand? Rather a long one, if you can provide."

'As I peeled off my greatcoat I continued in the same mad conversational tone. "Good Lord, man! How'd you manage to get yourself into such a pickle?"

'"Attempting to extricate a fellow officer from this quagmire, so, if you're minded to mount a rescue operation – have a care!"

'"A fellow officer? Where is he?"

'"I'm afraid I'm standing on him. He appears, involuntarily, poor sod, to be now preserving *my* life. For a few more minutes, at least."

'Holding firmly to the tails of my coat, I threw it out as far as I could over the soup. He made a grab for it and seized it by a flapping epaulette. I pulled, but the epaulette came away in his hand. He waved it at me as he sank another inch and laughed. "Bloody awful English tailoring!"

'They were all proud of their own smart *feldgrau loden*!' He smiled. 'I hauled the coat back and tried again. This time he grabbed the collar and, bit by bit, I reeled him in. There was just enough moonlight to get a look at each other close-up, and we stared in disbelief. Like me, he was unarmed; like me, he wore a cross around his neck. The belt of his field tunic carried the words *Gott mit Uns*. I was looking at my opposite number. The man was a German priest. He hunted about round the edge of the crater for the greatcoat he'd thrown off to facilitate his rescue attempt and put it about his shoulders. He was cold, wet, shocked, and at a low ebb. His attempts at cheeriness were, I thought, the last throw of the dice for him. We sat down, huddled together in the dry overcoat, in barely adequate shelter in the scrape of a shell hole and, in cupped hands, shared the last of my cigarettes and the emergency rum ration I carried. We talked away the rest of the night. He was – is – a scholar, a theologian and linguist. A Berliner, he'd spent some years in England researching his subject.

279

He was rather dismissive of English religious scholarship. "If we ever get out of this, my friend," he said, "I want you to come to Berlin and look me up. I will re-educate you! I will show you wonders!"

'Those moments of sanity and friendship were the only light in that black hell. And it was a human light. It owed nothing to a divine presence. Oh, we could quote chapter and verse of the Scriptures at each other in several languages, we could argue the finer points of theology, we could name our saints in order of merit – but when we looked about us, where was the supposed centre of all this? The Spirit that had moulded our lives? The Being whose name was on our lips and in our minds? Where was God? In that waste-howling wilderness not even Satan was present.

'Satan! I think if we'd caught sight of Milton's Fallen Angel striding about this Gustave Doré landscape –

'*A dungeon horrible, on all sides round*
As one great furnace flamed; yet from those flames
No light, but rather darkness visible
Served only to discover sights of woe
Regions of sorrow, doleful shades . . .

'– we'd have greeted him as a fellow soul in torment. We'd have spoken his language. But neither God nor Lucifer was there. And they hadn't fled the field – they'd never been there. The awful thought came to me that we were on our own and always had been. It was in that moment my faith began to crack and crumble. With the first streak of dawn we decided to make a run for it – in opposite directions. Before we parted, he took out his knife and cut off the epaulette from his overcoat and handed it to me. I hadn't noticed that he was still clutching mine in his left hand.'

'But you finished the war still a priest? The military cross was awarded to the Reverend Gunning, wasn't it?'

'I went through the motions. Like those wretched caterpillars that are paralysed and eaten away by parasites from the inside, nothing can be guessed from the outer shell. No one was aware of the inner void. You have been closer to me than anyone, Letty, over this last bit, and I don't think *you* noticed. In any case – no one was looking with much attention. I'm afraid we Anglicans were mostly despised by the troops – too many of us happy to dig in, in safe positions well behind the lines. We were not respected. You've probably heard the awful gaffe made by a chaplain addressing men bound for the front? "Well, God go with you, chaps! I shall be back here at base if you need me." True? I don't know, but it truly expressed the soldiers' verdict on the C of E priesthood. Now – the Catholic padres – they were a different kettle of fish. Many of them were – or had been – monks. Benedictine monks. Tough men! They seemed always to track the grief. They were up at the front line, they were back in the dressing stations, riding horses, driving ambulances . . . esteemed, listened to, sought after . . . they were there on the spot when they were needed. And they appeared to have more to offer than a slap on the back, a hearty bellow, and a squashed Woodbine.'

'But what tipped you over the edge, William?'

'The final realization came very easily, after months of mental turmoil. Oh, it wasn't one of the more dramatic scenes – the ones that have become fossilized into cliché: holding a man's stomach closed over his spilling entrails, looking into the still-living eye of a youngster whose limbs have been shot off, singing Sunday School hymns all night long with a quivering kid who was about to be shot by a firing squad of his own mates at dawn . . . No – I was just talking quietly to a dying soldier on the field. One of dozens that day. We both knew there was no point in trying to get him back to the trench. I suggested that in his last moments we called on God for grace. "Oh, that won't be necessary, Padre," he said calmly. "There's no kindness to be had in that quarter. But you're here. I'm

with a fellow man at the end. That's all the comfort I need."
He took my hand and held it until he died. Days later I put
my left foot on something ghastly. Invalided out, and
shortly after that the whole bloody business groaned to
a halt.'

'A double loss. You must have been bereft when you left
the hospital?'

'The physical damage was easy enough to repair. By the
end of the war, the surgeons had grown very skilled and
resourceful. The spiritual loss? Well, that was like throwing off a burden. Though I had thought it soldered to my
soul, I found the strength to jettison the dead grey weight
of it. I felt renewed, energetic again, intoxicated. I set off
into Europe to test out my new foot and my new freedom.'
His voice took on a distance and a chill. 'You would not
understand or condone my subsequent way of life.'

She was saddened by his revelation, but Letty had no
intention of allowing him to drag her down into his self-
pity. 'Pretty rackety existence, eh? Rattling around Europe
free from divine supervision, I expect you got up to all
sorts of mischief. I can imagine.'

He gave her a pale smile. 'I do hope you can't.'

As he spoke, his face, lined with bitterness and self-
loathing, conveyed all the suffering of all young men
thrust, unwilling, into that obscenity. And still, years after
the war, he was walking around, an open wound, incap-
able of healing. And what was a woman to do but offer
whatever balm came to hand? It was her mother's long-
forgotten childish endearments, murmured in soft French,
that came to her lips as she bent and gathered him into her
arms, cheek against his, rocking him gently.

One moment, he was reaching for her, clinging to her, his
head drooping heavily on to her shoulder, the next, with a
suddenness that alarmed her, he had raised his head and
pushed her away, eyes sweeping the thickets on the
perimeter of the glade.

282

'Ssh! There's something . . . somebody . . . moving about over there. Do you hear it?'

'No, William. No, I don't.'

He remained tense, on the alert.

'It's all right, William,' she said, finally. 'You can stand down and stop scanning the horizon in that stagey way. Calm yourself! My impulse towards you was no more than a misplaced maternal gesture intended to comfort and soothe. Nothing more challenging than that.'

He replied, not taking his eyes off the distant trees. 'Dash it! And for a moment I thought you were about to make the Ultimate Sacrifice.'

Regretting her sympathetic overture and not much liking Gunning's swift return to self-parody, she replied crisply: 'Time to go home, I think. Here, put this back where you found it, will you?' She handed him the photograph. 'Too embarrassing for Edmond if he found out that his touching gesture had been discovered.'

'And, if it comes to being discovered, it may seem a bit melodramatic, but I don't think we should be seen driving back together. I'll drop you on the corner by the Haras where I picked you up.'

They were a mile short of the town when, negotiating a bend, Gunning exclaimed and pulled the car over on to the verge of the road to avoid an oncoming cyclist. Pedalling demurely towards them, basket full of vegetables from the garden, came Marie-Louise. She wobbled to a halt and put a foot down, looking from one to the other in surprise. Taking in their dishevelled appearance, her surprise turned to chilly disapproval. 'Hello, there. Enjoying the evening air, I see?'

'Wonderful! I've been visiting the count's horse. He's gone off to Lyon – with his groom – leaving Dido in the low pasture. She's jolly nearly fully healed, you know, and I said I'd keep an eye on her, take her on a gentle circuit or two of the field each evening to keep her in shape. They keep a field bridle handily on the wall by the gate . . .' She hesitated as Gunning's foot crunched down on her toe and finished hurriedly, 'But it's an awful bother getting out there and the Reverend kindly offered to drive me over.'

Marie-Louise listened, wide-eyed, to the meandering explanation, and managed a stiff smile. 'But you could have borrowed Maman's bicycle! Just let me know if you need it.'

'Going somewhere interesting?' Gunning asked politely.

'Oh, no! Just taking these things to my aunt down the road.' She waved a hand at the vegetables. 'It's the courgette glut! You'll be having courgette soup for supper every day for the next week, I'm afraid.' She nodded at both of them awkwardly then cycled away.

'Marie-Louise looked a bit hot and bothered, wouldn't you say?' remarked Gunning as they drove off.

'Could it be that she was purple with suppressed rage at seeing us together out of context? Do you think she noticed your collar's on back to front and your trousers are damp?' said Letty.

'And that you've got a dead harebell over one ear and grass stains all down your shirt? No, I don't suppose so.'

'Still – fences to mend there, as my father would say,' murmured Letty thoughtfully.

Chapter Thirty

'Are you sure this is going to be all right, Stella?'

This was the third time Marie-Louise had asked the question, and her uncertainty was beginning to chip away at Letty's confidence. Panting with the effort and the heat, the two girls had abandoned the attempt to cycle up the slope to the château and were pushing the heavy-framed bicycles the last few metres to the entrance.

Letty took her bunch of keys from the bike basket and rattled them. 'These are symbolic, I know, and I wouldn't like to have to try to find the doors they opened, but just you wait – drawbridges will crash down, trumpets will sound, gates will swing open at our approach. You'll see!'

She prayed that the local schoolmistress was not on d'Aubec's ejection list. Though initially cool towards Letty the day after their encounter in the lane, Marie-Louise had responded warmly enough to her request, over breakfast, to borrow Mme Huleux's bicycle. 'If you're sure your mother wouldn't mind? It would be a godsend – save me having to bother the poor old vicar again. Tell you what – why don't you come too? I'm getting off work a couple of hours early – it's the new schedule. Paradee's making us start and finish earlier while the weather is so unbearably hot. When I've checked the horse, we could go on up to the château to round off the ride and be back in time for supper. There's something very ancient and very Burgundian I'd like you to see,' she had offered temptingly.

And Marie-Louise had presented herself ready for the outing, fresh and eager in a white pleated tennis skirt and pink blouse, hair held back with a pink flowered scarf. Divested of her straight-cut, sober serge, and wearing colours that set off her dark looks, she was a very attractive girl, Letty noted, and was saddened by the thought that a dreary cycle ride with her English guest should be the occasion for such bubbling anticipation.

She had watched as Letty had whistled up Dido in her pasture and checked her over, and then followed when she set off boldly up the hill. Halfway there, with the size and severity of the building looming over them, the French girl had lost confidence. Stopping to get her breath, she'd confessed that she'd never visited the château before. D'Aubec, although generous in other ways with both time and money, was jealous of his privacy and, as far as Marie-Louise was aware, no townspeople were ever invited to go up there. The last time a marauding band of villagers tracked up here, she confided, was in 1790 and what they had in mind was the looting of a château whose owner had fled with his family to London. Two further reassurances were necessary before she could be persuaded to present herself with Letty at the gate.

To Letty's relief the door in the wide wooden gate was opened on their approach by a manservant who recognized her: 'Ah, here you are, mademoiselle. We missed you yesterday. No – allow me – I'll take your bicycles.'

The housekeeper was waiting by the front door with a warm smile. Tea and iced lemonade were offered. Gaining rapidly in courage, Letty asked for it to be served in the library. 'My friend, Mlle Huleux, is a schoolmistress and shares my deep interest in books and local history . . .' she began to explain, but trailed off with the realization that no explanations were expected.

Mme Lepage acknowledged Marie-Louise with a polite tilt of the head. 'Of course. Guillaume Huleux's daughter. You are welcome, mademoiselle.'

'Mme Lepage is – perhaps you didn't know, Stella? – the sister of the pâtissier's wife, Agnès,' explained Marie-Louise, apparently encouraged by the encounter.

286

Letty tried to stroll as to the manner born along the corridors as they made their way to the library, pausing to wash their sweaty hands in the cloakroom. 'I know you – and the whole town probably – must have been speculating in a perhaps overheated way about my activities up here with the count,' she began, and hurried on when Marie-Louise smiled and seemed about to interrupt. 'I've dragged you out all this way to show you exactly what I've been working on.'

'We had rather hoped you'd been working on the count,' said Marie-Louise surprisingly.

'Great Heavens! Aren't you aware that he's engaged to be married to his cousin Gabrielle? Why, he's even now in Lyon fixing the date.' Her voice sounded evasive even to her own ears.

Marie-Louise was scornful. 'Not that again? It's been rumoured for years. We were hoping he'd forgotten about it. Changed his mind. The lady is not much liked hereabouts. Snooty, manicured, tailored, skittish as an overbred horse. She's a city girl by nature and hates coming out here to the depths of the country.' She eyed Letty standing, red-faced, in bush shirt and trousers. 'The town's money is on you, *ma chère*. We appreciate a woman with dirt under her fingernails, sweat on her brow, and the courage to square up to d'Aubec. The Revolution seems not so distant, you know, to some. We're not all the forelock-tugging yokels you take us for! Just over a hundred years ago we were busily chopping off the heads of the aristocracy and setting up altars to the Goddess of Reason. There's an old carpenter in the town – Bernard Dutronc. He's very old . . . he must be over ninety . . . and he well remembers his grandfather – also a carpenter – who worked on the construction of the local guillotine. It's said that Bernard keeps the original design for the contraption in his workshop to this day. My great-great-grandmother probably knitted at the foot of it!'

This little speech was delivered with relish.

287

'Great Heavens!' said Letty. 'I had no idea! I'll be sure to warn Edmond that you still have the skills, Citoyenne.' She was beginning to get the measure of Marie-Louise, she thought. The words 'republican, revolutionary, anarchic' occurred to her, though she drew the line at labelling anyone 'Bolshevik'.

Marie-Louise's reaction to the library was everything Letty had expected. After her initial gasp of appreciation, she'd begun to move about, excited but restrained, firing question after question, looking but not touching. Finally they settled to an inspection of the ancient books d'Aubec had left on the table.

'But these should be put away, surely, in safe conditions to preserve them, not just left lying about,' she protested, refusing to put a hand on them. 'If they are what you say they are they should be in a museum, properly cared for and available for inspection by anyone who has an interest in them. They ought not to belong to d'Aubec – they should be handed over to the nation.'

'I think that's exactly what he's got in mind. They seem to have worn well so far. I would guess that the conditions here in this room are congenial. It's north-facing, cool, and dry. He cares too much to let them suffer in any way. Don't worry about that, Marie-Louise.'

'But what about this?' Marie-Louise said, gingerly poking at the scroll of architectural designs which Letty had left between the two piles. 'This has no leather backing to protect it. It shouldn't be left here on the table for anyone to handle.'

'That one's not particularly old, you'll find – 1810 or thereabouts. Plans for the construction of the stable block and the chapel. All completed by Hippolyte, I'm told – the chap who escaped the attentions of Dutronc's device. He returned from exile with an English heiress on his arm and they proceeded to spend a great deal of money refurbishing and expanding. It won't crumble, I promise, if you want to have a look.'

Intrigued, Marie-Louise held open the sheet by its

edges and studied it, turning it this way and that. 'Ah, yes, here are the stables. And the architect's notes. More than a touch of Ledoux. Very grand. Just what a man eager to re-establish himself would spend his money on. He knew how to behave, this young man. He employed local labour, cared for the estates . . . Oh, and here are plans for a chapel. Of course. Defender of the old faith, a traditionalist, countering the forces of republicanism and anti-clericalism. A wise move. And your Edmond continues the good work. He has his friend the curé to dinner once a week and the bishop twice a year. But I had no idea there was a private chapel – d'Aubec and his mother both worship at the church of St Mary Magdalene. Have you seen this chapel, Stella?'

'No, I haven't.' As she spoke she realized her voice had conveyed a sudden doubt. D'Aubec had never offered to show her the chapel. The hesitation was instantly picked up by Marie-Louise.

'Ah! A *secret* chapel? Sounds intriguing! But, wouldn't you like to see it? I think you should! It may hold revelations regarding the state of his soul. Better find out before it's too late whether your count is a disciple of the infamous Gilles de Rais. Perhaps they keep it locked up, stuffed full of guilty secrets? Upside-down crucifixes, pentangles on the floor, severed heads in niches, you know the sort of thing . . .'

Marie-Louise fell silent in embarrassment as the housekeeper entered with a tray of tea things.

'Oh, sponge cake and strawberry jam! How lovely! You are too kind! Madame Lepage, tell me – the chapel – is it kept unlocked? We were just thinking how very much we'd like to see it,' Letty said brightly, aware that the housekeeper must have overheard. Good servants, in her experience, always listened to the last sentence uttered before they came through the door.

'Of course,' was the smiling reply. 'And you will find we change the flowers there every day – even when the family are not at home. You know where to find it, mademoiselle? Take the long corridor and it's right at the end, on the western side of the house.'

Madame Lepage withdrew and Letty waited for Marie-Louise to finish her slice of cake. 'Well? What about it?' she said. 'An assault on Bluebeard's lair? Are you up to this? You don't have to, you know.'

'Oh, do you think we dare?'

Letty laughed. 'For a girl who claims descent from marauding yeoman stock, you're not very adventurous, Marie-Louise. In fact, I'm not sure that your antecedents can have been the bold despoilers you'd have me believe! I have noticed that much of the pre-Revolutionary furniture and decorations are still in place. They appear not to have been stolen or defaced. Not so much as a moustache drawn on a portrait.'

'True, most probably,' Marie-Louise admitted. 'It's said that when the townspeople reached the gate it was flung open by the maître d'hôtel, who greeted them by name and politely but firmly sent them about their business. They were informed that they were not able to speak to the count, who was away in London, but he sent them his greetings and looked forward to seeing them on his return.'

'Well done, the maître d'hôtel! And I hope he kept his head! Pity there isn't a portrait of him to admire, but we can have a look at his liege lord. Come on! We pass him on the way to the chapel.'

Marie-Louise's awed enthusiasm for the portraiture slowed them down to a point where Letty had to mask her impatience. Starting with brother Guy, whom she remembered and said a prayer for, they progressed along the line, Marie-Louise's commentary more anecdotal and salty than the official introduction d'Aubec had given her.

'Oh, look! That must be old so-and-so ... Now it's strongly rumoured that every time he went to Paris ... Ah! The family face! Do look at those ears, Stella – you'll see the very same on old Gaston at the Lion d'Or!' And on down the line until she stood, enthralled, in front of

Hippolyte and Charlotte and the tumbling brood of round-faced children. 'Good grief! How many?'

'Well, there were more to come. Eleven all told, according to Edmond. He says this was painted in 1810 on their return.'

'But had they the time to produce so many ... five ... six ... seven ... little cherubs?'

'Oh, yes. He went off to evade the clutches of your mob in 1790-ish ... married and came back, let's say, in 1808? That's plenty of time for a d'Aubec to show his paces, I'd have thought.'

'And we can be certain of the date? Perhaps it's a year or so later than you calculated?' said Marie-Louise, her voice giving away the excitement of an art historian on the verge of making a discovery. 'We ought to be able to work it out exactly. Look at the background!'

Letty looked. And looked again. How had she missed it? The now familiar outline of hills partially obscured by the half-built stable block. 'Right for direction. Wrong for elevation,' Gunning had said. This angle was right for both. Her eye was being directed firmly beyond the rising wall of the stables to the dark encircling cliff side behind, a cliff side about to be concealed by the elegant golden stone lining rising in front of it.

'You must look past the flamboyant figures in the foreground, all showy silks and muslins, pink cheeks and smiles of satisfaction, and study the background,' Marie-Louise was advising in her schoolmarm voice. 'The stables are only half built, do you see? And we know the plans were drawn up in June of 1810 – did you notice the date on the plans? So there, that dates it pretty accurately, doesn't it? This was painted in late summer – look, she's holding on her lap corn, poppies, apples, late summer things. There's no way you could get the plans approved and a building team on site and work advanced to such a point in two months. No, this was done in 1811,' she finished firmly. Suddenly she grasped Letty's arm. 'Look – you can hardly make it out, but – isn't that an escutcheon, there, right over the centre, the place where the arched doorway appears on the plans? There's something written on it. A date perhaps? Get a chair, Stella!'

Not waiting for Letty to react, Marie-Louise dashed back along the corridor and returned dragging a Louis XVI chair. She put it in front of the picture, and, running a critical eye over Letty – 'I'm smaller and lighter than you' – she kicked off her sandals and climbed up.

A squeak of excitement a moment later was followed by a triumphant: 'Four words. In Latin. *Vera equis celatur dea.*'

'Very appropriate for a new stable block,' said Letty slowly, buying time as she first translated, then wondered at the text. 'Epona the Horse Goddess. You must be familiar with the d'Aubec crest?'

'Oh, yes. Very neat. Very Burgundian,' said Marie-Louise, replacing the chair. 'Completely horse-mad, that family. Heaven knows what we'll find in their chapel! Prepare yourself for a freshly severed horse's head on the altar!'

Marie-Louise's eagerness to see the chapel did not propel her past the remaining portraits, and Letty patiently conveyed the sketchy information she had to her interested audience. At last they reached the end of the gallery and turned, following the housekeeper's instructions, down a short corridor which led to the chapel.

A strong oak door, heavily carved and decorated with cascades of wildflowers and fruits that Grinling Gibbons would not have blushed for, stood closed before them. With a glance at her companion and a drawing-in of breath, Letty put a hand on the massive wrought-iron doorknob and levered up the latch.

The door swung open easily on oiled hinges and they slipped inside, closing it behind them.

Chapter Thirty-One

Unconsciously, the two girls reached for each other's hands and stood in mesmerized silence.

They had jokingly evoked a Gothic room full of dark secrets, and Letty was aware that the Catholic Marie-Louise with her almost superstitious dread of cults had been physically quivering with some emotion before they came in. Her hand even now betrayed her unsteadiness.

They stared about them, not exchanging a word.

It was the scent that Letty found disturbing. She had expected the usual ecclesiastical assault on the senses: a top note of church incense underlaid by beeswax candles and a base of damp and rotting stone. Familiar and reassuring. But she breathed deeply and drew into her lungs an enchanting blend of jasmine, roses, and wild honeysuckle. Not a trace of incense on the air. Mme Lepage's fresh flowers stood, a simple delight, in silver vases on table and window ledge.

There was no place, surely, for dark secrets in this airy room. The white-painted walls, bare of any decoration, gathered up the eye and took it vaulting to the apex of the roof, rewarding its leap with a gem of a gilded cherubic face beaming down from the central point. Ahead of them to the east stood an altar, if indeed it was an altar. A rectangular table covered in a white cloth discreetly embroidered with a frieze of green grasses held nothing more than a single vase of meadow flowers – moon-pennies and Queen Anne's lace. The seating before the altar consisted of a dozen or so chairs covered in green velvet. On the west wall behind them was a carved wooden disc, a zodiac she guessed, with painted sun, earth, and stars, connected by mysterious elliptical lines and circles. She'd seen one exactly like it in the ambulatory in Chartres cathedral.

But the drama of the room was provided by the stained glass windows on two sides, the north and the south. In the north window and fired by a gentle light, there glowed dimly a familiar figure. Mary Magdalene, as intriguing as ever, stood barefoot in her dark red dress, long fair hair tumbling about her shoulders. Tucked under one arm she held a jewel-encrusted unguent vase. And on the ground at her feet lay a simple earthenware pot. To the south, and still sparkling with a warm afternoon light, was a representation of the Virgin Mary, and it was towards this that Marie-Louise headed with an exclamation of excitement.

She dipped a curtsey in front of the Virgin, crossed herself, and beckoned for Laetitia to join her. Eyes wide with awe, she whispered: 'Do you recognize this, Stella?'

'Not sure . . . No . . . I've seen lots of similar pictures but not this one.'

Letty studied the image with the attention it compelled, astonished and wondering. Her first impression was that the style was very ancient. Madonna and Child. Byzantine? Yes, perhaps. The rounded and youthful face was almond-eyed with clear dark brows; the mouth had the slight pout of a mother who has just kissed her baby and is about to kiss him again. The nose was long and narrow. The line of her smooth chin was interrupted by the chubby right hand of her son, who grasped it in the centre – a gesture so natural and affectionate that it brought tears to Letty's eyes. The left hand of the small boy tugged playfully at a fold of the robe hanging at his mother's neck. Surely a painting done from life? The gestures were completely unstudied and accurately observed.

But it was the colours that drew and held the eye. The background was a wash of gold; a blue robe covered the girl from her head, hanging down in folds, with wide sleeves showing an under-dress of gold and pink. The sun streamed through a lighter, silvery patch on Mary's right shoulder, highlighting a single emblem. Letty moved closer and peered, trying to identify it.

Following her gaze, Marie-Louise whispered: 'Six petals. It's a rose. Mary's emblem.'

'No, it's not,' said Letty. 'Those aren't petals! Too narrow. It's a star. A six-pointed star.'

'You don't know the story, do you?'

Letty shook her head.

'You must have heard of Bernadette Soubirous?'

'Who hasn't? If you mean the little country girl who claimed to have seen visions of the Virgin Mary in a grotto at Lourdes and dug up a spring reputed to have healing powers.'

'Yes, that Bernadette. When she grew up she went to live with the Carmelite nuns in Nevers, and when asked why she refused all pictures of the Holy Mother with which she could have decorated her cell, she maintained that none of them looked remotely like the Lady she'd seen at Lourdes. She never called her the Virgin, or Madonna – always the Lady,' Marie-Louise added thoughtfully. 'And, one day, she was offered a fresh image. It was a copy of a famous icon from the cathedral in Cambrai. Bernadette accepted it at once, saying: "This is her! This is the Lady I saw!"'

'And now *you* are seeing her. The Madonna,' Marie-Louise said with the warmth and formality of one making an introduction. She was clearly looking for an appropriate reaction from the silent Laetitia.

As no words would come, Letty made the sign of the cross and gazed back in unfeigned admiration at the picture. This was not the place; this was not the companion with whom she could air her thoughts.

'This is a version in glass of that image in Cambrai. And, Stella, the fascinating thing is – the original icon, which is quite small' – she sketched out with her hands a size a little larger than a sheet of foolscap paper – 'came to France in . . . oh . . . 1400 and something . . . from Byzantium. But before it fetched up there, it's said, it came from the Holy

Land and was painted by Saint Luke himself! What do you think of *that*?'

Laetitia truly thought she'd recognized, in the slightly unfocused gaze and the gestures of maternal pride, an enduring image, a universal image. Mary, certainly. But also Isis or any one of man's visions of the Goddess-Mother.

'I believe it all,' said Letty, smiling. 'Whoever painted her and whoever she is, for *me* she's the Virgin, the Mother. I feel I've met her and yet she's inspiring and imposing. Wonderful!'

Marie-Louise appeared pleased with the reaction. She went to repeat her curtsey, murmured a prayer before Mary Magdalene, and then settled on one of the green chairs in front of the altar to look around her again.

The Good Catholic, then, appeared to have given the chapel her approval. Staring ahead at the expanse of the eastern wall beyond the altar, Laetitia wondered if her friend had responded too swiftly. Perhaps there was a third window piercing the white-painted stone wall? One certainly looked for an image of some significance in that place. Difficult to judge, since a linen curtain hanging from a black iron pole had been drawn across the entire wall. If there was a stained glass offering behind it, the effect must be very spectacular speared by morning light, Letty thought. She joined Marie-Louise and, head bowed, went through her familiar routine when praying by herself in French churches. She found, with some surprise, that she was offering up a prayer, a request for indulgence for William Gunning.

Raising her head when she thought Marie-Louise had finished her devotions, she gave her a gentle nudge. It was difficult to speak out loud and her voice came in a whisper. 'Look behind the altar, Marie-Louise. What do you suppose that curtain conceals? Do you think we could take a peek? I should like to. The other two windows are truly lovely and the third, if there is one, is in pride of place and probably even more spectacular. It must be well worth seeing.'

Receiving a doubtful nod as assent, Letty moved forward and pulled on a fold of the curtain. Light poured into the chapel as she tugged it clear of the window it had been hiding, and she was aware of puzzlement on Marie-Louise's face. Moving back to get the window in focus, she sat down again by her side.

'But what is this?' Marie-Louise hissed. 'I'm not sure what I was expecting to see, but it certainly wasn't this! I don't understand. Are we to imagine ourselves at Eleusis? Did the priests not close the Ceremony of the Mysteries in ancient Athens with just such a piece of nonsense?' She stirred uneasily, glancing to right and left, calming her doubts with the comforting familiar presence of the two Marys. 'An ear of wheat? Just an ear of wheat? Are we supposed to be impressed? I've seen more impressive symbols in a baker's shop! And what is that framework surrounding it meant to represent?'

Almost equally puzzled, Letty considered the window. Plain uncoloured glass for the most part, a dash of colour had been inserted towards the centre. A circular maze, delicately etched and tinted black, swirled in a continuous line around an open space. And in the centre was shown, in gold, the offending single ear of wheat.

'It looks very simple,' she agreed. 'All that plain glass . . . it's almost like a marker, a stopgap, holding the space for something more important to come. Striking, though, what there is of it.'

'Well, I think it's disappointing but at least it's not a pentangle.' Marie-Louise crossed herself hurriedly as the last word slipped out.

'And I'll tell you what else is missing,' said Letty, 'from our shopping list of religious arcana. Crucifixes. Not one, right way up or otherwise.'

Marie-Louise crossed herself again at the glancing reference to Satanism and said uncomfortably, 'Can we leave now, Stella? I'm pleased to have seen Mary, but there's really not a lot more here to claim the attention, is there?'

As they walked back down the corridor, Letty pursued her theories. 'All the same, the similarity with the cathedral at Chartres is striking, you know. No crucifixion scenes to be seen there, either – nor, I believe, in any of the Gothic cathedrals which shot up all over northern France in so short a time. And they were all rather bare of ornament originally and soaring like a symphony. When I was small, and left sitting by myself in the cathedral, I used to think that if I struck one of the columns with a tuning fork, the whole building would sing to me. I had much the same feeling in that chapel. And the maze . . . there is a maze on the floor in Chartres. I've walked it many times.'

All this cathedral lore seemed to be soothing Marie-Louise.

'I'm sure there was no pagan undertone,' said Letty. 'Just a nod to the Burgundian way of life. I expect the architect dissuaded Hippolyte from putting a stallion argent passant up there and the wheat was no doubt a concession. It could just as easily have been a bunch of grapes or a vine leaf or two, but I suppose that would have struck a wrong Dionysian note. At least there are frequent references to wheat in the Bible – all that sowing and reaping and falling on hard ground.'

'Well, anyhow,' Marie-Louise said, shrugging, 'there was something about it . . . It wasn't Roman Catholic.'

'With the Blessed VM well to the fore?' said Letty. 'You can't get more Catholic than that. And la Madeleine, the local patron saint, backing up on the right flank?'

'But I didn't quite feel easy there.'

'No. I have to say it: nor did I,' Letty admitted. 'But then, we were interlopers. It's a family place and we ought not to have been there. But – tell you what – there is a place we will feel welcome. We've got bags of time before supper and our road home's all downhill . . . would you like to inspect the stables before we leave?' She was eager to take a fresh look at the building in the light of the revelation in the portrait. 'And there's something special to show you,' she added, remembering.

Marie-Louise pulled a face. 'Oh, would you mind if we didn't? I don't care for horses very much.' And, catching Letty's disappointment, hurried to add, 'Oh, but I *would* be interested to see the architecture.'

They crunched over the gravel and stood in front of the symmetrical façade, looking up at the carved relief of silver-haired Epona above the arched entrance.

'"*Vera dea,*"' commented Marie-Louise. 'The true goddess. And I expect the rest of the building is a shrine to her. *Ça alors!* Nothing but the best for the horses! There are people in the town who have much less opulent accommodation.'

Before they started their tour of the stables, Letty looked in on Bella and her single remaining pup. To her joy, both animals came fussing forward to greet her. Marie-Louise was less enchanted. 'Ah. Dogs. I don't mind dogs. Those are pretty.'

She paid little attention to the horses themselves, seeming even to have for them an aversion she was trying to conceal behind an over-bright reading out of their names from the brass plates fixed over their stalls. She kept well clear of the bumping rear ends and watched carefully where she put her feet. 'How many can one man need?' she said critically. 'But at least I suppose they provide employment,' she conceded, watching as a groom came in whistling, greeted Letty, and began to attend to a chestnut hunter.

'Oh, Marcel!' said Letty. 'I wonder if you've made arrangements for Dido tomorrow? I understand there are going to be fireworks let off in the evening. I wouldn't want her to be alarmed and dash around damaging herself again just when she's so nicely healed.'

'All's in hand, Miss.' The countryman grinned with pleasure, eager to speak to her. 'We'll get 'er in from the pasture long before the junketing starts.' He rolled his eyes. 'The Saint Jean! It's likely to get a bit lively, like! And how that do go on! Begging your pardon, Miss, but I said young

Robert could go down to town and take a look around. He's still of bonfire-leaping age and unattached as yet. The count usually gives permission. There'll be two lads on duty here just to quieten any nerves. As per usual.' .

'Then I'm sure that will be fine, Marcel,' said Letty, bemused. 'Carry on. Bath time, is it?'

'That's right. He's been rolling in something nasty.'

'Where's he taking that animal?' Marie-Louise asked.

'To have a bath,' said Letty, enjoying her surprise. 'Oh, yes, they have their own bath! Well, washing pond – there's a reservoir a short way down the hill to feed it.'

'*And* their own piped water supply, I see,' said Marie-Louise, eyeing a water basin and brass tap.

'Horses need a lot of water – they're not happy to guzzle champagne like their master.' Letty was getting a bit fed up with Marie-Louise's socialist slant and critical eye.

'Sorry! This is all fresh and strange to me!' she said, tuning at once to Letty's mood. 'Do go on – I'm enjoying the tour. Tell me – how many grooms work here?' she asked, struggling to show interest.

'There are three at the moment, more in the high season. And there's Jules, who's usually in charge, but he's away in Lyon with the boss.'

'I see. And over there?' she asked, pointing towards the door at the end of the run of stalls. 'Is that where the grooms live? Does he make the men live with the horses?'

'No. They have their quarters over in a wing of the main house. This is the harness room.' Letty unlocked the solid oak door and Marie-Louise poked her head around and then entered.

'Ah! At last a room I can enjoy,' she said, sniffing appreciatively the scents of leather and cedarwood, approving the neatness and order. Glass-fronted cupboards held saddles in rows; pieces of metal harness were arranged on felt-backed boards fixed to the panelled walls; polished riding boots stood lined up, toes outwards; and a row of wild boars' heads glared down at them with small savage eyes.

300

But it was the wall backing up to the natural rock out-crop that encircled and defended the castle promontory that was drawing Letty. While wishing Marie-Louise and her iconoclastic eye a thousand miles away, she had to feel grateful to the girl for spotting the marker in the portrait: the second escutcheon, clearly indicating a place of inter-est – the place to which Daniel had been directing her all along. Letty paused and looked around to get her bearings, recalling the position of the escutcheon, and then she strolled along until she reached the spot where she cal-culated it would have appeared, halfway along the stalls and opposite the main entrance. And she saw there another sign so clear, so obvious, that for a moment she stood, frozen and staring.

Marie-Louise's voice over her shoulder made her jump. 'Is she special?' she asked. 'This horse? The pretty white one.'

'Grey,' said Letty automatically.

'Nonsense. She's pure white. What's her name? What do you bet it's "Snowflake"?' She peered into the stall which occupied the exact halfway point along the row and put out a hesitant hand to pat the silken flank of the mare, standing quiet and unthreatening. She read with some dif-ficulty. 'Ah! We'd lose our bet. It appears to be "Eponina". Daughter of Epona . . . well, what else?'

The lettering was florid, curlicued – of a bygone age. The brass name plate was so well polished, the letters were barely discernible. Probably of the same age as the stables, Letty guessed. And it looked unchanged. It occurred to her that every horse occupying that stall must have answered to the name of 'Eponina'. A long tradition of white mares? All the guardians of the goddess? *Vera dea celatur equis suis.* The true goddess is concealed by her horses.

A rush of frustration and longing swept over Letty. 'Edmond! Where are you? You should be here. Now.'

Her fingers closed over the notebook in her pocket.

* * *

301

'Supper calls, I think. We'll just let Mme Lepage know that we're leaving now.'

Letty led the way back into the château and along to the summer salon, where she rang the bell for the housekeeper. Letty thanked her for the excellent tea. 'We were particularly taken with the cake, madame. The *quatre-quarts*? Delicious! Your own recipe?'

'One I inherited from my grandmother, mademoiselle. But it is simple: a question of the best ingredients – eggs and butter straight from the home farm – and the exactness of the quantities.'

'Is it a secret or could you bear to give me the recipe? I should like to have a copy for my cook in England.'

At Mme Lepage's nodding consent, she tore a page from her notebook and handed it to Marie-Louise with a stub of pencil. 'Look – why doesn't the teacher take dictation for a change? Would you mind, Marie-Louise? I've remembered I promised to telephone Edmond to reassure him about Dido's condition. I'll dash down to the library and do that now. Oh, and while I'm at it – why don't I ring your father and tell him we'll be a little late for supper? What's your number? . . . Write it down here . . . Thanks . . . Be back in a tick.'

Letty smiled as she closed the door on Madame Lepage's authoritative voice. 'Take six eggs and their weight in butter . . .'

Chapter Thirty-Two

'Let me have men about me that are fat;'

D'Aubec recalled with an effort the few lines of the one play of Shakespeare's that he admired.

'Sleek-headed men and such as sleep o'nights;
Yon Cassius has a lean and hungry look;
He thinks too much: such men are dangerous.'

But just for once, Julius Caesar had it wrong, he thought, looking at the selection around the conference table. The two politicians would have found favour with Caesar, certainly. At first appearances, they had the comfortable fleshiness of the bons vivants they undoubtedly were, but their lapdog sleekness was deceptive. One French senator, one German – a disaffected member of the Weimar Republican government – it was hard to distinguish one from the other. Their eyes were shrewd and now, at the end of a gruelling two-hour session, remained alert. D'Aubec trusted neither one outside the limit of the control he exercised. The two reins of ambition and coercion that he held in his hands seemed to keep them on track. The pair of industrialists, however, had the rangy twitchiness of wolves. He didn't trust them, either. 'Cassius' and 'Casca', he named them privately. Just as well he had his own special means of ensuring their loyalty.

He disliked the pair of them but agreed with Constantine that they had much to offer. He recognized that the war could have been won three years earlier by the allies, had not the German cause been saved by – of all men – a chemist. Not a general, not a politician, not even an assassin. By unravelling the threads and tracing them back, he and Constantine had arrived at a point early in the war when it was clear that the lives of millions hung on the discovery of one man. If a man called Haber had not found out how to synthesize ammonia, German supplies of nitrate, essential for the production of explosives, would have run out as a consequence of the British blockade and their army would have been obliged to put up its hands in short order. No Somme. No Verdun. No Ypres.

And here at his table was another of these modern magicians: a chemist, German-born, distinguished, sought after by many nations. Tipped to receive the Nobel Prize, d'Aubec was assured. A man of exceptional ability, conscienceless, ambitious, he was tireless in the quest he had pursued since before the war. This was no less than to produce industrially a highly toxic acid which would prove a more reliable and effective weapon than the chlorine gas the German army had uncorked at Ypres. A gas dependent on wind for dispersal, the armies had realized, was uncertain, and the prevailing wind on the battlefield, on two days out of three, blew from west to east. Unfortunately, the day Edmond's brother Guy had been sent to the trenches had been a third day.

In the grey unnamed folder under Constantine's elbow, the one he privately called 'War Technology', were details of the scientist's brainchild, a sweet-smelling, highly toxic pest-control substance. Already tested and ready for production. And there the scientist sat, smoking a cigar and dropping names: '. . . my good friend Albert Einstein once confided . . . It's not generally known, of course, that the Kaiser is pathologically afraid of the dark, but . . .' Tedious upstart! The second guest, a Swiss, owned the factories and the resources to turn the formula into drums of poison gas.

And d'Aubec owned the Swiss.

Sharing a table with members of his family in his uncle's gracious town house, the newcomers had responded to the courtly good manners and warm welcome they had experienced. His mother, present as hostess, reassured them with her well-bred confidence and her openness. And who could fail to be impressed by the chairman, his uncle? D'Aubec exchanged a glance of weary amusement with Auguste. He owed everything to Auguste. The elderly aristocrat had taken in hand the distraught younger son he had been when, at the age of sixteen, he had acceded to the title on Guy's death. Auguste had understood the boy's grief and his urge to throw himself at once into the conflict, but he had successfully counselled against it, calling on the strongest motives. And, in the way of younger sons who have seen no action, d'Aubec had set about acquiring the panache he considered the world might expect of a descendant of the Dukes of Burgundy. Discovering that no one takes any notice of a sixteen-year-old even if he is shaving twice a day, he developed a peremptory bark and a decisive manner. With his uncle's guidance and the genius of Auguste's man Constantine, he had set about repairing the family's fortunes, sunk to a low ebb during the war. The unfathomable Constantine's first loyalty – d'Aubec was under no illusion – had always been to his uncle. And there he sat, his literal right-hand man, peacefully making notes and exchanging asides with Auguste.

D'Aubec examined their profiles, the elderly and the young. He could see no physical resemblance but, as he occasionally did, he played with the thought that Constantine might have a closer relationship with his uncle than had been publicly admitted. In the days of the *ancien régime*, illegitimate sons were given similar influential positions within a noble household. Constantine would have worn the splendid satin coat of a *gentilhomme servant* and been charged with the administration of the household. He would have had the ear of the lord and wielded considerable power. Nowadays he chose to call himself a secretary; he wore dark suits and stayed discreetly in the

305

background. But the influence remained. And so carefully was it managed that d'Aubec himself was never quite certain how far it reached. He knew neither the extent nor the quality of that influence. What he did know was that difficulties and difficult people were often ironed away as they arose, following a calm 'Leave this to me, Edmond.'

And perhaps he'd left too much to Constantine? Could he ever manage his enterprise without the man's acumen and his executive abilities? Probably not. D'Aubec had no delusions; he was clever enough to calculate and accept that his own intellectual powers were inferior to those of his secretary. And he was not unaware that to be the dashing figurehead of any movement was to occupy a dangerous and exposed position.

Well, today he intended to surprise them all. He'd had quite enough of standing at the prow, jaw to the wind, feeling but not occasioning the power surge and the direction changes happening behind him. Today the figurehead would suddenly show itself capable of acting as steering oar!

He looked around the table assessing alliances and allegiances and wondering in whom he could safely trust. Strangely, he'd have felt more confident with Laetitia at his side. She would support him, watch his back, make him feel less alone.

He'd enjoyed leading her on a wild-goose chase, a Gothic treasure hunt, trailing the lure of Daniel's clues to a secret that was no secret to him, and he felt no guilt at the deception. The distracting trail of ancient books he'd put in front of her had been an inspiration! And he'd dreamed up the scheme himself.

He pictured again the delight with which she'd fallen on the texts, tears of emotion in her eyes as she'd swept up her godfather's notes. She'd even secreted something from the wastebasket into her pocket when she thought he wasn't looking. It had been the work of a moment to bring out of storage the boxes of material Daniel had left behind and spread it out in a semblance of the disordered mess in

306

which he usually worked. And he'd obviously got it right. He remembered Laetitia's barely contained eagerness to grapple with the translation, so reminiscent of Daniel's enthusiasm. He smiled at the memory of their last evening when, with wide-eyed solemnity just failing to cover a bubbling glee, she'd revealed to him 'his treasure'.

And, much to his amusement, that's exactly what it had turned out to be – a treasure of sorts. He had felt proud to be the owner, the inheritor, of this nationally important cache of texts. Auguste had agreed with him that it should be exploited and as soon as possible. Their man at the Louvre had it in hand already, and the resulting news reports would have the power to knock any Egyptian Pharaoh off the front pages. The whole country would rediscover, in the most sensational way, a pride in its Celtic roots. Thanks to Laetitia, they'd taken the first step.

Unexpectedly, he had caught her fever. He'd fallen victim to his own manufactured excitement — been hoist with his own petard. Her instinct had been right and he was the more the fool . . . so unaware of what had been there in front of him, available yet ignored.

He'd shrugged off suggestions that he was spending too many precious hours in her sole company, but the pressure on him to 'resolve the problem of Miss Talbot', as they delicately put it, was increasing. Was she on their side or not? No halfway position would be tolerated. No objections or queries had ever been raised by his previous fleeting amours. He'd always dealt with the consequences himself, amicably, satisfactorily. Easy enough to do if one was circumspect. Upper-class, married, Parisian. This was the preferred order of qualifications – and all three, for choice. He stirred in his seat at an uncomfortable and usually suppressed memory. He'd made a mistake. Barely out of adolescence and testing out his newly acquired position, he'd fallen for and tempted a village girl. It would all have been a disaster if Constantine hadn't been brought in to negotiate with the outraged family, calm anger, and divert recrimination. This was the first occasion on which he'd been grateful to hear 'Leave this to me, Edmond.' And he'd defused the bad situation. D'Aubec was not encouraged to ask by what means.

But he wanted Constantine nowhere near Laetitia Talbot. He remembered standing with her before Guy's portrait, his arm about her supple waist, her blouse still damp from the spring, the delightful scent of the top of her head under his nose . . . herbs? grasses? . . . and a gentle female glow, at once reassuring and arousing. A woman who felt right at his side. A choice of the heart and the head. Perfect! He smiled to himself at the memory of her face in the grove at twilight, eyes huge with a blend of excitement and trepidation. He'd been a fool not to go through with it. He should have made certain of her there and then, as he'd intended, in the shade of the rowan tree. He shifted uncomfortably in his seat, feeling a rush of anger and regret. Yes, that would have done it.

A girl of her background – she'd have considered herself instantly committed to him. Undoubtedly a virgin. And you didn't expect an English girl to have acquired the sophisticated knowledge of someone like Gabrielle, with the addresses of discreet Parisian clinics in her notebook and their intriguing products secreted away in jewellery cases and powder boxes. He couldn't now imagine why he'd held off – she'd been very willing. Attracted to him, that was obvious; allured by his way of life but a girl not to be impressed by expensive gifts . . . He was sure he'd got that right. And if he'd insisted, they could have presented everyone with a fait accompli. He wasn't obliged to wait for Constantine's nod – or his mother's approval.

The old lady had had her doubts at first. 'Darling, are you sure?' she'd asked. 'My friends report that this English girl is somewhat . . . er . . . *farouche*. She goes around the town in trousers and boots with her hair all over the place and – they tell me – galloping about like a goatherd. Daniel gave us no warning of this, I'm quite certain.'

D'Aubec had reassured her that at Laetitia's appearance at the Lion d'Or, heads had turned; appreciative eyebrows had been raised at the sight of her severely elegant evening dress. Every hair of her blonde head had been in place, her manners impeccable. 'This is, after all, Daniel's daughter, Maman!' he'd reminded her with emphasis. 'Would we expect anything less than good breeding and charm?' And Laetitia had won his mother over, though Constantine remained impervious to the alleged charm.

As he watched, his secretary leaned to his right and made a comment to the old countess. She laughed and whispered something in agreement. Odd that; the man never said anything deliberately to amuse d'Aubec.

There was no doubting the parentage of the young man on d'Aubec's right. Very much his father's son, François had grown up with Edmond: his playmate, more of a brother than the cousin he was. François had just returned from a trip to the United States where he had plunged into a study of communications, particularly the possibilities of journalistic and cinematic propaganda. And he had returned invigorated and inspired. An ally, but more than that: his trusted lieutenant. Another young man unwilling to adapt his step to the slow march imposed by the Old Guard. His mother was supported in everything by her confidant, the priest Anselme. And their litany was unchanging: 'This is not the time. We are still in the era of the fish. We must wait, prepare, strengthen, pave the way ... There will be far graver challenges at a future time ... Another ninety years must pass ...'

Anything but take action. Edmond and François were ready. Fish? To hell with the fish!

D'Aubec had paid close attention to the scholarly Anselme's explanation of the ancient time patterns displayed by the astrological device to which his family paid such close attention. The Zodiac they kept on the wall of the chapel was the twin of the one discreetly displayed in Chartres. Such an obviously pagan symbol – he was surprised that it had not been routed out. He wasn't quite sure that it had a place in his own chapel, warning him of Sirius rising, red path intersections, ecliptic perihelions of the

Dark Star . . . mumbo jumbo! He'd tried to come to grips with it but, really, you'd need the mathematical brain of a Pythagoras to decipher it. And who was to say that some devious old Greek wasn't responsible for the contraption in the first place, or even – if Anselme's hints were to be taken seriously – an earlier witch doctor . . . some ancient Egyptian. He entertained himself briefly with the thought that the ardent amateur Egyptologist and archaeological scavenger Napoleon had sweated his rapacious way through the deserts of Egypt with his squads of scientists when such arcane knowledge had been all the while right under his nose in Chartres.

And if one of his savants had been able to interpret it and use it to unveil the future for him? D'Aubec wasn't entirely certain that it would have been possible even for a Champollion, but the Emperor would have been appalled at what he saw. Death and disaster in snow and in desert, on land and on sea. Loyal Frenchmen dying by the uncounted thousands for years in his service. And, at the end of all the slaughter – the bloody English, left strutting about, cock of the walk! Never again. The next attempt to secure supremacy – and the peace it would bring – would be short-lived, unexpected, and delivered with the precision of a surgeon's scalpel. Good thought! He scribbled on his notepad. Yes, he'd mention the scalpel . . .

Timing! It was all in the timing, and d'Aubec wasn't prepared to be restricted by the predictions of some worm-eaten old piece of astrological rubbish. He'd worked out a perfectly timed scheme without the aid of oracles or computation or even advice from anyone. A scheme that stunned by its simplicity.

François had been left gabbling with astonishment and approval when he'd confided it to him, and with his support he intended to put it before the gathering. Constantine was unaware; d'Aubec longed to see his expression when the plan unfolded before him. All the key players were here. A decision could be arrived at before they rose from the table. D'Aubec smiled, grim but elated. The security of Europe – perhaps the world – would be decided by his words in the coming minutes. He was no orator. He would keep it short and blunt. The substance of his proposal was shattering enough to pin them to their seats. He squared his shoulders, cleared his throat, and resolved to speak slowly.

His uncle caught his eye. 'And now, I believe Edmond has a proposal of a practical nature to put before us . . . Edmond?'

D'Aubec set aside his notes and looked around, waiting until all eyes were turned on him. The eyes were chill and reserved. He caught expressions ranging from outright suspicion to his mother's lightly questioning wariness.

'Gentlemen, you have your diaries? I'm going to ask you to enter some dates.'

At his prosaic opening, stiff postures began to relax. Diaries and workbooks were duly opened, fountain pens uncapped.

'You will already have noted an entry for July the fourth last year? The day of the National Socialist rally in Weimar? Larger than their Munich assembly in '23. The movement, as we had predicted, is growing at a pace to make our graphologists gasp. I want you now to note down the twentieth of August of this year.'

No one wrote. Pens poised, they stared at him, waiting.

'The third Party Conference is to be held this summer in Nuremberg. They have booked the Leitpold arena, where they are to stage what they are calling their "Day of Awakening" rally.'

François gave a knowing and cynical laugh. 'We have had sight of their arrangements. No secret. And their organization has never been difficult to infiltrate. Our information is of the best. François?'

His cousin rose and went to a display board installed at the end of the room and pinned up a poster-sized sheet. He returned to his seat. François had learned the importance of the visual image in manipulating perception. And the carefully chosen press photograph he'd had enlarged and printed spoke volumes.

D'Aubec allowed time for everyone to absorb the subject, noting the grunts of disgust and amused titters that ran round the table.

'A group photograph of the leading lights at last summer's shindig,' said d'Aubec. 'Hardly impressive. What a crew! Take a look at the circus-master in the centre. I leave a moment for you to fall victim to the pastoral charm of the costumes – the hearty socks, the woollen knickerbockers, the feathered hats. And – take a further moment to be entertained by the leader's theatrical pose. I've seen the same gestures on a flic directing the Paris traffic!' His tone was amused but full of scorn.

'But our instinctive reaction of frivolous dismissal, though understandable, is – unwise. It is less easy to speak lightly of the muscled, brown-shirted legions who step and strut before him in increasing numbers. No, we are not deceived. Nor is his government who look anxiously on, indecisive and impotent.' He waited for and received a regretful nod of assent from the German politician. 'His following grows. Thousands are expected to turn up at Nuremberg in August. The height of summer. The crowds will be in holiday mood. We may confidently expect to find there, packed into the arena, the whole of the Nazi party, their followers from every corner of Germany, and – since a recruiting drive for his SS brigade is to follow at the end of the proceedings – all the strong-arm bullyboys in the country who are sympathetic to his cause. For that one day, the city of Nuremberg will become the pest-hole of the western world.'

He paused for a moment, enjoying their puzzlement.

'Gentlemen, the rats will follow the Pied Piper. And on the twentieth of August they will all be conveniently gathered together in one place, cheering their leader, Herr Hitler. Gathered on to less than one square kilometre of German soil.'

Chapter Thirty-Three

Auguste exchanged sharp glances with Constantine. The countess looked fearfully at her son but did not interrupt.

'We have been watching this ... this ... boil grow and gather until it is bursting with pus! I reach for the scalpel! This is the moment.' D'Aubec spoke with calm certainty.

He nodded at each man around the table. 'Your gas, Erhard, will be delivered by one of *your* aeroplanes, Eric, using *your* detonating device, Claude, into the centre of this arena. No need to be concerned about the vagaries of the wind. Sufficient explosive power will be used to spread it over a neatly calculated area. In minutes we will have rid Europe of the menace of National Socialism. "Day of Awakening", gentlemen? "Hour of Oblivion" is perhaps the phrase we may expect to feature in their obituary in the footnote of history that will be accorded them.'

No one spoke.

'Eight weeks' preparation time is what we will have if we decide today on this action. We have the time, the resources, the skills, the right men with us, to achieve our aim. I need only to be assured we have the will. The practicalities will follow the decision.'

'But the scandal, d'Aubec!' objected the German politician. 'The aftermath! The Weimar Democratic Republic can not be expected to sit down and accept the wholesale slaughter of a section – albeit a despised section – of its own population! Enquiries would be made, reprisals taken. They would have to take action. Action involving the Great

313

Powers. You would not be taking on one small political group, d'Aubec. You'd be cocking a snook at the world!'

'And the world will seek you out and crush you,' added the French senator. 'I doubt anyone will mourn the loss of this vermin, but there must be a risk of obliterating innocent bystanders and we ... *you* ... will be pursued for indiscriminate slaughter. You bring your own country into danger, man! Can you not see that?'

'Of course, of course,' Constantine interposed, smoothly placatory. 'But, as I'm sure Edmond was about to explain ... if I may, Edmond? ... Two points. Firstly: our calculations will ensure a clean and clinical excision. The total loss will amount to a mere fraction of the casualties on any single day of combat in the last war. Millions of lives will be bought at the cost of a handful. Secondly: the plane we use will be German, flying, undisguised, in Weimar Republic livery. The pilot and his aide likewise, verifiably German. The machine will, sadly, crash – conveniently for the investigator – a few kilometres from the site, and the crew will be found dead in the wreckage. Nothing discovered at the scene of this disaster will lead back to us.'

Constantine's hard gaze silenced d'Aubec.

François picked up the baton. 'And, naturally, our newsmen will be on the spot to record the event. It is their photographs which will appear at once in the press, both in Germany and in France. Headlines all over Europe – and the world – will reveal the duplicity and desperation of the Weimar Republic, which found itself compelled to take this drastic step – to deal with this canker growing within its struggling state. The Great Powers who have watched from the sidelines – impotent leeches that they are! – will be loud in their condemnation, but they will heave a silent sigh of relief. We will be giving them news they want to hear. They will swallow the story with gusto! It'll slip down their gullets like the first oyster of the season!'

The young had all spoken. The older members had remained silent throughout, listening. Finally, all eyes on him, the chairman, Auguste d'Aubec, responded. He began to murmur approval in his rich, urbane baritone: 'We all acknowledge that we are engaged, not in a formal duel . . . rapiers at dawn in the Bois, eye-to-eye, toe-to-toe . . . or a medieval joust where our target is clear – and targeting us. We use the devices, the techniques, and the tactics the twentieth century has placed in our hands. And our purpose is to destroy a noxious growth which threatens to overwhelm a neighbouring country. We must look on this as part of our sacred duty. As part of our stewardship.'

'And then –' Edmond d'Aubec took up again, grateful for his uncle's pronouncement and eager to avoid alienating the older faction around the table: 'With this threat . . . this distraction . . . removed, an embattled and weakened democratic republic will be helped to struggle to its feet – once more.' He nodded to the Weimar man, directing his next comment at him: 'And perhaps, in the turmoil, there will rise to the top a more enterprising, more co-operative breed of politician? And a fresh government will have the chance to grow, uncontaminated. Other weeds may spring up – I suspect they are endemic in that soil – but we will be consolidating here and we will keep a watchful eye out. As my uncle says: This is our sacred duty,' he finished piously, pleased with the effect his speech had made on the company.

'And once free of this immediate menace,' Constantine was fast gathering up the reins, 'we can all turn our attention to achieving our real aims. A slower procedure, but the one sure way of making certain that Europe, with France properly at its centre, flourishes unimpeded, unthreatened, for centuries to come.'

If the young were intent on shaking the earth in a literal way, the older generation was working towards an earth-shaking shift in religious focus, with Constantine keeping the balance and the peace. Pivotal to the whole movement, in touch with both factions. Well, d'Aubec could pay lip service to this harmless pursuit of religious fervour. He knew that any energy could be channelled if you had the tools and the sense of direction to guide it. And he would

315

do almost anything to head off the schism he sensed was approaching.

The family was experiencing a divergence of aims. He glanced around the table once again, assessing strengths and allegiances. The chair his cousin Gabrielle should have occupied had been removed. As usual. And no loss. There was no support to be expected from her. She showed no interest in the family's business as long as her generous allowance continued to be paid. All the same, she had been the first successfully to challenge the older generation, he acknowledged with a rush of annoyance. The scene she had staged yesterday morning before the arrival of the guests had been alarming but impressive, and she had got what she wanted: the family consent to the official engagement she had set her heart on. And the wretched girl had instantly taken off to make her arrangements, which signalled an intensive shopping spree and endless telephonic gossiping with her friends. His mother and uncle had been doubtful and, predictably, had urged a further delay, but in the face of Gabrielle's determination and d'Aubec's compliance, they had conceded.

But at least he'd made sure the girl understood that in return for his lack of opposition – he could hardly call it support – she was now in his debt.

His mother was looking tired, he thought. He smiled encouragingly at her, sitting at the head of the table opposite Father Anselme. She rallied and, rising to her feet, issued an invitation to everyone to accompany her to the salon, where aperitifs would be served. Always the impeccable hostess, though increasingly weary. D'Aubec remembered the sacrifice of his mother's necklace of rose diamonds, a gift to a long-lost countess of Brancy from Cardinal Mazarin, a sacrifice which had set them on the road to financial recovery. One day he'd locate those stones and get them back for the family, whatever the cost. For a brief moment he allowed himself the sensuous indulgence of imagining them around the white neck of Laetitia Talbot.

He lingered behind as the room emptied and was joined by Constantine.

When they were alone, d'Aubec spoke casually. 'The senator is not with us . . .'

'I had observed. Leave it to me, Edmond.'

Reassured, Edmond went back to his vision of Laetitia. She was still in his thoughts when a manservant entered and sought him out. Leaning forward, he murmured that the count was urgently requested to come to the telephone.

Chapter Thirty-Four

'But it's the Saint-Jean, mademoiselle,' was the laughing and inadequate explanation given her by the young boy Letty questioned on Saturday morning. 'June the twenty-fourth,' he shouted over his shoulder, and ran off to join his friends. Strolling through the town, she'd been drawn to the hubbub in the central square, where half the town seemed to be milling about joining in the preparations for the evening's event. The other half was standing about offering advice.

The square had been cleared and teams of men and boys were constructing, with a good deal of Gallic drama, an enormous bonfire. One old man (it might well have been Dutronc of the Device, she speculated) appeared to be loosely in charge of the construction. The placing and sizing of the logs seemed to be crucial – six inches this way or that a vital matter – and the whole edifice was to be topped off with a tottering pile of brushwood. She hoped the town fire-service would be standing by.

She was enjoying the scene when a familiar sound drew her attention. Charles Paradee's van clanked to a halt by her side and he leaned out, glad to have spotted her in the crowd. 'There you are! Just move that spade into the back, will you, and get in! Excuse me – that is, if you'd like to go for a spin and don't disdain my old crate – accustomed as you are to something more grand these days, this will seem quite a comedown.'

How could she refuse this calculated invitation?

'. . . and good morning, Stella,' he went on with great good humour as they bounced their way down the cobbled street heading towards the hills. 'Didn't recognize you at first. Dressed like a native today, I see. I don't think I've seen you in a skirt before.' He ran an approving eye over her blue cotton print skirt and white blouse and the espadrilles on her feet.

'All bought in the local market. Charles – tell me – are you making off with me?'

'Yes.' He grinned, unabashed. 'I've an interesting proposition for you, young lady. I'm taking you out for a drink. It may even turn into lunch. We're going to a little café-restaurant I know where we can talk quietly. I often come here at the end of the day. Working with students can make a man feel very middle-aged and I like to escape when I can, even if my bolt-hole is only ten kilometres away.'

He sank into silence and Letty sat back, puzzled and distractedly watching the Burgundy farmland flow past her as they drove towards the hills. This was a road she had not taken before. They appeared to be heading northeast, climbing out of the valley. She glimpsed a crowded fan of grave Romanesque saints above the arched door of a church, its outline blurred by the thousand years that had passed since the pious monks of Fontigny first set it there to inspire and protect its surrounding village, as it slid past one window. Three small children escorting a supercilious Charolais cow slid past the other and, on a low hill ahead of them, appeared an ancient wall, a jumble of roofs, and, soaring above all, the solid outline of a defensive keep.

> 'Towers and battlements it sees
> Bosomed high in tufted trees,'

chirruped Letty, to break the awkward silence.

Paradee shook himself from his abstraction. 'I'm sorry, Stella. You were saying?'

'Trees,' she said. 'Tufted.'

319

He seemed suddenly to focus his attention on her, but had swiftly to look ahead to negotiate the narrow gateway in the old wall. He drew up, wrenching on the brake, in front of a café terrace in the centre of the village. Chestnut trees shaded the village square; wood smoke still drifted lazily from the ovens of the *boulangerie.* One or two old countrymen were already sitting at tables enjoying a drink and they greeted Paradee as a friend, exchanging comments on the weather and the state of his van. Seeing that he had a female companion, they tactfully cut short their conversation and exchanged swift smiles as Paradee made for a table at the far end of the terrace. He ordered a beer for himself and a lemonade for Letty.

She looked about her, enchanted. This village, like Fontigny, was *en fête.* Strings of bunting wound around the square from tree to tree and here too men were busy piling up a bonfire. She watched in silence as it grew, to the noisy accompaniment of shouted advice and expostulation. Letty pointed to a poster, one of many tacked to trees. 'They're having a dance followed by fireworks this evening. Is every village in Burgundy celebrating today?'

'In this area it's traditional, yes. Midsummer fertility rite, though they'd never admit it, of course,' said Paradee. 'It died out generally halfway through the last century but,' he shrugged, 'after the war, it started up again. People needed to reassert themselves, reaffirm their national identity, listen to good old Mother Nature urging them to do a little restocking, I suppose. Well, that's my explanation, delivered with my anthropologist's hat on and my tongue in my cheek.'

'So it's not an accepted Christian celebration?'

'Oh, yes, it is. On every ecclesiastical calendar. They've sanctified it by naming it the festival of Saint John, but underneath – and not that far underneath – the official label there's a pagan ceremony. They're actually celebrating the summer solstice. The boys jump over the fires, showing off their courage, but in the deep Celtic past – and beyond – one of the poor souls, the strongest and the handsomest, would have been chosen as sacrificial victim. He might well have been proud to be selected.'

'How would we ever know? We can dig up his bones, we can count his teeth, identify the killing blow, but we can never hear him speak,' said Letty. 'Was he screaming or praying when he died? Perhaps the work they're doing at Hallstatt or here at Alésia and Mont Lassois will tell us more.'

'I'm not sure his voice would have been very different from our own,' said Paradee, surprising her. 'We'll never know what a Celt would have said to his gods, because their language is lost, but I bet it would have been much the same as his ancient Greek or Roman counterpart, and what he would have said is: *Do ut des* ... I give, that you may give. It's all about fertility. Pleasing the gods, enriching the earth. We think of the ancestors as savages, but, really, if one young brave were to die tonight in every village, well, that's still a lot fewer than the millions sacrificed in the fields of Flanders.' He sighed. 'And, of course, you can't deny – it's effective,' he added slyly.

'What *can* you mean?'

He affected an air of innocence. 'The crops keep growing, don't they? The flocks multiply. And next March will be a busy time for the midwives. It always is.'

'Goodness! You mean ...?'

'Oh, yes. A lot of wine gets drunk, there's song and dance and a lot of showing off. The youths and maidens have a chance to take a look at each other and make their choice. I approve heartily,' he finished as their drinks arrived.

She sipped her lemonade slowly, much intrigued by Paradee's behaviour.

'You had a proposal to put to me?' she reminded him.

'A proposition, I think I said ... initially ... but you never know your luck,' he said, the boldness tempered by an engaging grin. 'Look, I'll come straight to the point.' And still, he hesitated.

'When were you ever less than direct, Charles?'

321

He gave her a long look and embarked on his speech. 'I've been watching you work for . . . how long now? . . . three weeks? Seems much longer. Well, you can always tell . . . three days is all it takes . . . I've been very impressed with the way you got your eye in so quickly with our project here. It's not exactly your preferred period or place we're investigating – you made that clear at the outset – but your professional approach has been noted and appreciated. You've learned fast; you've integrated well with all the other members of the team. They all have a good word for you and respect you. They've noticed, as have I, that you don't shirk any task, however unpleasant, and never seek to push yourself forward . . . Phil saw and reported to me the discreet way you let Fabrice take the glory for that Etruscan potsherd the other day . . . and I'd say that's typical of you. Anyhow, I want you to know that I shall always be delighted to recommend you to any archaeological outfit you care to approach in the future.'

Letty was barely listening. *I've been here before,* she was thinking miserably. *I've been sacked from the university, I can survive getting the sack from a job I didn't really want to do and am doing under a different name, anyway. It's Stella he's dismissing, not Laetitia Talbot – I must hang on to that. Surely I can take this?* But she was steeling herself for the hard words all this flannel was preparing her for. She decided she was not going to help him out. A familiar scorn for all the men who had meddled in her life, controlled her actions, decided her future, and perpetually underestimated her was beginning to bubble.

As he sank into silence again, she acknowledged that, to his credit, he was not finding it easy. She relented and threw him a life-line. 'I think I can guess what you're about to say, Charles. You're going to tell me it's time to pack my bags and leave? Time to go back to England?'

He looked at her gratefully, relaxing at once. 'As a matter of fact, yes, I *do* want you to pack your bags and leave. But to come back to the States with me.'

'I beg your pardon?' Her response was inadequate to express her astonishment.

'I'm pulling out, Stella.' His voice was bleak, his expression stony. 'I had a wire yesterday from our backer, "our very own Lord Carnarvon", as I jokingly referred to him when you arrived. Unlike the English lord, my own personal Maecenas has proved fickle. He's decided to invest his abundant cash in another project. He's following the frenzy to Egypt. Monastic architecture in a town no one's heard of in France has failed to fix his interest. Now, if we'd uncovered a Roman shrine to Mithras, his butterfly attention might have been engaged but – well, you know, as do I, nothing that glamorous is ever going to emerge here. So – before we're down to our last cent of support, I'm making plans to hand over to the French and see that the team members have somewhere to go next. As far as I can.'

'Charles, you don't have to make contingency plans for *me*, you really don't,' Letty protested.

'But I have. Listen while I lay them out for you,' he said. 'There's a possibility – more than a strong possibility – of an academic post in Chicago. I can use the time and the opportunity to write up the research we've done here . . . the outcome may not set the world on fire but the *work* we've done has more significance, I think, than the actual trench production might suggest. I want to write a textbook, Stella. An authoritative guide – no, the definitive guide – on how to carry out an excavation. So many examples and methods to draw on from the past – Pitt Rivers, Flinders Petrie, even old Schliemann can cast some light. And I thought I might give credit where credit's due to Thomas Jefferson . . . the third President of the United States but, in my book, the First Archaeologist. Some time before he took office – 1784 – he dug out and meticulously recorded the digging of a mound on his property in Virginia. A native burial ground. He devised stratification, realized the significance of skeletal remains, and recorded geological evidence. I thought I'd celebrate these heroes, outline their techniques, extract what is truly useful, and add a good deal of my personal experience.'

Letty was relieved to hear the familiar enthusiasm returning to his voice. She found herself, in spite of her personal disappointment and surprise at his news, taking fire from his brief outline.

'Well, if that's what you're about – I wish you would include in your gallery an Englishman I'm fond of,' she said. 'Captain Meadows Taylor. In 1850 he was using methods of excavation in India which are still relevant today. I wonder why so many military men have made a name for themselves as archaeologists? There's a question you might consider, too.'

'There you are! That's why I want you to come with me! You pick up my thoughts and run with them . . . Meadows Taylor, did you say? Never heard of the fellow. Say, Stella, how come you're acquainted with the techniques of an obscure Victorian archaeologist?'

'Ah. It all goes back to the murky origins of my interest in the subject. You've never asked me how an English flibbertigibbet girl-about-town fell into a fascination for dust and old bones.'

'I just assume everyone is as enthralled as I am, I suppose . . . More lemonade? Tell me about your dubious past.'

'It all started with an evil act. One of mine. At school. I've long obliterated the memory of what I did, so don't ask! But I'd seriously annoyed the headmistress. Miss Scott doled out the punishment: a gating. In view of my lengthening charge-sheet, she felt it her duty to administer the usual confinement to barracks but with additional refinements. So exasperated was she, she shut me up in solitary state in her office after prep every evening for a week and a whole weekend. She plucked from a shelf a selection of yellowing old journals and piled them on her desk. I was told to read through them – every word – and prepare myself for a test at the end of the week. They were copies of *Antiquities* dating from 1850 to 1916.'

'And I'm guessing her mean scheme misfired?'

324

'Spectacularly! I could never resist a challenge and was determined to pass her wretched test, so I set about the task. Really, if the magazines had been *Lepidoptery Weekly* or *Railway Modellers Quarterly* I'd have confounded her . . . but, by the end of the first volume, I was caught, entranced, addicted.'

'You passed?'

'With flying colours. I was even able to enjoy her expression when, on being discharged, I paused in the doorway and, as an afterthought, asked demurely if I might borrow further volumes of *Antiquities*. I specified volume numbers.' Letty shuddered. 'Heavens! I squirm with embarrassment when I recall what an arrogant clown I was. I'm amazed they put up with me. Well, of course . . . some didn't.'

Paradee's expression was indulgent but quizzical. 'Tell you what, Stella – have you ever thought your Miss – Scott, did you say? – may have . . .'

Letty laughed. 'It's taken you seconds, Charles, but it took me years to work out that her choice of punishment was not random! I did write to her to thank her when I settled on a career.'

'You'll be able to write again to tell the old girl about your next venture, then,' he said. 'Be my assistant! Help write up the notes on Fontigny. Your qualifications, your connections, your intuitive feeling for the work . . . you'd be the most enormous asset, Stella. But it would be good for you, too. I have powerful friends in the States and they would be your friends, too, if you'll come. Say you'll think about this and let me know tomorrow. I'm going home next week.'

'Next week? So soon?'

'Short notice, I know, but it will be a marvellous opportunity for you.'

The words were friendly, but there was something behind the friendship in his urgency. His eyes were shadowed by calculation, and Letty felt suddenly afraid that hidden issues were riding on her answer. She needed time to collect herself but she sensed that time was not to be accorded her. She felt that an abrupt refusal, or any refusal at all, would cause disproportionate offence.

'Charles! That's an amazingly generous offer. Look, I risk sounding like a Victorian heroine but I have to say it: this is so sudden! I'm devastated to hear your news but flattered by all you have to say, and I know we work well together. You guess rightly that I'm ambitious and I'm dazzled by the chance you're offering me, but even ambitious girls need time to . . .'

'A week, Stella. That's all the time you've got. There's a sailing from Cherbourg on the first of July.'

His voice was so tense as to be verging on threatening, she thought.

She stared calmly back at him. 'A week. Well, that should be long enough to get my laundry done. Now . . . while you've been agonizing, I'm afraid I've been lightly eyeing the menu board over your shoulder, Charles. The plat du jour is andouille à la lyonnaise and pommes frites! Shall we? And how about a pitcher of cool Beaujolais to drink to the future and wash down the sausages?'

His face relaxed, then creased into a grin of relief and humour – though triumph was an alternative interpretation. Whatever his emotion, the man sitting opposite was impressive – intelligent and ambitious – and their enthusiasms sparked and caught fire when they were together. There were many couples in the world of archaeology, not necessarily sharing a bed, according to gossip, but all famous, rich, influential, and hardworking. They could become another such; Laetitia knew it. He was offering her an opportunity which just one short month ago she would have seized on with squeals of delight.

He leaned towards her, face alight with affection, and said, 'Would you like mustard with that?'

Chapter Thirty-Five

'Are you saying he sees you as the next Sophia Schliemann or Katherine Woolley?' said Gunning. 'How exciting for you. What an opportunity. And there you were thinking it would take ten years to make your reputation. You may have done it in as many weeks. That's if it is indeed the reputation you were hoping for.' He tucked Letty's arm through his and they strolled together along the high street towards the noisy centre of activities.

'Don't be silly. It's obvious what he's up to. He's after my money,' Letty said with too much emphasis. She was shamefacedly trailing her suspicions before Gunning, hoping that he would contradict her and laugh her out of them. As he did not at once challenge her, she pressed on: 'Somehow he's discovered who I am and done a bit of research. Digging's his job, after all. And he wouldn't have to dig very deeply to find traces of me rising to the surface. You said it yourself, William – Phil and Patrick weren't taken in by the count's rendering of my family's coat of arms. They'd have reported back to Paradee, and one call to – oh, where do you suppose? The College of Heralds in London? Yes, that would do it – and he'd find out all he needed to know. His dollars have drained away and he thinks that by luring me to the other side of the pond, as he calls it, he can isolate me, perhaps even marry me – if he's not married already; I know nothing of the man – to get his hands on a little secure funding. Don't you agree, William?'

'I think that the speed with which all this has happened is disturbing and speaks of motives and compulsions of which we have no idea. But I'm inclined to share your suspicions.'

'To do him justice, he did hint right at the start that finance was a concern . . . and Howard Carter himself came within a whisker of being left in the lurch right on King Tut's doorstep. It's an uncertain world and I do think sometimes I oughtn't to be groping around in it.' She shot a sideways glance at him. 'But whatever his motives, this offer of an academic position might well provide a firm base from which my career could take off. I have to consider it objectively. Who knows? – under Paradee's wing I could flourish!'

She watched as the first of the rockets took off from the town square and burst into the darkening sky.

'And you could equally well fall back to earth, singed, a spent force, a blackened stick up your rear end the only souvenir of your brief glory.'

'William! I have detected an increasing laxness in your speech of late. I am not one of your fellow soldiers or your fellow tramps. You may not swear in my presence, and you may not indulge in these louche innuendoes.'

'May as well go back if I'm to have no fun,' he grumbled. 'I couldn't resist the timeliness of the image. I apologize.'

Letty was instantly struck with remorse. 'William, I *am* sorry! I invite you to come out for a walk in the gloaming on Saint John's Night and what do I do? I *gloom* at you! You could have asked Marie-Louise or any of the other suitable parties hereabouts to join you for the festivities . . . enjoy a little dancing . . .'

'Do shut up, Letty!'

Taken aback by the abrupt discourtesy, she fell silent.

'Cripples don't dance, as you'd realize if you gave it half a second's thought. But, look here, you don't have to apologize for contriving a few minutes alone with me. Need I remind you that my attention is being generously paid for by your father? Though what Sir Richard's reaction would be if he knew you were engaging me in the capacity of matrimonial-cum-employment advisor, I can't imagine. I congratulate you on the interest you have aroused amongst the eligible male population of Fontigny, with their dazzling offers of everything from matrimony (or was it concubinage? . . . I don't think the terms were made quite clear) to research assistantships. And let's not forget your arrangement with Laval – copper's nark, was it?'

She scowled. 'That's enough! You have my permission to go rattling on about the local topography, geology, mythology – whatever you like. Don't expect me to respond or even listen. I'm disappointed – though not surprised – you don't care to hear my deeper concerns. I'll keep them to myself. Ah, there goes the first bonfire – do you see? – on that hilltop. What is that village? Mortaine, do you think?'

'Did you notice they lit the fire the moment the sun dipped below the hills? Here in Burgundy –'

'I sense another of your -ologies coming out for a trot, William.'

'Just look on it as verbal wallpaper and return to your dark thoughts. I'm perfectly happy bonfire-spotting. There's another! How these customs live on in the country.'

'Yes, yes. Paradee told me all about it. The boy-sacrifices and all that.'

'An ancient figure. Adonis, Osiris, Tammuz, Christ . . . self-chosen often, a willing victim who goes, anointed and garlanded, dressed in mock-regal robes, only to be, when his appointed hour comes, stripped, mocked, tormented, and put to death. For the good of his people. His blood, his flesh, reinvigorate the earth and ensure re-birth. It's a very ancient theory.'

'That the dead should come back again, or at least some part of their essence, is a deeply disturbing if romantic thought.' Letty shivered.

'And what does Nature do but go on validating the truth of the myth?'

'Paradee said something similar.'

'Flanders fields are ablaze each year with a welter of bright poppies. And, of course, the superstitious claim that the spirits of the dead are rising up.'

'I sometimes think that never blows so red
The Rose as where some buried Caesar bled;
That every Hyacinth the Garden wears
Dropt in her Lap from some once lovely Head,'

said Letty, pleased to retaliate with a quotation. 'FitzGerald.'

'Balderdash! And these superstitions are continually shored up by religion. How many more centuries before people heed the evidence of their senses?' Gunning said bitterly. 'How long before they listen to men of science? How long before they recognize that a crop of poppies is the predictable result when land is churned up by military manoeuvres, that the soil has been fertilized by the blood of young men, and that this is an entirely natural process?'

Letty rounded on him in disapproving astonishment. 'You're saying that the blood of young men like my brother may be equated with . . . reduced to . . . no more than phosphate? Seaweed? A bag of Fish, Blood, and Bone Manure?'

'What else? The microscope would reveal no difference. Crop trials would show no emotional bias. There are no old gods to placate, Letty. And no new ones. They and their gruesome demands have only ever existed in our minds, can't you understand? They are our creation, a primitive human device for explaining the unseizable, the uncertain, and the terrifying aspects of life. We may be rid of their tyranny the moment we have become strong enough to admit that.' His voice took on a grating edge of anguish. 'The thought of the aeons of suffering that humans have inflicted on themselves through ignorance and fear, in an effort to appease these imagined monsters, makes me despair.'

Her reply when it came was measured but cold. 'Mr Gunning, I have to say, if there is one thing I feel grateful for, it is that you took the decision to vacate the pulpit. Any

330

church which has escaped your attentions by your quitting the cloth is a fortunate one. And the soundness of your decision becomes more evident, the more you reveal of yourself.'

Emotion finally burst through her imposed calm. She kicked savagely at a tub of geraniums projecting on to the pavement and swore. 'Bloody men! Damned hateful creatures! Isn't there a single one I can trust or admire?'

Even Gunning was alarmed to hear such language from a woman. 'I say! Too many hours spent in bad company, I think, Letty?'

Infuriated further by his reprimand, she poured out a torrent of words learned from an early age in the stables and stopped only when she noticed he was trying hard not to laugh.

'Well, you've made a good job of ruining a perfectly good pair of espadrilles. The flower tub, I'm pleased to say, shrugged off the attack. I wonder whose head you were kicking in? No – don't tell me.'

They drank glasses of the Green Lady at a café table, and enjoyed the crowds whirling excitedly to the lusty accompaniment of a country band. Young and old were there, grannies and children, singing, drinking wine, calling out greetings to people they hadn't seen since the last Saint-Jean. The fire blazed nobly, and, Letty was relieved to see, performed exactly to the requirements of the morning's careful construction. The fire crew came off watch and joined in the dancing. She waved to Marie-Louise, who waltzed by, flushed and excited, her eyes offering a flirtatious challenge to her partner, the Director of the Haras, Letty could have sworn, though it was hard to be sure when the chap was out of uniform and moving at speed. She briefly wondered what on earth the two were finding to talk about.

As the flames began to sink and the glow deepened, the crowds pressed closer. At last, with a hushing and a

331

murmuring, they fell almost silent to welcome a file of young men who came forward, gauche and embarrassed to begin with, falling over their feet, pushing each other, encouraging each other, egged on by friends in the crowd. Letty was sure she'd spotted Robert, d'Aubec's young stable-lad, amongst them.

They performed beautifully, she thought, these leaping youths, born too late to be sacrifices. Lithe, handsome, daring, and moving her to tears . . . and no part of her could condemn or wonder at the girls who took them by the hand, murmuring shyly of rewards in their ear. The press of people grew less with the collapsing of the fire and Letty realized that the square was emptying fast. She raised her glass defiantly.

'Here's to corn in the grange, cows in the byre, and babies in the cradles,' she told Gunning. 'By the next Beltane. Or Easter Day. Whichever is appropriate. Time we were getting back, William.'

The house appeared to be unable to shake off the heat it had drunk in from the June day. Letty had a cold bath, washed her hair, put on her dressing gown, and sat, too agitated to sleep, scribbling letters at her desk. The floorboards had creaked for hours with unseen people arriving, leaving, using the bathrooms. The hill villages had popped with fireworks until well into the night. She walked to the window and looked over the rooftops to the blue encircling horizon. It would be cool up there on the hilltops. She'd be able to think clearly, weigh her options. Making up her mind abruptly, she slipped on a short skirt and a fresh blouse and pulled on a pair of soft walking boots.

She made her way silently downstairs and hesitated by the front door, then opened the door, cringing at its treacherous creak, and slipped out. Walking had always cleared her head, and she set off rhythmically and determinedly towards the open country, promising herself that she would return with the answers to all her problems worked out. The streets were deserted; her soft soles made no sound on the cobbles. Speculating as to the lives behind the drawn curtains, hearing a baby cry or seeing a light suddenly break from an uncurtained attic in a dark house, she sped along, pausing occasionally to note a coat of arms over an arched doorway, glancing through an iron gate to a flagged courtyard and the dim radiance of an ancient lamp.

She walked into the deserted square, and stopped, startled, as peevish cries of protest rang out. Wretched jack-daws! She'd forgotten about them. She hurried on beneath the abbey spire and in front of the Haras. The houses were thinning out into farmland and fields and at last her mind was clearing.

He hadn't come back. In spite of her telephone call, her urgent need to see him. And with her usual self-honesty she admitted that the rebuff had hurt her more than she would have expected. He hadn't been fired by her enthusiasm. He hadn't sounded in the least excited by her revelation. Had she believed his excuses? 'Vital meeting tomorrow morning . . . Try to get François to deputize but I can't promise . . . I'll do what I can . . .' And he hadn't been encouraging when she told him she was there at the château with Marie-Louise. 'Didn't I say you were not to bring anyone else with you?' She'd frostily reminded Edmond that his list of out-laws consisted of two names only. 'Well, at least I trust you're charging an admission fee if you're opening up to the public . . . The woman's probably even now planning visits by crocodiles of sticky-fingered schoolchildren . . .' Preoccupied, detached, pompous.

Why was she surprised? The man had his empire to run. The sneaking thought occurred to her that the Emperor Napoleon whom he so despised had managed to do that and lead a romantic and involving love life through the ups and downs. Time perhaps to weed d'Aubec out of her life before the feelings she had for him put down serious roots in her heart. Very well, she decided – d'Aubec might well be returning on Monday but it would be to a château empty of *her* presence!

333

Good. That was one decision made. This walk was proving effective, it seemed.

She pushed through a gate, relying on the bright moonlight now to light her path, enjoying the profound silence broken here and there by the short questioning bark of a yard dog, and onwards towards the hills bathed in the white glow of the Mother Goddess, under a radiant canopy of stars. With a rush of feeling she stood and held up her arms to the silent but benign presence, smiling her homage. A simple little song came back to her from her childhood:

> 'Lady Moon, Lady Moon, where are you roving?'
> 'Over the sea.'
> 'Lady Moon, Lady Moon, whom are you loving?'
> 'All that love me.'

Diana? Epona? Isis? Names. Did it matter which one she spoke? It was the emotion surging in her that had meaning – a deeply human need to gush out wonder and praise. She knew the God she believed in would understand and approve her greeting the moon, loving the moon, as a divine presence. Though not a divine presence at all: a lump of planetary rock circling the earth, if Gunning were to be believed.

Unconsciously, she had been heading towards the château, she realized, and decided to turn back. Too late, the thought of her foolhardiness struck her as she paused for breath and looked back at the town. There was the town where Daniel had been murdered, the town where she had dug the pathetic, crouched corpse of a young boy from the earth, and here she was, walking its fields alone at night.

Alone? With a thump of the heart, it came to her that she was not alone. Not a sound, but a movement had caught her stretched senses. She turned and walked on a few more paces before whirling around to scour the field behind her. The branches of a hawthorn bush in the hedgerow about fifty yards away stirred although there was no wind.

Bending to pretend to tie her boot-lace, she hunted about and found a stout, short branch lying broken in the ditch. Checking it was not rotten, she clutched it to her side and stood up again. But, on lifting her head, she was confronted by another problem.

Was she staring at a sunset afterglow? At two in the morning? No. On the castle hill? Surely not. With the dancing radiance came a sharp acrid tang. A bonfire? She was certain that no Saint-Jean fire had been planned for Brancy, and on every other height the fires were lying, cooling grey piles of ash. The château or some part of it was on fire.

Where were the servants? The grooms? Sleeping off the night's indulgence? Perhaps she should take action? She was, after all, however halfheartedly, the key-bearer, the temporary châtelaine.

Which way to turn? What to do? Run back to the town and get help? She assessed the distances: the town was much closer. She'd run back. But between her and the town was a dark shadow lurking at the roots of the hedge. She turned around again to face the field and tightened her grip on the branch in her sweating hand.

Twenty yards now. The presence in the hawthorn hedge had moved closer.

Chapter Thirty-Six

The last inheritor of the fighting spirit of a long line of soldiers licked her dry lips, swallowed, took several deep breaths, and raised her improvised club. She had surprise on her side and would be attacking downhill. But these were the only practical advantages she could count on to back up the hot indignation pushing her to calculate the odds and then seize the initiative. With a Valkyrie scream she hurled herself down towards the menace lurking amongst the bushes.

'Put down that weapon!' The agitated hawthorn spoke with a crisp English officer's voice. 'Bloody hell, girl! What do you think you're playing at?'

A second later a scratched and bleeding Gunning emerged from the foliage and sank to his knees in front of her, head bowed at a suppliant tilt.

The sudden release from tension and fear left her rocking on her heels, her impetus no longer needed, the surge of fighting energy seeking a target which had melted away. She dropped her branch, grasped him by the hair, lifted his head, and smacked him soundly across his cheek.

'You nearly got yourself killed, you fool! What are you doing out here? Trailing about after me? Am I to think you shadow me everywhere, whatever I'm doing?'

He hadn't flinched when she hit him, just looked up at her with quiet defiance.

'Oh, for goodness' sake, get up! The grass is wet.'

His posture was ridiculous and irritating, but she acknowledged that it had probably saved him from serious injury at her hands. However roused, she could not have clubbed a man about his offered defenceless neck.

'Yes, I have followed you. Just about everywhere. As closely and as often as I could. Not always possible when you put yourself into questionable positions, but I have otherwise obeyed Sir Richard's instructions to the letter.'

Letty groaned. 'I shall have something to say to the pair of you. But that will have to wait. Had you noticed, Mr Snoop, that the castle's on fire?'

'Hey! What?' He got to his feet and peered at the sky, where an evil orange flower blossomed suddenly. 'Yes, you're right. So it is. Not the main buildings, I think. Yet. No sign of flames internally. It's silhouetting the bulk of the keep. It's coming from behind. Could it be coming from a courtyard? The stable block?'

'The stables! There's at least a dozen horses in there. And the dogs! No sound of an alarm being raised. And the town's asleep.'

'You're faster on your feet than I am. Run, Letty, and get the car out. Pick me up where this lane joins the main road and we'll motor up. See if there's anything we can do. Bang on the door of the fire-station on your way.' He shouted the last sentence at her as she disappeared at speed into the darkness.

'It's still alight but at least it doesn't seem to have got any worse,' Gunning shouted at her encouragingly when she braked to pick him up.

Knowing the road as well as she did, Letty was able to put her foot down and drive at the car's top speed up the hill. Just short of the coach road, she squealed in protest and wrenched hard on the wheel, pulling the Wolesley aside to avoid another car coming at them at a furious pace.

'Good Lord!' said Gunning, shaken. 'Well done to avoid that maniac! He's all over the road! Did you see who it was?'

337

'No. The headlights were blinding me.'

'I got a sight of his number plate. Lyon number.' He recited it. 'Let's remember that. Not a local car. Big Buick, I think.'

'I'm not giving chase,' she said, easing the car back on to the road. 'I'm not that good a driver and, anyway, we've got a fire to put out. I left a message with the fire-master's wife. She said she'd wake him and send one of the children for Capitaine Huleux. I do hope we're not starting them off on a wild-goose chase.'

'Stop, Laetitia! The gates are wide open. Not sure I like the signs . . . Turn the car around and leave it outside. I'd rather not be trapped in there.'

They hurried through the entrance and followed the gravelled sweep of the drive around to the stable courtyard.

'D'Aubec's back! There's his car! There – by the stables. Doors swinging open.'

The house itself was dark and silent, but the scene in front of the stables was alive with light and sound. Horses whinnied hysterically and hooves pounded against wooden stalls. The flickering light, now fading somewhat, seemed to have its source, not in the stable block itself but in front of it. Straw bales, which had been tidily piled last time she had seen them, were lying smouldering and burning half-heartedly, though renegade sparks and wisps aflame danced dangerously in the slight breeze towards the open door of the stable.

Racing across the courtyard towards the abandoned car, Letty stumbled, catching her foot on something unyielding lying halfway on the path and halfway into a flower bed. A few yards away lay a second huddled shape, equally still.

'Watch out, William!' she called, and then, bending, moaned, 'No! Oh, no! We're too late. They're dead!'

'Two bodies?' said Gunning. 'Who on earth? Oh, my God! Leave this to me, Laetitia.' He knelt over the first body, sprawled on its back.

338

A chauffeur's hat lay close by. The man was in uniform and still wearing his leather glove on his left hand. His right hand held a gun. 'Jules! He must have been driving d'Aubec back from Lyon. So the other corpse . . .' She hardly dared look.

'Dead. He's dead,' said Gunning, feeling a pulse point on the neck. He eased the body over, checking the wound. 'Gunshot wound through the heart, fired from the front.' He dropped Jules back on to the gravel, gleaming black with blood in the moonlight, and turned to the second body.

'What! Oh, no! Can't be! But how on earth? Letty, rouse yourself and come and look!'

She moved slowly around Jules's body and stood by the second man, staring, too astonished to speak.

'Hard to tell when he's not in uniform,' she whispered finally. 'Laval? It's Inspector Laval, surely?'

'Yes, Laval. He's a goner, too. Shot likewise. But what's he doing up here at night in plainclothes?'

'Trailing d'Aubec and Jules from Lyon?' Letty suggested half-heartedly. 'He said he never gave up. He said he always got his man.'

'Well, this time his man got him. Poor soul.'

'And if Jules is his man, that means . . .' Letty bit her lip hard to keep back her suspicions but Gunning voiced them.

'D'Aubec! Where's *he* in all this?' He checked the interior of the Hispano-Suiza and returned to her. 'Jules wouldn't have driven home by himself. His master must be lurking about the place. And he may be armed. What on earth is going on?'

'The fire's going on! Lucky so far it's only those collapsed bales alight, but they're smouldering and the sparks are drifting. The stables seem intact as far as I can make out. No real danger for the animals, but the horses are frantic. Some idiot – or villain – has unbolted the doors and thrown them wide open. Line of fire buckets over there on the stable wall, William,' said Letty, pointing.

339

She hung back for a moment watching Gunning stumble off through the smoke and returned to the body of Jules. His gun was still clutched in his ungloved right hand. She detached it from his fingers. An evil, purposeful pistol. A German souvenir of the war, she guessed. She'd handled a similar one before: taken illicit target practice under the amused but watchful eye of her brother on his last home leave. A Luger. Much prized amongst British officers. She checked it was loaded, slipped on the safety catch, and tucked it into her belt behind her back.

Before hurrying after Gunning she paused, uncomfortably aware that something was wrong. She peered down again at the dead right hand that had held the gun. Reluctantly, she bent over and pulled it into the light. Her senses had not deceived her. The thumb she had encountered in relieving Jules of his gun was broken. So, she thought with a feeling of nausea, the watcher in black she'd encountered in the market square had had her in his sights all along. Jules le Lugubre was d'Aubec's man. And the gun presently tucked into her own belt was the one so accurately predicted by Gunning.

Gritting her teeth in distaste, she knelt beside the body and tugged loose the belt of his chauffeur's uniform jacket. She pulled back the right flap. Yes, there it was. The holster Gunning had lurched into. Panting and almost unable to go further, she peeled back the left flap of the coat. And shuddered. Gleaming with ugly menace in the moonlight was a decorated metallic scabbard. She ran a hesitant finger over it, exploring its length and thin shape. The knife and the hand that had killed Daniel? She didn't doubt it. But this creature was himself no more than a weapon. Whose was the voice that had directed him to kill? At last she thought she knew for certain. She would somehow get the evidence of guilt. She got to her feet. For the moment she could go no farther. A closer examination of the evil stabbing knife would have to be left to the police.

The police? Letty felt suddenly sick with anxiety. She went to stand over the inspector's body. 'And was that what you were about to reveal, Laval?' she wondered, with a glance at the stiffening white face. His telephone number in her notebook had been reassuring: a last resort if she and Gunning got into serious trouble; a friendly official ear, if all went well, to hear her triumphant solution to the case. And now this life-line had been brutally cut. She felt bereft and, with no time to grieve for the man, muttered a hasty promise: 'I'll finish this, Laval. I'll finish it.'

'Letty! For God's sake!' The desperate cry came from Gunning, barely discernible in the cloud of steam his fire-fighting efforts were producing. She ran to grab a bucket and hurled the contents at a still-glowing bale. The water from the bucket line and constant refilling from the trough were enough to put the stables out of danger in twenty minutes. Letty and Gunning clung together, each supporting the other, panting and smoke-blackened.

'Stupid way to start a serious conflagration,' Gunning commented. 'Frightfully inefficient. Should have cut the bindings and loosened the straw – it would have taken hold better. Looks to me as though someone's kicked that one there at the end to bits and lit it. Most of it consumed and blown away, but the other bales caught light from it. No more than charred round the edges. The stables appear to be perfectly safe, for the moment. Dangerous behaviour though, and deliberate. Amateur arsonist? But who? Jules?'

'No. He'd never endanger the horses. Nor would d'Aubec. Whatever else they're capable of they would never set fire to the stables.'

'The horses! Better check on them. And where are the two grooms you said were supposed to be on duty tonight? I don't see *them*. Come on, we can steer a course through this mess now.'

A few paces beyond the blackened barrier Gunning stopped and put a sheltering arm in front of Letty. 'Stay back! There's another of them.' He pointed to a dark shape slumped in the entrance, lying in the shadow of Epona's arch. The goddess stared down, unmoved by the scenes of wild emotion played out below her horse's feet.

Letty ducked underneath his arm and dashed forward. 'Edmond! It's Edmond! Is he dead? He looks dead.' Her fingers went to the grip of the pistol in her belt and she watched as Gunning warily approached.

The skilful fingers went straight to the pulse. 'No, he's alive. Barely.'

The examination of d'Aubec's body and limbs was swift and ordered. 'Not shot. Wound on the head. There. A blow. He's deeply unconscious.' He looked into her face, pale and anxious in the moonlight. 'Not much hope, I'd say.' His voice was calm and professional. 'But let's see what we can do. Flashlight? Water?'

Letty raced to the stable and unhooked a hand lamp from behind the door. She dragged a clean towel from a pile by the water basin and filled a brass ewer with water. Gunning was gently palpating the skull when she returned to the still body. While she crouched behind, shining the light on the head, he took the towel, dampened a corner and began to wipe the blood away from the wound which revealed itself, curved, long, wide, and livid across the side of his head.

'I think we can guess what caused that!'

She nodded.

'Hold the light still. Look, I can't wrap this up. The skull appears to be intact but that's a powerful blow he's suffered. It will have caused bruising to the brain, most probably. When ... I ought perhaps to say *if* ... he regains consciousness, he may well not be himself. I say this because ... I know you've got fond of the bloke, so ... Well, prepare yourself for that. More water over here. Trickle some here where I'm pointing.'

The flow of cold water on his temple had its effect.

'Shit! Bloody hell! It's the godawful English vicar! What are *you* doing here, you carrion crow? Come to gloat? Read me the last rites? Well, you're too early. Bugger off!'

'Ah! He's with us again. And would appear to be very much himself,' said Gunning.

'Laetitia?' gasped d'Aubec, struggling to turn in her

342

direction. 'Where is she? Is she safe? Tell me they didn't harm her! What have you done with her, you buffoon? I want Laetitia.'

'I'm sure you do, old chap. Anyone would. The girl has many endearing qualities, but just for the moment you're actually better off enjoying *my* ministrations. I have some experience in treating wounds.' His voice was soothing but authoritative. 'Carnaval finally get fed up with you and lash out? This wound was made by a horseshoe. We must get you a doctor.'

Letty shuffled forward into his view, confused and hesitant.

'Laetitia! My love! We have unfinished business!' he reminded her, reaching for her hand.

With a rush of relief on hearing him speaking with clarity and his memory apparently unimpaired, she bent and gently kissed his lips. He grimaced. 'Thank God you're all right! Listen! The grooms – they're locked in the harness room. Get them out. Tell them to deal with the animals. Eponina and Atalanta are loose about the place somewhere. They're to round them up. Rouse Madame Lepage. She's a bit deaf and may not have heard the to-do. Her room's on the south side so she won't have spotted the flames. Ring the police and the doctor.'

He sank back exhausted, head cradled on her lap.

'Six commands in one breath,' said Letty. 'Yes, he's back. Look, I'll execute those orders, William. I know my way about and – honestly, if *you* were to confront the house-keeper looking like that . . . a stranger covered in blood-stains and soot . . . the old dear would have a heart attack. Enough corpses on our hands for one evening.' She gently transferred the weight of d'Aubec's head to Gunning's hands. 'And while I'm away, see if you can keep those long, sinewy fingers of yours off his throat. I know how annoying he can be.'

As she ran off, rehearsing her commands, it occurred to her that even in his battered condition d'Aubec had delivered them in the right order. Grooms first.

343

She flung shut behind her the four heavy doors of the stable to keep out the stench and plunged into the screaming turbulence. Passing the door to the dogs' room she opened it, dreading to find two hysterical animals, but the space was empty, the straw removed and all tidy. She closed the door with a gasp of relief, asking herself no questions. Nothing more could surprise her on this strange evening. She pressed on, dodging the lashing hooves between the rows, trying not to look at the white eyes and frothing muzzles, praying that the head halters would hold a while longer. She noticed, as she ran by the gaping hole in the panelling, the destroyed stalls where Eponina and her neighbour Atalanta had been housed. Later. Later.

She reached the tack room, hearing the desperate thumps and shouts which had been one insignificant strand in the skein of hysterical noise created by the horses. She turned the key and out tumbled two terrified men. They must have spent nearly an hour, she thought, smelling the fire, awaiting a terrible death, screaming with the horses. The smaller of the two seemed to be injured.

'Hurt his ankle, Miss, trying to reach the skylight from my shoulders. Walking wounded, though . . . I can get him along.' Marcel spoke bravely but was clearly shattered by his experience.

Laetitia told them the lord was back and passed on his orders.

'Dogs are all right, Miss. I took Bella and your young 'un back into the house yesterday. She only comes down here for the whelping. You'll find them in the back kitchen. But the horses! Two missing, you say? Better get them back first before they damage themselves.' Anxious to retrieve the situation, they set to work at once.

Letty called after them, 'Oh, Marcel, you will find there are two bodies in the rosebushes. Please leave everything in place until the police arrive.'

She was choosing the words to tell him that one of the dead men was Jules when he replied without surprise,

'Yes, Miss.' He gave a gleeful grin, sharing his pride and triumph with her. 'Boss got 'em then, did 'e?'

'Somebody got somebody – that's all I can say,' she added doubtfully.

Mme Lepage, when Letty could rouse her, was unflustered. In curlers and nightdress, she scrambled from her bed and asked Letty to pass her the green plaid dressing gown from behind the door. As she slipped it on she listened to Letty's brief and much censored account, commenting: 'The count rang to tell me he would be arriving late and that I should retire for the night. It would seem a regrettable decision. May I suggest you leave the telephoning to me and return to his lordship, Mademoiselle Laetitia? I know the numbers to ring. Perhaps you could write down the number of the fleeing car you witnessed? I will alert what is left of the staff – most are with their families in the town – and set them to their duties. I will then take up my place at the front gate. I observe you are armed, mademoiselle. Sensible precaution.'

'Ah. Yes,' said Letty. 'But perhaps a little too obvious,' and she pulled her blouse out from her skirt to cover the gun.

Mme Lepage nodded her approval, stepped to a long cupboard, and took out a shotgun. 'Ready?'

Chapter Thirty-Seven

Laetitia had resumed her place by d'Aubec and taken his injured head on to her lap when headlights announced the arrival of a vehicle.

'Reinforcements at last,' muttered Gunning. 'I wonder who we've got?'

After a pause at Mme Lepage's checkpoint, a van clanked a short way into the courtyard and braked. Out stepped six men wearing firemen's coats over their pyjamas. Their leader, the fire-master himself, marched over to the recumbent d'Aubec and saluted.

'Pardon us for intruding, Monsieur le Comte, but I need to know whether all persons on the premises are accounted for. Anyone in the stables?'

'No, Capitaine. There's no one inside. The horses are safe but alarmed.'

'No fire engine?' Gunning asked.

'The count keeps an appliance on the premises. My men,' he waved a hand at his scurrying crew, 'are familiar with it. We'll run a hose from the reservoir and douse this lot again just to be certain. And I'll go and cast an eye over the stable building.'

A moment later a lorry bearing the words 'Haras de France' arrived and six tousle-headed young soldiers jumped out. The commander presented himself, clicked his heels, and gave a crisp salute. 'I see you're busy, sir. I apologize for the intrusion. Capitaine Huleux thought you might need some help up here.'

'Much appreciated! But who's next? The Député, the

President? Laetitia, get me away from here. We risk being drowned, trampled, or saluted to death. Send Huleux to me in the salon when he gets here. Help me up. I think I can walk now.'

Between them, Letty and Gunning managed to move him along to the house, leaving behind them a scene of surprisingly ordered activity. They settled d'Aubec on a chaise longue and, more in hope than expectation, Letty tugged at a bell pull. It was answered by two maids, blinking like owls and hastily attired in their morning uniforms. Her request for coffee and iced water to be served and the same for the men working outside was noted and the girls hurried off.

She moved around the room, turning on lamps, wondering how – or whether it was wise – to break the news that his man had been shot and his stables pillaged.

'Jules?' he asked, solving her dilemma.

'Dead, I'm afraid,' said Gunning. 'Shot. By Laval. All the signs are of a duel at twenty paces.'

'Ha!' d'Aubec exclaimed viciously. 'Did the swine get away?'

'No. Jules shot him before he could get to his car. But his accomplice made off. Abandoned Laval and took off in the Buick. Damned nearly ran us into a ditch as we rode to the rescue.'

Letty was relieved to hear the men communicating with each other in a purposeful way; she just wished she could understand what they were saying. 'Swine'? – Laval? 'His accomplice'? She had a sudden feeling that they'd turned over two pages at once. Perhaps if she kept quiet a little longer she'd be able to make sense of all this?

'I got here as soon as I could, Laetitia,' d'Aubec said, involving her at last. 'It was your phone call that alarmed me – that and the thought that it was the Saint-Jean and the staff so depleted. I couldn't be easy. Jules drove me back. We swept into the courtyard and there was a strange car, a Buick, all doors open and something going on in the stables. Not sure how many of them were involved, I put

Jules to stand by their car in case they tried to make a break for it and went in by myself. Careless.

'They were waiting for me.' He grimaced. Pride had taken a battering along with his head. 'I was wrong-footed to be confronted by a policeman. I recognized Laval and assumed he'd been summoned to investigate. I thought perhaps you'd been a little over-zealous, Laetitia, and called him in. I hesitated. Fatally. Laval had the advantage. He grabbed and held me while his partner bashed me over the head with a horseshoe. Never a shortage of weapons in a stable! There's one in each stall,' he added with a wry grin. 'For good luck.'

'You didn't merit a bullet?' suggested Gunning.

'Too smart for that!' said d'Aubec. 'Don't forget this is a trained policeman we're dealing with. He wanted no traceable police-issue bullets in the body. What more accountable death could you find than that of a reckless owner who, suspecting intruders, ventures into a stable full of maddened horses? He's struck by a flying hoof, crawls into the yard for help, perhaps even starts a small fire to signal for assistance . . . perhaps the fire's been started by a stray rocket from the Saint-Jean and gathers strength? And – how sad – his body is consumed by the flames, which then spread to the stable . . . The man, in his semiconscious state, left the doors wide open . . .'

He shuddered. 'It would have worked. In the subsequent destruction even signs of the demolition work would have been lost.' He briefly touched his wound. 'Oh, yes. This was personal. A lot of force and years of pent-up hatred were behind this blow! I wasn't intended to survive.'

'Lucky we caught sight of the fire and got here in time,' said Gunning.

'Yes. And thank you for that. And perhaps at a later time you'll tell me how you came to be wandering about the town with Laetitia at two in the morning.'

'Your suspicions do you no credit, Edmond!' snapped Laetitia. 'Just be thankful that William saved your life.'

'Have you any idea what they got away with?' asked Gunning.

'Oh, yes. I can list the items down to the last candelabrum. All valuable. All well packaged. They can't have got everything into that car, although it was capacious. They'll have taken the choicest and the most portable. And I can check. When my ancestor concealed the goods from the abbey in the cave in the outer defences he had a steward at his elbow noting them down as they went in.' He smiled at Letty. 'That's what Daniel came across in the archives. The most significant item: the list. The hole in the rock was covered over and Hippolyte built the stable block in front of it as extra cover.'

'But I don't understand!' Laetitia almost screamed at them in her frustration. 'What has *Laval* to do with all this? Why did he try to kill you? Why is he dead? Why tonight? Who are "they" and how did they ever find out the location?'

D'Aubec and Gunning exchanged looks, neither one hurrying to explain. Gunning began to walk about the room. D'Aubec winced and pretended to swoon. They were not able to meet her eye.

Finally, Gunning said, 'Know the story of the Trojan horse, Letty?'

'Of course . . .'

'I'm afraid you yourself were that horse. They used *you* to get into the château and extract the information they needed, or confirm what they already suspected.'

'Me? But how?'

'Marie-Louise Huleux,' said d'Aubec bitterly. 'Vengeful, acquisitive hellcat!'

Chapter Thirty-Eight

Laetitia slumped into an armchair, her mind whirling, relieved to be distracted at that moment by the arrival of the maids carrying trays of refreshments. She took a few fortifying sips of the fragrant coffee before saying steadily, 'You're asking me to believe that this innocent and rather sad schoolmarm I've become friendly with over the last month is in fact a robber and a murderer? That she used our friendship to gain access to and information on the château? That she was, by some means I can't begin to imagine, working with the police inspector, Laval, to commit this horrible crime? That she bashed you over the head and nearly killed you, Edmond? No. I'm sorry. That is asking a lot. It's asking too much.'

Again, the furtive glances. It was becoming clear to Letty that the two men had, of necessity, exchanged information and established some sort of understanding while she'd been dodging flailing hooves and briefing the housekeeper.

'Starting with the easiest part of all that . . . Laval must have been known to her for some time. Through their police connections. Her father probably knew him. And it's likely that they were more than just partners who'd come together to perpetrate this crime . . .' Gunning paused, unsure how to proceed.

'They were *lovers*?' prompted Letty, impatient with his pace. 'Is that what you're trying to say? But how can that be? What nonsense! She's so . . . so . . . unworldly. All right then, I'll say it – virginal. She hasn't a clue how the world works.' Letty ignored d'Aubec's snort of derision. 'I know she goes into Lyon on her day off, so I suppose such an arrangement would not be out of the question. But – a policeman's daughter, a respected figure in the community? She would never contemplate such disgrace, such a crime. And even if she got away with it, it would cut her off forevermore from her family, her town, her roots.'

'Quite. I'd say that's exactly the result she was planning for,' said Gunning. 'And it was, if I've got this right, precisely her position in the community that launched her into this devilish scheme in the first place.' He looked a question at d'Aubec, who nodded confirmation and encouragement.

'People were destitute after the war. Things are still not good. And what do you do when you're on your uppers? You look about you for something to sell:

'"Wasn't there something in the attic put there so long ago and almost forgotten?"

'"That old book that nobody ever opens? The one with the painted pages and the foreign language . . ."

'"And what about Granny's ugly old crucifix . . . Probably just a bauble but perhaps we should polish it up . . . give it a closer look?"

'And to whom do you take the object for a clue as to its value and origin? To someone you trust and who will have an answer for you. Someone discreet, with standing in the town. Probably not the priest, who might well have been your first choice, because there was more than a chance that the objects themselves were of ecclesiastical origin and they risked being confiscated! No – the schoolmistress was the safe option. She knows about these things. And her father's a policeman. She's in a unique position to explain the rules about ownership and disposal of such goods. But *she*, in turn, seeks the opinion of a man who really *does* know the rules . . . For the obvious reason that it is his job to do so.'

'Laval. The Police Judiciaire are in control of the *trafic de biens culturels*,' said Letty. 'And if you know how to *prevent* the smuggling and illicit sale of valuable artefacts, I suppose you also know how to get around the rules. The safest way to export them. The right person to bribe. Perhaps even issue the correct documentation?' She paused, thinking furiously. 'And you'd know all you needed to know about fences!'

They looked at her in puzzlement.

'Isn't that what they're called? The shady gentlemen who deal in stolen goods?'

Gunning smiled. 'I think Laval had in his address book contacts of a much more elevated nature. Contacts with a direct but impeccable link to the great auction houses – remember the silver chalice and the illuminated manuscript? To say nothing of a list of discreet and very private clients on both sides of the Atlantic.'

'I think they probably started on a small scale – "Look here, Mister So-and-so, why not let me handle this for you?"' said Letty, angrily imitating Marie-Louise's prim voice. '"I've sought a legal opinion on this and find that you're quite within your rights to sell it . . . For how long was it in your cellar? Really? So long . . . Then there can be no doubt. Tell me, how will you manage the sale? You have no connections with the art world? . . . no, I suppose not . . . but listen, I could help you there . . . There will be a commission to pay, of course."'

'And the sellers hardly needed the warning to keep it all quiet,' said Gunning. 'Their neighbours would not have been pleased to hear that the abbey's wealth was being used to provide – oh, let's hazard a wild guess, shall we – the new extension to the Mayor's house? The blacksmith's son's new sports car? A surprising number of local folk have come into an unexpected inheritance or had a bit of luck at the casino lately, I notice.'

'But that was just the beginning,' said d'Aubec. 'Like every child of the town, she had heard the stories about great and secret matters being hidden away up in Brancy. A few items were not enough for her. She wanted the precious core. And to get away with it before the smaller local activities were uncovered, as would undoubtedly soon have been the case.'

'I know what Scott Fitzgerald's comment would have been,' said Letty, remembering. '"The victor belongs to the spoils." Beautiful, greedy, and damned.'

'A dangerous and desperate woman. I would never have allowed Marie-Louise anywhere near the place, but Laval got under my guard. At the time, for us, he was just a smarter-than-usual investigating officer and, as friends and contacts of Daniel whose murder he was investigating, he was welcomed and entertained by my mother. Who knows what he managed to learn? Good Lord!' he said, suddenly shaken. 'He looked through Daniel's things . . . this was, after all, the last known place Daniel visited before his death . . . my mother the last person he spoke to . . . Laval came back once or twice. Rather more than the situation justified, I believe. He interviewed the staff . . .'

'Marie-Louise was pleased that I seemed to be getting close to you, Edmond. Even sang your praises. Reassured me that you were not the ogre I might have thought. And her performance when she visited the château! Seeing everything with a jaundiced eye but – crikey! – that eye was everywhere. She inspected the plans for the stables, covering her interest with distracting questions about the chapel.' Letty's voice was rising in anger at the deception. 'I even held the chair for her when she climbed up to take a closer look at old Hippolyte's portrait! And she drew me in with her pretended interest in poor old William. By getting close to me and encouraging my closeness to you, Edmond, she was making links in a chain to the château. Oh, dear!'

'It's all right, Letty,' said Gunning. 'We were all of us deceived to some extent.'

'Well, I certainly was!' said Letty with a flash of anger. 'All that "borrow Maman's bicycle" and "hope you like courgettes"!' She was struck by an unpalatable thought.

'Yes, I'm afraid so,' said Gunning, catching her reference. 'She was trailing us about the place whenever she could, and the evening she caught sight of us motoring off to find d'Aubec's grove . . .'

353

D'Aubec exclaimed and looked from one to the other, with narrowed eyes.

'It's all right! You can stand at ease, old man! . . . She followed us. When she realized we were not bent on digging up treasure but sitting about enjoying the evening air and engaging in other innocent English pursuits – reciting Milton and Swinburne – she got bored and headed for home. By bicycling vigorously she'd got a good way down the road before she heard our engine. Out of sight round a bend, she turned her cycle around. We met her wobbling innocently along in the opposite direction, to all appearances surprised to see us.'

'And I gave her the grand tour of the château! Even the stables. She pretended to have no interest in the building and obviously hated the horses.'

'In that she did not deceive,' said d'Aubec bitterly. 'And there is the reason I'm still alive. She intended to set the stables on fire but couldn't summon up the courage to go back inside, the horses were making such a fuss. I think she has a genuine fear of them. She restricted herself to kicking a bale loose outside, setting fire to it, and hoping for the best.'

'Well, at least Epona and her horses have played their designated protective role,' said Letty. 'More than I did. I'm so sorry, Edmond.'

D'Aubec smiled his forgiveness. 'My goddess,' he said, reaching for her soot-blackened hand and kissing it.

Gunning coughed and choked and went to refill his coffee cup.

'Poor old things,' said Letty. 'Her parents, I mean. They didn't understand their daughter. They would have been happy with a homely canary, content to sit in a cage, but what they were given to rear was a skylark, beating its wings against the bars.'

D'Aubec snorted. 'If you're searching after a winged metaphor, my dear, try – *Harpy*.'

She ignored him. 'And Laval! Not just a thief and killer – he tried to deceive me into thinking poor old Paradee

354

was at the bottom of all this. He planted the idea in my head that Charles was using his plainly barren digging enterprise as a screen for a much more productive sideline. He flattered me by sharing his suspicions about the aureus he found clutched in Paul Morel's hand. And he didn't need to reel me in – I leapt aboard! And, after all this death and devastation, are we any nearer to finding out who killed Daniel?'

'Not so sure about that. Patience, Laetitia, patience.'

'That advice, coming from the most impatient man I have ever known, will go unregarded.' She favoured him with a sweet smile.

The doctor came and left, having confirmed all that Gunning had said. D'Aubec resisted his strong recommendation that he go at once to hospital but submitted to more probing, an application of unguent, and a dramatic bandaging. Letty threw a cushion to the floor and settled down protectively at his side.

'Huleux's taking his time,' said d'Aubec tensely.

'Oh, come on,' said Gunning. 'He's got rather a lot on his plate, communicating with Lyon. I would offer to make myself scarce, but I think he would probably prefer to take our statements on the spot.'

'Don't think of leaving!' said d'Aubec. 'Send for more coffee. Brandy? Eggs and bacon? What do you English like to have an hour before dawn?'

'Something you can't provide, old man,' said Gunning lightly, and yawned.

They sank into their own thoughts and were startled some minutes later by the entrance of the maid returning to announce that Capitaine Huleux had arrived and would like to see the count.

'Show him in, Thérèse,' said Letty.

D'Aubec's reaction surprised her. He took her hand again and turned desperate eyes to Gunning. '*Mon père!* Stay close by, will you? This is likely to be an uncomfortable interview. I should welcome your presence by me, if not your support.'

355

Letty and Gunning fixed him with enquiring looks until he explained: 'You may as well hear it from me, I suppose. There should be no secrets between us, Laetitia. Must be twelve years now, since the unpleasantness, but there was never a forgiving … Attractive girl, Marie-Louise, as I'm sure you'll agree. Well, I thought so when I was sixteen. Mistakes were made. I had thought the family had been more than adequately recompensed for their silence. The girl's chosen career was facilitated … Her respectable position in the community was assured.'

Laetitia sighed and tugged her hand free from his grip. Gently she tweaked his nose. 'I've a jolly good mind to finish off what Marie-Louise started. I just hope the inspector has remembered to bring his horsewhip with him. I shall offer to hold his coat while he beats you. Ah, here he is!' She stepped forward to welcome him. 'May I get you a cup of coffee, Capitaine?'

The polite phrases died in her throat. She had never seen a man so distraught. Normally ready with a cheerful word in every situation, he went to stand to attention in front of d'Aubec, icily silent, immaculately uniformed, assaulting the lord with his iron gaze.

'Guillaume, you must understand that –' d'Aubec began.

'I understand what I need to understand. And more than *you* can tell me.' The tone lacked respect, was barely polite. 'My officers are, as we speak, going over the scene of the crime. The double shooting. My commiserations on the death of your man. And Laval? God rot him! He is lucky he did not survive to answer to me or his colleagues in Lyon for his treachery.' Huleux turned to Letty. 'And thank you, mademoiselle, for relaying the number of the car involved in all this. It was recognized by the Motorized Division who set up a road block to intercept it north of Lyon.'

'*North* of Lyon? Oh – heading for Paris?'

'No,' murmured Gunning. 'Not Paris, I'm thinking. The Swiss border?'

356

Huleux nodded. 'You're right, *mon père*. We will be able to follow the thread back – or forward – starting with a particular dealer who will find he has surprise guests when he comes down for breakfast.'

They all fell silent, each willing one of the others to ask the unaskable question.

Chapter Thirty-Nine

'It may be of interest to hear,' said Huleux, breaking the tension, 'that the sole occupant of the Buick failed to stop when intercepted. The car, a heavy one and overloaded, careered off the road and, in the ensuing crash, the driver was killed instantly. Impaled on the broken steering wheel. The contents of the car, a number of wooden boxes and leather satchels, have been confiscated and, having a particular involvement, you will be notified of decisions taken regarding their disposal. Sir.'

They all imagined the scornful sharp click of the heels. When the policeman turned for the door, Letty hurried after him and touched his shoulder gently, tears scouring a path down her dirty cheeks.

He turned to her, his control ebbing, seeking understanding. 'She was too small to be driving that car,' he whispered. 'Much too small.'

'I'll show you out, Capitaine,' said Letty quietly, and led the way from the room.

At the door into the courtyard she paused and faced him, saying steadily, 'We have both suffered a loss ... yours far more acute than mine and more raw. You have my deepest sympathy and my understanding. We each have a task to complete. Mine, for the moment, demands my presence here in this wasps' nest. Our objectives may not be the same but our paths to them may cross. May I assure you that my role in this ... this tragedy ... is no more than that of one who seeks the truth and then justice for a wrongdoing?'

He looked at her and nodded his agreement.

'I may need to call on you, Capitaine, later . . .'

'You have my number, mademoiselle. There will be someone in attendance at all hours.'

'When you come to examine the body of the count's man, Jules, you will find at his left side a concealed weapon. An Italian dagger. The blade may well match the wound that killed Daniel Thorndon. My godfather.'

She had a feeling that this was not news to Huleux.

'We understand each other, mademoiselle. I am at your service. And thank you for befriending my daughter over these last weeks. You brought some excitement into her life. She craved excitement. She could never be satisfied with what she had . . . despised the provincial life and itched to get away from it. Her first attempt to better herself – a disastrous affair with that scoundrel in there – only anchored her more firmly into the town. And left her with a virulent resentment which, I think, turned her bad from the inside. Most girls would have just run away to Paris and gone on the stage in the time-honoured tradition, but . . .' He shrugged his shoulders, the tears starting again. '. . . Marie-Louise couldn't sing and she couldn't dance. So she stole.

'I don't have the words to speak of my daughter calmly for the moment but . . . I know that she admired you. You and the Reverend must feel free to use your rooms in the rue Lamartine, though you must fend for yourselves, I'm afraid. My wife has gone to spend some days with her sister. I shall be in Lyon during the day, most probably, and an empty house is not a good place for a grieving mother.' He straightened his shoulders. 'The stiletto, you say. On Jules. It has already been discovered and is being examined as we speak.' And he strode firmly out into the courtyard.

When she returned to the salon she went to the window and flung back the curtains, staring gloomily out at the countryside. A streak of saffron outlined the hills to the

359

east. 'I wonder how much longer we must keep ourselves available?'

Receiving no answer she turned and saw that both men were fast asleep. She paused to check that d'Aubec was still breathing, pulled a throw over Gunning's long limbs, pushed a silk pillow under his head, and crept from the room. She left a message with Thérèse for the house-keeper, saying that she had gone up to the room prepared for her and that the gentlemen in the salon were not to be disturbed.

The sun was high in the sky when Letty swam up from a deep sleep. Her first thought was that she would be late for work and Paradee would have her guts for garters. Her second was that today was a Sunday, her third that she was lying naked and filthy, cocooned in soft, white, lace-edged linen, much to its detriment. The lump under her goose-down pillow identified itself as a Luger pistol. In a pile by her bed were her underclothes, skirt, and blouse. With the realization that her situation would take some industrious unravelling, she pulled the eiderdown back over her head and tried to focus on the previous night's appalling events.

Half an hour later – bathed and smelling exotically of several of the bathroom's de luxe offerings, with lily strongly to the fore – she struggled back into her stained clothes and went in search of breakfast.

In front of the door to the breakfast room she paused and put her ear to it. Two male voices were raised in earnest conversation. In English and French. Not quarrelling but debating a point, she judged. Under cover of a sharp burst of laughter, she went in.

Her entrance stunned them into silence and Letty was the first to gain her poise.

'Great Heavens, darlings! Who've we got here? Bertie Belvedere and Emil Eglantyne. Opening in a musical at the Lyric?' She eyed the suave, shaven, silk-dressing-gowned figures lounging on either side of the breakfast table with

360

mistrust. How long had they been engaged in this amic-able discussion? Had they been talking about *her*? From the open quality of their instinctive welcome, she thought probably not.

'And Tyche Tantrum enters to a clever and distinctly roguish number by Mr Irving Berlin,' said Gunning. 'Good morning, Letty.'

D'Aubec, pale and bruised but cheerful, threw down his napkin and came to greet her with a repeated kiss on each cheek, murmuring his concern. 'Fresh as a daisy, my nose tells me, but, my dear! You appear in rags! What may I provide?'

'First things first – a huge breakfast. Then perhaps a shirt of yours – one of your informal ones? I can't exactly bor-row a little washing frock from the countess – she's much smaller than I am. But, tell me – am I wrong? – I don't detect a police presence.'

'You yourself gave the order, my angel. Did you not leave instructions with Madame Lepage that the gentlemen were to be left undisturbed?'

'Don't be fanciful,' Gunning reprimanded his host. 'The girl's quite big-headed enough as it is. The police, I don't believe, hang on her every word. With all the villains accounted for and the centre of enquiries moved to Lyon, according to Mme Lepage, the pressure was off. Huleux has announced he is to come back on Monday morning to conclude his enquiries.'

'So you will be my guests for what remains of the week-end,' said d'Aubec expansively. 'Gunning has been pro-vided with a room in the west tower. My family will be returning at some time during the day and I would like you both to attend the evening service with us in the chapel. I've sent a car for your things, Laetitia. Now, my dear – tea? Coffee? Croissants, toast, raspberry jam?'

'All of those, thank you. In that order.'

'And then, properly attired, of course, we'll venture out to the stables to assess the damage.'

* * *

361

In the end, both she and Gunning were thankful to the count for the use of his wardrobe. Gunning, being as tall, though not as broad, fitted easily enough into soft corduroy trousers and a plain white shirt. Letty, wearing almost the identical outfit, had done her best. Trousers were rolled up and tightly belted; a blue checked shirt flapped in a concealing way over the gun she tucked into her waistband. Her room was certain to be cleaned, perhaps even searched, and she had no intention of giving up the Luger. She felt she looked ridiculous, but she tried to walk like a duchess as they crossed the courtyard where the gravel and flower beds had been much churned up by police and emergency vehicles the night before.

D'Aubec's voice burst out in anger. He called to two men standing disconsolately by and demanded to know what they were doing, lounging about with so much to restore.

'Capitaine Huleux's orders, sir,' they said. 'Scene of a crime. Not to be disturbed.'

'He wants to take a look at it again on Monday,' said the other man. 'Seems there's a question of a missing gun, sir,' he confided. 'They couldn't find it last night. It might have gone off to Lyon or been thrown into a flower bed, or kicked into the gravel. Men and horses all over the place, there was. Huleux said not to worry – he had a good idea where he'd find it and would come back for it.'

Moments later they were picking their way through the blackened and wet approach to the stable block. Edmond listened to the groom who was standing on guard, accounting for the staff's activities, dismissed him, and they went inside. The horses not out at exercise were standing quietly, Eponina and Atalanta, her stablemate, re-housed in vacant stalls. The wooden stalls they had previously occupied, and the panelling behind the stalls, had been destroyed. The pieces were lying about, a pile of splintered oak. There was revealed in the background a stone wall, this also prised apart and smashed.

'There she is!' said d'Aubec, gesturing towards a large slab of stone lying flat on the floor.

And there she was. A second goddess astride a prancing horse, pointing the way to a gaping hole in the stonework. A hammer and a crowbar lay abandoned in the dust.

'Devils! Vandals! This is . . . *spoliation!*' d'Aubec hissed.

Gunning peered through the hole, with Letty close behind him. 'It's big,' she said excitedly. 'It's far more than just a hole in the rock face. It's a cave – a cavern. Come on, Edmond, give me a leg up!'

'A moment. Let me get a couple of torches.' He went over to the tack room and returned with two flashlights. Handing one to each, he cupped his hands to receive Letty's foot. She hopped once and was heaved up to the sill of the opening. The men jumped up beside her and stood for a moment contemplating the void before them.

'It's empty.'

'They couldn't get all of it into the car. Whatever was left, the police will have taken away for safer keeping, I suppose,' said d'Aubec. 'I shall check it against my list when it is returned to me. Interesting, anyway, finally to get a glimpse of Hippolyte's construction.'

The rock-cut cavern was six feet by ten but all that remained of the abbey hoard, it seemed, was a wisp or two of straw and a handful of shavings until Letty, shining her torch across the floor and catching a gleam of gold, picked up a coin about the size of an English guinea. She held it out to Edmond on the palm of her hand.

'A louis d'or,' said Edmond. 'Probably worth a few hundred francs. But what must have been the value of what is gone!' He added, gazing around, 'So this is the place the monks chose . . . I have to suppose they thought it would be safe up here in their summer retreat. And the compliant count of the day – the newly returned Hippolyte – obligingly built up the stables to cover the hiding place. They probably intended to retrieve it when the troubles blew over. But they never did. The monks were dispersed – sent packing by Napoleon. And their secret died with them. Or would have done, had not my ancestor employed a particularly vigilant steward.'

They stood in a row, playing the torches around the cavern, silenced by disappointment, trying to picture the grandeur of the treasures now hidden from view once more in a police vault in Lyon.

Suddenly Laetitia's torch shook. She pointed it over their heads and said in a steady voice, 'Edmond! William! Look there! Can you see it? This is only *half* a cave. It must have been twice this size when it was hacked out. You can see that if you look at the curve of the roof. There, do you see it? I've seen something like this in the Valley of the Kings! But more cleverly done. This is really quite obvious, wouldn't you say? And look at the walls. It's wood-lined, but the wooden planks end abruptly at the corners. And the far wall is plastered over. Pass me that hammer, Edmond. There! Old plaster but not ancient. Hippolyte again. Now, why would he plaster over the stonework or the wood? Bet he didn't! He's hiding something else.'

D'Aubec snatched back the hammer. He was sweating, uneasy, hesitant. 'No! I think that's enough for one morning. Beyond this we will not go.'

She rounded on him but spoke in a soft voice, quoting the phrases she remembered from the architect's plans, the same phrases Marie-Louise must have noticed: '"The worldly goods of Our Lady rest with the Lady of Ancient Days." You've known all along! She's there, behind that plaster wall, Edmond, isn't she? The Lady you're saving a space for in your chapel!' she exclaimed with sudden insight. 'The east window! Is she then to take pride of place over the altar? The Gallic face of the Triple Goddess?'

Tight-lipped and avoiding her gaze, he began to collect up the tools, preparing to leave.

When she spoke again into his silence, she was using the one persuasion she could think of that might shatter his brittle resolve and push him in the direction in which she knew he wanted to move. 'Hippolyte saw her. And now she's yours. She would not turn away three sincere worshippers, Edmond.'

For an agonizing moment the much-maligned figures of Belzoni and Schliemann sneered at her in triumph, and she heard her mentor Andrew Merriman hissing a warning. How could she have fallen into this trap? Yet here she stood, glowing with concupiscence, ready to tear at the wall with her fingernails if necessary.

D'Aubec caught fire from her tinder.

Pushing her aside, he hit the plaster with a mighty blow of the hammer. He groaned and staggered and Gunning, clucking sympathy and a warning, took it from him. After several more hefty swings, the hole was large enough to peer through. Letty shone her torch into the dark space beyond.

Chapter Forty

The wall yielded almost at once. Flakes of plaster flew and from behind these loose rubble began at once to disintegrate. Soon there was a hole through which they could pass. Squeezed together at the entrance, they stood on the threshold of the farther cave, staring about them.

'What is this? Tell us what we're seeing, Letty,' whispered Gunning.

When at last she could scrabble a few words together, she spoke quietly: 'It's a sanctuary. I think we're in a sanctuary.' She flashed her torch over the ceiling and walls, avoiding for the moment the central awesome display. 'Wood-lined, you see, even the floor. A large space . . . perhaps fifteen feet by ten. I think it's far earlier than the monks of Fontigny . . . I think it goes back to the very earliest days of all. It's surely a Celtic shrine. Look! Do you see? The row of skulls in the niche? Celts worshipped the head, and enemies defeated in battle would be decapitated and their heads used as triumphal ornaments. These have been set up in a religious ritual, I'd say.'

'And that monster?' asked d'Aubec, pointing.

The light danced off the surface of a huge and intricately wrought bronze vessel occupying the centre of the space. It stood five feet high and was terrifying rather than beautiful. Its handles were grinning heads, their tongues poking out in derision, and the riot of animals which encircled it seemed for a second, in the unsteady light of Letty's torch, to move in a wild ritual dance with the human figures interwoven with them.

Letty moved forward and gingerly touched the cauldron with her fingertips. Striving for, but not quite achieving, the unemotional and schoolmasterly tone of the guide who'd shown her around the tomb of Tutankhamen, she carried on with her commentary: 'Greek workmanship? But how did it get here? Hauled over the Alps? By sea and up the Rhône Valley? Perhaps in pieces and then re-assembled when it reached its destination?' The enquiring fingers followed the beam of her torch, seeking seams in the metalwork. 'This is too big to have been a crater for mixing wine,' she said. 'I would say it's a sacrificial vessel. A frightening thing when you look at it.' The grinning heads stared back at the intruders with sneering menace. Letty shuddered at the thought of the victims who had leant over it to have their throats cut in ritual sacrifice by the priests.

'But look! Over there. There's something beyond it.'

They moved forward, illuminating a huddled dark mass.

'A shrine, but also a burial chamber,' murmured Gunning.

They gazed in rapt attention, taking in the details of the body lying on its bier. Flesh long rotted away had left behind skull and skeleton, the bones still covered in places by the remains of a dark fabric. At the shoulder gleamed a brooch shaped like the new moon. But it was the skull which drew their eyes. Yellowed with age but intact and gently rounded, it evoked none of the dread which the time-honoured image traditionally arouses in the onlooker. The starkness of the bony outline was softened and made human by a fall of golden hair which gleamed still as Letty played the torch over it.

At the sight both men made the sign of the cross.

'Could it be . . .? Surely not . . . But who, then?' breathed Gunning.

'You'd better tell us, Letty, who you've found.'

'It's not Mary,' she said quietly, answering the question they were both avoiding. 'This lady is much, much older. She's a Celt. Look at the neck.'

367

About the neck lay a golden torque, the splendour of which drew a gasp from everyone as the light revealed it. Letty pointed a quivering finger. 'Look! It's exquisite! Solid gold and of an artistry that takes the breath away. So simple, so elegant. So Celtic. And do you see the terminals?' Spanning the angle between the golden globe at either end of the collar and the main arc of the torque, and linked to it by the finest filigree work, were rearing golden horses, no more than an inch long.

The woman's arms were folded over her breast. 'A princess or priestess, probably both,' said Letty. 'And I don't judge solely by the wealth of her ornament – the position of the arms – do you see? And here's a puzzle – I've seen that in Egypt. It's the traditional pose for royal mummies. Celtic, Egyptian, Greek,' she murmured, 'so many influences.' And she concluded: 'This was a very important lady.'

'Our Lady of Ancient Days,' said d'Aubec. He made to stretch out an arm in some sort of homage but Letty held him back with a whispered 'Careful now!

'And this,' she continued, pointing to a pile of smaller bones below the feet from which still dangled two ragged slippers, 'must have been her dog ... her hunting dog, perhaps.'

In death the lady had been provided with all she had needed in life: stacked against the wall were Greek wine jugs, Etruscan copper beakers, silver platters, an intricately worked bronze mirror, and the crumbling remains of a four-wheeled chariot, distinguishable by its gilded hubs and spokes. Letty carefully picked up an Attic black-figure drinking cup. 'I don't know much about Greek pottery but I'd say this might give an expert a date for her. And it would be earlier than ... oh ... 500 BC. This is all very amazing and wonderful, but, Edmond, do you suppose *that's* what we've been led to discover?' she finished in awed tones, lighting a niche in the far wall of the cave.

Again the beams reflected off metal and d'Aubec breathed, 'Epona!'

She gleamed darkly, tarnished by the centuries, staring through them as she sat astride her silver horse; at the feet of the horse there trotted a silver hound. The Horse Goddess. The earliest treasure of Fontigny. A secret kept through the ages. This sacred place had been guarded through the centuries. Letty felt herself an interloper.

'This is Our Lady,' she said. '*Vera Dea!* The true goddess. That's what the manuscript meant. The monks left the sacred valuables belonging to the Virgin Mary – the ones from the abbey – here in the one safe place they knew of – in the proximity and care of Epona. And her priestess, the embodiment of the goddess.'

'The monks – some of them were local boys with country memories and country beliefs – they knew she was here and would look after the treasure,' said d'Aubec. 'And she did. My ancestors colluded. They shared the secret. For a further two centuries, until Laval broke into her cave.'

A sudden rush of ancient fear and superstitious dread caught hold of Letty's heart and got the better of her professional absorption. They were intruding in this quiet, holy place, and she understood perfectly why the monks had paused to build up a partition before secreting their hoard on the other side. 'Let's leave her alone again. We have penetrated deeper, defiled more surely than Laval,' she said.

The two men did not object. It occurred to her that each of them had strong reason to withdraw and make good the damage they'd done. Even in their awe and astonishment, Letty was aware that both had kept a silence, each hoping that the other had failed to notice the plainest and yet the most significant object in the chamber. She wondered if it would be Gunning or Edmond – or neither – who would speak of it to her.

After a last swift look over her shoulder at the emotionless features of the goddess, Letty scrambled back through the hole.

* * *

369

She emerged, blinking, into the bright sunshine of the courtyard, glad of d'Aubec's steadying hand, devastated by their violation of that ancient place. But, outside, a further shock was waiting. It was as if a slip in time while they were inside had changed the stableyard into a different place. They had left it empty, but now it was alive with cars and well-dressed, chattering strangers.

There was the family Mercedes with Constantine standing in deferential formality at the door. A Citroën was parked askew with its doors open, and next to it a large chauffeur-driven Packard laden with luggage. A distinguished-looking Frenchman who must certainly be Uncle Auguste was on the far side of the courtyard escorting the countess into the château. They disappeared inside. A small red open sports car had just disgorged a young man and woman. Bookends, Letty thought; both looked very like d'Aubec. His cousins. The girl came in for Letty's close attention. She was tall and slender and dressed, improbably, in riding clothes. Tight white jodhpurs, black jacket, shiny black boots, and, around her throat, an elegant silk scarf. A marcel wave swirled expensively around her neat dark head. Letty, dishevelled and tripping over the drooping hem of her borrowed trousers, knocked a cloud of dust from her hair and stared in hatred.

The young man, whose name she thought was François, caught sight of them, looked briefly, then turned away and busied himself discreetly with the boot of the car. But the girl gave a shout of laughter and came towards them. D'Aubec's arm went protectively around Letty's shoulder.

'Edmond! Darling!' She laughed a tinkling laugh. 'What's this? Girl grooms now? Whatever next? Can't say I think much of the uniform, though ... And all the hay burned away, I see, so nowhere for you to have a nice roll!' Her fluting laughter echoed round the courtyard.

'Oh, I don't know,' said Letty easily. 'Who needs hay? So many cosy holes and corners to be found in a stable. If one is eager to seek them out.'

'Quite a squeeze for three, though,' drawled Gunning

370

provocatively, stepping forward from the shadows and dusting off his knees. He flung an arm around Letty's other shoulder and eyed Gabrielle lasciviously. 'Still – there's always room for one more on top – as we say on the London omnibus.'

Gabrielle gasped and took a step back.

'Edmond, old fruit,' Gunning pushed on, 'aren't you going to introduce us to this charming *amazone*?'

Edmond's voice, when it came, was in a higher register than his usual light baritone. 'Gabrielle, you misunderstand. I would like to introduce to you the English lady I was telling you of. The lady . . .' He paused to flash a placatory grin at Letty. 'The lady I would like you to greet as my future wife. Miss Laetitia Talbot of London. Laetitia, my dear, this is my cousin Gabrielle.'

Frosty nods and murmured greetings were exchanged.

'And may I also present Laetitia's cousin, the Reverend William Gunning? But – David? Where is David?' Edmond asked looking around. 'I should explain, my dear, that Gabrielle's engagement was announced this weekend – with my blessing – to a most unsuitable ruffian! A French air force officer, a pilot of the worst suicidal kind but great fun. I might have looked for him to fly to my rescue,' he added with a lift of the eyebrow.

Gabrielle's recovery had been instant. 'He was recalled to Paris. I'm sure he will be devastated to have missed this encounter. David has a strange appreciation of the English sense of humour,' she added sweetly. 'I was about to take my Sunday morning ride when the news of your predicament broke and we dropped everything and hurried over. Perhaps, as you are clearly firing on all cylinders, Edmond, and need neither my sympathy nor my succour, I might steal a ride on Carnaval . . . as I'm dressed for it.'

Letty glowered.

'I would guess he'd be delighted,' said d'Aubec politely, 'after the night he's had, to stretch his legs. You'll find him a lively ride, my dear. Just exactly what you like. And now, if you'll all excuse me, I have some things to clear up here

371

in the stables. Boring matters like tidying up after the burglars. I'll get a couple of stout chaps to make good the
damage done to the walls.' He gave a whistle and rapped
out instructions to the men who were swiftly in attendance.
'And now I'd better go and show my wounds to Maman
and Uncle Auguste. Laetitia, why don't you go and
change? I'm sure your things will have arrived by now.
And why not show William the library? I'll join you there
as soon as I can.'

'Golly!' said Letty, watching as their host strode off. 'I
seem to have acquired a fiancé and a blood relative in less
time than it takes to tell! *Cousin!*' she said, eyeing Gunning.
'Where does he get that from?'

'Could have been worse,' grunted Gunning. 'He could
have said "grandfather".'

'So that's it! The standard to which every Frenchman will
rally!' said Gunning when they met in the library.
'Spectacular! Quite spectacular!'

'Not sure I follow,' said Letty doubtfully. 'And I do hope
you're not about to make another lecherous comment
about my cousin-in-law-to-be. Really, William! Edmond
was frightfully embarrassed. You must understand, if you
are to take your place in society again, that the language
and manners of the Mill Road Shelter are simply not
appropriate.'

'Are you telling me you didn't notice it?' he persisted.
'You and your archaeologist's eye! Was that eye so dazzled
by the gold, the silver, the bronze, and the bones that it
didn't take in a simple piece of earthenware? The urn
standing in a position of honour at the priestess's right
side? Not, I think, contemporary with the burial. A later
addition, most probably. Placed there perhaps five hundred years after the original burial, but centuries before the
abbey treasures fetched up there for safekeeping, I'd guess.
It looked quite out of place amongst all those fancy Greek
pots and pieces of Etruscan ware.'

372

Laetitia turned on him a look of pure indulgent affection. 'First century AD pottery style? Eighteen inches tall by about twelve inches across, Greek form, perhaps, but undecorated? The original of the one we see today in the fresco in the church of Sainte-Madeleine? The urn that stands, significantly, I have to believe, on the soil of Burgundy, at the goddess's right hand? That urn?'

Chapter Forty-One

'The answers to all this lie in a very ancient papyrus.' Gunning's voice was urgent. 'It was discovered at Akhmin, in Egypt. Goodness knows how it got to Germany, but it fetched up in the Berlin Museum in 1896. My Berlin friend – Klaus, his name is Klaus – was helping to prepare a translation of the Coptic script before the war. The contents were stunning! They had got as far as actually publishing some copies. Unfortunately the stock was caught up in a wartime accident – the cellar the books were stored in was flooded, and all lost. And then the war broke out and everyone had other things on their minds.'

'Stunning?' Letty prompted.

'Oh, yes. Klaus had retained a copy and allowed me to study it. World-shaking? . . . Yes, I think I'd say that. The text was short – I learned every word. It was a Gospel. A Gospel written by Mary Magdalene, Christ's apostle, herself. Early. Very early. Possibly second century, which makes it one of the founding texts of Christianity. Suppressed by the early Church because its contents were explosive.'

Gunning was speaking swiftly, listening out for the sound of d'Aubec's feet in the corridor.

'It reveals her to be, as I mentioned before, the foremost of the apostles. I wonder if d'Aubec and his crew have any knowledge of this? You know, it's just possible they don't . . . She's shown to be the person closest to Christ, his chosen one. She knew more of his teachings than any of the male disciples. A question of intelligence, intellect . . .

perception. It's clear that her understanding went much deeper than that of Peter and the rest. She had access to sacred knowledge their minds could not encompass.'

'Not an easy situation, in a time even more oppressively male-dominated than our own?' Letty guessed.

'No. Having listened to Mary delivering a delicate, cerebral, esoteric understanding of Christ's teaching and hearing her answers to such questions as: "What is Matter? What is Sin? Lord, do we perceive you through our soul or through our spirit?" the disciples' response is the equivalent of "Eh? What was that again?" Andrew turns to the other disciples and says, "Will someone explain to me what this woman's been telling us? It's *my* opinion that the Teacher wouldn't speak like this. These ideas are unlike any we've heard before." And angrily Peter joins in the denunciation: "How can it be that the Teacher confided to a *woman* secrets of which we ourselves are ignorant? Are we expected to change our ways, our traditions, and listen to her? Did He really choose her and prefer her to us?"'

He waited for Letty to respond but she was thinking deeply, much disturbed by what she heard. Finally, 'Oh, I'm sorry, William. I'm afraid I'm with Andrew on this – "these ideas are unlike any I've heard before",' she said.

'You won't be surprised to hear that Mary's response was to burst into tears.'

Letty rallied. 'That would be tears of frustration and annoyance, I'd guess! We've all done that in the face of male thickheadedness! It's not a sign of weakness but despair.'

'But she did find support. Levi spoke up for her. "Peter, you've always been hot-tempered and now we see you rejecting a woman just as our enemies do. Yet if the Teacher considered her worthy, who are you to deny her? Surely the Teacher knew her very well, for he loved her more than us."'

'Well, good for Levi. But what am I to make of all this? What is the meaning in all this, William?'

'No less than a passing on to humanity of Christ's central message, his spiritual teaching.' He paused, silenced

375

by the gravity of his conclusion. 'Oh, it would take me a day to explain all this . . .'

A pair of lightly questioning, intelligent grey eyes fixed him until he blushed.

'I'm sorry, Letty! Echoes of Andrew there! The Gospel reveals a path of self-knowledge – gnosis – God in oneself.' He tapped his chest. 'We – every man and woman – are the incarnation of God, and those of us who have ears to hear, as Mary constantly says – "Let them hear!"'

'William, if I can lay hands on a translation of this manuscript I'm prepared to study it closely and write an appreciation for the *Women's Suffrage Weekly*, but I can't see what it has to do with d'Aubec and his schemes, even if the cremated remains of the saint may well be secreted in an earthenware pot on his property.'

'Have you forgotten the fever that went around the world following the discovery of the tomb of a very minor Egyptian king? One day his name was unknown and unpronounceable, the next the word "Tut" was on everyone's lips – even reduced to an affectionate nickname. Imagine the effects, worldwide, of a well-directed campaign by newspapers, radio, and film photography to broadcast this local discovery if d'Aubec cared to launch it! And I don't flatter this man with any esoteric sensitivity to a Christian icon. I have no idea what his inner spirituality consists of, but I'm prepared to guess at his readiness to use – and ruthlessly use – the *exoteric* power of what we saw this morning. With devastating consequences.'

In despondent silence their minds ranged over the possibilities for mayhem.

'You don't suppose, do you, William . . .?' said Letty hesitantly. 'No! Of course not! It's an insane notion . . .'

'Go on, Letty.'

'He might be proposing nothing less than a sea change in religion? A change in focus as significant as . . . as . . . oh, a switch in the Earth's magnetic poles? North becomes south overnight and everything is turned to chaos. We've had a change from agricultural societies who worshipped the Mother Goddess to the invasive, Father-God-worshipping, militaristic states, and humankind has suffered the consequences. Could Edmond be planning to start a movement back to the old religion?'

'Possibly. But not all the way, and not straightaway, back to paganism. Wherever you look in France, there are churches (increasingly empty and disregarded these days). The shrines are all there, in place! Many are already dedicated to a Mary – the Mother or the Saint. It would not be a devastating change to bring about – not nearly so life-changing as the utter obliteration of the orthodox faith by the Revolutionaries in the 1790s. And even those rascals had the sense to make the replacement a female entity – the Goddess of Reason.

'I think d'Aubec's icon, his banner, his siren for the soul, is an essence of female authority, an amalgam of three idols the French hold dear – the Mother, the Priestess-Lover, and the Goddess – be she wearing her Celtic or Egyptian or Greek garb. The Triple Goddess. Anselme has hinted as much.' He considered for a moment. 'Rather more than hinted. Taken me into his confidence, you might almost say . . . sounded me out . . . And you have to agree with him – how many people, disillusioned, bereft, rudderless, and . . . yes . . . frightened . . . would not find such an image appealing? Remember the Angel of Mons! Tell men and women suffering stress what they subconsciously want to hear, reinforce it with colourful pictures and miles of newsprint, and the upshot will be a fervent reanimation of a nation's faith. Give it the endorsement of a charismatic priest of impeccable character, a newsworthy and glamorous standard-bearer . . .'

'But you'd have to be mad, surely, in this masculine age, to rally to a female banner?'

'What? Mad like the followers of Boadicea? Of Elizabeth? Jeanne d'Arc? Victoria? Men fight all the more determinedly for such a cause. And, anyway, on a personal level – if it were to come to a choice between a "rich-haired, deep-bosomed goddess, bringer of seasons and giver of

377

good gifts" and a crazed, egotistical god who behaves like a spiteful child yet demands unquestioning obedience, I know which would have me on my knees! But I'd prefer that mankind learned to do without the prop of all this imagery.'

'That's all very well,' said Letty, 'but most men and women, like the disciples, need their external emblems. They need their parables to be able to approach the truth. They need the support of a physical image – a black virgin, a man writhing in torment on a cross, to focus their emotions. They need to stick their fingers in the wound. They need to hear bells and smell candles, worship on a given day, and have their sins forgiven.'

'D'Aubec knows this. He's blending all these elements in the crucible and passing through it a current of twentieth-century technology. Heaven knows what the result may be! Precious metal? Utter dross? Blackened faces all round? Stay away from the flame, Letty!'

Letty managed a laugh. 'Well, I enjoyed our canter through the realms of fantasy, William. You've spent too many evenings swapping ideas with Father Anselme.'

She began to move nervously about the room and turned to him to share her anxiety. 'We're prisoners here, aren't we, William? In the most correct and hospitable way, he's keeping us here.'

'Oh, yes. I think if we strolled down to the gates in our boots, we'd be politely herded back. If we tried to start the Wolesley, we'd find the engine mysteriously failed to function. If we asked to use the telephone, we'd be told regretfully that there was a fault . . . perhaps tomorrow when the engineer could attend? When did you realize this?'

'I went to my room to change. My trunk had been fetched. And unpacked. He'd had time to leave a note on the dressing table. "Suggest Talbot livery for dinner." D'Aubec's even telling me what to wear! It was at that moment I heard in my mind the creak of a drawbridge coming up. How long do you think he expects us to stay cooped up in the library?'

378

'Until the dressing gong sounds, probably. An hour perhaps? I've known worse places to be incarcerated. Settle down, Letty. You're making me nervous, pacing about like a panther. Want to play I Spy?'

She smiled and joined him at the table. 'How about a game of cards? A game for two? Piquet? I can just about manage at piquet. But I'm unbeatable at Snap!'

The unwelcome thought flashed through their minds in the same instant, and they stood and stared at each other until Gunning asked, 'Remind me, Letty – what did the countess tell you about that last evening Daniel spent here? Can you remember exactly what you told me? I had assumed that she and Daniel passed the time tête-à-tête?'

'That was the impression she gave . . . "We played a game or two of *belote* . . . we danced a tango . . ." She made quite a show of girlish embarrassment about that revelation. And now I know her better, I'd say that was definitely not in character. She was misdirecting me like a conjurer because she'd made a slip!'

'Yes. *Belote!* All the rage at the moment. Takes two to tango, all right, but for *belote* you need *four*. I wonder who were the other two around the card table that evening? The ones whose presence was never declared to Huleux and the police. The last people to see him alive. How would we find out?'

'We obviously can't just ask a d'Aubec. Tell you what, though! – the housekeeper knows everyone's movements. I don't think anything happens here that she doesn't know about. I'll go and ask her.'

'Are you mad? Why would she tell *you*?'

'Two reasons. As far as the staff are concerned, I'm the future châtelaine and they are not displeased by that notion – when, as far as they are aware, the alternative might be Gabrielle! And the second? I'd rather you didn't ask!'

'Your speciality, Letty? A slight touch of blackmail? I can't imagine that . . .'

379

'Madame Lepage's sister's husband, the town pâtissier, has just bought out the baker on the opposite side of the square. Now, I wonder where he came by the sudden influx of cash? If a public-spirited individual were to make a fuss ... demand an enquiry?'

Gunning groaned. 'They'll stuff you down an oubliette!'

'Listen! There's the dressing gong. I'll wait a minute to let all the guests get up to their rooms, then I'll pop along to her office and see if I can catch her before supper. If d'Aubec wants to know where I am, hiss out of the corner of your mouth, "Women's problems, old chap." I find it paralyses any man.'

Letty made her way confidently through a bustle of servants, along to what would have been called, in her home, the butler's pantry. The door was ajar but the room empty. She accosted a scurrying maid. 'Madame Lepage? Is she about?'

'Sorry, Miss. She's in the kitchens. There's trouble with the aspic. Shall I tell her she's wanted?'

'No. Don't disturb her. Aspic demands one's full attention.'

Letty ducked inside and looked about her with approval and familiarity.

She'd spent many hours as a child in just such rooms. Lonely, evasive, and quite often forgotten by adults, she'd passed the time cleaning silver, polishing glasses, mending broken crockery, and chattering to the butler. It was snug but well organized. In spite of the season a wood fire crackled in the hearth, dispelling the chill from the vaulted stone walls. A gouty sofa, a polished table, racks of patterned china, and a case of silverware. Everything had its place in such a room, and Letty looked for the desk. And there it was. On it, in solitary state, to her surprise and delight, stood a gold and black telephone.

Mme Lepage's link with her domestic suppliers, of course. She wondered whether the d'Aubecs even remembered it was here. She picked up the earpiece and listened, triumphant to hear a familiar buzzing. She gently replaced it. Later. Above the desk was what she had hoped to find: a shelf of leather-backed books. Ledgers.

She glanced at the titles handwritten in black ink on white card and stuck along the spines. *Recipes* . . . *Wages* . . . *Accounts* . . . She pulled down the one marked simply *Housebook.* It was carefully kept. At the back, guests and visiting family were listed in alphabetical order and their tastes and preferences noted. She would have been happy to spend time exploring this section but contented herself, as she riffled through to the front, to note an intriguing fact about Cousin Gabrielle. Never think you can keep secrets from the housekeeper! Mischievously, she stored it up for future use.

At last, she found what she was looking for. Today's cast list. Not quite the method of notation Dawkins used, but near enough. Carefully inscribed, in spite of the turmoil of yesterday, were details of everyone on the premises. Gunning appeared, booked in as Mlle Talbot's cousin. His room was listed. The family's arrival had been noted. Having got her eye in, she flipped back nine months and counted down to the day before Daniel's death.

There was his name: *Souper. Le professeur Thorndon (v).* Visiting for supper. Leek soup and potted partridge had been enjoyed evidently. And there was his hostess and alleged tango partner: Mme la Comtesse.

But it was the other two names that she was intrigued to see listed. Two men who had, over the card table, listened to Daniel, argued with him, quarrelled with him perhaps. She remembered her godfather had once overturned a card table in his wrath. And that quarrel had started with nothing more than an accusation of cheating. The cheat in question (herself aged eight) had at once admitted her guilt but could not understand the fuss – surely he would want her to win? Her mother had banned him from the house for a week for bad behaviour.

What then would be the punishment exacted from quick-tempered, upright Daniel for challenging this nexus with its sinister aims? She knew the answer: a dagger in the throat.

But the command passed down to the hand that wielded the dagger – to Jules – would, she guessed, have come from one of these two men. She thought she knew which of the pair would have given the order to kill. Laetitia rationed her seriously offensive swear words for special occasions. She used one now. 'Got you, you bastard!' she murmured.

Chapter Forty-Two

'Where've you been? Your fiancé is combing the castle for you.'

Gunning caught up with her hurrying back down the portrait corridor a few minutes before they were due to gather for aperitifs in the summer salon.

'In the chapel. Just saying a prayer, coming to an understanding with the two Marys, and . . .' she added mysteriously, 'doing a little stage-managing.'

A triumphant bellow from the foot of the staircase cut her short and they were instantly rounded up by d'Aubec and ushered along to the salon. He sent William in first and held Letty back for a moment. 'You look lovely, my dear,' he murmured, arms sliding around her slim body in its wisp of black silk. She was intrigued to find that, although she was well aware of his intentions in running eager hands over her, the embrace was disconcerting. Pleased with the response he had evoked, he moved a finger slowly under her gold necklace.

'Heraldically correct?' she reminded him.

'In every way correct. For me. I'm sorry for my cousin's behaviour, and I'm sorry I lied to you . . . a pathetic attempt to rouse the demon of jealousy, but I perceive he has no place in your heart?'

'Oh, he's there but lying dormant, I think,' said Letty. 'And I apologize for *my* cousin's behaviour. Well, shall we go in and dazzle them with the glamour of a happy couple?'

* * *

After five minutes of unobtrusive assessment, the countess relaxed. Laetitia was behaving impeccably. Talking lightly, moving easily from group to group, she was even observed to make a comment that provoked a spurt of laughter from Gabrielle and a warm response. After a conversation with the girl, the countess's brother-in-law, Auguste, had caught her eye across the room, smiled, and nodded. Yes, a good choice. But the Englishman was a bit of a mystery.

Edmond had assured his mother that the man's provenance – as he called it – had been scrutinized and found acceptable. In the course of the day, she had come to suspect, though Edmond would never admit it, that he admired the man. And for deeper reasons than the most obvious: that he had quite possibly saved her son's life. Edmond had never made friends readily. Surrounded by close family, protected, aware from an early age of his special status, he had been concealed and prickly with others. Not an easy companion. He had craved approval without possessing the qualities to attract it. Mistakes had been made. And corrected.

This latest pair – the Talbot girl and her vicar friend – were, in the countess's eyes, on trial this evening. Suitable company for Edmond? How would they be judged? She hoped Laetitia at least would impress – she fitted easily into their life and the countess had never seen Edmond so struck with a girl. Yes, she would hand over her keys to Laetitia Talbot with some relief and the sooner, the better. But where was the clergyman in all this?

She had insisted: 'But what is his connection with Laetitia? They seem very close?' And her son had replied casually enough: 'Do you remember, Maman, the Arab stallion Papa had before the war? The skittish grey that bit him? That horse was only at ease in his paddock when he was in the company of a moth-eaten old donkey. His friend.'

His mother had looked at him quizzically. 'But that is no moth-eaten old donkey! Never think it!'

Her eyes were drawn constantly to Gunning. According to Anselme, the man was open-minded and enquiring, and had a cerebral approach to religion rather than a profound and visceral belief. A man still choosing his path, was Anselme's judgement. And, of course, a man who understood the workings of the Church of England. Could be useful. Who knows? He might even prove to be the Saint Paul of their movement?

And her judgement had been upheld over the dinner table. Her niece, Gabrielle, seated uncomfortably between Gunning and Constantine, had been prepared to turn her attention anywhere but in his direction, but his undemanding charm had won through and before the first course had been cleared, there they were – smiling, heads together.

The countess sipped her Montrachet. It might not be the disastrous evening she had feared.

Towards the end of the meal, a footman entered and announced that Father Anselme had arrived and been shown to the chapel. The countess looked around the table, gathering attention and quietening conversations, and invited her guests to accompany her, adding, for the benefit of Laetitia and Gunning, that the service would be short, non-denominational, and in French.

The chapel was serenely waiting, and Father Anselme, with arms outstretched and a broad smile, welcomed them at the door. His long white robe and the green-embroidered stole draped about his shoulders were reassuringly formal. They entered and seated themselves to the sound of voices singing in Latin. A recorded sound. Gunning's comment about the current of technology sparking and transforming ancient ingredients was proving apt, it seemed.

Silkily, the ancient words were calling on Mary:

O Maria virginei, flos honoris,
Vitae via, lux fidei, pax amoris . . .

Clinging to Gunning's arm, Letty had chosen a seat by the door. Whilst the company settled, coughing and shuffling, Letty put her nose to a low arrangement of trailing ivy leaves and white roses on a table at her elbow, inhaling the calming scent and trying to still her shaking hands.

The curtain had been drawn back to reveal the stained glass labyrinth and the ear of wheat. The warm rays of the evening sun filtered into the chapel, spreading pools of honey and amber on the floor, casting a golden glow on to the faces around her, listening with reverent attention. Sunshine, honey, amber, gold. Timeless ingredients, a bewitching alchemy.

Letty allowed herself to become ensnared.

When the last pure note had faded, Anselme switched off the gramophone and spoke quietly, echoing the sentiment: 'Shining star, moon without darkness, sun giving great light, Mary of great beauty.' He walked to the lectern and began by announcing that he was present merely to lead the worship; as with the Quaker religion, the congregation was free to make contributions – in any language – even if that contribution were simply silence and thought.

So far, so familiar, Letty thought. Esmé could not have objected.

She was further lulled when Anselme began to read from a psalm which she'd heard many times before. At Harvest Festivals, she thought.

'Thou causeth the grass to grow for the cattle, and herb for the service of man: that he may bring forth food out of the earth.

And wine that maketh glad the heart of man and oil to make his face to shine and bread which strengthens a man's heart . . .

Oh, Lady! How manifold are thy works!

In wisdom hast thou made them all: the earth is full of thy riches . . .

All that thou givest us, we gather. Thou openest thy hand, we are filled with good.

When thou hidest thy face, we are troubled; when thou takest away our breath, we die and return to dust.

386

When thou sendest forth thy spirit, we are created and thou
re-newest the face of the earth . . .
Lady, hear our praise!'

The worshippers repeated the last line then joined him
as he finished:

> *'Our words falter.*
> *The Goddess sings a hymn of silence*
> *And we are silently singing.'*

The certainty in the firm voice was persuasive, the phrasing hypnotic. At that moment it seemed entirely reasonable
to Letty that all these good things – grass, corn, wine, the
fruits of the earth, and the earth itself – should have been
created by a female deity.

Letty stole a glance at Gunning. He had the attentive but
slightly strained expression of a doting father being
required to hear a child recite the thirteen times table.

The silence was broken by the countess. The first to rise
to her feet, she turned to face the image of the Virgin,
curtsied, and spoke in a clear voice: 'We thank you by
singing your greatness; we reach towards your bright light,
perceived only by the intellect; we recognize you, true seed
of humankind, the womb pregnant with all life to come.'

The others began to chant:

> *'Mother of Creation, Fountain of Goodness,*
> *From you we will be born again.'*

Five further eulogies of varying lengths and degrees of
conviction followed, until all had spoken but for Letty and
Gunning. With a shake of the head, Letty indicated that she
was content to remain silently singing. She was alarmed to
see Gunning getting to his feet and she put out a hand to
restrain him. She had sensed him by her side growing
increasingly tense.

Shaking off her grasp, he strode towards the lectern. No self-conscious comments offered from the body of the Church for him, Letty thought, annoyed, but she acknowledged that he was a man performing in a setting very familiar to him. He was playing a part he had been trained for and had practised for years in English churches and on French battlefields. The lack of a dog-collar and priestly garments was disconcerting at first, but his elegant dinner jacket, borrowed from d'Aubec, gave him distinction and authority. Uneasily, Letty identified the sudden rush of emotion she felt as pride. The firmness of his hands on the lectern, the amusement in his sharp blue eyes as they made contact with every person in the congregation, the absence of notes, all spoke of a growing confidence. Letty hadn't the faintest idea what he would do: tear down the temple or shout hallelujah – neither would have surprised her.

Father Anselme went to sit down, leaving Gunning in possession of the stage.

Chapter Forty-Three

He chose to speak in English, confident that his worldly audience would have no difficulty in understanding him. A good decision, Letty thought. An Englishman struggling with the French language is a comical figure and Gunning needed at this moment to be taken seriously.

'Under the challenging gaze of the Magdalene' – he bowed to her stained glass image – 'I am prompted to speak to you, her devoted followers, in no less than the Lady's own words. Words with which I don't believe you will be familiar.'

His audience was intrigued and eager to hear more. They were not disappointed. His account of the discovery in the desert of an ancient and tattered manuscript, its passing through the hands of scurrilous dealers and thieves to fetch up in the safety of a museum where its miraculous contents had at last, after years of dusty neglect, finally been understood, was, Letty thought, a little highly coloured, but there was no denying its power.

Surprise and anticipation were on every face. Father Anselme smiled and looked modestly at the floor as his protégé held them in the palm of his hand. Auguste cast a questioning glance at Constantine, who looked blankly back at him.

'And the words she speaks are Christ's own, transmitted through the clarity of her own sharp intellect, undistorted by ambition, fear, jealousy, or doctrinal wrangling. And she had some very fundamental questions to put to the mouthpiece of God: "What is matter?" she asks him. "Will it last forever?"

'And Christ answers: "All that is born, all that is created, all the elements of nature are interwoven and united with each other. All that is composed will eventually decompose; everything returns to its roots; matter returns to the origins of matter."'

Nods of agreement greeted this uncontroversial statement. They were all certain they'd heard it before somewhere. Gunning seemed to be treading a well-worn path.

'And again, Mary asks (and who knows the depth of personal need which prompted it?) a question the answer to which we all thirst for: "What is the sin of the world?" And his reply is clear: "There is no sin. It is you who create sin when you act according to the habits of your corrupt nature; this is where sin lies."'

He's making all this up. Surely? thought Letty. *How can he know? Has he gone over to them*?

His glance towards the vivid figure of Mary on his right was agonized, seeking strength, and suddenly Letty was ashamed of her suspicions. She was closer than she had ever been to getting a glimpse of the man at the centre of the protective layers he had built around himself over the years. He was speaking from the heart – the heart she had thought atrophied within him.

'But Mary has a message for you. A message against which all your ears are stopped.'

And, of course, at the challenge, each listener unstopped his ears and paid even closer attention.

'You will not want to hear, you will not want to accept the truth she hands down to us: the Lord calls on us to become *anthropos.* I offer you the Greek since we have no word subtle enough to express this, in French or English. Fully human, accepting and rejoicing in our humanity, perhaps. "Be vigilant," Mary warns us. "Allow no one to mislead you by saying – 'Here it is!' or 'There it is!' For it is *within you* that the Son of Man lives. Go to him. For those who seek him, find him."

390

'Some spark of the creating deity is within each human. We should not seek outside ourselves for external symbols of faith. Those who offer them, who set up objects of veneration, idols, prophecies, promises of divine intervention . . .' – Gunning waved a hand round the chapel – 'are misleading mankind, are denying him progress by chaining him to his Stone Age beliefs. We are not primitive hunters, dwellers in caves who do not understand the workings of our planet and must explain them with stories of the supernatural.'

The audience was beginning to stir uneasily. Auguste's looks in Constantine's direction were increasingly flinty. No emotion played on Constantine's stern features, but his right hand had settled in his pocket. They all flashed anxious glances at the countess and for a moment Letty was reassured. Would they risk a violent scene in front of an old lady whose health was known to be failing?

But now they know where he's going with this, they'll surely find a way of silencing him, Letty thought, despairing. *He's leaving them no choice.* And she saw clearly why Daniel had died.

They had attempted to recruit him to their cause, just as they were even now trying to capture herself and Gunning. Daniel would have gone along with it in a spirit of intellectual enquiry – that was ever his style: debate, listen patiently to your opponent, get into his skin, then, having understood him, play devil's advocate, tie him in philosophical knots. But, agnostic humanist that he was, Daniel would, when he finally grasped the enormity of what they were about, have poured scorn on their plans to use religious fervour as a means to their sinister goal. Once he had understood their intentions, he would first have ridiculed them and then flung down a direct challenge. Metaphorically, faces would have been slapped by Daniel's glove. He would have threatened them with exposure. Letty shivered. She could imagine the old cavalryman's challenges: 'My friend the Archbishop must hear of this . . . the Pope would expect to be made aware . . . His Majesty's government and our allies the United States will take a dim view!' He might even have invoked his old pals at the War Office.

No, it had not been a peaceful exchange of views, a cosy foursome round the card table. There had been no sentimental tango. One of the four players had picked up the gauntlet. She looked around the assembled company and identified her target.

'But this is what you are proposing,' Gunning was storming on. 'To mislead humanity. With velvet-lined handcuffs you will chain him to his superstitions. You attempt to distort man's highest impulses and use them to forge no less than a tool of social control. You propose to take the finest images of man's faith – the Mother, the Virgin, the Giver of Good Gifts and Bringer of Seasons – and blend them into a heady cocktail for a thirsting people. What you are seeking after is a nation which, inebriated and inflamed, will hurl itself mindlessly into action against an enemy chosen for them by you yourselves. By a gang of nationalistic tyrants!'

Letty cringed. She had seen, in the park one Sunday before the war, a crowd at Speakers' Corner attack a pacifist. They had pulled him from his soapbox and begun to kick and pummel the lad. The police were calculatedly slow to come to his assistance and Letty had been dragged screaming from the scene by her father. Gunning was in far greater danger than that young man.

Auguste's ascetic features were becoming increasingly strained. François raised a disbelieving eyebrow to his cousin Edmond and shrugged his shoulders. Anselme's fingers twitched, anxious to clasp a rosary he did not carry.

'Patriotism!' Gunning's voice was rasping with scorn. 'Love of one's country! What are these? Virtues? No! Nothing but a sleek mask for nationalism – the evil which has brought Europe time after time to the edge and made it stare into the pit. Tribalism by another name. Have we made no progress since the Celtic Aedui fought their neighbours, the Germani, here in these hills? Have we

392

learned nothing in two thousand years but that our young men are born to be sacrificed to the God of War?

'Our warrior no longer runs naked into battle welcoming a hero's death, fighting hand to hand with a single enemy, the image of himself. Our new Achilles lurks in the shadows, slaughtering hideously and indiscriminately from a distance. He doesn't see the light leave a man's eyes, he doesn't hear his death gasp, doesn't feel his last breath hot on his cheek. When this warrior strikes it is not one man who falls nor yet an army but a whole people.

'And you would put Nationalism into harness with *Religion* to power the charge of the unreasoning masses? You plan to replace God with yourselves! Do I need to remind you of the name of the last being to attempt this?' he said, turning his unearthly blue gaze on d'Aubec. 'His name was Lucifer!'

At last it came and Letty, alert to every changing expression on the faces around her, was astounded to catch the slight nod that gave the order to silence him. The signal without which no one would have taken action came from a totally unexpected quarter but there was no mistaking it. It was accompanied by the flash of a great ruby in a ring too massive for the emaciated finger that wore it.

Chapter Forty-Four

All eyes had been looking in the countess's direction – Letty had been aware of this – concerned, she had supposed, for the old lady's health. But with the peremptory gesture she understood at last that, at the centre of the web around her, there had always been the countess. The Lady. Who else? The cornerstone of their matrilineal tribe. The one they looked to for command.

And this command was translated into furious action as Constantine, released at last, leaped forward, cosh in hand, and laid Gunning low with a single vicious blow behind the ear.

With everyone's attention on the slumped figure of Gunning lying motionless at the foot of the lectern, no one saw Letty's hand reach out and snatch the Luger from under the concealing sprays of ivy and roses at her elbow.

Anselme dashed forward and fell upon the body of Gunning, covering him protectively with the folds of his white robes. Constantine and François advanced on him menacingly, shouting at the priest to move away. Gabrielle shrieked and the countess watched, impassive.

Letty was confused; she despaired of getting the attention of this circus. She could have shot any one of them dead where they stood but they milled about, oblivious of the menace in her hand.

She took a deep breath, found her target, raised the Luger, and aimed for the left eye.

The crash of the shot in the enclosed space was deafening.

All movement ceased and all sound save for a small whimper from Gabrielle.

'Bad shot!' said Letty. 'I hadn't meant to destroy the whole face.'

What remained of the gilded plaster cherub's head at the apex of the roof stared down blindly at the group below. They coughed and swatted at the dust and shards that rained down from the ceiling.

'Jules's Luger,' she said concisely. 'I'm sure you're familiar with it. Nine millimetre, butt-loaded, well maintained. Seven bullets, two now used up, which leaves me five. And I have six targets. Oh, dear! I shall be one short.'

They saw the firmness with which she held the angled grip of the gun; they eyed the menace of the steel-grey barrel trained unwaveringly on the countess's heart; they flinched before the purpose in the steel-grey eyes directing her aim, and they stayed very still.

Constantine tore his gaze from Letty and raised his head to examine the eyeless cherub, assessing the shot. He looked back at her and spread his hands in a placatory gesture.

'Anselme! Get Gunning out of here. Send for a doctor,' said Letty.

The countess looked at her thoughtfully. Letty had not asked for the police to be called and she calculated that the wise woman was guessing the significance of the omission: they had already been summoned. Letty managed by a superhuman effort to keep her attention on the group and ignore the limp body of Gunning as the priest tugged it by the armpits through the door and out into the corridor.

D'Aubec took a step towards her, arms outstretched, alarmed and loving. 'Laetitia, my darling! Your loyalty does you credit, but this man has battened on you, used you, filled your head with silliness. He's obviously unhinged. You heard him ranting just now ... Neurasthenia, perhaps? He has suffered. Poor chap! But dangerous ... We ought never to have asked him here.' He threw an apologetic glance at his mother. 'He's not dead.

Constantine has merely silenced him for the moment. We'll look after him.'

'I'm sure you will. Look after him by throwing him from a height to cover the blow to the head? From the battlements? Perhaps if you can revive him, the countess would like to dance a last tango with him? Every bit as fatal, I think. Go and stand behind the altar table, all of you.'

The gun remained steady while they moved with varying degrees of co-operation. Auguste gave the countess his arm and they made their way to the far side of the altar with the insouciance of a couple setting out for a stroll in the Bois de Boulogne. Constantine took up a position on the edge of the group, tense as a tiger, ready to spring the moment her attention wavered. D'Aubec stood on the other side looking at her with affectionate amusement. In their different ways, each was a danger.

'Darling, that gun's far too dangerous a toy for you to be playing with. Why don't you just hand it to me, and I'll make it safe and give it to Huleux, who must be searching everywhere for it . . .'

'Shut up!'

'Children! Children!' scolded the countess. 'Do you think we could all do with a cup of tea?' she suggested brightly. 'Or a tisane, perhaps? All this dust is making me thirsty.'

'What about a game of *belote* while we're waiting?' said Letty. 'We've got enough players. You need four, I understand. Just as on the night Daniel died. You were there, madame, with Daniel. And, hurrying from Lyon to deal with the emergency my godfather was creating – your lieutenants. Your brother-in-law Auguste and Constantine. The Top Brass. All three of you alarmed to discover finally the depth of Daniel's disgust with your plans. He must have made you aware, in his honourable way, of his intention, if you did not at once abandon them, of shouting the truth from the rooftops.'

They listened to her with polite attention, in silence, becoming more relaxed as the seconds ticked away. Letty

396

was conscious that she was following exactly the same lethal path as her godfather and was filled with exaltation. No possibility of a retreat now and her present position was untenable. Her finger was growing rigid on the trigger. She was not sure how much longer she could hold the heavy gun convincingly at the ready.

She knew the peril she was in. This group was thinking as one entity, and they had realized that time was on their side. They simply had to wait. Avoid attracting her attention. The gun or her spirit would inevitably droop. And one moment's loss of concentration and she would be disarmed. Seconds later, Gunning would die. How much longer?

Gabrielle began to examine her fingernails. Auguste studied the stained glass. The countess coughed pathetically into a lace handkerchief. Waiting. Waiting.

'Keep going, Letty! Don't look back!' Daniel's voice.

Forward then. There was only one course open to her. Break the deadlock. She had to provoke an attack to which she could legitimately respond. One last attempt at retribution for Daniel. She would have to shoot one of them. She looked along the group and made her choice.

'It was of no importance that Edmond was not present that evening.' Her voice was calm. 'No loss. Decisions can be taken without him. Edmond – the dud of the family . . . the howitzer shell fitted with a useless one-hundred fuse . . . all thunderous delivery and no explosion.'

Letty's shot rang out the instant d'Aubec leaped towards her, screaming his fury, catching him in the right shoulder, hurling him backwards, and spinning him round. He crashed to the floor, blood spurting between the fingers of the hand he held over the wound. Letty watched his expression turn from incredulity to agony. He turned away from her and through clenched teeth he muttered, barely audible, one word: 'Maman!'

The countess, oblivious of the gun, dashed forward and threw her arms around him, murmuring.

397

'*Mater dolorosa*,' Letty whispered, her gun now pointing at Constantine. Then, more firmly: 'Madame, your son's bleeding. Use the altar cloth.'

Three agonizing minutes later, the door burst open and Huleux, accompanied by two armed officers, came in, open-mouthed with horror but training revolvers steadily on the group behind the altar. Huleux rapped out a few commands and warnings, and it was some time before Letty realized that most of these were addressed to her. Sensing her paralysis, he approached and gently touched the hand holding the gun in a frozen grip.

'It's over, mademoiselle. Let me have the gun. We were just entering the building when we heard the first shot. Go to the vicar. He is conscious and calling for you.'

Chapter Forty-Five

'I'll drive, William. I think you would do it very badly,' said Letty as she put the last suitcase into the car. 'Two hours out of hospital – you can't be feeling very sharp.'

'*Au contraire!* I'm feeling very chipper! Really, four days chained to a hospital bed was excessive.'

'It's funny – I was in such a lather to get to Fontigny and now I can't wait to be back in England. I'm never sure where I want to be.'

'You'll find your place one day, Letty. For the moment I'm just thankful you're apparently undamaged and free to be taken back to your father in Cambridge.'

'In one piece and having done what I came to do. I found her, William. Daniel's killer.' She fell silent. Not quite ready to move off, she paused before starting up the engine. 'But I'd thought no further than that. What happens now? They still use the guillotine for capital crimes, don't they? You don't suppose, do you, that I'll have sent someone to the guillotine? I couldn't bear it! I wouldn't like to think that old Dutronc and his infernal machine were to have the last word! And I think even Daniel would say I'd over-steered. He was quick-tempered but not the least bit vindictive. He would have wanted to see their guns spiked, but not blowing up in their faces.'

'It won't come to that. Families of this consequence no longer end up on the scaffold or even in a court of law these days. They have friends in high places. I wouldn't put it past them to be pulling a few strings we know nothing about.'

'I think they've started already. Whipping up local and national sympathy. Were you aware that the old girl's dying? They've all gone off to Lyon to be by her bedside at the clinic. She's known for some time, apparently. And, of course, the whole world rushes to forgive an ailing, grieving mother. Not sure I believe a word of it. That's what they're good at, after all – propaganda, they call it. Lying, in other words.'

'I wouldn't dismiss the idea. It does go some way to explaining why she was so eager to see that son of hers settled. She saw herself as the guardian of the faith . . . *they* saw her as the guardian. They had manufactured a belief in the Mother Goddess, after all. Not surprising, then, to find at the centre of the system a woman. A priestess? Almost an object of veneration herself. But not immortal! And the time was coming to hand on the torch. A choice had to be made.'

'Gabrielle would have been their first choice, but she ruled herself out, I think! Deliberately? I wonder.'

'Yes. The old girl had no illusions about her son. He needed a steady hand and a quick mind to guide him, and if they came accompanied by various other agreeable attributes, the countess was well pleased. Perhaps she would have hung on long enough to see the family line was assured? That there was a new countess in place to guard the flame? Someone to train on.'

'A frightening notion! They'd have had me tied up, tricked out, and stuck on a spike as a corn dolly to be thrown away when her time was up! Evil creatures! Oh, William!' Letty seized his hand. 'Thank God you were there! Several steps ahead of me all the way. Showing me where to put my feet. Putting up with my nonsense. I was rash . . . and it was my carelessness that nearly got you killed. I'm so sorry.'

Too late she realized that, though he could deal with any amount of thoughtlessness – rudeness even – contrition and a show of emotion were still unwelcome.

'No need to apologize. Nothing personal, I'm sure. I look

400

on you as a Force of Nature, Letty. Next time I hear a warning rumble, I'll put on my tin hat and hop into the nearest trench.'

'But I think we've left them in some disarray, at least, don't you? D'Aubec's shoulder was smashed, apparently, and he's going to take some months to recover. He's taken sanctuary with his uncle Auguste and a battalion of lawyers. And when I've told Sir Richard about their political activities and he's made a few phone calls to Whitehall, enquiries will follow. The family will find a few more spokes have been stuck in their chariot wheels. It will take them some time to recover their momentum.'

'Yes, but don't go off watch yet! Organizations of that age and strength are not easily killed off. Their roots go deep, and we have done no more than lop off a couple of branches.' He was struck by an uncomfortable thought. 'Good Lord! We know what the effect of that can be! I do hope, Letty, that our efforts amount to more than a little judicious pruning!'

She looked across at him, suddenly doubtful. 'There was a moment, William, when I wondered whether I ought to . . . whether it was my Christian duty to attack this monstrous growth from the inside. I could have got inside, you know. I could have fought from that favoured position to neutralize, to disarm . . . I could have done *something*.'

'It had occurred to me that you were planning a self-sacrifice of that kind. Though the "favoured position" – by which I suppose you mean marriage to d'Aubec – might not have been exactly what most people understand by "martyrdom"! I think you'd become fond of him?'

She looked away, hiding her face, unable to answer.

As they neared the turn-off to the castle road, Gunning persisted, determined to extract an admission, though the pain of the extraction was etched on his own face: 'Your last chance to come clean, Letty. Are you going to regret leaving him behind?'

'I should never have risked starting a relationship, I know.' She smiled and glanced up at the imposing silhouette of Brancy. 'Too deeply rooted. Too Burgundian. He might well not transplant easily. Still, in the circumstances, I thought I had to give it a go. William, I want you to wait here for a moment.'

She braked outside the lodge cottage at the end of the carriage drive. Hearing the car, an elderly lady called a greeting from the doorway. 'He's ready and waiting for you, mademoiselle. I'll just fetch him!'

'Marcel's mother,' Letty explained to Gunning. 'She's done me a huge favour. I didn't come away empty-handed from all this.' She jumped from the car and walked down the path to talk to the groom's mother and take from her hands a travelling box.

'Can we find room for another passenger in the back?' she asked him. 'Or would you like to have him on your knee?'

'Good Lord! I was hoping you'd forgotten about *that*,' said Gunning. 'Are you sure you know what you're doing?'

'No. Not sure of much any more. Marcel seemed keen for me to take him away and offered his mother's services. He's a good dog. Well worth having. And I did earn him! He can join the pack back home. We've got cows he can herd.'

'What's his name?'

'Oh, something grand and Burgundian . . . "Dagobert", I'm afraid.'

'Crikey! Imagine calling that across a soggy Cambridge meadow!'

Gunning opened the box and took out the small form wriggling with excitement. Letty noted that he allowed his thumb to be chewed.

'He's going to be brown. Why don't you call him "Bruno"? . . . Bruno! There, you see – the tail wagged. That's decided, then.' He held up the dog and spoke into his face: 'Now, mate, if you'll take my advice you'll go back to sleep again in your box. We've a long journey ahead and I won't have you tearing holes in these trousers – or worse.'

As they drew off, he changed the subject, conceding that it pained her to bring up her feelings for d'Aubec. 'Let's not forget that the Lady's still up there, asleep in the hillside ... charged with the same patriotic duty as King Arthur but, unlike him, we know she exists. And will we ever know what the urn contains? Charred horse bones? Mouse droppings? A trace of spikenard? Or the ashes of a very important woman? It's all still in place, Letty. Waiting.'

'And Paul Morel?' she said as they chugged past the entrance to the Allée du Parc. 'I should have realized from the moment I saw d'Aubec beating that poor boy that he was a man of ungovernable temper. But – I'm too hard on myself, had you noticed? I rather think I did realize. A violent man. A man with two characters. Esmé would understand, I think. I can't imagine why they decided not to charge him with Morel's murder. As soon as d'Aubec was safely in custody, the lad's friends came forward to speak out. Why did no one listen to them?'

'Ah, I can tell you that. Old Huleux came to see me in hospital and cleared up a few things for me. He had to speak slowly in words of one syllable to penetrate my headache but I think I got it! They did listen to the boys who, themselves, had been very concerned at the trouble young Paul was getting into. You knew he'd been serving an apprenticeship with Jules? Yes, well, he was receiving a training in more than care of horses; he was learning the trade of the assassin into the bargain. It took two of them to murder Daniel. Paul was there. He saw it all, he told his mates. When he started to make life difficult for the boss, Jules was ordered to finish him off and bury him in your trench.'

'Make life difficult? How could he do that?'

'After the shaming public beating at the hands of d'Aubec it was understandable, perhaps, to brag to your friends that you intended to get even by speaking to the police – revealing the family's part in the killing. Understandable but not very sensible. Morel was a loose cannon. D'Aubec had to defuse him and chuck him overboard.'

'And why waste a good corpse?' said Letty bitterly. 'He used the boy's body to divert suspicion. The watch and the wallet. D'Aubec was really psychopathically vindictive, wasn't he? He had to gild the lily. Wasn't content just to implicate Paul Morel in Daniel's murder, he had to plant that gold coin – from his own collection, no doubt – to bring Paradee into disrepute. Killing two birds with one stone.'

Letty stared straight ahead as they drove past the deserted dig, covered with tarpaulins. Deliberately, Gunning drew her attention to it.

'You'll miss all that, won't you? I've always been aware of the attraction the digging had for you . . . of your ambitions in that field. A pull rather stronger than anything young d'Aubec could conjure up, I had thought at one time.' And, probing further: 'Anything more known of Paradee? You don't hear much gossip from a hospital bed!'

'Oh, he skipped off one step ahead of the authorities. Leaving debts behind him, according to Phil. His backer refused to honour any of the bills and it's left a very nasty atmosphere in the town. It will be a few years before anyone else is welcomed to do any excavating. Phil and Patrick are going off to the Levant. I think they're to join the Woolley dig. Paradee was as good as his word in that – he did make arrangements for his team . . . In fact, I really think he and I – we could have made a go of it . . . Oh, William! I had a narrow escape!'

'Oh, yes? About as narrow as the Atlantic! Don't be so silly! Your personal Mr Plod wouldn't have let you get away.'

She smiled. 'Mr Plod turned out to be a bonny fighter!'

'But inadequately armed! Words! The only weapon I can call on. Not much use, I'm afraid. It takes the blast of a

Luger and a bullet through a cherub's eye, I hear, to get the attention of a man like d'Aubec.'

'Don't underestimate the power of words, William.'

'I'm just going to stop off at the church before we leave town. Do you mind? I'd like to have a last look at Mary. I'd like to seek her blessing . . . see whether she condemns me or whether she understands . . .'

She stayed for several minutes in front of the fresco, in silent conversation with the saint. Finally, she spoke to Gunning: 'William. There's something I want to do in London, something I've been planning while you've been away in Lyon. Would you mind awfully taking me to our house in Fitzroy Square when we get back? I don't want to go straight home to Cambridge.'

Gunning looked with silent speculation at the blush spreading over her cheeks. Her face, vivid but secretive, strangely echoed the enigmatic features of the Magdalene. He turned from one fair head to the other in puzzlement, and then he raised his hand in an unpractised gesture. Clumsily, he made the sign of the cross, his eyes questioning Mary's.

They parked on a cliff top watching the ferryboat making its way into harbour, and Gunning made up his mind to speak. 'I have to tell you something, Letty . . .'

For a moment she heard the old, grating hesitancy.

'You know you brought me back to life again? Perhaps you don't even now realize how far gone I was when you came upon me. I wouldn't have survived a week in the House of Correction with their medieval methods of punishment. Not another one. And I knew that. Lacking the moral strength to kill myself, I was prepared to allow others to shoulder the sin of doing it for me. A cowardly act but I was set on it. And then I came face-to-face with a bossy girl who bought my life for half a crown.'

405

'A bargain ... though she didn't at first know that.'

'She picked it up, handed it back to me, and then helped to carry the burden of it. Grumbling the while! I have a good deal to thank you for.'

'No, William. It's I who am thanking you. And not just with this ...' She turned and kissed his cheek and hugged him. 'There's a little gift for you in the glove box.'

He opened it and took out a brown paper parcel, holding it awkwardly.

'You've forgotten what to do with presents! You pull the end of the string like this ... here, let me ...'

He gasped as the contents slid into his hands. 'Thoreau's *Walden*! But it's the book you took into Heffer's to sell! The very copy.' He opened it reverently.

'I just pretended to sell it. I put it away in my bag and came out flourishing three pound notes and boasting about my haggling skills. I could see that you lusted after it! ... William?'

And into his continued silence: 'Words failing?'

'Silently singing.'

He turned his face away from her, the salty breeze from the Channel stinging his eyes.